ALL FOR A ROSE

JENNIFER BLACKSTREAM

SKELETON KEY PUBLISHING

HE'S FALLEN IN LOVE WITH HIS PRISONER

"You once told me I make you nervous. Tell me, do you find that —like the sprites—you are less...nervous, in my presence now?"

Maribel's mouth went dry, the rumbling bass of Daman's voice drawing her attention to his bare chest. It wasn't until that moment that she noticed he'd removed his shirt—the clothing that he'd started wearing for her benefit—apparently to keep it from getting destroyed as he shot around on the ground after the invading sprites.

Now there was nothing to hide the strange combination of unblemished human skin and glittering scales that traced the ridges decorating Daman's face and chest before disappearing in the cascade of scales that composed his draconic lower half.

She followed the lines of sinewy muscle over his pectorals, up around his biceps and the sharp lines of his throat. The scales should have given him a monstrous appearance, but at some point in the last week or so, they'd become less foreign. Now they were familiar, a defining feature that only served to decorate the already handsome veneer of the isolated lord.

The blue and green scales were warm, despite their icy appearance, slick under the pads of her fingers. She trailed a finger over one of the large ridges that traced Daman's collar bone, turning sharply at the line it met and following it up his neck.

I'm touching him.

Every muscle in Maribel's body seized at once, shocked and outraged at her own behavior. Tendons whiplashed, recoiling her hand with a speed surpassed only by creatures beyond the veil. She didn't remember moving, didn't remember reaching out to touch him. Dear gods, what had she been thinking?

His hand closed around her wrist, keeping her from retreating. She swallowed a squeak, her heart leaping into her throat.

Author's Note:

From time to time I will have a short story in an anthology that is time-sensitive. To view those stories, see the BOOKS page on my website at www.jenniferblackstream.com

Skeleton Key Publishing

All for a Rose

ISBN-13: 978-0692577592 (Custom)

ISBN-10: 0692577599

©Copyright Jennifer Blackstream 2013

Cover Art by Clarissa of Yocla Designs © Copyright July 2015

Edited by Sharon Muha

www.skeletonkeypublishing.com

Published in 2012 by Skeleton Key Publishing, Norton, Ohio, United States of America

❀ Created with Vellum

For those who are brave when love demands it...

ACKNOWLEDGMENTS

Dragon, you can always make it better.
Sib, you are my *cuelebre*.

All for a Rose

JENNIFER BLACKSTREAM

CHAPTER 1

"Wait, that doesn't make any sense."

Maribel paused and swiped a hand across her sweat-dampened brow, leaving behind a thick trail of mud as the earth from her hands happily clung to her skin and the lock of brown hair that had pasted itself to her forehead. She squinted at the book propped up on a tomato plant in front of her, pointing to the faded words with her gardening spade.

"Mountain arnica... Paste made from its leaves eases bruising and muscle pain... Poisonous if it comes in contact with the skin." Maribel tapped her knee with the spade, ignoring the clumps of dirt that flung themselves with wild abandon in every direction. "Well, which is it? Does rubbing it into bruised skin heal you or kill you?" She plucked a cherry tomato from the plant beside her, chewing savagely as she glared at the text.

One didn't get this sort of ambiguity with cooking. A plant had a certain flavor and that flavor mixed with other flavors, lending its unique qualities to the overall experience of the dish. There was no question on whether or not something was poisonous, it either killed you or it didn't. Maribel snared another cherry tomato, admiring the sleek, perfect red skin before popping it into her mouth. The frustrating herb lesson faded from her mind as her taste buds sang their praise of the sweet flavor that only came from sun-ripened fruit. Her gaze slid to the side, snagging on the thin beige shoots that stuck out of the ground in the garlic patch, letting her know the small bulbs were ready to harvest. Sliced tomato sprinkled with minced garlic and drizzled with olive oil. A dash of salt and pepper, perhaps some finely grated cheese…

"Good morning!"

Maribel coughed, seeds from the tomato she'd been enjoying threatening to fly up her throat and out her nose. That voice. Warm, but firm, ringing clear and strong through the air. A shrieking laugh immediately followed and Maribel closed her eyes, slowly counting to ten before pinning a smile on her face and rising to greet her visitor.

"Good morning, Madame Balestra." Her gaze fell to the two-year-old boy barreling ahead of her approaching neighbor like a warning shot from the cannon of an unfriendly ship. "Pierre, how lovely to see you again."

The toddler ignored her and fell like a plague on her cherry tomato plants. Grubby hands flew through the air like windmills, snagging her precious fruits by the fistful and shoving them into his mouth. Pierre's cheeks bulged like a greedy chipmunk's and he fell to sit beside a particularly heavy plant, eyes locked firmly on the cherry tomatoes he planned to consume next.

"Pierre, please, you must ask Maribel before you help yourself to her tomatoes."

Maribel's skin ached as she forced it to maintain an expression of welcome despite her fervent desire to chase after Pierre while banging on a pot—the same method she used when crows landed in her cornfield. His mother's voice was anything but disapproving. Madame Balestra had been the one to give Maribel her first cherry tomato plants, had been the one to show Maribel how to tie them to supports so the fruit didn't drag on the ground. Had Maribel known that the price for the plants and advice would be letting her neighbor's spawn eat his fill whenever he happened by, she might have elected to get her starter plants from someone else—perhaps someone who would take money for them instead of taking the fruits of her labor from her family's mouths.

"Oh, no, please, he can help himself." She stroked a nearby tomato plant, as if she could offer it the comfort she herself needed in the face of the ravenous child. Her gaze slid to the interloper with the bottomless stomach. "The little darling." *Enjoy the diaper rash, you tomato thief.*

"On my oath, that child could eat his weight in fruit," Madame Balestra muttered, shaking her head. She prodded at one of the ruby-skinned fruits, touching at least five of them before finding one that seemed to meet her standards. Juice trickled from the corner of her mouth as she chewed and she dabbed daintily at it with a faded, but clean white handkerchief she pulled from her apron. "I'm so pleased the plants I gave you are flourishing so."

"I don't know how I can ever thank you enough," Maribel said sweetly. *Because apparently, it is never enough.* She cleared her throat and knelt beside the tomato plant closest to her. She opened her skirt and gathered cherry tomatoes as slowly as her annoyance would allow. "I was about to take some inside myself. If Corrine enjoys them half as much as our young Pierre, it might be just the thing to put a smile on her face."

"Ah, yes, where is your sister?"

Maribel tensed as Madame Balestra put on a show of searching the garden.

"I don't see her," Madame Balestra continued. "I would think that on a lovely day like today, she would be only too excited to be out working in the sunshine."

"She's tidying up inside." *But not in the corners, because there could be spiders there.* "You know how dusty a house can get out here."

"Oh, yes. I only wish I too could limit my duties to tidying up the house." Piercing green eyes met Maribel's. "But that is not the life of one who works the land to survive, is it? One must push oneself to care for not only the house, but the land. It is a great deal of work—especially when left for only two people such as yourself and your dear father."

"Corrine's not feeling well," Maribel said tightly. She yanked a cherry tomato off the plant hard enough to rock the stick it was tied to.

"Still?" Madame Balestra plucked another tomato and held it in front of her face, though her attention was obviously on Maribel. "I'm so sorry to hear that. It must be so difficult for you to always have her work to do out here on top of your own. I can't recall the last time I saw your older sibling tending the land."

"I'm sure she would love to be out here working with us," Maribel forced out through clenched teeth, her pleasant expression becoming brittle on her lips. "I often think of how horrible it must be for her to be housebound even on gorgeous days such as the one the gods have blessed us with today."

"Such a shame nothing can be done to help the poor child," Madame Balestra continued, her monologue unimpeded by Maribel's interruption. "And so unusual. My niece was touched with the Evil Fire as a child, had horrible convulsions and delusions—used to scream that she could see her auntie who had passed away. But she outgrew it in a few months. I've never known anyone to suffer with it so far into adulthood. The demons' grip must be strong on your sister, bless her soul."

The cherry tomato in Maribel's grip died a gruesome death as Maribel clenched her hand into a fist. Seeds and sticky red juice trickled from between her fingers.

"Maribel? Maribel!"

Maribel closed her eyes and cursed under her breath. *Not now, Corrine!*

"Ah, here comes the poor dear now." Madame Balestra threw

the cherry tomato to the ground as she focused her full attention on Corrine. Her tone dripped with the false sincerity that struck so many of the villagers around Maribel's family. "Such a lovely dress."

The older woman twisted the knife in Maribel's back with practiced ease, and Maribel surrendered. Her shoulders slumped as she faced the direction of her sister's musical voice. Corrine's tone was slightly breathless, something that could mean she was feeling particularly unwell today, or that she'd been calling Maribel's name for some time and Maribel had been too preoccupied to hear her. Maribel half-wished it was the former. Perhaps if Corrine came stumbling up the hill with the pallor of a fresh corpse, Madame Balestra would stop harping on her absence in the fields.

"If you ever decide to come to one of our town's social events, Maribel, perhaps your sister would let you wear one of her dresses."

Madame Balestra was in rare form today. Maribel fought not to react as she brushed as much of the dirt from her skirts as she could. The blue material had faded from a brilliant sapphire to a muted robin's egg, dragged even further from its former glory by the layer of dirt that spoke of the garment's reassignment as gardening wear. It was hard to believe the gown had once been a beacon of class at society balls, a sign of Maribel's family's wealth and status. The condition it was in now, it was more believable that the dress had been sewn together from worn bedskirts and discarded scraps—old scraps, not even fit to be saved for rags. Still, neither Maribel nor her dress missed those days.

The same could not be said for her sister Corrine.

Maribel peered over the tomato plants, casting her gaze down the hill at her family's small farmhouse. Corrine was trudging up the slope, her slender body so pale that she stood out like a ghost amidst the gleaming colors of the garden. Her silk and velvet gown rustled audibly even from this distance as she fought her way up the slight incline, the reflection of the sun off the fine silk nearly blinding Maribel.

"If I'm perfectly honest," Madame Balestra mused, "I've never quite understood your sister's dedication to fashion. Even if she doesn't intend to work the field with you and your father, that sort of attire is hardly appropriate for wearing around the house, or in bed."

"She doesn't stay in bed all day." Maribel offered the protest, but it was half-hearted. Corrine only made things more difficult for herself, stubbornly wearing her precious gowns even while traipsing around the outdoors. It would have been one thing if she were as indifferent about her wardrobe as Maribel was of hers, but Corrine valued every stitch of her clothing as one might treasure a child. It was one more way Corrine clung to the past, fighting tooth and nail against her family's new and humble circumstances

"It's a wonder she can breathe coming up the hill in that corset," Madame Balestra observed.

Corrine arrived at the summit of the gentle hill with a gasp, one hand clutched to her chest. She heaved in breaths as deep as her gown would allow, her brown eyes locked on Maribel with a physical intensity, as if holding her in place until she could regain her breath.

"Maribel," she gasped finally. "We need to go see Mother Briar."

Instant irritation ate at Maribel's nerves like an army of fire ants. "We saw her yesterday." She gestured around the garden at the weeds that were trying to strangle her tomato plants. "I have to do something about these weeds or I won't have enough— Are you going to faint?"

The spade fell from Maribel's hand to land with its sharp side buried in the moist earth as she rushed to her sister's side. Corrine swayed on her feet, the back of one trembling hand pressed to her forehead and her eyes fluttering. The sent of copper tickled Maribel's nose and she noticed that Corrine was cradling her other hand against her stomach.

Madame Balestra sucked in a sharp breath. "Oh, my."

Maribel's stomach rolled as she got a good look at Corrine's hand. The flesh of her palm was red and raw, blackened ends curling in places to reveal skin wet with blood and other fluids. The mess leeched into Corrine's gown as she clutched the injured limb to the trunk of her body. The fact that her sister gave no attention to her gown's state of ruin frightened Maribel nearly as much as the wound itself.

"Corrine, what happened?" Maribel put one hand on Corrine's shoulder to steady her as she peered at the wound. "Is that a burn?"

Corrine swallowed hard, her face growing even paler. "I had…another episode. I was trying to pick up the rug in front of the fireplace so I could drag it outside for dusting. By the time I came out of it, I was lying on the floor, and my hand was against the hearth."

"You shouldn't have come up the hill," Maribel chastised her gently. "And you're in no condition to go traipsing through the woods to visit Mother Briar. Come back to the house and I'll tend your burn."

Corrine jerked away from Maribel, nearly sending herself tumbling to the ground. She stumbled to get her feet under her, glaring at Maribel all the while. "No! I need to see Mother Briar."

"Your sister is right, dear," Madame Balestra spoke up. "You should get that tended to as soon as possible, here and now if you can. The trek to Mother Briar's will only give it time to get worse."

Corrine snapped her head to the side as if she hadn't noticed Madame Balestra until now. "Wasn't that your son I saw rampaging through my sister's snow peas next to the house?"

Madame Balestra swiveled her head around like an owl who'd lost the mouse that was to be his dinner. "Pierre? Pierre!"

Maribel had to give the woman credit. Most parents would have showed some sign of embarrassment or muttered a bit of self-deprecating slander against themselves if their child had wandered over a hundred yards away without them noticing—to plunder a neighbor's food-stores no less. Madame Balestra stalked off down the hill as if Maribel's family had lured her poor child to their home with promises of candy and then forced him to sit in the garden and eat until he ruined his supper.

"I hate that woman." Corrine kicked the abandoned garden spade, sending it to thunk against one of the tomato plants so the beady red fruit trembled and threatened to fall. "She was talking about me again, wasn't she?"

A stab of guilt lanced Maribel's stomach as she remembered her earlier thoughts, how she'd hoped Corrine appeared worse for wear so the nosy neighbor would be shamed.

"Corrine," Maribel said over the sound of her own thoughts, "your hand is badly burned. It'll be a miracle if it doesn't get infected from rubbing against your gown. You need to let me treat it."

The mention of her gown's demise should have distracted Corrine, but her sister's gaze zeroed in on Maribel with the same intensity as earlier.

"Mother Briar will treat it."

Irritation took the edge off Maribel's guilt like sandpaper over roughly hewn wood. She fought to keep her gaze on her sister's face instead of staring around at the garden and all the work waiting to be done. "The sooner we take care of it, the sooner it can start healing."

"Is it really such a burden to take me to Mother Briar's? It's not even a mile away, Maribel, surely that's worth having someone who actually knows what she's doing tend to me?"

Maribel's lips parted, shock momentarily stealing her voice. She opened and closed her mouth as a hundred words fought for space on her tongue.

"Corrine…"

Corrine's brown eyes sparkled with unshed tears, reminiscent of the puddles that pooled in the garden after a hard rain. "I know what Madame Balestra thinks of me. Did you agree with her when she went on about how lazy and worthless I am because I can't do as much work as you do?"

"I never said that!"

"Not to me," Corrine countered evenly.

The denial faltered on Maribel's lips, her brain working furiously to comb through her memories of every conversation she'd had where she'd mentioned her sister. Yes, sometimes she thought Corrine could help more than she did, but she'd never said that out loud to anyone. She hadn't—

Too late, Maribel realized her hesitation had betrayed her. Corrine's gaze dropped to a tomato plant and she ripped one of its leaves off, crushing it in her fingers until the scent of ruined greenery filled the air between them.

"You could work more if you wanted to." The words were sour on her tongue and they left an unpleasant taste in Maribel's mouth, but it was too late to pretend now. As much as she pitied her sister and the illness that had plagued her since childhood, there were times she thought she and her father had coddled Corrine too much. Perhaps a little tough love was in order.

Corrine fell back as though Maribel had struck her. She must have tightened her hand into a fist or something, because she cried out, eyes squeezing shut and her face twisting in pain. What little blood she'd had left in her cheeks drained away and sweat broke out in a fine sheen on her forehead. The fingers of her burned hand curled into claws and she sucked in a sharp breath through her teeth. Maribel lunged in an instinctive move to support her, but Corrine bared her teeth at her and hunched over her hand like a wounded animal.

"I wish I could be more like you," she choked out. "Out here digging in the dirt, snacking on the fruits of my labors and dreaming of all the wonderful things I'm going to cook for dinner." She stepped back, the movement uneven as she fought not to fall over the churned earth. "But I can't. I don't know when my limbs will freeze, when my mind will go spinning off into…"

She pressed her lips together until pale white swallowed the pink. A glint of something hard flashed through her eyes and she dropped her gaze to her hand. "I don't want to cut my flesh open on a gardening tool during a spell, or fall onto the stove because I thought it was a bed. I don't want to put my hand into a boiling cauldron because in my mind it was a wash basin, or be caught talking to a cat as though it were a human being because I thought it had spoken to me first." Her voice wavered and she raised her good hand to point at Maribel. The wind tousled her brown hair and for a moment she appeared wild, untamed. "If you think for one second that I wouldn't trade places with you if I could, then you don't know me at all."

Maribel tried to push away the images Corrine's words raised. Her sister wasn't wrong. Her…episodes, had put her life in danger more than once. Her gaze was pulled unwillingly back to Corrine's burned hand and the fight melted from her tense shoulders.

"I'm sorry, Corrine." She ran a hand over her face and then shoved it back through her hair. "I know you would help if you could, really I do. I just get frustrated sometimes, and—"

Corrine stomped a few steps away, leaving deep footprints in the soft soil of Maribel's garden. "Are you going to walk me to Mother Briar's or not?"

Maribel's gaze fell on the tomato plants around her. She had so much work to do…her share and Corrine's.

She returned her gaze to Corrine, ready to offer one more protest. Corrine's face had faded from the color of warm eggs to the sickly pallor of a discarded caul. The burned mess of her hand was starting to smell, scalded flesh, blood, and pus poisoning the fresh spring air between them. Maribel swallowed her objections.

"All right, let's go." A sharp ache in her spine reminded her of how much time she'd spent that morning bent over the plants she was now abandoning. "But I can't stay long. I need to get back here and finish my chores."

Corrine's shoulders sagged. "Good. Good. Thank you."

Maribel stayed close enough to Corrine that she'd be able to catch her sister if she fell, but not so close as to risk bumping into her injured limb. They trudged slowly down the rolling hill and crossed over the well-tended pasture to the edge of the woods. Trees towered over them like sentinels, filling the air with the sweet smell of new blossoms and the singing of baby birds. Despite her stress and the weight of the chores waiting for her, something inside Maribel loosened, eased as though a fist had been closed around her gut and was only now letting go. Nature was twirling around her with open arms, and despite everything, she couldn't feel anything but blessed to be in the midst of it all.

"If only I could be more like you."

Maribel stumbled and almost fell over a coil of wild vines. After a head-spinning moment of wind-milling her arms, she managed to keep her balance. Her sister's gaze was fixed solidly ahead of her, her footsteps slow, but determined. Maribel's heart softened and she put a sympathetic hand on Corrine's shoulder.

"Corrine, you can't help being sick. I'm sorry I—"

"I'm not talking about being sick." Corrine halted abruptly, tearing herself free of Maribel's offered comfort. Putting a little more distance between them, she resumed her pace, staring resolutely ahead.

Maribel gave her sister some space even as she tried to see past the mask Corrine had schooled her features into. She tried to remember the Corrine she'd known when they'd lived in the center of the kingdom, been in the midst of the bustling activity and the thriving social scene. A time when the lines around her sister's eyes had been laugh lines, her tears few and far between. Corrine had always had episodes, always struggled now and then, but it was nothing like it was now out here on the outskirts where they had to work to survive. They'd been milder, manageable.

Maribel trailed a hand down the bark of a tree as she passed. Loose dirt coated the pads of her fingers and she rubbed them together. "Other than your illness, what difference is there to envy?" She offered a tentative smile. "It's my recipes, isn't it? You're jealous of my buttermints."

The corner of Corrine's mouth twitched, but the humor didn't reach her eyes. "Yes, Maribel, I envy you your buttermints." She paused and frowned. "Great, now I'm craving sugar."

"I knew it!" Maribel smiled, but the joke pittered out, dying all too soon. She bit the inside of her cheek. "I'm sorry, I guess I really don't understand."

"No, I guess not." Corrine stroked her gown with her uninjured hand, dancing her fingers lightly over the intricate embroidery done in shades of silver that glittered in the sun. A roughened edge on the side of her fingernail snagged the material. Corrine stumbled as all her attention shifted to her dress, her breath catching in her throat the way it might if she'd suddenly dropped an infant.

Maribel kept her gaze ahead, but studied Corrine out of her peripheral vision. Her sister held her breath as she eased her finger away from the skirt, carefully examining the material for damage. Her fire-ravaged hand was all but forgotten in her concern for the garment, and Maribel was once again struck with the sense that there was more going on with her sister than she realized.

"Corrine, please talk to me."

Apparently satisfied that her gown was fine, Corrine slanted a glance at Maribel. "About what?"

"Anything—everything. I want you to be happy."

"Ha," Corrine barked. "Happy, you say." She snorted, shaking her head. "You might be thriving out here in the middle of nowhere surrounded by plants and animals instead of people, but I *liked* the life we used to have, I belonged there. Out here..." A muscle in her jaw clenched as she swallowed. "I feel worse with every second that passes. Every day it's harder to remember a time I was comfortable, that I was *happy*." She surveyed her dress. Her brown eyes lost their shine, despair dragging her shoulders down. "Every day the things I have left fade a little more."

"Oh, Corrine." Maribel tried to embrace her sister, but Corrine pivoted out of the way, putting more space between them. Maribel bit her lip. Suddenly Corrine's obsession with her gowns didn't seem quite so frivolous as before. "I'm so sorry. I know this has been hard on you. You had so many more friends than I did, and—"

"Friends," Corrine spat, kicking a pile of leaves. The scent of wet earth filled the air along with the faintest hint of frost left over from winter. "*Friends* wouldn't have shunned me when I needed them. *Friends* wouldn't have shut their doors in my face and talked about me behind my back after I lost everything. Where were they after all of Father's ships were lost to pirates? Where were they after we lost our house, our land?" Her features hardened, giving her the appearance of a fierce marble statue. "I have no *friends*."

The hair on Maribel's arms stood up. There was a certain... promise in Corrine's words. A seed of desired action in the lament that made it more than blowing off steam. *Perhaps I should be paying more attention to the magic Corrine is learning from Mother Briar.*

Old stories of madwomen driven to magic out of a thirst for revenge filled Maribel's mind with macabre images and she shoved them away, not wanting to see Corrine's twisted by such dark intent.

"You know, Corrine, I was thinking," she said lightly. "I know that Mother Briar said my talents lay with plants and medicine and such, but perhaps she wouldn't mind if I sat in on one of your magic lessons? After all, we are sisters. Who's to say I don't share some of the same potential she sees in you? You didn't know you had the potential for magic until—"

"No."

Corrine stopped so suddenly that Maribel nearly crashed into her. She pinwheeled her arms, trying to keep from falling into her sister's injured hand. The uneven ground offered no help, but she managed to regain her footing in time. Breathing faster, she blinked at Corrine. "What?"

Immediately, the sharp lines that had spread out from the corners of Corrine's eyes a moment ago vanished. Corrine smiled, though the expression was strained to the point of being a grimace.

"You know what Mother Briar said. Magic can't be taught to someone who doesn't have a natural affinity for it. She read your aura, and she saw that you have a kinship with nature and that's why she limits your studies to botany and medicine. And if you want to learn about plants, the best thing to do is surround yourself with them. The best thing for me is to have a quiet space alone with Mother Briar to practice what little magic I'm capable of learning."

Maribel shifted on her feet, trying to ignore the roll of unease sliding over her stomach. Her annoyance at constantly being left outside to "study" while Corrine and Mother Briar retreated into the witch's cottage was now shifting into unease. Corrine didn't want her seeing her lessons with Mother Briar. Why?

Corrine hesitated, good hand twitching against the fold of her gown, then pulled Maribel to her side. She tucked her arm into hers, holding it too tight. "Thank you for trying so hard, Maribel. I know you're only studying plants with Mother Briar so you can make medicines to help me." She nudged Maribel with her shoulder. "I know you'd rather drop those herbs and flowers into some sort of stew."

Maribel ducked her head at her sister's teasing tone. "If this is about the raspberries last week—"

"Raspberries were obviously meant to be eaten, not brewed into medicinal teas," Corrine interrupted smoothly. "I don't resent you for eating them and Mother Briar was wrong to make you feel guilty about that." She laid her head on Maribel's shoulder, her dark brown hair brushing against Maribel's arms like a braid of silk. "I'm sorry. I'm sorry I don't help more, and I'm sorry I took out my pain and frustration on you. You didn't deserve that, and I know you aren't like that awful Madame Balestra. I want you to know that I don't know what I'd do without you. I wish there was some way I could repay you for all you've done for me."

The knot in Maribel's chest loosened and she rested her cheek briefly on top of her sister's head. Corrine's dark hair held on to the sunlight until it practically burned against her cheek. "I study plants because I want to. You know I like playing in the dirt." She lifted her head and nudged her sister until Corrine met her eyes. "And don't talk about yourself like you're not great with magic. I've seen the twinkle in Mother Briar's eyes when she looks at you. She's as proud of you as if you were her own daughter."

"Don't sound too excited." Corrine toyed with a loose thread in the embroidery on her gown. "It's not like I can spin straw into gold or anything. At this point I'm not even sure if what I'm doing works. Maybe the old witch only came up with this 'absorbing energy from the air' thing to make me shut up about how wretched I feel."

"What exactly is it you want to be able to do with magic?" Maribel ducked under a low hanging branch, the air filling with the crunch of dry sticks as she and Corrine tromped together over a fallen limb.

"I want security," Corrine answered immediately. She let go of

Maribel to fist her skirts and step over the remains of a rotted tree trunk. "I want to be surrounded with people, like we were at home, our real home, not alone in the middle of nowhere where we could die and it would be months until anyone noticed." She kicked at a pine cone, sending it skittering over the half-frozen ground. "I want enough money to make sure no one ever has a reason to snicker behind my back, enough money to make sure I never have to worry about starving again."

Maribel gripped Corrine's arm. "You will never go hungry again, Corrine, I swear it."

For a moment they were both silent, lost in the same memory. Those first days after their father had lost everything, after every one of his ships had been taken, leaving him with no cargo and no means to transport more. They'd always been so wealthy, one would have thought it would take more time for it all to vanish, but vanish it had in the blink of an eye.

Debtors had showed up from all four corners of the kingdom, friends had turned their backs. They'd had barely enough money to purchase the small farm, far from the main village, and in the most undesirable territory in all of Sanguennay. Winter had fallen on them like a hungry wolf, chewing their bones and rattling the old farmhouse with its howling winds. They'd nearly starved, surviving only because the old witch in the forest, Mother Briar, had taken pity on them and taught them to forage for edible wild plants. She'd even shared some of her own personal stores to get them through.

It had been a poor substitute for the feasts they'd been used to, and none of them had felt it so acutely as Corrine. Her delicate sister with the sweet laugh had died that winter, replaced by a pale, brittle woman with hard eyes and a haunted expression that never truly left her. It had been Corrine's idea to seek out Mother Briar after that winter and beg to be taught more than just how to forage for food.

"Hello, girls."

Mother's Briar's raspy voice broke into Maribel's reflections and she nearly jumped out of her skin as she realized they'd arrived at their destination. Her hand flew to her chest as her gaze darted around the trees, finally landing on the old woman standing amidst a tangle of flowing ivy, the long green vines spilling over the roof of her modest cottage to tickle the sides of the stone on the way to the ground. They writhed like the tentacles of a living beast as the witch disentangled herself and stepped to meet her visitors.

Ebony eyes gleamed as she brushed her graying hair out of her face and dusted off the simple brown dress she wore under her green cloak. Between her garments and the ivy covering her house, both the witch and her cottage were practically invisible.

"I'm sorry we're late, Mother Briar," Corrine said immediately.

Maribel frowned and glanced at her sister. *Late? This visit was planned?*

"No sense waffling on about it now." The witch gave Corrine's burned hand a disapproving glance. "You were near a fire today. Another episode, I suppose?"

Sweat beaded on Corrine's brow and patchy redness crept up her neck like a sickening sunrise. Corrine's brave front wavered, the pain revealed in her moment of weakness. Maribel took an instinctive step closer, but Corrine stepped away, nearer the witch.

"Yes."

If Mother Briar noticed how unsteady Corrine was, she didn't show it. "We'll need to step up your lessons. From now on, you'll see me every day." She glanced at Maribel and produced a book from somewhere under her cloak. She handed it off to Maribel and pointed at a circle of thick green bushes bedecked with broad-petaled purple flowers. "Maribel, take the book and go study those plants there. When I come out, I want you to tell me what kind of plant that is and be able to give me three ways to use them in healing."

Maribel bristled at Mother Briar's dismissive order. She parted her lips, ready to give the witch a piece of her mind—starting with what she could do with her book. The words halted on the tip her tongue as Corrine tensed, her eyes flashing too much white and a stricken look seizing her features. Maribel pressed her lips into a thin line and swallowed her irritation like a bitter potion.

"Actually, Mother Briar," she started tightly, "I had a question first." Maribel brushed away the tickle of unease as the witch focused her intense stare on her and squared her shoulders. "I was reading the book you gave me the other day, and I don't understand Mountain Arnica. It says it can heal bruised skin, but it also says contact with skin can be poisonous."

"Well?" Mother Briar prompted impatiently.

"Well? Which is it?" Maribel tried to keep the frustration out of her voice for Corrine's sake, but she really wasn't in the mood for Mother Briar's mystique today. Especially not now that she had the distinct and growing impression she was being kept in the dark about something. Something involving her sister's magic lessons.

"Depends on who you are. Mountain Arnica is also called Holy Herb. It's used by humans and the bright creatures beyond the veil for healing. In other places, it's called Demon's Bane, and it is quite poisonous to those creatures closer to the other side of the grave. I wouldn't recommend it for demons, vampires, and the like, but for humans, *sidhe*, and that sort of creature, it can be quite helpful."

"The book could have said that outright," Maribel muttered.

"This is why it's important to study with someone who knows what they're talking about instead of relying solely on books."

A book you *gave me and told me to study.* Maribel bit back her retort, giving in to the plea in Corrine's eyes. She graciously accepted the new book the witch offered her, gripping it tightly to keep from giving in to the urge to whack the old biddy with it. Corrine practically ran inside the cottage without so much as a backward glance at Maribel and the witch shuffled after her. For a heart-stopping moment, Maribel thought Corrine was going to crash into the doorframe, but she managed to twist at the last moment and stumble safely into the house.

Again Mother Briar appeared unperturbed by Corrine's worsening state. She strode into the house with the meandering gate of someone who hadn't a care in the world, leaving Maribel to glare at her back. Her ire went unnoticed as Mother Briar shut the door behind her.

Alone again, Maribel let out a breath of resignation and trudged with her book over to the plants the witch had indicated. It didn't take long to identify the plants as blue elderberry and she plucked some of the flowering tops to prepare a tea later. She was about to close the book when she spotted a particularly beautiful bloom filling a page in her peripheral vision. She opened the book and flipped through the pages until she found the flower that had caught her eye.

"Rose of the Mist," she read aloud. "A rare and beautiful bloom that shines gold in the sunlight. One of the rarest flowers known to man, the Rose of the Mist is said to endow those who consume a tea steeped from its petals with the radiance-absorbing qualities of the rose itself."

A flare of excitement burned fast and bright, briefly stealing her voice. She quickly scanned the rest of the page, her hopes rising higher and higher with every paragraph. A Rose of the Mist had been found in a part of the forest between here and the main village of Sanguennay less than ten years ago. If there'd been one then, perhaps there were more.

If I could make Corrine a tea from that rose, all she'd have to do is sit outside in the sun and she'd never feel weak and exhausted again!

Slamming the book closed, Maribel slumped back against a

resilient young sapling. Nervous energy twitched over her skin like creeping vines and she fidgeted in her makeshift seat of tender leaves. There was no way she could go on a journey today. She had to get back home and start preparing dinner so her father had something to eat after he came in from the fields. And then there were all the chores she'd been forced to abandon so she could accompany Corrine here. There wasn't time to go wandering around the woods searching for the rose.

"Tomorrow," she promised herself. "I can find it tomorrow."

Waiting for Corrine to finish with the witch was pure agony. The usual pleasure Maribel found in these spare moments, searching for herbs to cook with that had nothing to do with eating and everything to do with flavor, failed her. All she could think about was that rose, the difference it would make for Corrine.

"I'll need to fix some food that will last a day or so, something that won't spoil while I'm gone." She plucked a raspberry from a nearby bush and chewed as she thought. "I don't have time to dry any meat. Bread would be all right, and there's always vegetables—"

The door to the witch's cottage opened and Maribel's thoughts ground to a halt. Corrine and Mother Briar were talking as they left the cottage, their voices hushed, too low for Maribel to make out the words. Maribel tucked the book against her body and dashed over to Corrine.

"Corrine! Come on, we have to go. Mother Briar, may I borrow this book?"

Corrine stared at Maribel as if she'd grown a second head and Mother Briar's stern features pinched in confusion.

"Yes, take the book," she said finally. "Study it and return it when next we meet."

"Thank you!"

Maribel barely remembered her sister's injured hand in time to keep from grabbing it and dragging her sister off. She glanced down at Corrine's palm, impressed to find it covered in shiny pink skin, all traces of blood and blackened flesh gone. The fingers of the hand were curled into a half-claw, but the improvement was undeniable. She snatched up Corrine's good hand and hauled her sister off Mother Briar's front porch.

"Come on!"

"Maribel, slow down," Corrine wheezed, yanking her arm from Maribel's grip. She stopped with her hands on her hips, her chest heaving as she fought to regain her breathing. Her dark hair fell in wild disarray around her shoulders, the natural curl doing its best to survive against the tugging fingers of the wind. "Why are you in such a hurry? Is missing one afternoon of chores really such a setback?"

Maribel bit off the urge to point out that she was, in fact, doing the chores of two people and that an afternoon made an incredible difference. *Just get the rose. Everything will be fine if you can get the rose.* "I don't want Father to worry about us," she said instead. She waited for Corrine to catch her breath, shifting from foot to foot as her nerves urged her to run ahead. The picture of the rose hung in her mind, whispering promises of how much better life could be if she found it.

"Father will be in the field until dark," Corrine pointed out. She waved at the sky, still gloriously bright. "We have plenty of time."

"But I left that book in the field, the tomatoes still haven't been weeded, and I need to get dinner started if it's going to be ready to eat by the time Father comes in."

"If you keep running like this, we're going to relive your little trip down from the well when you were eight. Remember that?"

Maribel winced, slowing down to wait for Corrine. "How could I forget? That stupid duke's son, what was his name? Jack? I never should have let him goad me into that race down the hill."

Corrine grinned. "You did win."

"Technically, neither of us won since neither of us had any

water left in our buckets after the tumble down the hill. Though I suppose since Jack ended up with his scalp split open and I just had a few bruises, I did come out better off."

"Maybe someday I'll race down a hill. On purpose, I mean, not falling down because I had an episode on a steep slope."

There was a wistfulness in Corrine's voice that tugged at Maribel's heart. She opened her mouth to respond, though she had no idea what to say. It hadn't really occurred to her that Corrine wanted to do those sorts of things. Corrine hated to run.

Awkwardness swelled between them and Corrine put on a burst of speed, as if the pressure was too much. Her gait was uneven, hindered as she tried to run with her injured arm still cradled against her stomach, but though she tilted a bit, she didn't fall.

As they rounded the top of the hill that marked the northern boundary of their land, both girls came to a sudden halt. A strange man was riding away from the farmhouse, his stern features and plain clothes unfamiliar. Their father stood on the path to their front door, rooted to the spot, his graying brown hair tousled by the wind and his gaze locked on a crisp parchment he held open in front of him. If he hadn't blinked, Maribel would have worried he was suffering one of Corrine's episodes. It was eerily similar to Corrine's posture when her sickness held her prisoner in its grasp.

"Father, what is it?" Corrine scurried the rest of the way to their father's side, injured hand scrabbling at her skirts to try and hold them up as she went. Her eyes widened as she abandoned the skirt to point at the official port master's seal on the message. "Father?"

Their father slowly raised his cloudy blue eyes, the hand holding the letter beginning to tremble. "A ship. It… One of my ships…survived. It…came into port."

Corrine twitched and a small sound halfway between a gasp and a squeak escaped her throat. Maribel snared an arm around her waist in time to keep her from sliding to the ground, grunting as she took her sister's full weight. Corrine's eyelids fluttered as she clumsily tried to get her legs under her. It took her two tries to speak.

"What... What does this mean?"

"It could mean nothing, it could mean everything." Their father rolled up the parchment, his eyes avoiding the paper as if the mere sight of it raised his hopes so high it hurt. "I must go to the harbor. I need to see for myself if this is truly my ship, if its cargo is safe. If it is..." Tears glistened in his eyes. "My daughters, we may be able to get back what was lost to us."

Corrine burst into tears and threw herself into her father's arms. He gripped her tightly, mouth moving in a silent prayer. He gestured for Maribel to join them, lips pressed together as if too emotional to speak. Maribel offered a feeble smile as she allowed her father to gather her into the shared embrace. There was a strength in her father's body that hadn't been there the last time he'd hugged her, as though the thought of going back to their old life had revitalized him. Meanwhile, Maribel's stomach had fallen out and suddenly the last thing she wanted to think about was dinner.

He'll sell the farm.

Images paraded through Maribel's mind. They would be back to high society, back to the endless social functions and false niceties, back to having servants to do all the work Maribel had only recently realized she loved doing. She would be back in tight-laced gowns, restricted from activities that might damage her fine clothes. There would be parties full of people—people who had shown their true faces in the wake of her family's misfortune, but who Maribel would be forced to socialize with nonetheless if they returned.

The thought of facing all those people again, the ones who had abandoned Maribel's family in their time of need but who would welcome them all too willingly once they were once again rich enough to deserve respect... It turned her stomach.

"All right, all right." Their father pulled back, his eyes shining with excitement. "I will bring you both something wonderful. Tell me what you want, anything!"

"A new dress," Corrine answered breathlessly. "My old ones are so worn, and they don't fit me properly since we've been starving out here. I want something with silk and lace, something that will let me remember what life used to be like when we were happy."

Her sister's words stung. Maribel had worked hard to learn to cook, had slaved over a hot fire for months trying to perfect her recipes, digging in the forest for herbs that would bring rich flavors to the food she cooked for her father and sister. Yes, there'd been that first winter, but Corrine certainly hadn't "starved" since then. Maribel had actually dared to hope that her culinary skills had gotten quite good, perhaps enough to appreci- ate. *Only compared with starving, apparently*, she thought bitterly.

"And, my Maribel, tell me what I can get for you? Would you like a new dress too? Jewelry perhaps?"

Maribel tightened her hands into fists, trying to smother her frustration. A dress. What on earth could she want with a new dress? Another uncomfortable entrapment to hinder her in her chores, a reminder of the wretched life waiting for her with the nobility, a life she'd escaped and was now doomed to go back to? She didn't want a dress. She didn't want anything, damn it!

Her grip closed around the book she still held and inspiration struck. She hefted the book and flipped to the page with the rare rose.

Her father examined the picture. "A dress for my Corrine and a rose for my Maribel. I will do my very best." He handed the book back to Maribel and headed back to the farmhouse. "I must prepare for the journey now, I want to leave immediately. That ship is sitting in the harbor, I don't want to leave it there for one second more than is necessary!"

Corrine threw her arms around Maribel and hung there like a sticky cobweb. "Oh, Maribel, it's almost over. I can feel it, everything is going to be better now."

Maribel hugged her sister back as guilt ate her alive from the inside out.

CHAPTER 2

Something is burning.

Daman wrinkled his nose at the thick, woodsy scent of smoke slowly filling the air around him. For a moment, he wavered, torn between holding on to his meditation and finding out where the scent of smoke was emanating from. It had taken him hours to work this far into the meditation, hours to feel anything even resembling calm. He was very nearly at the end, the most difficult part, the part where he always failed. That moment where he would have to call up an image of the witch who had stolen his life and hold her in his mind without feeling anger or hatred, or the uncontrollable urge to destroy—

A memory erupted like an iron spike through the bedrock of his concentration, shattering the calm, meditative state he'd fought so hard for. His temper burst forth like hot lava exploding from the earth and he hissed, blood heating with his fury. It was like coming out of the water after a long swim, taking a deep breath after holding it for far too long. His eyes flew open, his clawed hands flexing as he scanned the room with quick, sharp glances, searching for the intruder who had so easily shattered his efforts and left him wallowing in the suspended fury that had been his permanent state of mind for the last year.

At first he saw nothing. He examined the crimson pillar candle nestled in a gold plate on the stone floor in front of the rug he'd curled up on to meditate. The flame wavered as if something had stirred the air, but remained smooth, resting calmly on its wick. No black smoke danced above the flame.

Daman swiveled in place, muscles protesting as they were forced out of the position he'd been holding for the last two hours. He rolled his aching shoulders, the thick lines of scales trailing down his neck and over his shoulders tugging as he tilted his head from side to side. As he worked the tension from his taxed muscles, he followed the scent of smoke. Someone had invaded his home, his privacy. When he found them, they would find out why all living creatures had fled his property, why he was the only being left on this entire damned estate. His claws ached, sharp white crescents itching to bury themselves in the intruder. The fangs folded against the roof of his mouth tingled, ready to drop into position.

A small spout of flame caught his peripheral vision and he focused on the large fireplace on his left. Thin tendrils of black smoke twined through the air above the remains of the last fire he'd lit in the hearth during the final days of winter. The brownies that crept in to clean his house in the wee hours of the night didn't dare to enter this room, and he certainly didn't care enough to do it himself. A flash of silver disturbed the shadows, something metallic reflecting the dim light of Daman's candle. Another tiny spout of flame bathed the logs, licking at their sides, coaxing them to glow with a faint orange radiance.

"Who's there?" Daman twisted to fully face the fireplace, the scales coating the coils of his lower body silently sliding against the thick rug underneath him. He flexed the muscles of his tail, drawing himself up higher and leaning until he formed a large 'S' as he peered at the fireplace from his new vantage point.

A tiny rounded head poked up from behind the logs. The meager light provided by Daman's candle was more than enough for his sharp eyesight to make out that the creature was reptilian —a snake? The beast blinked beady black eyes, pink tongue flicking out like a sliver of pale pink ribbon.

"I wasss trying to light a fire. It'sss freezing in here."

"It's warm enough." Daman tilted his head, eyeing the small creature peering unfazed at him from the hearth. "Who are you and what are you doing here?"

The creature slithered out from its nest of logs, its thin body sliding over the glowing embers as if the searing heat meant nothing. The scent of burning oak rose from its path as it loosened bits of the logs, sending tiny showers of sparks into the air behind it. It paused on the stone hearth then twisted its head around, sending another blast of flame at the logs. Finally, they caught, the small but steady glow of embers catching into cheery flames that formed a nest for the smoking logs. The snake nodded its satisfaction and continued to glide over the floor toward Daman. Something glittered on either side of its body, a faint iridescence.

Wings.

"You're a *cuelebre*." Daman didn't bother to keep the surprise out of his voice, though his annoyance kept his tone sharp. "What are you doing in Sanguennay? Shouldn't you be in Meropis?"

"Yesss. At leassst in Meropisss, they know that firesss are not jusssst for winter. Ssspring isss not ssso far along that the night'sss chill doesssn't lassst far into the day."

"I'm not cold." Daman's tail lashed behind him, striking something metallic. The sound of metal hitting the wall clanged against Daman's nerves. Another sound that suspiciously resembled hard wax being crushed ratcheted his frustration up even more. *So much for the meditation candle.* "It's my home, so I don't heat it unless I feel there is a need. I certainly don't keep it going for the comfort of guests I don't have—or want."

The *cuelebre* slithered around Daman, the tip of its tail flicking back and forth behind it as he inspected Daman's form. Daman bristled as the shining black eyes took in his mostly human torso and followed it down to his waist where thick scales cascaded down the muscled coil that constituted the lower half of his body. The *cuelebre* tilted its head.

"You are a dragon," it observed. "A *wyvern*, to be precise, yes?"

"Descended from *wyverns*," Daman corrected stiffly. "I'm a *naga*."

"*Nagasss* have human formsss asss well asss ssserpent and half-ssserpent. Do you alwaysss ssspend your time in half human-half ssserpent form?"

Daman clenched his hands into fists, ignoring the sharp points of pain as his claws dug into his palms. He sucked in deep breaths of blood-scented air through his nose, trying to remember the meditations he'd been performing in an attempt to hold on to his rapidly fraying temper. This was his first interaction with another flesh and blood being in nearly a year, perhaps the gods were offering him a test.

Remember your humanity. More man than beast. Humanity cannot be taken away, it can only be given up.

"Did she send you here to torment me?" he bit out. "Have you come to remind me of what she did, perhaps offer to lift the curse if I meet her demands?" Daman lashed against the floor with his tail, twining his body in a sharp circle that brought him around the *cuelebre* faster than the creature could follow. He snatched its tiny body from the floor and clutched it in his fist, closing his fingers until he could feel bones beneath scales and muscle.

"Ssshe?" the *cuelebre* gasped. "Who isss ssshe?" A strangled sound escaped its throat and its tail thrashed wildly as it struggled in Daman's grip. "Let go!"

"Unlessss you want me to crussh you, you will tell me what you are doing here." The sibilance coming from his own lips further reminded Daman of how far she'd pushed him. *She sent me a cuelebre—a serpent to remind me of all she's taken from me. Cold-hearted witch.*

"I'm here to help you with your guessst." The *cuelebre* writhed in his fist, tiny face stabbing up into the air as it tried to slip from his grasp.

"I have no guesst. I haven't had a guesst ssincce sshe curssed me." The sibilance of his voice grew thicker, his forked tongue flicking out of his mouth to taste the air. The *cuelebre* wasn't afraid, the sickly sweet flavor of fear was absent. Daman closed his eyes for a moment, trying to rein himself in, but it was like clutching a boulder in the center of a raging river.

"Open your eyesss. Look outssside. You have a guessst."

Without releasing the *cuelebre*, Daman threw the heavy coils of his lower body over the ground, powerful muscles propelling him to the window. His silver scales grated on the stone floor. The sound echoed in the air around him, adding to the *cuelebre*'s presence and fueling memories of the woman who'd cursed him to remain in this form. The reason he had to meditate every day, the reason he'd had to send away everyone he'd ever cared about.

The *cuelebre* gagged and Daman relaxed his grip as he realized he'd nearly crushed the delicate creature. The *cuelebre* took advantage of his moment of distraction, shooting out of his grip and zipping across the room like a horizontal bolt of lightning.

A noise outside caught Daman's attention and he gaped, disbelieving, down at the path leading up to his front door. A figure stumbled toward the manor, body hunched against the frigid early morning spring air. The kiss of winter was still fresh in nature's memory, the wind still smelling of ice and melting snow despite the green grass and blossoming trees.

The ragged garments the man wore would give him next to no protection against the bite of such a morning. It was barely past first light, too early for the man to have come from any inns nearby. Leaves and small twigs clung to the creases in his clothing and the wisps of graying brown hair sticking out from underneath his hat. Dirt coated half of his body like some sort of mangled pelt.

He must have slept in the woods.

"Who is that?" Daman demanded, keeping his eyes on the approaching figure even as he spoke to the *cuelebre*.

"I don't know."

Daman slammed a hand down on the windowsill, rattling the glass in its pane. "What do you mean you don't know? You're the one who told me I had a visitor, you said you're here to help me with him."

A visitor. Human by all appearances. A delicate human. Here.

The air around Daman grew thicker, harder to breathe. His lungs ached and his vision tunneled. He examined his hands, the white claws curving out from his fingertips like bleached sickles. An image of the old man helpless and terrified in his grip flew into Daman's head. He winced, closing his hands into fists.

"He can't be here. It isn't safe."

"I am here to help," the *cuelebre* reminded him.

"What good are you?" Daman pressed the tight knuckles of one fist to the window frame. "What good will you be to him if—"

The knock at the front door should have been muffled from this distance, but the sound thudded in Daman's ears like a manic heartbeat. A visitor. He didn't have visitors, couldn't have visitors. He couldn't even have servants.

"Anssswer the door."

"No." Daman backed away from the window. He gritted his teeth. "No, he can't stay here."

"Isss your control ssso poor? Isss that why you sssent everyone away?"

Daman's fingers tingled with the urge to catch the *cuelebre* again and puncture its skinny body with his claws. "Who are you?"

"If you ever want them to come back, then you mussst ssstart sssomewhere. Let the old man in, let your human ssside have a sssay."

Daman shot forward, his face burning as his blood boiled and he grabbed for the *cuelebre*. This time, though, the serpent was ready for him and with a flick of its wings, it zipped along the ceiling, careful to stay beyond Daman's grasp.

"Who ssent you here?" Daman choked out, blinking past the red haze growing in front of his eyes.

"He isss cold and hungry," the serpent pressed. "Will you truly turn him away?"

"You would rather I go down and frighten him to death?" Daman rose up to his full height, stretching the muscles of his serpentine lower body until his human half rose to the next best thing to eight feet tall. His wide, plated scales glowed dully in the firelight, pale blues and greens.

The human flesh of his upper body was too pale to be fully human, the same blue-green hue of his scales tinting his skin until he nearly glowed in the dim light. Thick scaled ridges crept down his forehead on each side, falling from his hairline, coiling along his brow ridge and curling to the side of either eye. The sides of his neck were pinched into scaled ridges as well, tracing down over his shoulders.

The scales bled out from the ridges, fading so they barely marked the flesh of his throat. His upper body was human enough, but his draconic heritage left no doubt that he was anything but. And if the dragon ancestry made apparent by the scales didn't scare the beggar to death, Daman suspected his curved serpentine canines and slitted reptilian eyes would finish the job.

"You are not ssscary during the timesss your temper isss not controlling you." The *cuelebre* settled on a wall sconce, settling in as though his life weren't in jeopardy. "You can be a graciousss hossst. Many of your friendsss would have ssstayed if you'd let them."

Daman pushed away the images the intruder's words threatened to drag to the forefront of his mind. He didn't want to think about the friends that had once surrounded him, didn't have to remember how he'd sent them away. There'd been no choice. Better they left than remained behind with him and his pathetic control.

Groping for anything to distract him from his own miserable past, Daman allowed an image of the beggar sitting down to a decent meal to fill his head. Perhaps this was a sign from the gods, a way for him to reconnect with his humanity—to remember who he'd once been.

This could be a gift.

Slowly, he smoothed a hand over his scales, claws dancing over the shimmering surface. "Very well. I will help him." He fixed the *cuelebre* with a hard stare. "But I will remain unseen. Go open the door for him. Lead him around the manor to give me time to set out a meal."

He rushed from the room without giving the tiny serpent an opportunity to offer its opinion. It took no time at all to arrive at the kitchen, and since there were no servants in the manor, Daman was free to fix a meal as he usually did for himself. Though he would have liked to offer the man a hot meal, it would take too long to cook anything, and his skills with food were limited. If only Moira were still here. Moira with her warm smile and her gods-given gift of making the most sumptuous meals any mortal being could ever hope to enjoy.

Bittersweet memories threatened to pour over him and he shoved them away, concentrating on the meal he was preparing for his guest. The brownies that cleaned his home often left him food, but mostly they provided ingredients and left the actual preparations for Daman to do himself. A loaf of hard-crusted bread and a generous helping of fresh butter, a small bowl of ripe strawberries, and a plate of cold beef. The meat was somewhat undercooked, and haphazardly seasoned, but it would fill an empty belly well enough.

He put a pot of black tea to boil and set out a cup along with a bowl of sugar and a small dish of lemons. It was perhaps not the grand feast of roast duck and glazed potatoes Moira might have managed, but surely for a man half-frozen and fresh from a night on the forest floor, it would be a blessing?

"You're thinking of Moira, aren't you, master?"

Daman didn't bother looking at the speaker. The talking teapot had stopped seeming strange long ago.

"Is it that obvious?"

"Your mouth is watering," the faded crockery pointed out. It swung a bit on the hook where it hung over the dark embers of the last kitchen fire, the flames casting a glow over its cloudy white surface with chipped blue flowers. "A bit early for lunch, isn't it?"

"This isn't for me."

As soon as the words were out of his mouth, Daman regretted them. The teapot stilled immediately, and if it'd had a face, Daman was sure its mouth and eyes would both be wide open.

"Master, this is… This is *wonderful*."

"Silence yourself." Daman spoke through clenched teeth, trying to hold on to the warm feeling he'd had while preparing the food. "It is nothing."

"How can you say that?" The teapot swung gently as if in deep contemplation. "Is it Jacque? I hope it's Jacque. He was so hurt when you sent him away."

Daman gripped the tabletop, claws digging into the wood. "Be. Silent."

"I know he tried to hide it, and goodness knows the man had a face like stone at the best of times. Apropos for a captain of the guard, I suppose."

"Do not speak of Jacque." Wood creaked and groaned as Daman's grip on the table tightened.

"He cared for you like a brother. And I agreed with him, you know, you could easily have continued your noble duties even after what the witch did. I know you don't think so, but you're really not that scary."

A split second later, Daman had snatched the teapot from the hook, and stood blinking at it through a red haze.

"Another word," he said hoarsely, "and I will shatter you into dust."

Footsteps echoed on the stairs leading down to the kitchen. Daman hastily put the teapot down on the table and rushed to hide in the hallway beyond the small eating area. His temper died as he held his breath, waiting for the first glimpse he'd have of another person in over a year.

From his shadowed position behind the partial wall, he watched as the beggar wandered in, led by a flicker of light that must have been the *cuelebre* moving too quickly for his eyes to follow. The man's knitted brows parted as he spotted the meal, his pupils dilating and an audible rumble coming from his stomach. A small prayer of thanks fell from his lips as he practically collapsed into the chair at the table.

A pleasant warmth spread over Daman as the man consumed the meager feast with the gusto of someone who hadn't eaten in days. It had been a long time since he'd brought happiness to someone else, and he allowed himself to cherish the feeling, holding the moment to him so he could use it in meditations later.

"I don't know who set this meal out," the man said aloud after he'd finally slowed down. He pulled his tattered hat from his head. "If truth be told, I can't even be certain it was for me. But whoever you are, wherever you are, please know that I am grateful."

Daman leaned against the wall, allowing himself a flare of

pride. Hope rose like a rare bird inside of him, delicate, but welcome.

Perhaps...

"Go out and ssspeak with him."

Daman snatched the *cuelebre* from the air beside him and held him solidly against his chest, using his other hand to cover its mouth. Given the disparity in their sizes, his hand practically encased the *cuelebre*'s entire head and he held the miserable creature still, holding his own breath as he waited to see if the old man had heard.

Blessedly unaware that he wasn't alone, the beggar stood from the table and wandered out of the kitchen. Shoulders sagging in relief, Daman followed at a safe distance, keeping the squirming *cuelebre* firmly in his grip. Every once in a while the man would call out, asking if anyone was home, and the *cuelebre* would resume his struggles, but Daman remained silent. It was a strange feeling, having someone in his home again. A living thing that wasn't...well, a thing.

"All right," the man finally called out. "Whoever you are, it seems you prefer to remain anonymous. Please know that you will forever have my gratitude."

Something in Daman's chest eased, and he took a deeper breath than he had in a long time. The *cuelebre* renewed its struggle in his grip and Daman glanced down. The *cuelebre* stared hard at him and Daman could feel the creature willing him to talk to his visitor. Daman hesitated, but shook his head. He would rather keep the pleasant memory he had than risk poisoning it with the man's fear should he see exactly who—or what—he was thanking.

Remaining silent, Daman stayed with him as the man meandered through the garden. He trailed a hand over some of the new buds, green leaves barely parting to reveal the brilliant pinks, yellows, and blues that would soon light up the garden. The air was already perfumed with the promise of new life and

Daman couldn't help but draw in the spring air, filling his lungs.

"Hello!" a voice called out.

The man shouted, one hand flying to his chest as if to stop his heart from escaping. Daman winced in sympathy. He'd had a similar reaction the first time he'd wandered through this garden after the witch's curse. The amount of raw magic the foolish magic user had poured over the land had not only affected things like crockery. It had also seeped into the soil of the garden—with similarly odd results.

"Who... Who's there?" the old man gasped finally. He swiveled his head in all directions, gaze scanning his surroundings.

It won't help to look, Daman mused. *You'll never guess.*

"I'm here!" came the same voice.

"What...?"

Daman waited for the man's eyes to follow the voice down. A small purple bloom bounced its petals, tiny green leaves along its stem waving merrily in greeting.

"Hi!" it said excitedly.

The old man blinked. Daman settled closer to the ground, his amusement tempered by sympathy. It was hard to stay confident in one's sanity when first confronted by a talking plant.

"You... You're a talking...flower?"

"Yes!"

Daman rolled his eyes. Of course it would be the violet. The seedling was always shouting.

"But...how?"

"I don't know!" The plant tilted its head, its leaves stilling for a moment. "Are you going to stay here? Are there others?"

"No, I... It's only me." The old man paused. "Is there anyone else here?"

The flower swiveled its petals in a complete circle, slowly surveying the garden. "No."

Daman snorted. The stranger should have asked the petal if

anyone lived here. The loud weed wasn't the brightest color in the garden, and it tended to take questions rather literally.

"Oh."

The violet fell silent and for a few long moments, it and the old man just stared at one another. Suddenly the old man brightened.

"Hey, perhaps you could help me."

"I'd love to!"

The old man's face creased in amusement as he hunkered down next to the plant, old leather boots creaking with the movement. "I'm searching for a certain flower. A rose."

"The roses are closer to the manor, on the trellis," the violet supplied graciously.

The man glanced back at the house. "No, I'm talking about a special rose. A Rose of the Mist."

Daman's muscles seized, shock singing through his body in crackling waves, followed by a hot flood of rage as realization dawned. *Fool! Idiot!* He threw the *cuelebre* through the air, the need for secrecy forgotten as he shot over the stone path. He slammed into the intruder, knocking him to the ground with enough force to make the beggar's body bounce off the cobble-stones of the path.

The beggar choked on a scream, the sound heavily laced with pain. He rolled to a stop and groaned, raising a hand to the bloody gash on his head where it had struck the stones. Swaying slightly, he pushed himself to his hands and knees, struggling to roll over. A violent trembling seized him as his gaze fell on Daman.

"How *dare* you!" Daman bellowed. "I let you into my *home*, I *fed* you, and thiss iss how you repay me?"

"I-I-I-I-I d-didn't m-mean any h-harm!" the beggar stuttered. "I-I-I only—"

"You thought to ssteal the Rosse of the Misst?" Sibilance drew out his syllables. "My hosspitality issn't enough for you, you would ssteal from me to increasse your own power?" He stared at the man's poor clothing, seeing it now for the disguise it was. *I've been fooled* again! His tongue flicked out as he struggled to keep from rending the man to bloody shreds. A familiar taste was in the air. Something sweet, smoky...

The witch. Daman went deathly still. His tongue flicked into the air, tasting it again, needing to be absolutely sure. Straw, aged wood, smoke, and old silk. The man smelled of the witch.

Tender human flesh gave easily under Daman's claws as he gripped the terrified man by the neck and hauled him upward until his feet left the ground. Wet gasping sounds came from the intruder's throat and his hands scrabbled at Daman's fingers as he struggled not to be strangled by the unforgiving hold. Eyes bulging like soap bubbles about to burst, face painted a dangerous shade of red, the man floundered in Daman's grasp like a fish in its death throes.

It was so hard not to squeeze, so hard not to give in to that urge to end the miserable thief's life. He could send his body back to the witch as a warning.

"If you want to sspare your life," Daman said softly, struggling to get the words out past the burn of his own anger, "you will tell me why the witch needss the rosse. What is sshe planning now?"

The man gurgled, eyes bulging from his skull. Daman gritted his teeth and relaxed his grip enough so the man could speak.

"I-I d-don't know w-what y-you're talking about!" the miserable creature rasped, his words grating past his damaged throat. "I-it is only a r-rose!"

"It iss not a mere rosse, as well I ssuspect you know." He tightened his grip again in small increments, the blood under the man's skin turning his flesh purple. "You will tell me what your mistress is planning. Or you will die here in great agony." He released the pathetic intruder, letting him crash to the stones. Part of him wanted the man to try and run, wanted the thrill of the chase he hadn't experienced in far too long, a release for his perpetual rage.

"I didn't know it was magic!" the man gasped, body curling in on itself in pain. "I swear! I have no mistress! I know no witch!" Tears streamed down the false beggar's face and he scrambled to kneel at the base of Daman's body, his entire frame trembling as his knees left a smear of blood on the stone through his thin clothing. "My daughter asked for the rose, she showed me a picture. I only wanted to bring this gift back to her—she asked for so little."

His voice was hoarse, every other word nearly lost as it was forced past the bruising of his throat, but he continued to ramble. He pressed his forehead to the ground, abasing himself in front of Daman. "I thought my fortune had returned and even though she said she needed nothing, I demanded that she ask for something—anything. I've been such a failure, I only wanted to prove that I could still give her the life she deserves."

"She has given you a pathetic story that will seal your fate if you do not abandon it." Daman slid back a few paces, giving the man some space to collect himself. His story was a bald-faced lie —the Rose of the Mist was as well-known among magic users as it was rare. The potential in its delicate blossom was enough to make even the most moral of witches salivate and think thieving thoughts.

He cursed himself. He should have known something was amiss after the man had left through the back door to leave through the gardens instead of leaving out the way he'd come. He should have scented the witch on him sooner. He should have *known* she would try something again. His temper rose higher, choking him until it was all he could do not to crush the thief where he lay.

"I thought one of my ships had escaped the misfortune of the others—that perhaps the pirates hadn't taken everything from me," the man rambled. "We lost our house, our home. I was such a wealthy man, a provider. Now I am too poor to buy nice dresses for my daughters, to offer a proper dowry. I've failed at so much." He sobbed. "It was only a rose."

Every word out of the man's mouth confirmed Daman's suspicions and he leaned over the man, claws tingling. He'd heard that story before, listened to a woman give him that same sorry recounting of her fate. He eyed the old man. Yes...now he remembered. This fool was the witch's father. He'd seen him when he'd gone to investigate her tale of woe, the day he'd discovered her lies.

His tail lashed from side to side and he pushed himself higher into the air, towering over the simpering beggar. His forked tongue flicked out of his mouth.

What color the man had left drained from his face and left him white as a ghost. A tiny voice of doubt whispered through his mind. Perhaps... Perhaps the fool truly hadn't known about the rose. Considering who his daughter was, the poor man could be an innocent patsy, someone to take the fall for the theft if caught. His fear was real enough.

Daman clenched his clawed hands into fists, concentrating on the bite of his own talons as they dug into his flesh. He didn't want her father. He wanted the witch. For the thousandth time, he wished he could go after her himself. If only he could take his human form one more time, just long enough to pass through the town without frightening innocent villagers. He wanted to see her face before he stained his hands with her blood.

But she would never come back here, never risk his wrath. Daman paused, gaze sliding to the man groveling on the ground. Unless...

Daman coiled his lower body tighter, bringing his chest closer to the ground so he didn't tower quite so high about the terrified man. "You tried to steal something very valuable from me after I was kind enough to offer you hospitality. I would be within my rights to keep you here as my prisoner to punish you for your crime." He took a deep breath, holding on to his temper as best he could. "But I am willing to make you a deal."

"A d-deal?" the terrified man stammered.

"Yes. A deal." Daman gripped the stones beneath him, trying to keep his voice calm. "Go home. Tell your daughter what has transpired. If she will agree to return here with you—and stay here for as long as I so desire—I will reward you with riches and allow you to go home and begin rebuilding all that you lost."

Daman remembered the witch, remembered how badly she'd wanted money, wanted the life she'd lost after her father's money had been taken. "Understand me, I will make you a rich man. Rich enough to climb even higher in society than you were. Tell your daughter that and tell her that her time here will not be forever and no harm will come to her."

Those last words tasted foul on his tongue, but he forced them out. More than the witch's death, he wanted her to lift the curse. If she would agree to do so, he would spare her life. "Make it clear to her that if she refuses my offer, then you must come back here alone and remain here as my prisoner."

The trembling of the old man's body grew worse, until it was a wonder the flesh didn't fly from his very bones. "What do you want with my daughter?"

She doesn't deserve your protection. Daman tried to keep his voice level. "That is my concern."

"I... I understand." The old man half-collapsed on the ground, his head apparently having grown too heavy to hold up anymore.

"Good."

Excitement swirled in Daman's veins, anticipation of finally having the leverage to force the witch to break her curse filling him with hope. A deep satisfaction curled inside of him. She'd once begged to stay here, claimed she wanted to be with him more than anything. Well, she would get her wish.

She would stay here all right—but it would not be in the lap of luxury that she'd wanted so badly. She would lift her curse on him or he would make her suffer. There were things far worse than death—especially for witches who pined for the finer things in life. "Go to the front of the house and wait there. I'll send a horse and carriage to take you home."

Without waiting for a response, Daman shot down the path through the garden, riding a wave of adrenaline, feeling light enough to fly. Birds flew screaming into the air, and dirt scattered in all directions from the savage thrusting of his tail as he hurtled over the field in the direction of the stable.

He'd had no need for horses in some time, but he'd never been able to part with the last one. The ebony stallion had been the jewel of his stable, completely fearless—an attribute that had never been more clear than when it had been the only animal in his stable not to shriek in terror the day Daman had come to release them after the curse had taken his legs. Even now, with his heart pounding and what he knew must be a wild light in his eyes, the beast blinked at him, not bothering to stop chewing its hay as Daman entered its stall. Its velvety nose quivered as it snorted at Daman—unimpressed.

The equine was reluctant to leave his lunch, but he amiably allowed Daman to lead it out of the stall and over to a carriage covered in a year's worth of dust. An undeniable feeling of indignation radiated from the beast as Daman hitched it to the carriage without cleaning it off first, but after a few tosses of its head, it snorted in resignation.

It took mere minutes for Daman to drag the heavy carriage from the confines of its dusty shelter and get the straps fastened snugly around the mild-mannered beast. He had to be particularly careful in his work, determined not to injure his noble companion with the sickle-shaped claws curling from his fingertips. When the final strap was secure, Daman breathed a little easier, patting the animal on the rump.

Cool scales slid over Daman's shoulder, followed by the flicker of a slim pink tongue.

"That wasssn't very niccce."

The horse's ears pressed flat against its head, but that was the only indication it gave that it registered the *cuelebre*'s presence. Daman gave it a swat on its silky hindquarters. The stallion shook out its mane and rolled one eye at the *cuelebre* as it trotted off down the path. The beast was well-trained, it would go to the front of the main house where it had once waited for Daman in his human form on those occasions he'd seen fit to go into town. The carriage, while unused for some time, was solidly built and barely swayed as it was jostled down the path.

"You know nothing of this situation. I have reasons for what I've done."

"You want the witch."

Daman faced the *cuelebre* with renewed interest, flexing his hands until his claws clicked against one another. "What do you know of it?"

"I know what a *naga* isss. You aren't in thisss form by choiccce."

The door to the stable creaked in protest as Daman's hand tightened on the handle. He inhaled slowly, closing his eyes and counting to ten before closing the door with as much restraint as he could manage. "What is your purpose here?"

"I am here to help." The *cuelebre* tapped its chin with the tip of its tail, contemplating Daman for several long seconds. "You have a plan," it said finally.

Daman waited, but the *cuelebre* said no more. Its black eyes were reflective black pearls, offering Daman no hint of its thoughts, only shining his own image back at him. "I do have a plan. But I will not require your help."

The *cuelebre* bobbed its head. "That'sss how it goesss. The bessst laid plansss…"

CHAPTER 3

"Everything is about to get better. I can't believe this nightmare is almost over."

Maribel remained silent as she stood stirring the pot over the fire, adding a dash of dried spices now and then. The aroma of salty chicken broth, fragrant onion, and tender carrots and celery fresh from the garden wafted up to envelope her in a pleasant, steamy embrace. Chicken soup was one of her father's favorites, a simple, but comforting recipe. It would be exactly what he needed after his long journey, especially if he'd had to travel at night. Nothing chased the chill from one's bones like a good soup.

"We'll have a real roof over our heads, not this miserable patchwork," Corrine continued. "There will be people all around us all the time. We'll have true friends this time, not people who will abandon us at the first sign of shifting fortune. Our clothes will fit properly and we'll never be hungry again."

Maribel forced herself to relax her death grip on the wooden spoon she held before she snapped it into useless twigs. *She doesn't mean to be insulting. She's just used to a certain lifestyle. She needs a different lifestyle to feel secure. It's no reflection on how hard Father and I work to make her comfortable.*

Squaring her shoulders, Maribel forced a smile to her face as she glanced over to where Corrine sat huddled under a thick quilt beside the fire. The chair had been pushed farther back, a testament to caution after Corrine's last episode. "If you're hungry, I can fix you a bowl of soup? It's already done, I'm just letting it cook longer to make the flavor richer."

"Do you remember our first winter here? How cold it was, how fast our food ran out?" Corrine rubbed the corner of the quilt against her cheek, the way she'd cuddled her coverlet when she was a child. Tendrils of fraying threads stuck out from the corners, betraying the blanket for the second-hand charity it was. Nothing like the silks and furs Corrine and Maribel had snuggled into when they were kids. She tugged at it, pulling it tighter around her, the damaged skin of her injured hand stretching with each movement.

"I remember." Maribel stopped stirring, lost in the dancing flames of her cooking fire. Cold touched her back, the memory of that winter still fresh in her mind despite the cozy atmosphere in the cottage.

"Strange that the winters never seemed quite so cold before. Back at home there was always a roaring fire, plenty of hot tea and warm meals. I remember we used to sit at the windowsill wrapped up in furs and blankets, holding hot chocolate and watching the snow fall. It was always so beautiful, and those are some of my best memories. But here…"

Corrine pulled the quilt up over her head until she peered out of it through an opening the size of her palm, her voice muffled by the worn fabric when she spoke. "I thought I was going to die, Maribel. The wind came through a thousand cracks in this miserable shack and each one was a knife cutting into my skin. For a moment I was the same pathetic creature I was as a child. At Death's door. Not strong enough to live."

"A lot different then now, isn't it?" Maribel broke in, trying to snap Corrine out of her depressing reverie. She winced at her tone and focused on the soup, stirring faster as if her body was trying to keep up with her racing thoughts. She hadn't meant for her voice to be so sharp, but she'd heard Corrine say the same words so many times. Her sister was forever trapped in the memory of that one winter, a victim no matter how good her life became. *Corrine, I love you, but, demons take it, things aren't that bad!*

Corrine's silence was so thick and sudden that it sucked the ambient noise right out of the room. Maribel yanked the spoon from the soup and rapped it violently on the edge of the pot. The loud clanging made her nerves spasm, the sound like a voice in her head shouting at her that she was losing her temper and she'd regret it.

Get a hold of yourself, Maribel.

Slowly, she put the spoon on the table beside her, careful to lay it down gently. She concentrated on the warmth sizzling against her face, the almost-burn that came from standing this close to the fire. The steam from the soup wafted over her, chasing back the memories Corrine was trying so hard to drag out of her.

"Do you ever see the faces?"

"Faces?" The hairs on the back of Maribel's neck stood up, something in Corrine's voice sending a chill up her spine despite the fire's heat. "What faces?"

Corrine didn't answer. Her brown eyes held a reflection of the hearth, glittering where they gazed out from the hood of her quilt. The shadows on her face flickered and jumped, seeming almost alive…

"Corrine?" Maribel's voice came out louder than she'd intended, startling her more than Corrine. She cleared her throat. "Corrine, what faces?"

"Faces everywhere. Watching. Waiting." Corrine startled, body twitching as though coming out of a daze. She blinked owlishly at Maribel, then suddenly she seemed to realize what she'd said and busied herself with pushing the quilt off her head and smoothing it around her again. "Or maybe it's only the episodes putting strange images in my head."

Maribel let out a breath she hadn't realized she'd been holding. "Oh. Yes." She groped beside her for some peppercorns, her mind picking over Corrine's words.

"Faces everywhere. Watching. Waiting."

Something sour churned in Maribel's stomach, a sense of unease. Against her will, whispers she'd heard in the past breathed through her mind.

"There goes the farmer's daughter. I heard she was possessed by the Evil Fire."

"Aye, touched by demons that one is. Studies with the old crone in the woods."

"Mother Briar is helping you with those episodes, isn't she?" Maribel dropped the peppercorns into the mortar, wrapping her hand around the base as she lifted the pestle to begin grinding them to powder.

Corrine lifted one shoulder in a half-shrug. "I suppose. But what I really need is to get away from here." She leaned her cheek against the edge of the chair. "I want to go home."

And we're back. Maribel smashed the pestle down with unnecessary force and one of the peppercorns shot out of the mortar like a tiny black cannonball. "Corrine, do you really hate our life here so much?"

"Yes," Corrine said without a moment's hesitation. "I know you like being close to the land, combing through the dirt with your fingers." She finally tore her gaze away from the fire to meet Maribel's eyes. "But, Maribel, don't you ever lie awake at night wondering how long it will be until our crops fail, or the hunting turns sour? How long it will be until we have another winter like that first one?"

"No, I don't." Maribel tapped the pestle against the mortar to loosen the clinging bits of pepper then placed it on the table beside her. Wiping her hands off on her apron, she went over and knelt by Corrine, taking her hands in hers. "We aren't the same people we were back then, Corrine. We came here knowing nothing about how to fend for ourselves, spoiled by always having the money to pay someone else to take care of us. We know better now." She brushed a curl of sleek brown hair behind Corrine's ear. "I promise, I will never let you starve."

Corrine opened her mouth like she wanted to argue, but suddenly horse hooves clattering on the stones outside the house drew both girls' attention. Corrine scrambled free of the blankets like a rabbit desperately escaping a net, arms and legs akimbo as she fought free. In seconds she was out of her chair and through the door. A muscle ticked in Maribel's jaw.

Shaking off the bitterness that pressed her lips into a thin line, Maribel gave herself a moment to regain her composure. She brushed her hair back from her face and settled her apron into smooth lines. Composed once again, she rose to leave the house.

She hadn't even made it to the door when her father stumbled inside. His clothes were covered in dirt and clumps of drying mud, his hair was in wild disarray around his face, and his skin was red from the frosty air. Maribel went still as she noticed her father's eyes were swollen…as if he'd been crying. Corrine trailed behind him, tears streaming down her cheeks.

Maribel swallowed her questions as she clasped her father's arm and helped him to the table. He fell into the chair more than sat and she set about getting him settled in, all the while fighting down a rising sense of dread. She retrieved one of the blankets Corrine had been using and wrapped it around her father, rubbing his shoulders and arms until the friction warmed the blanket. Corrine collapsed into another seat at the table, staring forlornly at the worn wood. Maribel poured a cup of tea from the pot keeping warm by the fire and set it down in front of her father.

"What happened?" she asked quietly, taking a seat.

Her father's face folded like an ancient parchment, tears glistening in his eyes. "Everything's gone. Claimed as payment for old debts." He pressed his lips together and swallowed hard. "There is nothing left."

Maribel firmly tamped down on the part of her that rejoiced at the news, the part that wanted more than anything to stay on this farm, to live this new life. Instead, she concentrated on her father, letting her sympathy for his loss show on her face. "Father, it's all right. We'll be fine here. We have each other, that's all that matters."

A sob escaped her father's throat and Maribel stared as tears spilled over and slid down his face. She'd expected him to be disappointed, even sad, but this... For the first time, Maribel noticed the deep purple bruising on her father's neck. Her lips parted in shock and her stomach dropped.

"Father, what's wrong?" she asked carefully.

"I was only trying to bring you your rose," her father sobbed. "And now I've doomed us all over again."

"What?" Corrine's face drained of all color and she swayed in her seat. "You... You've lost the farm?"

Their father wrapped his hands around his teacup as if it were the only thing holding him to this world. "No. No, you will keep the farm, both of you. But you will have to keep it...without me."

"What?" Maribel gasped.

"It's the only way." Their father didn't lift his gaze from his teacup. "I was on my way back from town. I heard wolves in the forest and I tried to take a new path, one that led farther away from the beasts. It shouldn't have taken me out of the way, but my mind..." He lowered his voice. "I wasn't paying attention. I got lost and before I knew it, I had arrived at the abandoned manor near the lake at the bottom of the mountain."

Corrine inhaled sharply, but Maribel kept her eyes on their father. "There are stories about that manor. I've heard rumors that the lord that ruled that house still lives there, but that he was cursed by a witch. They say he's—"

"A beast!" her father choked.

He met Maribel's gaze and her chest tightened at the wild light in his eyes.

"At first I was afraid, but there seemed to be no one there. I… I went inside—to get out of the wind. There was a meal laid out, fresh, with tea still hot. I called out, but no one answered, so I sat down to eat." His head drooped. "I thought perhaps there was someone there looking out for me." He raised a trembling hand to his face, dragging it over his jaw. "I was almost right."

He spread his fingers out on the table, pressing his palms to the worn surface as if gathering himself to finish the story. "I left the manor through the garden. And on my way, I…" He stopped, barked out a laugh. "I can hardly even say it. It's not possible."

"What?" Maribel prodded, her heart in her throat. A garden. Surely the bruises… No. Who would attack a man over a flower?

"There was a talking flower."

Maribel's eyebrows met her hairline. Beside her, Corrine went deathly still.

"A… Father, are you sure?"

Her father nodded, not meeting the eyes of either of his daughters. "I asked it about your rose, Maribel."

The anxiety that had laid like a weight in Maribel's stomach writhed, growing thicker and heavier. She held her breath, not wanting to hear the rest of the story, but needing to know. "The rose. What happened?"

"*He* showed up." A shiver ran through his frame, hard enough he tilted in his chair. "A more frightening sight I've never seen. Half man-half dragon, he had the upper body of a mortal man, but his skin, his eyes… They were a color no human ever possessed. He had no legs, only a tail… There's dragon blood there, I'd bet my life on it."

His voice broke and he swallowed twice. "He was furious with me for seeking that rose. I thought he would kill me there, and I'm ashamed to say I babbled like a fool. I tried to explain why I needed the rose, tried to beg his forgiveness. But I only succeeded in prompting a worse fate. He told me I had to either come back to him and be his prisoner forever, or give him one of my daughters." He let out a sound somewhere between a laugh and a sob. "As if any man would make such a sacrifice."

Maribel's heart sank deeper in her chest, her guts wrenching tighter. Her mouth opened and closed, but no sound came out. All she could do was gape at her father, her heart twisted by the way his hands shook so badly that most of the tea in his mug sloshed onto the rough wood of their table. *My fault.*

"He was truly frightening to behold, and ferocious in his anger, but up until I took the rose, he was kind enough to feed me. I don't believe he will harm me as his prisoner. I will be all right." He choked on a sob. "I only wish I could stay here and care for you. I don't want to leave you to fend for yourselves, not when I've already been responsible for you losing so much."

"This is all because of me." Maribel's voice sounded hollow even to her own ears.

"Father, there must be another way. You can't mean to leave us. Perhaps we could compensate this lord in some way." Corrine's voice was higher than usual, her eyes showing too much white. She swallowed hard, fidgeting with the skirt of her dress. Then suddenly she stiffened, visibly shaking off her panic. She whirled to face Maribel. "What rose did you ask for?"

"A… A Rose of the Mist. It was in one of Mother Briar's books." She groped for Corrine's hand, needing to see understanding in her sister's eyes. "I thought it would help you. The Rose of the Mist has magical abilities… It would have made you stronger."

"You asked Father to retrieve a magical plant?" Corrine held her hand back from Maribel's questing fingers, disbelief in her brown eyes.

"The book didn't say anything about it being guarded! I had no reason to think any harm would come from asking. I thought he might find it at an herbalist's or the apothecary's." The words sounded ridiculous now. A rose that rare with that much power… She'd been a fool.

"It is not your fault, Maribel." Her father snatched Maribel's hand from the table, clutching it fervently to his chest. The dirt from his own hand and clothes was irrelevant in light of the soil permanently embedded under Maribel's fingernails. "I am the one who has failed you both. If I had been more careful with my business… I lost all those ships to pirates, and now the last one has been claimed to repay debts. There is nothing left."

Exhaustion weighed his head down and his shoulders slumped. "And then to enter a strange manor—no matter how abandoned it appeared to be. I should have been suspicious, should have known something was not right." He cleared his throat, a fresh well of tears glistening in his eyes. "I will stay long enough to teach you both the work you will need to do in my absence."

"No." Maribel raised her other hand and brought it down to cup her father's between the two of hers. "No, I will go."

"Maribel!" Corrine grabbed Maribel's shoulder, spinning her to face her. "Maribel, you can't go!"

"It's all right." Maribel patted her hand. "Father said the lord promised I wouldn't be harmed. Perhaps all he wants is a servant." She glanced back at her father. "You said there were no servants, but that the manor was very large. Perhaps he intends to have me clean and cook for him."

"You have no idea what he wants!" Corrine knitted her eyebrows together, her grip tightening on Maribel's shoulder. "He could mean you harm, no matter what he says. And even if he didn't mean to hurt you, would you really go and be servant to a monster?"

"Hard work doesn't bother me."

Corrine flinched and Maribel winced. "Corrine, I didn't mean—"

"I know what you meant," Corrine said stiffly. "You do all the work around here anyway, so being the servant of a monster wouldn't be any different, is that it?"

"I didn't mean it that way." Maribel's voice hitched, stirred by a traitorous thought stabbing into her consciousness. If she were to go away, then she would still work hard, yes, but perhaps she could find some peace, could enjoy her toils if she didn't have Corrine looking over her shoulder, making her feel guilty for any stolen moment of happiness when her sister was so miserable…

"If you truly don't want to leave, then don't." Corrine's voice was a plea. "Maribel, I need you here. You know how much I need you."

I need me too. Through the guilt, an insidious hope took firm root, taunting her with images of gardening at the grand manor, feeling the soil in her hands and the sun on her back. Enjoying working with nature without pretending to miss the life they'd had. Maribel stood and retook her place in front of the cooking fire, not trusting her face not to betray her thoughts.

"Corrine, I can't let our father take responsibility for my fool-ishness." She picked up the abandoned mortar and tilted it until powdered peppercorns drifted down into the soup. "It is only right that I should go."

"Maribel, that is not the truth of the matter," her father broke in. "It is not your foolishness, it is mine. I lost our fortune, I entered a strange mansion. I have brought this on us. It is not for you to fix this. I'm an old man, I've lived a good life. Let me serve out the rest of my days with this lord, I will gladly be his prisoner if it means you two can stay here together."

"We can't work this farm by ourselves!" Corrine protested, her voice rising until it took on an edge of hysteria. She shot to her feet and stomped over to Maribel. Ignoring her sister's protest, she yanked the spoon from her hand, flinging hot soup in an arc through the room as she flung it to the table. "Come on. We'll go see Mother Briar. Perhaps she knows something about this beast, something that will help us escape him."

"Yes!" Their father sat up in his chair, red-rimmed eyes brightening with sudden hope. He pointed at Corrine. "Yes, go and see Mother Briar. Ask her if she can help us avoid this horrible choice." He met Maribel's eyes. "But if she can't, then I will go."

"No." Maribel pulled against Corrine, digging her heels into the floor as her sister tried to drag her out of the house. Her heart pounded wildly, a dizzying whirlwind of emotions rushing around inside her mind. She settled a firm gaze on her father, a man who up until now had always been vaguely disapproving of Mother Briar and the magic she wanted to teach his daughters. "Father, it's all right, just let me go."

Maribel's words fell on deaf ears as Corrine dragged her across the floor.

"Come on, Maribel. If there's anyone who can help us, it's Mother Briar. We're not going to let you go without a fight!"

Every word out of their mouths meant to comfort her and reassure her of how much they wanted to keep her with them only fed the flame burning steadily inside Maribel. The flame of hope, of anticipation. She was more certain with every passing second that she wanted to go, that perhaps there was more freedom to be had as a servant of this lord than there was here with her own family.

As Corrine kept a firm grip on her hand, pulling her forcibly through the door and into the woods, Maribel imagined that every branch that slapped at her shoulders, every bristle that caught her skirt, and every root that stuck up from the ground to catch her feet were all trying to warn her not to seek Mother Briar's help. In her mind, she was already packed and on her way to the beast's manor.

It was strange to proceed all the way up the stone pathway to

Mother Briar's door. Usually the old woman met them outside, and Maribel was usually left to work outdoors amongst the plants while Corrine and Mother Briar retired inside to practice other magical skills. This time, though, Corrine tugged Maribel right along behind her until she arrived at the door. She banged on the thick wood and the door swung open after only a few moments.

Mother Briar peered out at them, grey eyebrows arched. "Hello, girls. What a surprise, I didn't expect you for another—"

"We have an emergency." Corrine pulled Maribel to stand closer to her, infusing her voice with an intriguing mixture of desperation and authority.

"Indeed?"

"Our father has run afoul of the monster who lives in the abandoned manor. The beast is demanding that Maribel come to him to take our father's place as his prisoner. We need your help."

"Father said himself that the lord showed him kindness," Maribel insisted meekly. "I'm certain he will not harm me."

Mother Briar's eyes sharpened and she leaned closer to Maribel with an intensity that had her taking a step back. A strange scent drifted from the old woman's clothes, something metallic and musty. Blood and feathers?

"The lord of the abandoned manor… What did he look like?"

"Father said he looked like a dragon." Maribel bit her lip. "He said that he was half man, half serpent."

For a brief second, Maribel could have sworn a message passed between Mother Briar and Corrine, a conversation without words. Mother Briar shuffled back and opened the door wider. "Come inside."

Though she'd been inside once or twice in the past, stepping inside the witch's house was like stepping into a whole new world. Plants and herbs hung from strings all over the walls, filling the space with the dust of yellowed leaves and the cloying scent of dying blooms. The skeletons of small creatures were scattered about flat surfaces, some of them with bits of flesh still clinging feebly to the blood-stained bone. Sharp blades glinted from the shadows, polished but somehow still managing to hint at their gory tasks, as though the blood hung on the steel like a shadow. A thick black cauldron hung in the fireplace, a liquid bubbling inside that didn't smell like any soup Maribel had ever come in contact with.

After they were all seated at the small table in the witch's kitchen, Mother Briar focused her full attention on Maribel. "Now, tell me exactly what happened."

Maribel resigned herself to the situation and leaned heavily on the table. "Father received a message saying one of his ships had come in, and he asked Corrine and me what we wanted. I tried to tell him I didn't want anything, but he insisted. Finally, I remembered a rose I'd seen in one of your books. A Rose of the Mist. I told him I wanted the rose and showed him the picture. I thought he could get it at a florist or an apothecary, or maybe even from the woods—the book said the rose had been found in these forests near here before." She closed her eyes, her stomach rolling as she forced herself to think of all that her father had been through—because of her.

"This lord has a Rose of the Mist?" Mother Briar breathed.

A gleam came into her eyes, a shine that emphasized the darkness of her irises rather than lightened them. Maribel had to fight not to rub her arms to rid herself of the sudden crawling sensation over her flesh.

"A Rose of the Mist is very valuable," Mother Briar mused, half to herself. A flash of disapproval lit her eyes. "And if you'd read the book in its entirety, you would know that it does not occur naturally. The Rose of the Mist is created from an ordinary rose that has been subjected to intense magical forces—wild, uncontrolled magic. They cannot be created on purpose, only by accident. That is what makes them so rare."

Again the old crone's gaze slid to Corrine as if trying to

convey something important. Corrine's brown eyes remained ice cold, her face set in sharp lines. Maribel opened her mouth, ready to ask what was going on, what the two women weren't telling her.

"I've heard stories of this lord," Corrine said tightly. "Mother Briar, I'm *sure* you'll be able to confirm them. I've heard that this lord was cursed into a bestial form because he turned away a weary old woman who begged shelter during a wicked storm. She wanted to teach him a lesson, but the lord was too cruel and selfish to learn. I heard that he killed everyone in his manor—down to the last servant."

Mother Briar held Corrine's look for a moment longer then faced Maribel. "I've heard those rumors as well. And indeed, we must not dismiss them too easily." She paused. "However..."

Corrine choked, but Mother Briar ignored her.

"If your father says that this lord fed and sheltered him, then perhaps he has learned from his past mistakes. In fact, I had heard that in order to break the curse upon him, he must learn to love and trust another, and earn their love and trust in return. Perhaps that is why he has sent for you, suggested this trade. It is possible that he wants an opportunity to break his curse, and he simply feels that his appearance is too frightening for him to get the chance any other way."

Maribel's lips parted. "You mean... You think he wants me to stay with him so that he can...woo me?"

Corrine's fingers gripped the wooden table so hard her nails drew furrows in the surface. Mother Briar continued to ignore her, her unwavering gaze locked firmly on Maribel.

"I think he wants a chance to prove that he's changed, that he is not the beast inside that he is on the outside," the witch confirmed. "Do you think you could see beyond his appearance and give him that chance?"

Maribel blinked, shifting uncomfortably in her seat at the witch's lack of subtlety. She folded her hands, urging herself to get a grip. The witch was probably toying with her, filling her head with ridiculous fantasies so she'd embarrass herself in front of this lord. Mother Briar had never liked Maribel. "I'm sure we'll get along fine," she told Mother Briar, her will to remain polite strained to the point of discomfort. "Thank you for the advice."

"No!"

Corrine's shout drew the attention of Maribel and Mother Briar simultaneously. Veins pulsed in her sister's temples, straining against her skin. The hair on Maribel's arms rose as some sort of ghostly wind flowed from her sister. The brown tendrils of Corrine's hair danced as though stirred by a breeze, and there was a disconcerting vibration rolling off her body. Maribel held her breath as she realized that for the first time, she was getting a taste of Corrine's magic.

"Mother Briar," Corrine ground out, "surely there is some information you can give us that would let Maribel escape the lord's grasp? We need her on the farm."

Mother Briar gave an exaggerated sigh. "I'm afraid I can think of nothing. In my mind, the best thing for your sister to do is to go to this lord, save her father, and perhaps see if she can't get to know the man within the monster."

Corrine looked like she'd swallowed a live toad and Maribel shifted uneasily in her seat. The vibration from her sister grew stronger, and the sensation on Maribel's skin was...unpleasant. Not for the first time, she wondered exactly what happened in this cottage while she was outside among the plants. "Corrine," she said gently. "Please. Everything will be all right, you'll see."

Corrine shot out of her seat and practically flew through the door. Maribel raised her hands to cover her face, suddenly wanting nothing more than to be alone with her thoughts.

"She will be all right," Mother Briar assured her. "There comes a time in everyone's life where they must travel their path alone."

"I suppose so," Maribel mumbled.

"Your sister relies on you, Maribel, but she is stronger than even she thinks. Go to this lord, save your father—save the beast. Do not worry about Corrine." The witch's voice shifted, taking on a tone somewhere between a promise and a threat. "I will take care of your sister."

Suddenly Maribel had to get out of the witch's cottage. She offered Mother Briar a half-hearted wave goodbye and, without making eye contact, followed the path Corrine had taken. For the first time in Maribel's life, she ran to catch up with her sister.

CHAPTER 4

The vase exploded against the wall, shattering into a thousand pieces and littering the rug with glistening dust and jagged fragments of broken ceramic. The nerve-scratching sound of the crash did nothing to appease Daman or the tempest raging inside him. His blood still boiled in his veins, a red haze hanging in front of his eyes and clouding his vision. His chest rose and fell rapidly with his heavy breathing as he faced the window again, watching the new arrivals emerge from the carriage and start up the path.

"That iss *not* the witch," he seethed. "The old man hass played me for a *fool*."

"You didn't know the witch had a sssissster?"

"Of coursse I knew!" Daman ground his teeth, the increasing sibilance in his voice grating on his nerves, taunting him with his loss of control. "It made ssensse that the witch would be the one to want the Rosse of the Misst." He tried to keep his voice level, his tone even. "I vissited her home a year ago—I ssaw no ssign that her ssisster practicced the craft."

"How long did you obssserve her?"

Daman drummed his fingers along the windowsill, white

claws clicking against the stone in a sharp staccato pattern. "No longer than I obsserved the home of anyone who came to me sseeking ssanctuary. It didn't take long to esstablish that the witch wass not being abussed, wass not misstreated by her family. Sshe didn't sseek my help becausse her life wass in danger, sshe merely wanted an eassier life and sshe thought I would give that to her."

The rest of that particular memory tried to creep into Daman's consciousness, but he shoved it away. He couldn't afford to lose his temper completely. Not now that there were people here, people who could bleed, could be injured.

He stewed silently. The old man was a wreck. Even though he wore clean clothes now and had obviously eaten and slept much better than the last time Daman had seen him, his hair was sticking out in tufts where he'd probably shoved his hands through it. His face was lined with worry and his eyes were red from tears. He held his daughter to him as he trudged up the path, lips moving the whole time. No doubt whispering words of comfort.

Or perhaps trying to convince her to leave.

The woman for the most part appeared determined. Her jaw was set in a stubborn line, though her eyes flicked nervously, taking in her surroundings with the caution of a cat approaching a rustling bush. Daman's eyes lingered on her, taking note of her fair skin, her beautiful chocolate brown hair. Her body was thin, but the curve of her hips suggested that her slender state had more to do with a peasant's diet than any decree of the gods. She would probably have luscious curves if fed properly, the kind of curves a man could cup in his palms...

The scrape of claws against hard stone grated on his ears, drawing Daman out of his burgeoning fantasy and back into stark reality. He stared down at his hand, his skin spotted with bluish green scales, fingers tipped with sharp white claws. Not the hands one held a woman close with. Pain washed over him, followed quickly by a welcome rush of hot anger. Yet one more thing the witch had stolen from him then.

"I have to ssend her away." He flowed for the door like a churning tide, his scales scratching over the stone floor. Even with his back to the window, he could still see the woman's brown hair with deep red highlights glistening in the sun. An image from a year ago, the same woman kneeling in the dirt, face smudged with soil, humming happily as she tried to coax a tomato plant to lean properly against the stick she was trying to tie it to, brushed across his mind. He'd thought her beautiful then too. He'd had his human form then, he could have spoken up, introduced himself...

Frustration pulled his skin tight and threatened to urge his temper to stone-shattering depths. Daman sucked in air through his nose, letting it out of his mouth silently as he dashed through the hallways down to the lower level. All of that was done, in the past. He couldn't change it now, and a fleeting attraction to the woman didn't change anything. She couldn't stay here.

Why couldn't it have been the witch? It should have been her.

His head throbbed, a loud buzzing in both his ears making him clench his teeth. He needed to meditate, needed to get a handle on the rage building inside him. He'd thought of the witch too often these past few days, had allowed memories of her to feed his fury for too long. He had to get rid of his unwanted guests so he could retreat to his sanctuary, his loneliness. It was the way it had to be.

His hand closed over the doorknob, claws scratching at the polished metal, and he ripped it open, muscles already propelling him to meet his guests. Shock broke over him as he realized they'd progressed farther than he'd anticipated and were directly in front of him, standing on the doorstep.

His serpentine reflexes were the only thing that kept him from colliding with the man and his daughter, his lower body constricting and pushing upward so that his momentum was redistributed into rising up higher as his tail uncoiled more than usual and lifted him instead of shoving him into his new arrivals.

The end result was that he filled the doorway, looming over his visitors from nearly eight feet in height. The old man cried out and curled himself around his daughter, putting his back between her and Daman. The girl sucked in a startled breath and squeezed her eyes closed, cowering into her father's arms.

Fear me, of course you fear me. Their reaction broke something inside Daman, the last of his tenuous control. He roared, a loud, bellowing sound that rattled the windows on either side of the door. The girl whimpered, eyes still tightly closed, and her father gritted his teeth, clutching her tighter.

"What gamess are you playing, old man?" Daman demanded, heart pounding wildly in the flood of adrenaline pouring through him. His tongue flicked out with every sibilant syllable—a fact that only fed his rage.

"Y-you said—"

"You were to bring me the daughter that assked for the rosse!"

The girl peered over her father's shoulder while still huddling in his protective embrace. Her blue eyes revealed far too much white.

"I," she started, her voice hoarse and broken. She cleared her throat. "I am the one who asked for the rose."

Daman gripped the doorway, digging his claws into the wood until it groaned, threatened to splinter. The girl flinched, but kept her eyes on his.

"You?" His tongue stabbed the air, tasting it. He growled. "You are no witch. You—"

Daman went perfectly still, the taste of the girl's scent on the air fully registering. Instinct seized control of his muscles, sliding him closer to the woman, his tongue slipping out again to confirm what his senses were telling him. He ignored the old man's shudder, focusing on the woman.

She is a changeling. How did I miss that before?

He studied her for a moment, his gaze flicking from her to her father. The old man cared for her, that much was obvious. It was impossible to tell if he knew the woman in his arms was not of his own blood or if he, like so many others, continued to believe the lie of the new babe in the cradle.

Rage still bubbled inside of him like a pot left too long over the fire. It wasn't until his brain registered the trembling of the changeling on his doorstep that Daman realized exactly how close to the edge of the cliff he was standing. She was a changeling, a member of the people he had given his oath to protect—a child left by fey parents in exchange for their human babe. That she saw him as a threat was the greatest blow to his honor he had ever born.

Exerting his will over his temper was never easy, but those blue eyes gave him the strength he needed to reach deep inside himself, to search for the elusive thread of humanity wavering in the wind of his temper. He snatched it up and held it close to him, sucking in long, deep, slow breaths. He pictured his rage like a fire burning inside of him, and he kept breathing in a controlled, even fashion as he pictured the flames dying down until the image became his meditation candle. One small flame.

Something of his new calm must have shown on his face, because the old man gathered his bravery enough to face him with unblinking eyes. "Please reconsider. Let me take my daughter home."

Daman opened his mouth, fully intending to grant the old man's request. "A deal is a deal. The woman will stay, and you may go." The words came from a part of him not controlled by his brain, catching him off guard. He blinked then moved quickly out of the doorway, back into the house so he could gesture for his guests to enter while simultaneously hiding the bewildered expression he knew must be on his face. "Go up the stairs and into the first room on your right. There is a trunk inside. You may load the trunk with as much treasure from the room as you like."

"Keep your treasure and let me keep my daughter," the old man begged.

"Father, please. It's all right."

Daman glanced back. The man hadn't moved from the doorstep and was still standing there clutching his daughter. The woman's voice was soft, but confident, not a trace of the uncertainty screaming from her posture huddled in her father's arms. She didn't look at Daman, but edged away from her father, easing out of his protective embrace. She stepped over the threshold and marched for the stairs.

"Don't ignore his generosity, Father. Please, take the treasure and use it to hire help. Corrine will need someone to take care of her."

Corrine. The name sent a shiver down Daman's spine, caressing his temper and urging it to rekindle. He averted his eyes, not wanting to frighten the woman with the scowl he could feel tightening the lines of his face.

"Load the trunks," he said, his voice only slightly hoarse and mercifully free of sibilance. "I will bring it down to the carriage after you're done."

Without another word, Daman left the room, moving as fast as his scales would carry him. He kept going until he was safe in the sanctity of his own chambers. Light poured in through his large, arched windows, casting a golden glow on his bed, revealing the nest of torn blankets and shredded sheets—a telltale sign that this was another room the brownies did not dare to enter. Their absence was felt keenly in the shattered statues, shredded paintings, and broken glass that desecrated every surface, every wall. A shrine to the madness threatening the lord of the manor.

Thoughts and memories swirled faster and faster inside Daman's head and he slammed the heavy door behind him. The sound of the solid wood crashing against the doorframe thundered through the room, a satisfying, but empty sound.

Corrine.

The name echoed in his head like ripples in a pond, growing larger and more powerful as they spread. *Corrine. Corrine. Corrine.* More ceramic shattered against the wall as Daman heaved a statue of a dragon across the room. The heavy sculpture shattered into large chunks, filling the air with fine white dust. It coated Daman's nostrils as he sucked in ragged breaths, flailing around for something else to throw. His hand closed around a brass bookend carved to resemble twined serpents and he cast it outward. It hit the window, shattering the glass and then sailing out into empty air.

What have I done? What was I thinking, demanding she stay? His gaze flew wildly around the room, his breathing ragged. *The witch's sister—her* sister!

Every scale on his body grew heavier, reminders of what he was, what he would be as long as the curse held him trapped in this form. Neither man nor beast. Unfit for human company. The meditations were already pathetically ineffective at managing his temper. With that woman here—*reminding* him…

"You're upssset."

Daman whirled to find the *cuelebre* peering up at him from the floor, tiny from Daman's vantage point. It flicked its tail from side to side, like a dog greeting its master.

"What are you doing here?" Daman snarled.

The *cuelebre* snaked its tongue out and blinked. "I told you. I'm here to help you with your visssitorsss."

"You are in my private chamberss." Daman slashed at the *cuelebre* with the heavy coil of his lower body, cracking it against his diminutive intruder. The *cuelebre* sputtered as it was sent skittering over the floor.

"It iss the *wrong daughter.*" Daman shoved a hand through his hair, not caring that his claws drew ragged, bloody furrows across his scalp. "He wass ssupposed to bring me the witch."

"Did you tell him to bring the witch?" the *cuelebre* asked. It stared intently at him from a cave created by a large and mostly undamaged section of down comforter. Only its pink tongue slithering out as it spoke gave away its position.

Daman flexed his fingers as he imagined squeezing the miserable pest in his fist. "No. But sshe iss the one who had reasson to want the rosse. It sshould have been her."

"Well, sssend thisss one back and sssee if you can exchange her for her sssissster."

"Do not mock me!" Daman thrust against the stone floor, sending his body hurtling to the bed. There was a startled burst of flame and the comforter caught fire as the *cuelebre* shot into the air, wings beating furiously.

"Don't be mad at me." The *cuelebre* sailed across the room and wrapped itself around a wall sconce, clinging stubbornly as if daring Daman to try and remove it. "It'sss not my fault that your heart ssspoke for you."

Daman trembled with the urge to strike out again. He tried to clear the haze from his eyes so he could focus on the *cuelebre*. "What iss that ssupossed to mean?"

The *cuelebre* snorted. "I heard you. You sssaid you were going to sssend her away, but when it came time to do it, you forccced her to ssstay. You want her to ssstay." The serpent stabbed the tip of its tail in Daman's direction. "It wasss not your head that made that decisssion."

"It wass a mistake." Daman rolled his shoulders, tilting his head from side to side to ease the muscles in his neck. "A sslip of the tongue."

"Ssso you intend to go back to her father and tell him he can take hisss daughter home?"

Daman looked away, focusing on the dark, empty fireplace. His gaze slid across the room to the shattered statue, the gleaming shards of the broken window. For a moment, the temper receded, leaving him unspeakably tired. His shoulders sagged. "I am better than this."

Scales sliding against metal signaled movement on the *cuelebre*'s part, but the serpent said nothing.

"The girl is a changeling."

"Ah. Ssshe remindsss you of your passst purpossse."

Daman slid his gaze to the *cuelebre*, the skin around his eyes twitching. "Not passt. It iss sstill my purpose, however incapable I may be of fulfilling it at the moment. And what do you know of it?"

The *cuelebre* scrunched up his body, pressing a coil to the side of his head in a serpent's version of a shrug. "I know what a naga isss. Your people are protectorsss, guardiansss. If I remember correctly, upon maturity, a naga choosesss a protectorate, a people he will dedicate hisss life to. You were well known in thisss land for being a sssavior of changelingsss. I have heard of them praying to you to deliver them from cruel parentsss." The *cuelebre* paused. "You're ssstill well known, of courssse. Only now, people fear you asss a monsssster." It tapped its chin with the tip of its tail. "Though I think there are ssstill prayersss—"

"Sstop." Daman clenched his hands into fists, sucking in deep breaths as he battled his temper back down. An image of the girl waiting in the treasure room filled his mind. He could see her face pale as she peered at him from the questionable safety of her father's arms. Even as terrified as she was, she'd spoken with calm confidence to ease her father's worries, to assure him that she would be all right. The knowledge that he'd frightened her, that a creature that beautiful and kind-hearted had seen him not as a savior, but as a threat...

"Do they only know me as a monster now?" He had to wrench the words from his vocal cords, dreading the answer.

The *cuelebre* inched closer, tiny scales glittering with the movement. "No. They know who you truly are. They remember." He tapped his tail against the floor. "They wait."

The blood drying on his scalp itched and Daman examined his claws. Brittle flakes of blood drifted down from the sharp points as he flexed his fingers, falling to the ground like macabre snowflakes. He silently moved to the dresser beside his bed and the wash basin with its chipped pitcher sitting next to it.

The *cuelebre*'s gaze was a tickle between his shoulder blades, a tangible weight. He moved mechanically through washing his hands, pouring the water from the pitcher, trailing his claws through the water. The liquid turned pink as the blood released its grip on his skin and scales, flowing through the bowl like eerie fog. When his hands were clean, he dried them on a scrap of linen that had once been part of a bedsheet.

"I can be that man again. I can be the knight instead of the dragon in the eyes of those who need my protection."

The words lacked conviction, but hope flickered inside of Daman, meager though the flame was. If he stared hard enough at his hands, he could see the human limbs they had once been. He could remember.

"Isss it your intention to sssave the changeling girl?" the *cuelebre* asked curiously.

Daman pressed his lips together in a fine line. He slowly slid his hand down his armor, feeling the supple chainmail and strips of heavy, worn leather. It had been part of the armor he'd worn in human form, one of the few pieces that he could wear even in this stage of his transformation. It settled him, reminded him of honor, his discipline. "The day the witch came to me a year ago, she pretended to be a changeling, pretended to be the victim of an abusive host family. She had blood on her arm—the blood of a changeling."

Daman replayed the memory in his head. The beautiful girl crying in his foyer, holding out her bloody arm as she pled for sanctuary. He could still remember the passionate urge to protect that had swarmed over him, the rush of tenderness he'd experienced as he'd comforted her. There had been no attraction, only the passion of his cause, the satisfaction of knowing he was doing exactly as he was meant to do. The zealousness of the righteous.

"She fooled me until I sent her to get cleaned up. She didn't realize that I would visit her home, that I would go to see for myself what circumstances she was escaping from. It didn't take long to learn that she'd lied. Her bedroom was the nicest room in the house, full of beautiful dresses and thick, comfortable blankets. Her father and sister did not have the look about them that comes with cruelty to others."

"What doesss thisss have to do with the sssisssster?"

Daman picked up scraps of bedsheets from the floor, gathering them in his arms. "Corrine had bandaged her arms by the time I arrived back at the manor, but I already knew the wounds were fake. The scent of changeling no longer hovered about her." He straightened with his arms full of ruined fabric, his gaze sliding to the door as he pictured the changeling who was in his home now. "She must have gotten that blood from her sister. I heard the woman tell her father to take the treasure I offered him and use it to hire people to care for Corrine."

"Ssso?"

"So, there is nothing wrong with the witch." Daman's grip tightened for a moment, crushing the fabric to his chest until he could feel the pounding of his heart through the thick material. He inhaled deeply and let it out slowly, imagining his meditation candle, picturing the gentle flame. His posture relaxed and he dropped the load of cloth into a pile near the wall. "She's obviously taking advantage of her sister's good nature, probably working her like a slave."

"You can't know that," the *cuelebre* pointed out.

"You didn't meet Corrine." Daman gathered the largest pieces of shattered ceramic and splintered wood. Every bit of debris he removed from the floor calmed him, order returning to his mind as it returned to his environment. "When she first came to me and the taste of the blood on her arm led me to believe she was a true changeling, I told her I would relocate her, find her a loving family. She insisted that she wanted to stay here, with me." He snorted. "Tried to seduce me. She didn't want safety, she wanted wealth. One look at her hands and it was clear she'd never worked a day in her life."

"That doesssn't mean ssshe isss cruel to her sssissster."

"Her sister is *sidhe*."

The *cuelebre* stilled, its beady eyes growing wider. "*Sidhe?*"

"The *sidhe* exchange children with humans to keep their bloodlines strong, to bring in new blood. But they don't abandon their true children. I've never known a *sidhe* family that didn't check up on their child after leaving them, to make sure they weren't being mistreated. This changeling tastes of *sidhe*, but she does not have the same aura. It is muted, weakened. Someone is trying to hide her from her true family. What reason could they have to do that if they aren't afraid of what her family would do if they found her, discovered her circumstances?"

"Perhapsss the humansss are trying to hide her from her family becaussse they believe her family will hurt her?"

"Perhaps." Daman dumped what he'd gathered in the same pile as the shredded bedsheets. "But until I am sure, I will keep her here."

"Isssn't that dangerousss?" The *cuelebre* curled around the wall sconce. "You sssent away your ssservantsss, your warriorsss, all becaussse you believed they would be in peril if they remained here with you. Do you not think that you are a threat to the girl asss well?"

Daman focused hard on the stone floor. "It is my purpose to protect changelings. I stopped helping them because I can no longer take my human form and when I tried to continue on in this body, I frightened them too much. But this girl is already here." He squared his shoulders, though he still didn't look at the *cuelebre*. "Perhaps this is a sign, a chance to remember how I once was."

Daman nodded at the improvement in his room. It was still a disaster, a few moments of clearing debris wouldn't change that, but the act of cleaning had been symbolic. If the gods were giving him another chance, then he needed to show he could change. It was time to stop living like a demented hermit, a monster too destructive to be trusted in human company. He was a man. He needed to act like it.

Before the *cuelebre* could say anything to change his mind, Daman swept out of the room to join his visitors, nervous energy singing against his skin. He entered the room slowly, head held high and posture as formal as though he had strode in on two legs. He ignored the way his visitors cowered as he approached, offering them a slight bow of greeting.

The old man groped behind him for his daughter, an instinctive need to protect his offspring, but the girl appeared to notice the change in his manner. She tilted her head slightly, watching him steadily with only the slightest hesitation in her body language.

Encouraged, Daman gave her what he hoped was a pleasant smile, grateful that his fangs remained snugly retracted against the roof of his mouth so his expression was human rather than draconic. The girl returned the smile, albeit shyly.

They'd filled the chest with riches, as he'd instructed them. The enchanted wardrobe had been as kind to them as he'd expected and the chest not only contained gold coins and jewels, but gowns of fine silk and lace. It was enough to please even the greediest witch...

His temper leapt up at him like a leviathan coming up for air, the full weight of his rage all too ready to reappear as an image of the witch roared into his mind. Copper burst on his tongue and Daman tamped down on a fresh wave of irritation as he realized he'd bitten his tongue grinding his teeth. It was fortunate his fangs were retracted against the roof of his mouth, else he likely would have ended up with a second fork in his tongue.

He offered his guests a small bow while he got his facial expressions under control. The man clung to his daughter as though desperate to protect her from Daman. They stood silently as Daman lifted the heavy chest with ease and carried it out to the waiting carriage. It took more effort than he wanted to admit to ignore the tears shining in the woman's eyes as her father climbed into the carriage and drove away.

She stood there, hands worrying the folds of her worn blue skirt. In all the years he'd been rescuing changelings, Daman had seen many of them cry—but never because of him. He had never once forced a changeling to leave their home, it had always been their choice.

It was still her choice, Daman reminded himself. A small voice in his head scoffed at him.

He cleared his throat. "What is your name?"

"Maribel." She didn't take her eyes from the horizon where the carriage had disappeared. "And yours?"

"Daman."

Slowly he turned back to the manor, gesturing for her to walk with him. She tore her attention from the horizon and locked it firmly on the ground as she followed obediently. At first he thought she was lost in her own wondering. He wouldn't blame her if she were thinking of the life she'd left behind, perhaps wondering if staying had been the right choice. But something about the brittle set to her body, the utter stiffness in her neck... Realization dawned. She was trying not to gawk at him.

He stiffened. "If you want to stare, then just do it and get it over with."

She flinched and closed her eyes for a moment. Her hand drifted to a pocket in the apron she wore over her dress and she withdrew something too small for Daman to make out. Her hand rose to her mouth and she popped something small and red onto her tongue. As she chewed, she opened her eyes, attention fixed firmly ahead.

She said nothing.

A cherry tomato? She brought food? Daman swallowed a growl. She'd probably expected him to starve her, to be some sort of monstrous beast that would relish her suffering and inflict torment on her at every opportunity.

So, show her she's wrong. Barking at her certainly won't disavow her of such dismal notions. He took a breath to muster an apology for his harsh tone. Before he could speak, Maribel came to an abrupt halt, her back stiff as a board. Daman reared back slightly as she whirled to face him. With a defiant flash in her eyes, she proceeded to look him over from head to toe.

For a moment, Daman didn't know what to do, so he stood there, letting her look her fill. Maribel's gaze took in every minute detail, starting from the ridges of his face and following every glittering scale down his neck and over his chest. She hesitated at his waist and Daman had an odd flash of gratitude that he'd thought to put on his armor. He had no real need for clothing in this form, especially since there was no one around to dress for. He'd only put the armor on today because he'd known he'd have visitors. And he'd expected one of them to be an enemy.

As she examined the thick coil of his tail, Daman clenched his hands into fists. Already his mind tortured him with images of the disgust that would pinch Maribel's face at any moment, the terror that would send her running from him in tears. Like the others.

"Can I... Can I ask what you are?"

He crossed his arms, realized he looked defensive, and dropped his arms to his sides. "I'm a *naga*."

"Oh. I've never heard of a...*naga*." Maribel bit her lip, her gaze sliding down the length of his serpent-like lower half, taking in the bluish-green scales as thick and large as dinner plates. "Are you from Sanguenay?"

"I am from Barzakh, an island far off the shores of Dacia."

"Oh."

An awkward silence fell between them, their pitiful attempt at conversation gasping its dying breath. Agitation teased the skin between his shoulder blades and he fought to shrug it off. He wanted to say something more, wanted her to say something more, but it appeared neither of them knew how to keep the conversation going.

Frustrated, he surged in the direction of the manor, leaving her to follow him into the mansion and up the stairs to a long hallway that led to her room. The space was mostly bare, the curtains having been shredded and the busts of old generals smashed long ago during the worst of Daman's rampages. The brownies had cleared away the debris, but had never attempted to replace them.

Daman kept waiting for her to say something else, ask him more questions, but she remained silent. He tried to think of something to say, anything that would break the wretched silence, but nothing would come to him. He bit back a growl. There'd been a time when conversing had been easy for him. He'd dealt with timid changelings, earned their trust, put them at ease. But apparently it had been too long. The skill had withered away.

"This will be your room," he said finally, having given up thinking of any other conversation.

He gestured for Maribel to enter, an annoying case of nerves making his heart beat erratically as he waited to hear what she thought. The room he'd chosen for her was pristine, untouched by him or his temper. The bed was draped with thick down comforters with the winter furs folded at the foot for nights that still dreamed of winter. The wall sconces were polished until they shone even without the sunlight. Thick curtains hung on either side of the broad windows, framing the gauzy material that muted the daylight until the heavier material was drawn.

He wasn't sure what he wanted, a gush of praise over the room's elegance, delight at not being held in a dungeon like a prisoner. Anything would be better than the silence that left him with only his own thoughts for company. After a few moments, she offered him a timid smile.

"It's lovely, thank you."

Despite her words, she didn't meet his eyes.

"What is it?" he demanded. "Would you prefer a different room?" He flung a hand out, gesturing down the hall. "It is only you and I here, you may have your pick of any room that pleases you if this isn't good enough."

"Oh, no, the room is wonderful. I just…" She shoved her hand into the apron pocket again and popped another cherry tomato into her mouth. Her jaw worked as she chewed furiously, perhaps buying herself time to think. Finally she faced him. "I was just wondering why you want me here? I mean, what is it you want me to do while I'm here? Cook? Clean?"

Daman opened his mouth, then snapped it shut. "I— No. That is, I didn't bring you here to be my servant. Brownies clean the house. I usually cook for myself." The words fell out of his mouth of their own accord and his temper flared at how foolish he sounded. He crossed his arms and tried not to look confused.

"Brownies?"

Her voice rose with the question. Daman narrowed his eyes. She was *sidhe*, he knew she was *sidhe*. How could she not know what brownies were?

"Brownies. The fey folk?"

She blinked, another cherry tomato hovering in front of her lips. "Fey folk? You mean like fairies?"

Daman eyed the ruby-skinned fruit. *Nervous eater?* He settled down on his coils, trying to get closer to eye level with Maribel to read her face better. "Sort of. Brownies are a type of fey. They're small, mostly harmless creatures. They love to clean and they take great pride in their work. I...did a favor for a family of them once, and they repay me by cleaning the manor."

"Where do they stay?"

He waved a hand. "They don't live here, and they won't come while anyone is awake in the house. You won't see them. They don't like to be acknowledged for their help." He paused. "You don't know about the fey folk?"

Maribel shrugged. "Not really. I mean, I know to be careful where I throw out the bathwater, and I try to leave cream and honey out now and again if things are going particularly well." She bit the inside of her cheek. "Of course I know about the vampires that rule Dacia. I guess..." She shrugged again. "I suppose I've never run into any creatures from beyond the veil." She stopped abruptly, eyes flicking about as if she'd said something embarrassing.

Daman slid his tail around, deliberately scraping it over the floor so that Maribel had to strain not to look down or move away. "Until me, you mean."

She cleared her throat, still not meeting his eyes.

The way she avoided eye contact grated on his nerves, as though he were some wild animal that would attack her if she challenged him, however inadvertently. "You don't need to be so skittish. I'm not going to hurt you."

Now he had eye contact.

"So you'll just continue to shout at me, is that it?"

"I'm not shouting," he said, forcing the words through gritted teeth.

"You've been yelling at me since I got here," Maribel corrected him, her voice holding nearly as much frost as the air outside. "And I don't appreciate it. This hasn't been a great day for me either so the least you could do is keep a civil tongue."

A red blush sprang to her cheeks as her last word seemed to register, but she didn't take her eyes from his. Daman relished her discomfort, flicking his forked tongue out of his mouth just for spite. Served her right for being cross with him.

"My father said that you were very kind to him, that you fed him. I had hoped that you and I might get along."

Daman's amusement abruptly died at the gentle tone in her voice. Fighting with her had been easier than trying to put her at ease, a fact he didn't want to dwell on. Resigned to the impending challenge of social niceties he hadn't bothered with for over a year, he pulled his tail back behind him and tucked his forked tongue out of sight.

"I was the one who asked him for the rose," Maribel continued, fingers toying with the ends of her hair. "He didn't know anything about it. He was only trying to make me happy."

Daman shifted uncomfortably. He wasn't quite ready to believe that the request for the magic plant had been entirely innocent. Even if Maribel didn't intend to use it, there was no way for him to know if Corrine had manipulated her sibling into getting her the flower. Still, Maribel was his guest, and she was a changeling. Treating her poorly wouldn't serve anyone.

"What did you want the rose for?" he asked instead.

Maribel dropped her arms to her sides. "My sister. Her health is very poor and moving from the village to a farm was hard on her. I read about the Rose of the Mist and it just seemed like the answer to everything. If I could have brewed her a potion from those petals—"

"You intended to give the Rosse of the Misst to the witch?"

Daman fisted his hands at his sides, struggling not to throw anything, destroy anything. So this *had* been the witch's doing. Not only had she protected herself by sending her father for the rose, she'd managed to get her changeling sister to make the request. How neatly she'd managed to shelter herself from the consequences, from him.

Maribel took a trembling step back. "How did you know my sister was a…" Her eyes narrowed and she planted her feet firmly on the floor, her chin jutting out in defiance. "My sister practices some witchcraft—so do I. We aren't evil, whatever the villagers might tell you."

Aren't evil. Daman's hands opened and closed. "I know *you* aren't evil."

Something flared in Maribel's eyes, a heated spark of her own fury. "Are you insinuating that my sister is?"

Daman fought to hold the sneer from his face, to keep back the words that so readily sprang to his tongue. "Perhaps. What sort of magic does she practice?"

Maribel hesitated, her defiance dimming slightly. "I don't know. My studies are separate from hers. I study plants and how they can be used to heal. I'm not sure—"

"So you don't know if your sister is practicing black magic or not?" Daman sneered. "And yet you would give her a Rose of the Mist, increase her power?"

"What do you care? You got what you wanted. You scared an old man half to death, made him feel like a common thief for a simple mistake. He's given up one of his own daughters out of fear of you and now my sister will have no one to care for her while he's out in the field. The spoiled witch will have to do the work herself, perhaps end up with another hand burned beyond recognition, or another scar on her head from a nasty fall. Are you satisfied?"

Daman opened his mouth to point out that he had, in fact, given her father more than enough money to hire help to take care of the spoiled witch, but then the rest of Maribel's words registered. Badly burned? Scarred from a nasty fall? He'd seen no such marks on the witch. Then again, he hadn't looked too hard once he'd discovered she was lying. *Did I miss something?*

"You said this is to be my room while I'm your prisoner, is that right?"

Daman opened his mouth, ready to object to her reference to

herself as his prisoner, but then thought better of it. He nodded instead.

"Good." She turned her back on him, crossing her arms over her chest. "Then get out."

"Get…" Daman's mouth hung open and he gaped in disbelief. One clawed hand rose into the air, fingers flexing, yearning to grab the changeling and shake her until she understood he wasn't the enemy, that it was her sister who deserved her disdain.

When he didn't move, she pivoted back to him, arching one delicate eyebrow and looking pointedly from him to the empty hallway. She didn't spare so much as a glance to the hand raised against her, the wicked points gleaming in the dim light.

Frustrated anger boiled in Daman's veins, painting a red haze before him. He lowered his hand, skimming it close to her body, watching her face for some flicker of fear, some sign that he frightened her.

The warmth of her skin teased him through her clothes, the body heat of another person an alien sensation. He closed off the part of himself that wanted more, that wanted to shake her hand, hug her, do all the little things people took for granted. Then again, her expression suggested such gestures would not be welcome even if he were so inclined to try. If not for the pulse straining the delicate skin of her throat, the icy façade she'd painted on her face would have fooled him into thinking she didn't even notice how close his claws were to her vulnerable flesh.

Leave. Walk away. Don't be a child.

Daman gritted his teeth and closed his hand around the pocket of her apron. He made a fist and was rewarded with the sticky juice of crushed cherry tomatoes soaking through the worn material. Maribel's jaw dropped.

One flick of his tail against the floor sent him hurtling down the hallway, the sound of Maribel sputtering in disbelief following him all the way.

CHAPTER 5

"Oh, dear."

The shopkeeper's voice buzzed against Corrine's skin like an annoying insect. Reluctantly tearing her gaze from a row of fresh pastries, she shot the squat bald man an irritated glare and drew her new silk-lined fur cloak more firmly around her.

"Look at the hem of your fine garments," the man continued, pointing at the floor with a finger the size and shape of a malformed sausage.

His voice didn't quite match his words, the frosty tone suggesting it was her cloak and not the floor he found distasteful. Corrine tensed and quickly formed her expression into as blank a mask as she could manage. "It's fine," she assured him coolly.

"Oh, no, Corrine." The shopkeeper's muddy brown eyes held more ice than a Dacian winter, and more poison than an adder's spit. "My shop simply isn't fit for the likes of you."

"Indeed it isn't. But since it is half a day's journey to the next grocer, I'll have to make do." Corrine resumed her assessment of the man's wares, refusing to give him the satisfaction of seeing her flinch. Her stomach growled and she bit the inside of her cheek hard enough to draw blood as she was forced to admit none of the delicacies she was seeing would be coming home with her.

"I'm afraid I must insist."

A grubby hand landed on her arm and Corrine hissed and clutched the pendant hanging around her neck in her left hand. The scarred skin creaked in protest as she closed it into a fist, but she ignored the discomfort. Power pulsed from the scarlet gem in the center of the talisman, filling the air with the scent of a coming storm. The fine hairs on the back of her neck danced in an invisible wind and she breathed easier as the magic filled her with the confidence that came from someone holding a *very* big stick.

The vendor flinched and yanked his arm away. She held his gaze, pouring out as much derision as she could muster up. The shopkeeper's flesh paled to an unhealthy shade of green. He backed away so fast, he fell over his own feet and tumbled into a display of apples. Fruit bounced and tumbled to the floor around him, the flow of red spilling down appropriately symbolic.

"You would do well not to lay a hand on me." Corrine kept her eyes locked on his as she slowly bent down and picked up an apple. The shopkeeper's eyes burned with muted fury as she lifted the fruit and sniffed. She wrinkled her nose and glanced down at the food with disgust. "Spoiled," she sneered, tossing the apple to the ground. It wobbled as it rolled across the floor to bounce against his leg. Corrine gave him her back.

"Get out of my shop, you witch!" The shopkeeper choked. "I don't want your gold or your black soul darkening my shop!"

A dull buzzing sound crept into the shop from outside. A crowd was beginning to gather. The space between Corrine's shoulder blades itched and she had to fight not to look back and make sure the shopkeeper wasn't about to launch some sort of projectile at her. Someone shuffled near the door, one of the braver villagers opening it to get a better glimpse at what was happening. Corrine waited until the door was all the way open, then raised her voice.

"What is that horrible stench?" She made a show of sniffing the air and waving a hand about in front of her face. "Oh, dear, it's your wares. How dare you try to pass off such rotten fare? What fool would pay for food with such a smell?" She put her hand over her face as though being overwhelmed by a foul odor and strode for the door. "I can't bear to be in here a moment longer. I'll be taking my business elsewhere."

The old woman who had been brave enough to open the door watched Corrine without an ounce of shame. The rest of the people parted hurriedly as she plowed ahead, lowered voices buzzing in her wake. Corrine firmly kept her eyes straight ahead. Her bravado was starting to fail her and she needed to get as far away as possible before her façade crumbled and she had to face the fact that she had once again failed to obtain food for herself.

"Maribel, forgive me for not appreciating you as much as I should have," she whispered.

She walked as briskly as she could, using every ounce of her self-control to keep herself from running. The forest path ahead of her loomed like the gateway to salvation, offering peace and privacy. When she was finally hidden from view, she stopped.

The shaking of her shoulders brought a swell of rage rising up like a dark tide inside of her. Corrine pulled the hood of her cloak up, hiding her face from the world as hot tears burned her eyes. The soft fur of the silk-lined cloak caressed her face almost as if it were offering her comfort. She took a slow, deep breath and ran her hands over the supple midnight blue velvet and silver fox fur. The richness of the fabric told people she was someone of importance, of influence. It was pleasant to the touch, and thick enough to keep her warm no matter how heavy the chill in the air. It was the sort of cloak that offered protection. Only the fact that it was a gift from her father kept it from being perfect.

Bought with the money the monster paid him. The price of keeping my sister.

Corrine stared ahead, unfocused on her surroundings. She wasn't seeing trees and grass right now. She was seeing her father. She could picture him so clearly, bustling around his cursed farm. The old fool had come home with enough money to buy half of Sanguenay, but what did he do with it? Hired people to work the farm. Hired people to build a new farmhouse. Hired people to cement their miserable lives on this damned piece of land so far from society that it may as well be an island in the middle of the great sea! That money should have been their way out of this life, their ticket back home, *but what had he done with it?*

Snatching the silk gloves from the pockets of her cloak, Corrine tugged them onto her trembling fingers. She caressed the silk in short, too-quick strokes, ignoring the hysterical scream tickling the back of her throat. If her father thought that buying her new clothes was going to make up for keeping her a prisoner in the middle of nowhere, he had another think coming. She would not rest until they left this nightmare behind them.

"Those are some fine garments you're wearing. Very fine."

The old woman's voice jarred Corrine out of her thoughts so suddenly she had to bite down on a shriek. Heart pounding like an angry dwarf on a particularly cemented diamond, she whirled around to face the intruder.

An old crone stood less than ten feet away from her, the same nosey old woman who'd shoved her way into the shop to witness Corrine's humiliation. Her burgundy cloak was worn, but clean, the plain brass clasp too dull to glint in the sunlight spearing through the forest canopy. The hood was down and her wild grey hair danced about her, fighting with every breeze that passed. Warm brown eyes peered from a face creased with more lines than a prospector's map.

"Are you all right, dear?" she asked politely.

"I'm fine." Corrine brushed her hair back from her face,

smoothing the waves as best she could. "Though I might be a touch *startled* because someone snuck up on me and shouted."

"Shouted?" The old woman rubbed a hand over her jaw, one corner of her mouth quirking up.

Corrine pulled the cloak tighter around her, trying to gather her thoughts enough to reestablish the haughty façade she'd worn in the shop. She tried to look down her nose at the stranger. "If you're here to steal my 'fine garments,' I'd advise against it. I'm a powerful witch, you know."

The woman barked out a sharp laugh, the lines creasing her face deepening in genuine amusement. "A powerful witch, eh? Oh, my, they didn't tell me you were funny."

"They?" Corrine stiffened.

"Oh, don't you mind them, dear. People will talk. After all, they must do something to entertain themselves. Common work can be quite tedious, you know."

"Is that some sort of joke?" Corrine demanded, her face heating. "Are you a friend of Madame Balestra's? Has she told you all about Maribel's lazy sister who never helped on the farm a day in her life?" She clenched her hands into fists, the tears pricking at her eyes as they attempted a valiant effort to return. "Did you have a good laugh?"

The amusement abruptly vanished from the crone's face and she eyed Corrine with a hint of disapproval. "You're a fine, healthy girl and you could do far more if you had a mind to."

"You know *nothing* about me," Corrine spat. "I—"

"You were a very sick babe, nearly died in your mother's arms 'ere you'd seen your first birthday. Ergotism from bad wheat. A tragic truth, to be certain." The old crone took a firm step forward. "But you are no longer that child. You are a grown woman, and you are far stronger than you give yourself credit for."

Corrine's jaw dropped. Anger fought with shock for dominance as her mouth opened and closed several times without letting a sound escape. Ergotism, she'd said. How long had it been since anyone had named her illness by it's scientific name, the word it seemed only the doctors used? It was far more common to hear the disease's more colorful nomenclatures. Evil Fire. Demon's Fire. A sickness that marked someone who practiced the dark arts. Nevermind she'd been a child. *You're never too young to be damned.*

"Who are you?" she demanded finally.

"Haven't you heard? I'm a witch, my dear." She sniffed, managing to look down her nose without even stretching to her full height. "A *proper* witch."

It was Corrine's turn to bark out a laugh. "Oh, are you now? Well you're not a very good one. You haven't said a thing that every busybody in this village hasn't said at one time or another. And like all of them, you have no idea what you're talking about. I'm as sick now as I ever was, only now I don't have parents hovering over me and asking for prayers."

The last sentence twisted her heart, a reminder that even her father doubted her now. Sometimes she wished she still had the physical signs of her illness that she'd had as a child. Something that she couldn't be accused of faking.

"Malarkey. You're more than capable of anything you put your mind to. You merely lack the courage."

Anger bit at Corrine's nerves like an army of fire ants. She thrust her burned hand out toward the witch, letting the light shimmering through the leaves dance over the shiny pink of her scarred flesh. "I have episodes that steal my mind and body, leave me vulnerable and more often than not in excruciating pain. Hallucinations take hold of me with such unrelenting strength that even falling with a hand in the fire isn't enough to let me fight my way out of it."

The memory of lying there, face against the floor at the

perfect angle to watch her flesh burn in the embers of her own hearth, tried to take over. Sensory memories started to rise and she quickly shoved them back down with a shudder. She couldn't relive that again. "It's a wonder I haven't woken up dead."

The witch snorted. "Woken up dead. Clever girl. But those episodes aren't a sickness, dear. And if you'll let me, I can teach you to overcome them."

"Overcome them?" Corrine shifted from one foot to the other, studying the witch more closely. Pieces of town gossip were coming back to her, snatches of conversations she'd heard on the few occasions she'd come into town. "You're Mother Hazel."

The witch bowed her head once in acknowledgement. "I am."

"Well, thank you for the offer, but I've already got a mentor. Mother Briar. I don't need your help."

"*Mother* Briar," the witch spat. "She has done nothing to earn that title. She'll teach you no more than serves her, and you'd do well to be rid of her."

"What is this, some sort of professional jealousy?" Corrine mused. "Do you often try to pilfer the students of other witches?" She crossed her arms. "No honor among crones, is that it?"

Mother Hazel opened her mouth as if to fire off a retort, but then pressed her lips into a thin line. Her brown eyes narrowed as she looked Corrine up and down, and it took Corrine more effort than she wanted to admit not to squirm under the intensity of the witch's assessment. She gritted her teeth and stuck out her chin, forcing herself to meet the crone's eyes.

"You have a great deal of strength," the witch said finally. "You will find it soon. When you do, you will have a choice to make about what path you will travel. Choose wisely. Such choices are often only made once."

"How delightfully cryptic," Corrine said, her voice dripping with sarcasm.

Mother Hazel snorted, but there was a twinkle in her eye. Her hand vanished under her ragged cloak and withdrew a wrapped parcel. She held it out to Corrine. "Here."

Corrine eyed the package, searching for some sign of its contents, wary of the possible tricks the witch might play. "What is it?"

"Bread. From the shop you visited moments ago."

Corrine recoiled. "I want no part of that man's wares."

"Yes, for a moment I thought he felt the same way. I could have sworn he'd been rude to you—rude to a *witch*, can you imagine? However, I was ever so pleased when I spoke with him and he *assured* me that he would never do such a thing."

There was something in the witch's voice. A sort of…kinship? She met Corrine's eyes and there was a kindness there now, an understanding. But that wasn't all. There was a promise. Something in her eyes told Corrine *"I've been where you are, and if you let me, I'll help you get to where I am."*

The material of her cloak filled Corrine's palms as she squeezed it, determined not to be swayed by pretty words and promises. "Nice try, old woman," she muttered. "I don't know what you want from me, but you won't get it. I don't need your help or your food." She averted her eyes, stroking the silk of her gloves over and over. "I'll send a servant to the shop later."

"I see. Well, I'll just leave this here then, perhaps some birds will find it."

The witch placed the wrapped loaf of fresh bread on the ground and Corrine imagined she took great care not to let any dirt trickle under the wrapping. The scent of warm yeast and melted butter curled through the air to wrap around her nose like an affectionate cat and Corrine's stomach tightened with sudden yearning. She quickly looked away as the witch stood.

"When you want to find me, I'll be there."

There was a surety in the witch's voice. When, not if.

Corrine clenched her jaw, then whirled back to face her. "Is it part of being a witch to speak so—"

Corrine trailed off as she found she was alone. She ran her gaze over the surrounding trees, searching for some sign of the meddling witch, but saw nothing. No moving leaves, no figure forging a path through the frost-tinged brush. Nothing except the bread lying on the ground. Still covered. Still hot. Still smelling decadently of butter.

Forcing herself to wait five minutes to be certain the witch was truly gone was one of the hardest tasks Corrine had ever forced her mind to. She counted in her head, trying to distract her stomach from the baked goodness lying within reach, half-flying to it as soon as her self-imposed time limit was up. She held it to her with the same care one would cradle a newborn babe as she lowered her gaze and marched back to the farmhouse.

She kept her head down as she trudged past the workers building the new farmhouse and the recently hired help plowing the fields and tending the garden. Eye contact would only invite meaningless conversation and she'd already had enough of that.

She made it to her room without being accosted, breathing a sigh of relief as she bolted her door behind her. Clutching the loaf of bread to her chest, she focused her attention to the trunk on the floor at the foot of her bed. A feeling of security settled over her as she approached the trunk, the sight of the heavy wood and thick iron lock soothing her nearly as much as a new gown.

The lid opened soundlessly on well-oiled hinges, but a knock at the door stilled her hand, startled her out of her thoughts.

"Corrine? Corrine, may I come in?"

Corrine cursed as the sound of her father's worried voice broke into her room and she fumbled the loaf. The crusty surface of the bread cracked, spilling crumbs into the trunk. The bulk of the bread hit the edge of the chest, tumbled down into her skirts, and then rolled to the floor, leaving an accusing trail of crumbs. Her heart pounded, a thundering echo in her ears as she hurriedly retrieved the loaf and tucked it into her trunk. The smell of mold tickled her nose and she sneezed.

"Corrine?"

She quickly closed her trunk, locked it, and arranged pillows and blankets on top of it. She swept the crumbs under her bed as best she could with her hands, her heart pounding as she scanned the floor for any she'd missed. After she'd gotten rid of as much evidence as she could, she stood there staring at the trunk.

Her father was at her door, he would want to come in and check on her. What if he opened her trunk, found her food? Nausea rolled through her like a sickening wave. *Hurry up, Corrine! The door isn't locked, he'll let himself in any second if you don't say something!* She quickly sat on the lid of the trunk, half falling as her knees gave out. The sound of the door opening sent her heart into her throat and she just managed to fold her hands in her lap before her father's face peeked in.

"Corrine, are you all right?" he asked carefully.

Corrine shoved all thoughts of food from her mind. "Yes. Yes, of course, I was just…tidying up."

Her father opened the door slowly, revealing more of his tired face inch by inch. Maribel had been gone for weeks, and every day of that absence was etched on her father's haggard countenance. His hair stuck out in sharp tufts from where he'd tugged it, perhaps without even realizing it. Even his new clothes hung limply from his body, as if his flesh flinched away from the finery the monster's money had bought him.

Her father's bedraggled state sent a creeping tendril of dread through Corrine's stomach. This was not a man that could take care of her. This was a man who was going to waste away to nothing and leave her alone and helpless. Without him, how long would it be until the strangers he'd hired turned on Corrine, using the fact that she was a witch to justify cheating her out of her home, her land, maybe her life?

"You're upset."

Her father stepped inside and Corrine managed to ignore the thoughts racing through her mind enough to notice he was holding his hat in his hands, worrying the smart, freshly delivered cap until it was barely recognizable. A throbbing beat began in her temples sending ripples of pain to settle in the back of her skull. *He has more bad news then.*

"How are you feeling? Really?" he asked, a pleading note in his voice.

Maribel, how could you leave me alone with this shadow of a man? She tightened her hands in her lap, resisting the urge to strangle her father for his weakness. "Exactly how you would expect me to feel. Scared, sick. Maribel is gone, a prisoner of some monster who's keeping her for the gods know what reason. I'm left alone in this house with no one to notice if I keel over and crack my skull, no one to find me if I'm lying on the floor bleeding to death." For the second time that day she had to fight off the memory of watching her own hand burn. She bit the inside of her cheek, focusing on that small pain, refusing to give in to the panic eating her alive.

Her father paled, his fingers tightening on his hat until they went white. "He said he would not harm her."

"He might have lied."

"I... I've been working, hiring more help. I was a good businessman once, I can be one again. I'll buy her back from him—"

"Please tell me that is not your plan?" Corrine's arms went limp at her sides, her lips parting. "You don't seriously think you'll pay for my sister with gold—buy her back from a lord who lives in a manor that could house half the village, who has *enchanted chests full of treasure.* Surely you cannot be that foolish?" She wrinkled her nose in disgust, hardly able to look at her father. "Why can't you just admit you're too afraid to fight for her? Too afraid to even *visit* her."

The fresh tears that shone in her father's eyes stabbed at Corrine, reflecting her own furious visage back at her. Not for the first time, she looked at her reflection in her father's eyes and didn't like what she saw. Answering tears welled up in her own eyes. She was just so frightened. Surely he could see that? "Father," she started, her voice gentler, more like a daughter than an accuser.

"I've tried to hire people to stay in here with you, but you won't have them," her father interrupted tersely. "After the new house is built, there will be quarters for the servants, but until then, if you are going to have company, you must agree to let them reside in your sister's room."

Corrine shot up from her seat. Servants in Maribel's room, sleeping in her bed, touching her things? *Never!*

"Let them stay here? Here where I sleep—where I'm *helpless?* Are you truly that blind?" she gasped. She shook her head, searching her father's face for some sign that he was truly as oblivious as he sounded. He blinked slowly, his eyes dull without a spark of enlightenment. She tightened her hands into fists, straining the fine silk of her gloves. "You have no idea, do you? No idea of how I'm treated by everyone outside this family. I'm a *witch*, Father. I can't even buy a loaf of bread in the village, they won't serve me. I'm lucky I'm not stoned to death for strolling down the road."

"You should have taken the carriage," her father mumbled.

"Should have taken the... What is *wrong* with you?" Corrine screamed, grasping her hair and tugging at it ruthlessly, using the pain to ground her emotions as they spiraled out of control. "I tell you they want to kill me and your response is to tell me *I should have taken the carriage? Stupid man, ignorant man, pathetic man, howcanyoupossiblybethisnaiveohsweetgoddessmaribelhowcouldyouleavemewithhimi'mgoingtodie.* Her thoughts raced faster and faster until they blended into one solid sound buzzing in her head. Hysteria lit up inside her, painting frantic lights over her memories, creating nightmarish images in her mind's eye. Her pulse struggled like a living thing trapped beneath her skin, desperate to get out.

Corrine ran her gloved hands over her skirt, concentrating on the supple material, the comforting constriction of it. Her insides were churning, acid eating at her stomach, bubbling up in an attempt to spill out her mouth. If she didn't calm down, she would lose herself to another episode.

Deep breath, one, two, three, deep breath, one, two, three...

It took several long minutes, but finally Corrine thought she could speak without losing herself to hysterics.

"The horses are afraid of me," she said slowly, careful to keep her voice calm. "I cannot take the carriage."

Her father hung his head, misery etched into his features. "Corrine, I'm sorry. I ... I don't know what to do. I keep failing you, no matter what..." His voice hitched. "I wish your mother were still with us."

"I don't want to talk about Mother." Corrine's heart constricted into a tight, painful ball in her chest, the reaction she always had at the mention of her mother. The woman had died giving birth to her sister—her real sister, not the changeling her father believed was her sister. Corrine hadn't realized what had happened until she was older, and by then Maribel was her sister, in every way that counted—she still was.

Still, what would her mother think if she knew that the fairies had claimed her last earthly act? What would her father think if he knew his precious Maribel was not his flesh and blood, that she was one of the fair folk, and his own daughter was off somewhere behind the veil with her fairy parents?

Perhaps he'd never know. Her father had been a fine businessman once, he had a head for math that was unrivaled, and a feeling for the market that bordered on prophetic. But when it came to people, he was completely, utterly hopeless. And as far as knowledge of the creatures beyond the veil... He probably didn't know what a changeling was.

Corrine certainly didn't plan to tell him. Mother Briar was right, if her father didn't have the sensitivity to magic that would let him feel how different Maribel was, then it was more likely that he would brush off Corrine's claims as jealousy or some other such nonsense. Besides, revealing Maribel's true nature would lead to questions. Questions about why Maribel seemed so human. Why she had no gifts. For those educated in the ways of the world beyond the veil, it would lead to questions about why her fairy parents had never checked in with her, never came to spy on their abandoned babe.

Corrine's breathing came faster—too fast. Sweat broke out on her forehead and her hands trembled as if she were freezing. A tickle sprang to life at the back of her mind. Terror closed around her throat, digging unforgiving talons into her flesh until she couldn't breathe.

"Corrine?"

Her father's voice came from far away. Corrine tried to scream, but no sound would come out. Her body wouldn't move, no words could squeeze past the constricting of her chest, her throat. Reality shattered around her like a broken mirror and she was falling, falling into the chaotic nightmare of another episode.

Everything around her changed. It was as though she were still viewing the world, but a different Dreamworld had been laid over top of it. Normal, everyday objects suddenly radiated with strange lights, shards of colors that poked out like multi-hued spines. Outside the window, the trees were full of clinging monsters, black-furred bodies hunched over as pale human-like hands gripped thick branches and pale faces with flat, slitted noses, long, pointed ears, and glistening, drool-coated teeth eyed her hungrily. She tried not to concentrate on the shadows, her lip trembling at the thought of what she knew she'd see there. Spindly forms twisted around like melted metal, fiery eyes and tense limbs, waiting for an opportunity to pounce.

Her father's face appeared in front of her. Corrine wanted to look away, tried to look away so she wouldn't see her father through this horrifying lens of fantasy, but it was useless. Her body may as well have weighed a thousand pounds and been hammered to the floorboards beneath her. She could only stare at her father's face, wet and lined with tears, his head bald in places where his hair had been torn out. She could barely make out his chest in her peripheral vision and what she saw there twisted something inside her.

Her father's heart beat weakly in his chest. Every feeble throb sent blood pulsing through the organ—blood that was leaking from a hole on the left side. Her father's heart had a hole in it, a black spot like an open mouth spewing blackish blood in a macabre fountain. She couldn't say how, but Corrine knew that the hole had been caused by Maribel being taken away, that her father experienced that loss as a physical and psychic blow.

Pressure built behind Corrine's forehead, the spot between her eyes burning, itching. Her finger twitched, the only response her body gave for Corrine's efforts to lift her hand. The pain grew, climbing, climbing. Her father's lips moved, but no sound came out. There was nothing but the images of the nightmare, and the horrible ache between her eyes that kept growing and growing...

"*Corrine!*"

Her father's voice exploded in Corrine's ears as the spell broke, throwing her back into reality with enough force that she was certain her flesh would bear bruises. She closed her eyes, bracing herself for the chaos that was coming for her. The pain between her eyes faded in time to be replaced with the violent strikes of the floor against her arms and legs. Her body thrashed against the wooden planks like a fish cast into the bottom of a boat, her limbs smacking against the hard surface with unforgiving intensity. She tried to fight it, she always tried to fight it. And as was always the case, her efforts were futile.

She didn't know how long the seizure lasted, time had no

meaning for her now. Tears welled in her eyes as the violent spasms finally released her, leaving her to lie on the floor in a puddle of her own pain. Her father gathered her into his arms and Corrine cried out, his touch too much for her battered body to take. She shoved him away with hands shaking so badly she could scarcely see individual fingers. She tasted blood and knew she must have bitten her tongue again. The pain added to the misery cradling her and she pressed her lips together to muffle her sobs. She hiccupped and lurched to her feet.

"Corrine, wait!" Her father scrambled to his feet, arms reaching for her as she stood.

"*Leave me alone!*" Corrine screamed, humiliation burning her cheeks. She stumbled as she regained her feet and half-fell against the door.

"Corrine, please, let me help you," her father begged, tears thickening his voice.

"You can't help me," Corrine bit out, scrabbling at the doorknob. The smooth metal mocked her as the scarred flesh of her hand slipped against its slick surface. "You've never been able to help me."

She bolted out the door, leaving her father's protests behind her. Furniture conspired to keep her trapped in the house, lunging out of nowhere to bang into her hips and thighs. Her heart beat harder as pain blossomed on each fresh strike, the blood pouring from the cut in her mouth welling up until she gagged. Whimpers were falling from her throat as she finally put a hand on the front door and forced it open.

She ran out of the house as fast as she could. The land flew beneath her feet, her surroundings a blur as she desperately raced for the forest that held Mother Briar's old hut. All around her, her father's new employees stared, not bothering with subtlety or basic human manners. She could feel their judgment, the hairs on the back of her neck rising as if warning her how dangerous it was to turn her back on them with their sharp farming instruments. She was a witch, untrusted, unwanted. It was only a matter of time before one of them decided they could no longer work for a witch. Before they decided they needed the job too badly to simply quit.

Her head ached, the panic riding her like a demon, urging her faster and faster. She needed help and she needed it now. Maribel was gone. She was slow, too slow. Surrounded by enemies. *Starving…*

Corrine didn't know if Mother Briar used magic to alert her to visitors or if the old woman had a sixth sense, but however it came to be, she was standing on her front stoop as Corrine burst out of the trees into the clearing that held her home. The witch stood with her hands on her generous hips, steely eyes tracking Corrine's progress. She inclined her head to Corrine as she ran up the pathway then retreated into the small hut, leaving Corrine to follow her.

"I've been expecting you." Mother Briar approached the fire and took up a large wooden spoon. She stirred something in the giant black cauldron hanging over the flames, filling the room with the sour aroma of stewed cabbage.

Corrine's stomach growled loudly even as her nose wrinkled in distaste. She put a hand over her belly and sank into a chair at the table, too tired to be embarrassed anymore or to care what manner of food was offered to her. Mother Briar scooped whatever was cooking into a bowl and set it in front of Corrine along with a few slices of bread and a cup of water.

Shredded cabbage cooked to within an inch of its life floated in an oily broth. Lumps of meat—pork?—floated here and there, nearly lost to the quagmire of cabbage. Corrine wanted to reject the foul-smelling food, but her stomach screamed at her, her body withering as she hesitated.

Starving…

The word echoed from somewhere inside her mind, and with it came an uncontrollable hunger so intense it threatened to fold her in two. Corrine fell on the food like it was a lifeline, her disgust forgotten under the force of her body's need.

Juice dribbled down her chin and she had to put her face down until it nearly touched the bowl to avoid spilling more food than she swallowed. She shoveled thick chunks of meat into her mouth, scarcely bothering to chew. Mushy cabbage slid down her throat whole and she choked. Still she didn't stop until she saw the bottom of the bowl.

The food was real, the bowl was real. She wasn't in that horrible dream anymore, her body was her own again, obeying her commands. Her gaze traveled to the cauldron. Who knew when she would eat again? She eyed Mother Briar, waiting until the witch wasn't' looking, then slipping the bread into the pocket of her cloak to save it for later. Finally the panic faded to a manageable level. She put both hands, palms down, on the table and fixed her eyes on her empty bowl.

Mother Briar said nothing, merely waited in silence for Corrine to speak. Corrine had all the time in the world to put her thoughts in order. She waited until she thought she could keep her voice steady before she spoke.

"You lied to my sister."

The old woman sat across from Corrine, her chair creaking like an ancient tree branch under the weight of a looming vulture. "Oh?"

Corrine raised her face, letting the hot anger flickering to life inside her show in her eyes. "You know full well that the curse on Daman has nothing to do with love or trust. Maribel can't break that curse—only I can."

"I'm the one who taught you that curse, Corrine," Mother Briar said calmly. "I am fully aware that you are the only one who can break it."

"Then why did you tell her that?" Corrine grasped the sides of the table with her hands, fingers white with the effort. "How could you send her away from me, filling her head with all that rot about saving him with love?" Corrine slid her hands onto the tabletop, clenching her hands into fists. "I *need* her."

"Yes. I'd imagine it is quite hard for you to drain your sister's energy now that she's so terribly far away."

Instinctually, Corrine rubbed at a spot over her heart where the arcane mark was drawn on her skin, ink and blood mixed together. Touching it should have let her feel the invisible thread that connected her to her sister, but she felt nothing. It was as though the distance between her and Maribel had stretched the magical bond so thin that it was intangible, even to her magic sense. Completely absent of the thrum of energy she so depended on. Useless. "Don't say it like that. I'm not trying to hurt her."

"You *can't* hurt her," Mother Briar corrected her, her tone condescending. "The spell I taught you doesn't work that way. The bond between you only allows you to share her energy, not to drain it from her. Despite her ignorance, she is *sidhe*, and as long as she is more powerful than you, you will not be able to take more energy from her than she can spare."

"I would never take more than I need." Corrine's heart pounded against the wall of her chest in a bruising rhythm. "Why did you send her away? You're the one who taught me the spell, surely you don't begrudge me using it?"

"I could not care less what you do to your sister." Mother Briar waved her hand as if to brush away the suggestion. "But for now, she is of greater value to me if she remains with Daman."

Corrine gritted her teeth at the mention of the monster's name. She never wanted to hear that name again—ever. "*Why?*"

Mother Briar's eyes flashed, an unearthly light glittering in eyes gone black as obsidian. "Daman stole my daughter from me. I want her back. Your sister is in a position to earn his trust and find out where he took her."

"He took your daughter because you treated her as your slave," Corrine spat. "You were a fool to mistreat her in the territory of a *naga* sworn to protect changelings."

"She is a goblin!" Mother Briar met Corrine's gaze, beady eyes fairly glowing with ire. "The goblins stole my child and left one of their own miscreants behind! If I hadn't kept the goblin brat busy, she would have been a danger to everyone. Daman had no right to judge my mothering—especially when he knew what she was."

"I notice you're not so interested in finding your own daughter—the one you actually gave birth to." Corrine rested her chin on her hand, propped up with an elbow on the table. "What's the matter, humans can't work as hard?"

"Obviously," Mother Briar sneered, giving Corrine a pointed look. "Isn't that why you need your fairy sister to come back? So she can be your slave?"

Corrine pressed her lips into a thin line. "I do not treat her as my slave. She is my sister. I love her." *Why doesn't anyone understand that?* She shoved that thought away. It didn't matter what anyone said, Maribel knew Corrine loved her.

Mother Briar didn't argue, but something in her eyes made it clear what she thought of Corrine's declaration of familial love. The dismissal tightened something in Corrine's stomach despite her attempts to reassure herself, and the stew she'd gobbled down so ravenously soured inside her.

"There is no reason for us to fight, Corrine," Mother Briar said finally. "We can work together and we will both get what we want. If you help me get my daughter back, I will teach you magic stronger than any you have ever dreamed of. I will give you the strength to steal energy from anyone around you, the power to bend people to your will. You will be able to find a rich husband and take him for all he is worth. You will have the land, the money, and the power to support yourself—forever."

The crone's words wove around Corrine like a new dress, corset strings pulling into a snug fit that hugged her closer than any human ever had. *Security.* That's what Mother Briar was offering her now. Magic was only a means to an end, a means to be absolutely certain that she never starved again, was never alone again, never *weak* again.

Corrine blinked, realizing she'd been leaning forward more and more as Mother Briar spoke. Her heart pounded and images of herself sitting in a grand house, surrounded by servants, smelling the sweet aromas of a sumptuous feast, kept floating through her mind. She searched inside herself for that power that let her sense magic, that let her use magic. Surely the witch must be using some sort of compulsion spell on her. Surely her desperation couldn't be this strong?

The magical sense rose like a pet greeting its mistress, coming to her call and dutifully sniffing for any traces of magical manipulation. She kept feeling around, but came up with nothing. Mother Briar's words were just words. There was no force behind them.

"You've suffered so much, Corrine," Mother Briar continued gently. "Your family doesn't want to admit it, they don't want you to feel badly, but the fact is that you are a pathetic creature. You're nothing but skin and bones, and sometimes I'm amazed that you can walk all the way here from your own poor farmhouse."

Pathetic. Skin and bones. Poor. Corrine averted her eyes, trying to force her brain to think past the strange muddle it had become. Her skin was suddenly clammy with sweat, and if she rubbed her hands together, she could swear she felt the bones grinding against one another. The horror built inside her as she noticed the way her dress sagged against her flesh, sharp, skeletal points tenting the fabric where her bones stuck out. She swayed in her chair. *So hungry...*

"Oh, you poor child. Let me get you another bowl."

Mother Briar snatched up Corrine's bowl and refilled it with the disgusting concoction. Corrine fell on it like a starving wolf. It didn't matter that the cabbage was overcooked to the point of losing all cohesion, or that the pork was tough and burnt. Her stomach was cramping, her head spinning, her entire body aching as though she hadn't eaten in days. She *needed* this food.

"Corrine, if you won't do this for me, then do it for yourself." Mother Briar put her hand over Corrine's, her meaty paw making Corrine's fingers appear even more fragile. "My dear, you won't survive this life much longer. You weren't meant for it."

She's right.

Corrine was only half surprised to find her food was completely gone. She kept her gaze fixed on the bottom of the ceramic crockery, forcing herself not to cast a mournful stare at the pot on the stove like a dog begging for more scraps. She was tired of being pathetic.

"Go to your sister. It has been weeks, and she is such a charming girl. It will only be a matter of time until she has the power over the beast to leverage the information I need. Use your influence over your sister. Get me that information. It is your only chance."

Corrine swayed in her seat, blinking slowly as Mother Briar's words echoed in her head. "I'll do it." She stood up, proud of herself that her legs only trembled slightly. She met Mother Briar's gaze. There was a spark of pride there, and Corrine's spirits rose. She tried to remember why she'd ever been angry with the witch, but couldn't think of a reason. "You're certain Daman will let me see her? After what I did…"

"Corrine, I've already planted the seed in Maribel's mind that Daman needs love and trust to break his horrible curse. I'm certain that Maribel's kindness and Daman's own guilt over his horrid temper will be more than enough to make him give her whatever her heart desires." Mother Briar scowled. "Besides, the beast has such a soft spot for changelings. I've yet to hear of him denying one of the creatures anything they asked for."

Corrine gritted her teeth. "He certainly doesn't care that way for anyone who *isn't* a changeling. He had no problem whatsoever telling *me* no."

"Yes, he was cruel to you, wasn't he?" Mother Briar moved to stand behind Corrine, hands rising to rest on her shoulders. "All you wanted was the same security he so willingly offered those pathetic changelings. He has no wife, no shortage of treasure. You're a beautiful girl, a girl who's been brave in the face of more adversity than any woman should have to bear. He had no right to *mock* you like he did."

The flames below the large black pot danced in her vision as Corrine's mind drifted back to the first time she'd met Daman. "He was so kind at first, but it was only because I had Maribel's blood on me and he thought I was a changeling. For a moment I actually thought he cared about me."

"He only cares for creatures from beyond the veil." Mother Briar snorted. "He obviously has no respect for the suffering humans must endure. Who knows what sort of terror those changelings wreak on their new homes after he's relocated them?"

"You are no changeling. You have a good life, you are just too spoiled to appreciate it. Go home, human, and be grateful."

Daman's words echoed in Corrine's memory. She could still see his flashing silver eyes, the harsh lines of his face, the cruel twist of his handsome mouth as he'd practically thrown her out of his manor.

"Make your sister understand that Daman is not the man she thinks he is, that he is a selfish beast who kidnaps changelings and sends them away from the people their own families chose to raise them. If she is the kind-hearted soul we know she is, she will help me find my daughter." The witch moved to the side and settled into a chair next to Corrine. "And then, my child, I will teach you all you need to know to get the life you want—the life you *deserve.* You can trust me. Only me."

Anger burned hot inside Corrine as Daman's face hovered in

her mind, mocking her, her pain, and her dreams. Her heart cauterized in her chest, the decision solidifying inside her like a lump of coal squeezed into a diamond. "I'll do it."

"Excellent." Mother Briar stood up, brushing her skirts off. "Now, let me wrap up some bread up for you to take home."

"Thank you." Corrine waited for the witch to turn her back and then plucked an apple out of the bowl on the table and tucked it into the other pocket in her cloak. She was so hungry…

CHAPTER 6

Maribel jabbed the knife into the slab of meat and began viciously sawing off the fat and flinging it into a bowl. It landed with a wet *plop!* The sound was not nearly satisfying enough to appease Maribel's growing temper.

"I wasn't staring." She savaged the piece of beef into small chunks, hurling them into the oiled cast iron pan heating on the oven. "Why would I? It's no big deal." Her teeth clenched in frustration. "Half... Half..." She pursed her lips and slammed a fist down on the cutting board. "Oh, for pity's sake. Say it. Half *serpent.*"

The word hung in the air like an accusation. Maribel drummed her fingers on the cutting board, jaw jutting out as she glared at nothing in particular. After several moments of silence, her shoulders slumped and she cast a glance at the oven.

She should have been more excited that Daman had an oven. She hadn't seen one since her family had been wealthy enough to have a full kitchen, and even then she'd spent limited time in that area of the house. It hadn't been until they'd lost all of that and she'd begun cooking for her family herself that she'd started dreaming of using one. Now she finally had her chance, and she couldn't enjoy it properly because she couldn't quit thinking about her sour host. She grasped the knife.

"It's been weeks," she informed the would-be stew. "*Weeks,* and every time he deigns to speak with me I get to bear the brunt of his atrocious mood swings." She stabbed the raw meat and resumed butchering it. "If he didn't want to go on a walk, he should have said so! It wasn't as though I was trying to underline the fact that he..."

She tripped over the words in her mind, tiny voices in her head screaming she was being rude until she forcibly shook off her embarrassment. "Don't be a ninny, Maribel," she told herself firmly. "Say it. He hasn't got any *legs*." The knife thunked into the wood on a particularly enthusiastic jab. "That's no reason we can't get along. I'm not judging him for it, there's no reason for him to be so blasted sensitive."

The meat sizzled, oil flying off in angry sputters, wrenching Maribel out of her reverie. She gritted her teeth as the oil splattered against her arm, tiny droplets burning her skin. "If anything, *I* should be the one who doesn't want to try and get along with *him*," she told the vegetables. "Every chance he gets, he steers the conversation to Corrine. I'm sure he thinks he's being subtle, but men in general are lost when it comes to subtlety and that's apparently even more true for men who are..." She glared at the angry red spatters on her arm. *Say it, Maribel, it's no big deal. You've already said it once.* "Half serpent," she finished.

"Wyvern."

A squeak exploded from Maribel's lips. She whirled around with the knife held out in a defensive pose, silver blade shining in the light pouring into the kitchen from the open door and the great cooking fire in the hearth.

Daman loomed in the doorway, his strange silver eyes glinting in the light like polished silver coins. The draconic scales of his lower body shimmered as muscles shifted, and Maribel cursed the blush that heated her cheeks as she became painfully aware that Daman was naked. The fact that he had no…parts, showing should have made it easier—but it didn't. The arm holding the knife sagged as she scrambled to tear her mind away from wondering things no lady had any business wondering about a man who was not her husband.

"What?" she demanded.

"Wyvern," he repeated evenly. His deep voice rolled into the air like approaching thunder. "Not serpent."

Maribel tried to follow the conversation and failed. The fierce heat of her embarrassment had obviously boiled her brain past the point of functioning. Anger obligingly rose to take the place of logic, but before she could let loose a scathing comment, Daman spoke again.

He gestured at his lower half. "I'm not half serpent, I'm half wyvern. Serpent could just as easily mean snake. My ancestry is dragon."

Maribel started to cross her arms, realized she was still holding the knife, and pressed her lips into a thin line. He'd heard her then. Shame rose at being caught insulting her host, but she viciously squashed it down. What business did he have spying on her anyway? She returned her focus to the chunks of meat sizzling in the pan, careful to brown them evenly. "What's the difference?" she shot over her shoulder, forcing nonchalance into her tone.

"Careful, child," Daman warned, the now-familiar warmth of his temper heating his tone.

Maribel whirled around. "I'm not a child. I'm a grown woman."

Daman held her gaze, silver eyes steady and unnerving. "What's the difference?"

A thousand contemptuous retorts fought for dominance on Maribel's tongue. She'd come to the kitchen to find some peace, to lose herself in doing something productive. It wasn't fair for him to follow her in here, to spy on her and try to paint her a fool. Not when he avoided her so well the rest of the time. She diverted her attention away from Daman and back to the meal she was preparing, jabbing at the chunks of meat and dusting them with pepper.

"What are you making?"

Maribel tensed, grip tightening on the knife. "You did say I was free to go wherever I wished on the property. You have no cook, I assumed it would be all right for me to feed myself."

"I did not mean to suggest you were doing anything wrong. I was simply...curious."

The hairs on the back of her neck rose as he moved closer. Her stomach fluttered and she had to take a moment to settle herself before answering. "I'm making a stew."

"Stew?"

Maribel glanced over her shoulder, brows rising to her hairline as she found Daman examining the vegetables she'd chopped, poking through the bowl of carrots and potatoes and the separate bowl of celery, onion, carrots, tomatoes, and garlic. Her inner chef preened at the expression of appreciation in his eyes as he surveyed the stew's ingredients. She started to say something, but suddenly his forked tongue flicked out of his mouth, killing the words before they could escape her lips. It was only for a second, but it was...unnerving. Generally speaking, such tongues were usually very tiny, belonging to snakes significantly smaller than Daman. Seeing a tongue the size of a human's —forked like a serpent's—was...strange.

Daman finally raised his attention from the ingredients. Maribel jerked her attention back to the browning meat, hoping he hadn't caught her gaping at him.

"Go ahead and stare, it's all right."

Maribel tensed. His tone held no heat, but after being here for weeks, the words were familiar—and they'd never been pleasant. "I was *not* staring."

Scales rustled against stone. "I wasn't accusing you, I was telling you it was all right."

Again his tone *sounded* sincere. The meat hissed as Maribel flung the thick pieces about in the pan. "So you think I want to stare at you, that I'm that rude? That's what you think of me?"

"You're behaving like a child again." Daman snatched up a potato, squeezing it in his grip until his claws disappeared into the brown-skinned flesh. "I was trying to be nice. I'm aware you've never seen a *naga* before and you're trying not to stare, but frankly it's more annoying to see you tense up every time I'm in the room because you're trying *not* to stare. The first time obviously wasn't enough, so just get it over with, satisfy your curiosity."

Now there's the sourpuss I remember. Maribel spun around, the spoon clenched in her grip as her arm trembled with the urge to fling it at her host. "Has it ever occurred to you that I'm *tense* around you, not because I'm trying so hard not to stare, but because I'm bracing myself for whatever vitriol you're going to fling at me? Perhaps you'd like to disparage my sister some more?" She pointed at him with the spoon, feeling a sense of empowerment with the utensil that usually only came from brandishing a weapon. "I don't know what has your tail in a twist, but I'm sick of you taking it out on me."

She whirled back to the stove before the color rising to her face could steal her victory from her. It had taken every ounce of willpower she had to mention his tail, and she didn't want to ruin the moment by letting him see how much effort it had taken.

The stunned silence behind her was incredibly satisfying. Maribel smirked at the stew meat. There was an exhalation of breath behind her, a ragged sound dragged up from the depths of his being.

"I'm sorry for what I said about your sister," Daman muttered.

"Sorry because it's not true, or sorry because it caused our 'little feud?'"

A low growl rumbled up from Daman's chest. "I do not want to fight with you."

"Then get out of the kitchen." Maribel grabbed the pan holding the meat and dumped the browned beef into a large bowl. The pan clanged onto the stove as she slammed it down. She kept her eyes away from Daman as she stalked over to the vegetables she'd prepared and threw the carrots, garlic, onion, and celery into the pan still coated with oil and residual fat from the meat. The vegetables sizzled, echoing her temper.

There was a short silence and then Daman's voice again. "It has been some time since I've...entertained," he admitted grudgingly. "Perhaps we could start over. Get to know one another over dinner."

Maribel went still, a cup of pulverized tomatoes in her grasp. "Are you completely serious?" She glanced back at Daman, torn between outrage and shock. "Are you inviting yourself to share a meal with me? A meal *I'm* preparing?"

For a moment, she caught him with his guard down. His stiff mask of indifference had broken and he was gazing with something akin to longing at the food cooking on the stove. As soon as he registered her attention, he stiffened. Haughty arrogance returned to mask his emotions and he pulled his claws free of the potato and thumped it down onto the table, holding her eyes as if daring her to comment. She swallowed the sharp words she'd been about to hurl at him and tapped her spoon on the pan.

"Do the brownies cook for you?"

His eyes twitched, but remained on her. "They gather fresh produce from the gardens, but they don't cook and they don't hunt."

Maribel couldn't help dropping her gaze to the claws on the tips of his fingers, glancing from them to her injured potato. "So you...hunted for this meat?"

"One doesn't 'hunt' for cows." Daman made a face as though

he'd bitten into something sour, then sighed. "I mean, yes, I slaughtered the cow for that meat."

Her temper, which had flared up at the first part of his sentence, quickly calmed as she acknowledged he was at least trying to be less insulting. "Well, I suppose it would be rude of me to cook your food and refuse to share it with you."

The hope that lit Daman's eyes was humorous. "That is very... kind." He slid closer, scales grating over the stone. "It's been so long since I've had a grand meal such as this."

Maribel tensed, the camaraderie of the moment threatening to shatter. "Are you *mocking* me?"

Daman's slitted eyes widened slightly. "No."

"A stew is grand?"

Again Daman gazed longingly at the pan of vegetables. "I've been cooking for myself for some time. I'm afraid I'm rather basic when it comes to meals—meat, bread, and whatever fruit the brownies harvest from the garden. I'm not much of a chef."

"A stew is a fairly simple meal," Maribel insisted, annoyed with herself for the curl of pleasure that spiraled inside her at the compliment.

"It smells amazing already." Daman moved closer, arching his neck to peer into the pot. "What are you adding now?"

"Tomato paste." Maribel scraped the thick red substance into the pan and stirred the vegetables into it. She let it cook for a moment and then grabbed the large bottle of red wine she'd found in the cellar. Part of her waited for Daman to stop her, to say something about the wine being too fine for such a paltry use. But the...*naga*, just watched, fascination lighting his features.

She dumped the wine into the pan, relishing the sizzle as the alcohol evaporated and the bouquet of the wine scented the air. Daman remained silent, though he slid closer. His body heat caressed her back through the few inches that separated them and Maribel's nerves danced with awareness. The butterflies swarmed back to life in her stomach and she realized she was holding her breath, anticipating... What?

Snap out of it! Maribel forcibly shook off the ridiculous fantasies trying to play out in her head and snatched up the bottle of balsamic vinegar. She poured it into the pan and Daman's tongue flicked out again. Maribel jumped, her arm jolting with the motion and pressing against the hot cast iron.

A sharp inhalation of pain escaped her lips as she dropped the spoon and clutched her arm. The skin shrieked in objection at her touch and she quickly yanked her hand away, holding the injured arm out into the air and clenching her teeth against the pain.

"I'm sorry." Daman's voice was terse, tight with an emotion akin to self-admonishment. He vanished with unnerving, inhuman speed, then returned with a jar of honey. "I startled you." He snorted as he unscrewed the lid, filling the air with the sweet, sticky scent of honey. "No wonder Moira never wanted me in the kitchen."

Maribel held still, trying to concentrate on his words, on the jar, anything but the throbbing pain of the burn. Equally to be avoided was the sharp stab of jealousy that lanced through her at the mention of some woman named Moira.

Forcing her mind away from that baffling train of thought, she held her breath and let Daman smear some of the thick, viscous fluid on her arm. "Honey?" she breathed, more to distract herself from her own thoughts than anything. She closed her eyes against the sting of pressure on the wound.

"It is a natural disinfectant and will ease the pain."

She opened her eyes. "I know, I..." The traitorous blush returned with a vengeance.

Daman arched an eyebrow at her. "You didn't expect me to know that. Because I'm a man or because I'm a *naga*?"

This time there was no doubt that Daman saw her embarrassment. She kept her gaze on her arm, pathetically unable to meet his eyes.

The sight of his finger sliding so gently over her arm mesmerized her. It wasn't the fiery red condition of her own blistered skin, but the unmarred perfection of his. For some reason, she'd expected his entire body to be covered in scales, thought that if she got close enough, she would see the fine diamond pattern common to snakes. His skin had appeared smooth, but she'd assumed the scales were simply more refined on his upper body.

Now that she had an opportunity to see his skin up close—in a situation where she could study it without appearing rude—she realized that for the most part, from the waist up, he was the same flesh and blood as any human she'd ever met. Though, granted, his skin was a pale blue and did bear some scaled ridges.

Her gaze landed on his neck and the lines of thick scales that fell like braided silk down either side of his throat and ended just after the curves of his shoulders. A circular swirl of scales sat at the base of his throat, tendrils of the thick scales sliding out in a line on either side to almost, but not quite, connect with the ridges that ended at his shoulders. The bottom of the circle was connected to another ridge that fell down his chest, branching out into two delicate lines of ridges that cradled his ribs on either side. The main ridge down his chest continued past his taut stomach until it blended seamlessly with the scales of his lower body like a glistening river meeting the rippling waves of the ocean.

The honey grew tackier as Daman continued to spread it. He dipped his finger into the jar for a fresh scoop. As he applied more honey to the burn in the same slow, soothing motions, some of the tension leaked from Maribel's shoulders. The even strokes he used to apply the balm were hypnotic, calming. The pain faded into the background and her mind continued its unimpeded consideration of her host.

His fingers were tipped with short, but wickedly sharp and

curved white claws. He was obviously taking great care to keep from scratching her as he used the middle of his finger to spread the honey. Her gaze travelled to his hand and up his arm, and she noticed for the first time how thick his muscles were, the tempting swell of his biceps.

She must have made some sort of sound, because when she finally tore her attention away from his torso, Daman was staring at her, his face less than a foot away from her own. His mercurial eyes were dilated, the reptilian slits wider, round enough to be human. He'd stopped spreading the honey and now held her arm in a gentle grasp. His grip was warm and strong, and Maribel was suddenly incredibly aware of exactly how close they were.

"Does that feel better?"

His voice was deeper than it had been, absent the sharp edge she'd grown used to hearing from him. Rough and textured, a tangible sound, like rich, thick bed furs on bare skin.

He has a very human face, really.

The thought came out of nowhere, but it lodged itself in Maribel's brain, dragging her attention to Daman's face, the line of his jaw. He had very angular features, strong and solid. His mouth was perfectly normal, his lips…

Maribel had a sudden image of his forked tongue flicking out, his reptilian eyes intense. The strange spell rising between them shattered like overheated glass.

"Thank you," she said hoarsely, tugging meekly at his grip on her arm. Her heart pounded so hard she thought the pulse in her throat would cut off her air.

There was a strange look on Daman's face, as if he were debating whether to let go of her arm or pull her closer. Hyper-awareness reminded her how much strength was in those broad swells of muscle, how much power was in that sculpted body. His eyes that had appeared so human to her a moment ago were now stark reminders that the man beside her was a predator. And she was behaving like prey.

The sound of blood rushing through her veins was so loud in her ears it shut out all else. She had to swallow three times before she could speak.

"I... I should get back to cooking."

She held her breath and tugged at her arm again, inordinately grateful as he released her without protest. Then she practically dove for the spoon she'd been using to stir the pot, focusing on mixing the simmering concoction as though it took all of her concentration. Every nerve in her body vibrated with awareness as she waited for some sound behind her, some indication that Daman had moved. There was nothing but silence.

"I don't want the vegetables to burn," she babbled, focusing hard on the stew that didn't need the attention she was giving it. "It has to cook like this for hours, and then I'll add the bowl of carrots and potatoes and they'll have to cook for another two hours... It takes so long, I know, but I used to make this all the time on the farm because I could leave it to cook while I..."

The complete and utter silence that met her incessant stream of rambling knocked against Maribel's awareness like waves against the hull of an abandoned boat, and she forced herself to stop. She concentrated on taking a few subtle, slow breaths, trying to regain her composure. By the time she finally got the nerve to glance over her shoulder, he was gone.

She searched the kitchen, checking the doorway and waiting a full five minutes before letting out her breath.

"Stupid," she muttered to herself.

"What did I do?"

Maribel screeched and yanked the spoon out of the pot, sending a spray of broth in a heated arc toward the wall. There was a flash of silver in the air and Maribel's lips parted as some sort of...snake, leapt into the air and swallowed a droplet of stew before landing in a metallic coil on the butcher block.

"Mmmm," the serpent hummed. "Can I have sssome more?"

Maribel clutched the spoon to her chest as her heart threatened to shatter her ribcage. "Who..." She blinked. "Daman...?"

The snake twisted its upper body so it was peering behind itself. "Where?"

Not Daman, then. Maribel let out the breath that had lodged itself in her throat. Her brain had managed a mind-boggling leap from utter distaste to a disturbing attraction to her scaled host. She wasn't sure she'd have been able to handle him turning into a full snake. Especially one as small as her visitor.

Not that size matters. Don't think about size. Size of what? Stop thinking! "Who are you?" she asked loudly, practically shouting from sheer desperation to drown out her own thoughts.

"Not ssstupid," the little serpent said pointedly. Its tiny pink tongue flickered out.

"Stupid?" Maribel tried to gather her wits back into some semblance of order. "Oh, no, I'm sorry. I was talking to myself."

"That'sss all right then. Asss long asss you realize I am not ssstupid."

"I'm sorry, did you burn your tongue?"

The snake tilted its head. A moment later, it opened its mouth and a small flame shot from its throat. It closed its mouth again.

"Probably not then." Maribel cleared her throat and continued stirring the pot. *I am not having a nervous breakdown. Nagas, vampires, brownies. Why not a talking snake?* She glanced at the snake. *With wings.* "I'd be glad to get you a...bowl when you're ready, but I must say, it would be worth the wait if you let me finish it first. It has to cook for a long time, but after it's done, the meat will melt in your mouth."

"Ooh, that sssoundsss good."

"Are you a...friend of Daman's?"

"Are you?" the serpent countered, its beady black eyes following her spoon as she stirred.

"Am I what?"

"Daman'sss friend?"

"I…" Maribel paused and cleared her throat, firmly shoving away the memory of Daman's fingers sliding over her skin and her subsequent perusal of his body. His naked body. She tightened her grip on the spoon. *Stop thinking about that!* "We haven't known one another long," she managed finally.

"You ssseemed clossse."

Maribel tapped the spoon on the edge of the pot and set it on the butcher block. The snake lowered its head as if intending to lick the spoon and she twitched and jerked it out of the way. She pressed her lips into a disapproving line and deliberately put the spoon on the other side of the stove.

"I don't know what you think you saw, but it was nothing. I burned myself and Daman was…helping me."

"But you do like him?"

"I'm not sure yet," Maribel sputtered. She crossed her arms. "Honestly, I'm having trouble making up my mind. He has rather pronounced mood swings, if you must know, and I'm not sure I care for him when his temper gets the better of him." She narrowed her eyes suspiciously. "What do you care?"

"Jussst making sssure everything isss going according to plan."

"Plan?" Maribel tensed, dropping her arms to her sides. "What plan?"

"I don't like to tell everything at onccce," the snake said casually. "It makesss it difficult to know."

"To know what?"

"If thingsss happened naturally or if you forcccced them to happen."

"Ohhhh," Maribel breathed. "You're talking about his curse."

The snake lifted its head higher, and if it'd had ears, they would have perked up. "You know about hisss cursssse?"

"Yes. Mother Briar told me about it."

"Ssshe would know," the snake agreed.

Maribel shifted uncomfortably. "I don't know what your stake is in all of this, but I'm not here to fall in love with a perfect stranger." The words tasted odd on her tongue and for a moment she felt foolish.

The snake blinked. "Did you sssay fall in love?"

"I know that's how to break the curse, but love doesn't happen like that." Maribel slanted a glance at the doorway Daman must have left through. Part of her wished he was standing there. "Besides, so far we don't seem very compatible."

"Are you talking about the mating assspect?"

Maribel nearly swallowed her tongue as she whipped her head around to gape at the snake. The serpent still sat there calmly, its body coiled in a pile on the butcher's block.

"What did you say?"

"The mating assspect," the snake repeated slowly. "You sssaid you weren't compatible. Did you mean—"

"No!" The heat rushing to her cheeks was making Maribel's head spin and she half-stumbled across the kitchen to fall into a chair. "I most certainly didn't mean—"

"Becaussse you don't have anything to worry about there," the snake continued. "Even if he doesssn't break the curssse, he isss fully capable—"

"If you finish that sentence, I'll make you sorry you ever sat down on a butcher's block," Maribel choked.

The little snake froze, then glanced down at where it was sitting, seeming to notice the large butcher's knife for the first time.

"Interesssting."

Maribel covered her face with her hands, mortified as her mind followed the path the snake had started down with its outrageous insinuation. She hadn't thought about it—of course she hadn't thought about it. He'd basically taken her prisoner, he'd threatened her father, insulted her sister... He was half *snake*, for goodness' sakes!

Not snake. Wyvern.

She paused, realizing that she wasn't entirely certain what a wyvern was, and this talking, fire-breathing snake might be her chance to ask without having another awkward conversation with Daman. It would also change the subject.

She opened her mouth to form the question, but when her gaze landed on the butcher's block, the serpent was gone.

"Must be a reptile thing," she muttered.

CHAPTER 7

Daman leaned against the edge of the lake, lashing his tail lazily back and forth through the water. Ripples flowed out from him, soothing in their graceful outward path, the way they kissed the shore and disappeared. The water was haunted with the memory of winter, but the sapphire depths held no chill for him. His scales were thick, his body easily able to adapt to changes in temperature...and his blood was still overly warm from the pleasant sensation of Maribel's skin under his fingers.

He lifted his hand out of the lake, fat droplets of water falling from his fingers. He imagined he could still see the honey even though it had been hours since he'd washed it away. Maribel hadn't recoiled from his touch, hadn't flinched or shied away from him. She was still very nervous around him, even after being at his house for over two weeks, but he was starting to wonder...

"Fool." He slapped at the water, sending a glittering arc through the air. "You are far too old for such self-delusion."

And it had to be delusion. The way Maribel's breath had come faster as their eyes had met—that all came from nerves. What woman wouldn't be anxious around a beast such as himself? He wasn't even a *naga* anymore. His temper had pushed him from the ranks of his noble kin, barricaded him behind bars of his own creation. He was a danger to anyone who came near him, and he'd been a fool to keep Maribel close. He had to send her away.

It didn't matter that his temper tantrums had been limited to harsh words and admittedly inexcusable rudeness. It didn't matter if her touch calmed him. It didn't matter if seeing the flush on her face, the pink tint flowing down her neck and below her dress, had stirred a heat inside of him that had nothing to do with his temper.

"Daman?"

The sound of her voice tore his attention from the water so quickly that he had no idea what was showing in his eyes, what emotion he hadn't had time to wipe away. Whatever it was, it robbed Maribel of her words, left her standing on the shore of the lake with wide eyes. He wanted to say something, ease the tension, but no words would come. His brain was far too occupied with how her blue eyes sparkled in the sunlight, how her breathing was hard enough to make her chest rise and fall in the most…distracting manner.

"The… The stew is done. I thought you might like to come inside and eat."

Her voice was more breath than tone, though if that was because of the trek to the lake from the manor or something else, he couldn't be sure. He blinked, surprised to find the sun so low in the sky. Had he truly been lounging in the lake for the entire day? Had he lost himself so completely in his thoughts?

Again he tried to speak, but no words would come. Part of him was afraid to speak, afraid that he would say something to make her leave. He tried to hide his awkwardness with motion, swimming across the small lake to the opposite side where she stood. She watched him swim as if mesmerized, her gaze flicking to his tail, following it up his body to his bare back. Something warm stirred inside him at the way she didn't run, but simply stood there with that...intensity in her eyes.

Waiting for him.

A desire that hadn't stirred inside of him for years, even before he'd been cursed, filled him with wild energy, buzzing over his nerves, invigorating his blood. He met her eyes, holding her gaze as he emerged from the water. The delicate skin at her throat fluttered with a rapid pulse, her chest rising and falling faster. His scales slid easily over the wet grass, bringing him closer to her. For the first time, he moved without self-consciousness, without concentrating on what her reaction might be.

Her entire face tensed, her eyes suddenly firmly fixed on his face in an obvious attempt not to stare. A familiar flicker of temper threatened to draw his face into a scowl, but he batted it away. Not now, he would not lose his temper now. Not over something so insignificant. Not in the midst of these other feelings, other emotions, tempting him with the promise of something...more.

He stopped less than a foot away from her. "How is your arm?"

Maribel blinked at that, though she still didn't take her gaze from his face. "Better, thank you."

Her voice was breathy and higher than normal. It was a balm to the masculine pride that had suffered along with his cause this past year. Daman kept his eyes on hers as he took her arm. She didn't fight him, allowed him to raise it to examine the wound. His fingers slowly curled around her biceps as his other hand held hers. The burn was still an angry shade of red, but the skin wasn't blistering or broken. He imagined it was painful, but she would be fine.

"I'm sorry if I made you uncomfortable earlier." He spoke partly to reassure her and partly to distract himself from the thoughts taking root in his mind. Apparently even a day spent in an icy lake was not enough to cool what had started to burn between them earlier. He was already holding her arm. Her soft, supple, delicate arm. It would be so easy to slide a hand around her waist, pull her to him. It had been so long since he'd been around anyone, so long since he'd basked in body heat like hers. Even longer since he'd wanted to...

A tiny voice in his head screamed that there was a very good reason it had been that long, but he shut it out. The sensations running through his body were too delicious, the vibration of her thundering heartbeat too mesmerizing to stop now.

"No, it's all right. You don't make me nervous," she protested.

He couldn't help the quirk of his mouth, the outward betrayal of his amusement. "Liar."

A spark flared in her eyes. "What you call nervousness is no more than a perfectly normal reaction for a lady when her male host stands so close to her—*naked*."

His eyebrows shot up. She hadn't said anything that wasn't true, but he hadn't thought she had it in her to bring up that particular subject. But was it a complaint? He pressed his lips together for a moment, firmly resisting the urge to slide his tongue from his mouth to taste the air. He so desperately wanted to know if her heartbeat was thundering from fear...or something else.

"Draconic anatomy is an oddly dignified thing." He kept his focus on her face, searching her features for hints to her thoughts. "Clothing is largely ornamental, even in mixed company. Unless of course you continue gawking at me like that, standing so close—"

The slap caught him completely off guard. His cheek stung where her hand had connected with his flesh, a warm throbbing that didn't hurt nearly as much as it had surprised him. He let go of her arm and she took advantage of his distraction and whirled around to stalk back in the direction of the manor.

He moved before his brain could process what he was doing.

In seconds he was in front of her, her body flinching backwards, startled by his sudden movement. She opened her mouth on a gasp as she stumbled and nearly fell. Daman grabbed her around her waist and jerked her against him to keep her from falling. Warm flesh met scales that still held the chill of the lake. She shrieked and he had to tighten his grip to keep her from leaping away and falling over again.

"Hold still or you'll fall and break something," he ground out, his brain still trying to catch up with what had happened. "I'll let you go as soon as you're calm."

Maribel went completely still in his arms, her lips pressed in a line so tight they'd gone white. Fury sparked in her eyes, making them flash like the center of a raging bonfire.

She's even more beautiful when she's angry, he thought, reluctantly releasing her. He expected her to scramble away from him, but she flitted away just long enough to grab a large, broken tree branch from the ground. She brandished it like a club, eyes hot enough to burn. Furious.

"I don't know why you want me here," she ground out, her voice only trembling slightly. She pointed the makeshift weapon at him. "But if you think I'm going to warm your bed—"

"Warm my…" Daman sputtered.

His own temper flared to life and he streaked forward as fast as his coils could launch him. The rough surface of her club dug into his palm as he closed his fingers around it and tore it out of her hands. Her scent teased his nose, a mouth-watering bouquet of vegetables and spices—the stew she'd made. He hesitated, remembering why she'd come out here.

"Perhaps we could start over. Get to know one another over dinner."

Maribel released the branch with a pained yelp that was quickly followed by an angry shout. Daman tensed, his focus sharply returning to the present. His temper still scratched along the inside of his skull, riled by Maribel's insinuation. He clenched his teeth and backed away, holding the branch up between them.

He snapped it with one quick tug, exerting no more effort than it would have taken to break a toothpick.

Maribel flinched at the sharp crack that shattered the silence, but she didn't retreat and she didn't quit glaring at him. In some part of his mind, Daman was aware that her lack of fear should have comforted him. Instead, it only made him angrier.

"I have never suggested such a thing—nor would I." He hurled the broken pieces of wood away from him. "A monster I may be, but I assure you I have not grown so desperate for female company that I would drag an unwilling maiden into my bed." He turned away from her, not trusting what his face might reveal of the emotions roiling inside of him. "I don't want anything from you."

"Other than my freedom," Maribel bit out.

Tension sang through his muscles, pulling them taut. Now. Now was the opening he'd been waiting for, the time to tell her she could go home. He should release her from the bargain she'd struck on her father's behalf, pack another trunk full of treasure, and send her back to her family.

"Yes. Except that."

Again, the words flowed from his mouth without permission, coming from the very depths of his being, a place far from wherever good intentions originated.

If he'd had any sense, he'd have used his superior speed to get back to the manor before she could respond. The dinner that had been supposed to give them a fresh start seemed highly unlikely now, and the gods only knew what other words were waiting on his tongue, ready to fly off without any acquiescence on his part. Why he faced her again he didn't know. Certainly it wasn't to see her face, to read her expression. It wasn't some deep need to see what her reaction was to being told she still had to stay.

Maribel stuck her chin out and crossed her arms. The tempting curves of her breasts were shown in a most flattering manner by the stance, but the agitation sparking in the air around them was far too stifling to allow that thought to proceed very far. The way Maribel planted her feet and straightened her spine did not bode well.

"I know you need someone to fall in love with you to break your curse," she told him, only a slight waver in her voice betraying her nerves. "But if this is your way of going about it, then you're dooming yourself."

He'd been prepared for a lot of things, but that hadn't been one of them.

The flame of his temper died under a flood of confusion. Daman's lips parted, eyebrows knitting together until his forehead ached. He opened and closed his mouth a few times, but words failed him.

"Fall in love?" he echoed finally. "Who…?"

"It doesn't matter how I know," Maribel rushed to add. Her cheeks grew redder by the second. "The point is, I know."

Daman tapped a claw against his scales, mind working furiously to figure out what the blazes she was talking about. What lies had the witch told her sister? Was this how she'd convinced Maribel to come in her place? Had she filled her head with stories of a beast who could be changed into a prince if only a woman would fall in love with him? Did Maribel envision herself as the future mistress of his manor as well?

That last thought cut too deep. Daman swore at himself, furious he'd once again missed what was right in front of him. Of course there had been a reason Maribel had agreed to stay. Whether she'd been manipulated into coming here by her sister for Corrine's own purposes, or she'd come here with her own grand plan, Daman promised himself he'd have no part of it. And to think he'd…

"My curse can be lifted at the witch's will, not by any… emotional *pity* you might try to bestow upon me," he said stiffly. "Trust me when I say, I have *no* designs on either your body or your heart. You may rest easy on that score."

The flash of hurt on Maribel's face was a trick of his mind, a cruel prank. If she felt anything, it was probably disappointment that her task would be harder than she'd anticipated.

"Well I'm certainly relieved to hear that," she shot back.

Her voice lacked the venom the statement called for, but Daman assured himself he heard no disappointment in her tone. Still, there was no point in continuing this ire. There was still a possibility that Maribel was an innocent changeling, a victim of her sister's machinations. And if that were the case, Daman had a duty to her, a duty that should mean more to him than his own petty fears and pride.

"Now that that's been cleared up," he managed, keeping his voice calm. "I suggest we put it all behind us and go back to the house to partake of the lovely meal you've worked so hard on."

"Typical male." Maribel snatched up a leaf that her broken branch had lost upon its death. "You insult me as much as possible and then invite yourself to share in the meal *I* cooked." She narrowed her eyes at him. "*Again.*"

"The meal you made with *my* food." Daman plucked the leaf from her hand. "It would be most impressive if you could keep me from it."

Maribel yanked the leaf back and ripped it down the middle. "My, my, not holding back, are we? You just come right out and say if I don't willingly share the meal, you'll take it anyway."

Daman ignored the shame blistering his ears and folded his arms. "Yes."

Maribel pursed her lips, contemplating him for several long moments. Finally, the corner of her mouth twitched. "Well, you can take the food by force," she said lightly, shrugging one shoulder. "But if you can't be nice, then I won't make the dessert I was planning."

"What kind of dessert?"

He absolutely hadn't meant to say that. Maribel's lips slid into a full out smile, flashing white teeth.

"Keep being rude, and you'll never know."

Daman barked out a laugh, the tension between them shattering with the rough, unexpected sound, leaving him feeling lighter than he had in some time. He eyed Maribel, amusement playing with his voice, robbing it of some of its abrasiveness. "You're not afraid of me, are you?"

Maribel startled as if he'd torn her from some deep thought. He leaned closer without meaning to, suddenly very curious about what she'd been thinking so intensely about.

She started back toward the manor, robbing him of the opportunity to glean any clues. "No. Not really." She cleared her throat. "When you get angry, I get a bit...nervous," she admitted. "But I think that would be true of any man of your stature. You simply have a lot of weight to throw around."

Daman blinked, slowly starting to follow her. "Are you saying I'm overly large?" He studied himself as he asked the question. He was considerably smaller than he'd be in his dragon form, but he'd never compared his form now with his human form—not in terms of size, at least. Was he larger than a human?

Maribel started to look him up and down, then seemed to remember he wasn't wearing any clothes and immediately locked her gaze on his face again. "You are an impressive size."

A masculine voice in Daman's head preened at that last comment, but Daman brushed the innuendo away.

"You aren't frightening," Maribel offered after a few moments of silence. "The...lack of legs is a bit...different." She shrugged. "But other than that, you're not all that different from other men. Actually, with your light blue skin and those silver eyes you're... rather striking."

The last words came out in a rush, as if she'd had to work up her courage to say them. A rush of pleasure curled upward inside of him and he moved closer to Maribel. A sudden bolt of realization struck him, logic rearing its ugly head.

Fool me once, shame on you, fool me twice, shame on me. There is no reason to believe that this seduction is any more sincere than her sister's.

"This form was not meant for attracting a mate," Daman said, carefully putting more distance between them. "This is an in-between form. The more powerful of my people can hold this form mid-transformation, but for most it is merely passed through during the shift from human to dragon. And even the most powerful of my people never held this form for great lengths of time."

"Why not?"

Daman clenched his teeth. "Because it requires a great deal of focus and energy to balance the mind of a man and the mind of a dragon. It is...challenging at the best of times. To remain in between for so long..." He didn't want to finish the sentence. There was no need.

"And you're trapped in this form because of a curse?"

Daman opened the door to the kitchen and gestured for Maribel to precede him inside. "Yes."

"That seems like a strange curse."

A heavenly aroma filled the room, curling into Daman's senses until his stomach rumbled loud enough to drown out the unpleasant thoughts being stirred by the unfortunate turn in conversation. Maribel went to the stove and Daman noted with interest that she'd already set out two bowls. Apparently, she'd taken his suggestion that they dine together seriously from the beginning. She ladled stew into each of them and brought them to the table.

"Why did the witch curse you?" Maribel asked as she sat down.

A surge of temper interrupted Daman's appreciative inspection of the red wine infused broth flowing around tender bits of meat, carrots, and potato. "Because I would not give her what she wanted. She was a spoiled, selfish woman and she wanted me to give her a comfortable life. She wanted to rule over my manor and lands, to immerse herself in wealth she had not earned. She used trickery to gain access to my home, and after I discovered her lies, she tried seduction. The curse was her revenge for my rejection."

"So now you hate all witches."

Daman picked up his fork and stirred his stew, avoiding eye contact. Maribel wasn't ready to hear the truth about her sister, that much was obvious. He would have to earn her trust before she would even begin to be open to the truth. And that wasn't likely, all things considered.

"I do not hate all witches. But I do think that the ability to use magic brings a great responsibility that few are truly prepared for. It is too easy to let one's fears and needs rule your decisions, and with magic at one's command, a great deal of damage is often the result."

Maribel dropped her gaze a little too quickly, failing to hide the flinch that twisted her features. Daman smothered the desire to push her, to find out if that look meant what he hoped it might —that Maribel herself had concerns about her sister's magic.

"This stew is excellent," Daman said instead.

Maribel perked up, a small, pleased smile lifting the corners of her mouth. "I'm glad you like it."

"Indeed. The vinegar complements the garlic nicely."

"An impressive palate," Maribel observed.

"My sense of taste in this form is extremely developed. In many ways it can replace my sense of smell. I can follow an enemy's scent by tasting the wind the same way a wolf might use its nose." He paused, his mind flowing back to a time his manor had been full of people, friends and servants alike. He could practically hear the bustling sounds of an active kitchen, Moira's voice bellowing the way only a head cook could. "I think perhaps this is something I missed most," he said, slowly prodding at a chunk of beef. "The meals my cook used to prepare." He cleared his throat. "And the company."

Maribel's attention fell to her bowl. "Yes, you mentioned that you isolated yourself—that you didn't feel you were safe to be around."

Daman's spirits sank. The question he'd avoided was hanging in the air between them now, weighted and foreboding. Maribel's unspoken inquiry echoed in the silence. *If it's not safe to be around you, why are you keeping me here?*

He tried to think of something to say that wasn't the truth. Telling her that he'd demanded her father bring his daughter because he'd been expecting Maribel's sister and he'd wanted revenge on the witch would not endear him to Maribel. And telling her that he'd kept her here after realizing she wasn't who he'd thought she was because...

Why *had* he kept her here? Why hadn't he sent her home?

Because you want her here.

The thought threatened to set off a chain reaction, and Daman barely kept himself from letting himself admit more than he should. "If I thought you were in danger from me, I would send you away," he said finally, feeling his words out carefully. He met her eyes, willing her to believe him even as he willed himself to believe what he was saying. "I would never hurt you, Maribel."

Maribel held his gaze, her blue eyes boring into him as if weighing the truth of his words. Finally she nodded. "All right. I'll trust you then. Until you give me a reason not to."

CHAPTER 8

Maribel shrank away from the sides of a dark cave. Solid rock rose up all around her, cold and damp. Moisture hung in the air, coating her skin in a layer of slime and infusing her body with a bone-numbing chill. She rubbed her arms, but no amount of friction could chase away the icy touch, the eerie grip of air that had never seen the sun. There was water nearby, a lake, or perhaps a stream. The bubbling sounds called out to her, beckoned her like a familiar voice.

Stones scattered as Maribel stumbled, her hand scrabbling along the slick stone as she carefully moved through the darkness. Her heart pounded out a staccato beat, the hairs on the back of her neck standing up.

There was danger here.

The darkness thinned, chased back by a glow from somewhere ahead of her. Maribel moved faster, careful not to trip over anything even as something inside her screamed at her to get closer to the light, to hurry. She tumbled into a new cavern.

Light radiated from the bottom of a lake, the rays blunted by the watery depths. The water was a crystalline blue, shining as though sunlight streamed down on it, though there was no discernible source of light inside the cave. Something thick and silvery, coated with scales, slid under the water. Ripples flowed to the edge, making the water lap gently at the smooth rock. Despite the strangeness of the scene, there was something mesmerizing about that lake. Maribel wandered closer, floating as if in a dream.

Water gushed upwards as something reared from the depths of the lake. Maribel's heart stuttered and her breath became a solid weight in her lungs. Whatever was thrashing up out of the lake, it was enormous. Shining scales reflected the light and a large snout opened to reveal rows of needle-sharp teeth. Reptilian eyes glittered at Maribel as the sinewy draconic body twisted in the air and dove at her. She screamed. Something jerked the monster back. It bellowed in rage as some invisible force dragged it back under the water.

Maribel's heart beat with bruising force against her chest. It hurt to breathe. She held her hands to her skin as if she could physically hold her heart inside her body. The surface of the water foamed where the beast had crashed back down into the depths, and she could still make out the heavy body roiling under the surface. Angry.

"It can't escape."

The voice ripped Maribel's attention from the water and brought a scream rising into her throat. She whirled around, falling over as her feet slid on the slippery rock. She landed hard, crying out in pain as her entire body jarred with the force of hitting solid rock. Chains rattled against stone and something about that sound sent the terror inside of her spiraling out of control. She let out a broken sob and scrambled away from the lake and the wall where the voice had come from.

The sound of the chains abruptly stopped.

"I'm sorry," the voice said softly. "I didn't mean to frighten you. I only wanted you to know the beast will not harm you. Cannot harm you."

Maribel's bottom lip trembled as she fought the burn of tears. She sniffed, hating how the sound gave her away, broadcast her fear so clearly for the stranger. He remained silent for awhile, letting her compose herself. After a long minute, her eyes finally adjusted to the dimmer light away from the lake.

A man was chained to the wall. Lean muscles cast sharp shadows on his arms, chest, and legs. His skin, what she could see of it, was pale. Not the ghostly pallor of illness, but an ethereal shade that reminded Maribel of fey creatures she'd only seen in books of fairy tales. Golden blond hair was cut short, close to his head on the sides, but sticking up at the top, mussed in a way that suggested he often ran his hands through it. Maribel sucked in a breath as wicked thoughts leapt into her mind, an image of what it might be like to run her own hands through that hair. He was beautiful, like carved marble brought to life by the gods. She wished he would look at her so she could see if his eyes were as perfect as the rest of him.

"Who are you?" she whispered.

"A prisoner," the man replied.

Maribel tore her attention from his physique, noticing the chains holding his wrists and ankles. The metal appeared black in the dim light, an abomination against all that perfect, pale skin. "Whose prisoner?"

His shoulders tensed and his head twitched as if he'd started to face her, but then he kept his face locked firmly on the cave floor. "You wouldn't believe me if I told you."

Maribel crossed her arms over her chest as the air around her grew even colder. Goosebumps spread over her arms like darkness swallowing the evening sky. A trembling rattled her entire body as she huddled on the floor. "Why wouldn't I believe you?"

"It's someone you trust. Only when that trust is broken will we be free."

"Who? Whose trust?" Maribel demanded, a sour feeling curling up in the pit of her stomach. "Who's we?"

MARIBEL'S EYES flew open and immediately shut again. The

morning sunlight streaming through her window seemed deter-mine to drill into her eyes until she couldn't see, stabbing at her from the sky like a vengeful spirit. She growled and rolled over. Too awake now to go back to sleep, she sat up and slid her legs over the side of the bed.

The images from the nightmare taunted her, filling her mind with questions she had no answers to. She'd had the same night-mare for the last three nights, and she was no closer to under-standing it now than she'd been before.

An uneasy feeling crawled up her spine as she considered the fact that the nightmares had started the night after she'd told Daman she trusted him.

"You look upset. Is everything all right?"

Maribel squeaked and grabbed the sheet from the bed. She nearly wrenched her arm out of the socket yanking it closer to cover herself and her flimsy nightclothes as she frantically searched the room for the source of the voice. It was feminine, so not Daman. But who else was here?

"I'm sorry, I didn't mean to startle you."

The voice was coming…from the wardrobe?

"Who's there?" Maribel asked, trying to keep her voice calm.

"It's only me."

Said the furniture. Maribel inched closer to the wardrobe. With every step, she firmly cemented to herself that there was no such thing as talking carpentry. "Who? Who's in there?"

"Well… No one's *in here.* It's just me."

Gathering her courage, Maribel grabbed the handle of the wardrobe and flung it open.

Empty. Nothing but clothing greeted Maribel's gaze, and there weren't so many gowns that it wouldn't have been obvious if someone were hiding in there.

"That was a bit rude," the wardrobe chastised her gently. "After all, I don't go around flinging your arms to the sides, now do I?"

Maribel leapt back. "You... I... You..." She closed her mouth and blinked. "No, this isn't right."

"Well, I can't really argue with you there," the wardrobe admitted. "Perhaps there's a lesson in there for magic users."

I'm still dreaming. Dear gods, please, tell me I'm still dreaming. Maribel closed her eyes and rubbed her temples in slow, soothing circles. "I'm talking to furniture," she mumbled. "I've been alone too long."

"Well, you're not *alone*, are you?"

There was a certain sly tone in the wardrobe's voice that raised Maribel's eyebrows. "And exactly what are you insinuating?"

"I'm not really insinuating anything. I'm only saying that you and the master have gotten very close."

"And how would you know that?" Maribel tightened the sheet around her. "I most certainly have not entertained him in my bedroom."

"The brownies are a gossipy bunch. Apparently the teapot was full of stories."

"The teapot," Maribel said flatly.

The wardrobe hummed confirmation. "The way to a man's heart is through his stomach," she agreed. "And apparently you are quite the cook."

Maribel averted her eyes then jerked her gaze back with a scowl. *I will not be embarrassed by furniture.* She eyed the wardrobe, its pristine white paint and expertly crafted doors far too normal for the situation. If she had any respect for her sanity, she would leave now. Get dressed, and be off on her merry way—perhaps to the kitchen or the garden.

On the other hand, it couldn't hurt to linger a moment in this nice room Daman had been kind enough to provide her. And it wasn't as if she didn't know for a fact that magic existed. Was it truly so much of a stretch that this wardrobe had been gifted with the ability to speak? Besides, perhaps it would be nice to have someone to confide in. Someone she could be sure wouldn't go gallivanting about the town spouting her private business. Maribel cleared her throat, trying not to think about the fact that she was taking on an inanimate object as a confidant.

"I'm only here for my father." She crossed her arms and stuck her chin out. "It was my fault he was here, my fault he made Daman so angry. It would have been wrong for him to be the one to stay here. Of course I would go home if I could, that's where I belong, after all." She looked around the room, taking in the rich furnishings and comforts that had been provided for her. Her shoulders sagged. "Not that he's been a bad host, necessarily. The past few days have been…nice."

The wardrobe didn't move, but nevertheless gave the impression of listening closely.

"I…" Maribel paused, snagging her lower lip between her teeth as she stared into space, her mind flowing over the past week or so. "He's in such a foul mood most of the time, but it almost seems…involuntary. It's like he wants to be nice, but he's…" Her shoulders slumped. "I can't think of any other way to say it. He's just in a bad mood, all the time."

"*All* the time?"

"Well, not *all* the time." Maribel smiled. "He's actually quite pleasant when he sits out in the garden with me." She glanced at the wardrobe. "I suppose you wouldn't know, but Daman gave me a very large plot of land. He said I can plant whatever I wish. He even asked the brownies to bring me some seedlings."

"How lovely."

A pleasant warmth blossomed in Maribel's heart the more she thought about it. "In the garden with me, he's happy. Sometimes he helps me with the planting, but other times he seems content to lie there in the sun and talk with me."

"Well, he is a reptile," the wardrobe noted. "Sunning is what reptiles do. My memories of being a tree are old, to be sure, but I remember all manner of snakes and lizards creeping out of the brush to sun themselves on rocks on days the weather was warm like this."

And just like that, the fuzzy feeling was gone. Maribel retreated to the bed and slumped down on the decadently deep mattress. *He is a reptile, isn't he?* She clasped her hands firmly in her lap and studied the dirt permanently embedded beneath her fingernails. *Does it matter?*

"I had heard that in order to break the curse upon him, he must learn to love and trust another, and earn their love and trust in return."

What if Mother Briar was right? What if Daman's curse could be broken if Maribel would... Would what? Let these warm feelings bloom into something more? Into what? And what if Mother Briar was wrong? What if Daman would stay as he was forever no matter what feelings she held for him?

Does that matter?

Maribel bit her lip again, thinking of Daman. Silver eyes that glittered with every emotion, pale bluish skin that gave him the appearance of carved marble during those times he held so inhumanly still. Strong muscles that were as intriguing as they were frightening...

"You look asss though you're thinking very hard about sssomething."

Maribel shrieked and clutched the sheet to her again. The little silver snake she'd spoken to the other day was peering out at her from under her covers, its beady black eyes blinking sleepily.

"How long have you been in there?" she demanded.

The snake snuggled farther into the blankets. "It'sss very warm in here. Very niccce. And you ssslept in late."

"How. Long?"

"You ssseem to be getting along well with Daman. Are you content here?"

Maribel opened her mouth, then closed it. "I— What do you care?"

The serpent curled into a tighter coil, tucking its head into the center as though it intended to have a nice nap. "Jussst trying to keep up. Want to make sssure you're both getting along. The *naga* lord hasss a temper, he isss not easssy to be around. Wouldn't want you to get upsssset and leave prematurely."

"Prematurely?" Maribel leaned forward, struggling to read any emotion in the serpentine intruder's face. Excitement crackled along her nerves, urging her heart to beat faster in burgeoning expectation. "You make it sound as though I should be waiting for something. As if something is going to happen?"

The serpent's eyelids drooped, its tongue flicking out. "Yesss."

Maribel waited, but the creature didn't offer anything more.

"Well?" she prodded, annoyance sharpening her tone.

The serpent opened one eye all the way, the other remaining closed. "Well what?"

"What is it I'm supposed to be waiting for? What's supposed to happen?"

"I'm sssure I don't know. It doesssn't matter asss long asss it happensss."

"That doesn't make any sense!"

"Well," the wardrobe broke in, "what do you expect to get from a conversation with a *cuelebre*? They aren't the most helpful creatures."

The *cuelebre* raised its head and eyed the wardrobe. "You ssshouldn't be talking. You're wood. Dead wood," he added.

"I've as much right to talk as you do." The wardrobe sniffed, a neat trick since it had no nose. "I'm sure I'm more helpful than you."

"Do you know what's supposed to happen?" Maribel turned a hopeful face to the wardrobe, wishing it had eyes so she knew where to look.

The wardrobe hesitated. "No. The master wants the witch to change him back, but I don't know what that has to do with you. Or why you're here."

"You know who cursed him?" Maribel held her breath, her heart pounding as she fought the urge to shake the wardrobe.

"Of course, everyone knows that."

"Who?" Maribel's voice came out a whisper, the sheer magnitude of what she was about to learn threatening to steal her voice. If she could find out who had cursed Daman, perhaps she could find a way to make them undo it. And then…

"That isss not for you to tell her," the *cuelebre* hissed. "Let her asssk Daman."

The wardrobe creaked as though shifting to face the snake. "What difference does it make who tells her?"

"It makesss a differenccce."

The wardrobe fluttered its doors. "Very well."

"No!" Maribel glared at the *cuelebre* as if she could set the pest on fire with the strength of her fury. "Tell me now."

"I won't tell you, and neither will the wood," the *cuelebre* said calmly.

Maribel whirled back to the wardrobe. "Tell me. Please," she begged.

"It won't tell you. It'sss too afraid I'll burn it to assshesss if it doesss."

"Well, actually, I hadn't even considered that you'd do such a barbaric thing," the wardrobe grumbled. It creaked again as though sagging in resignation. "But as that is the case… I'm sorry, Maribel, I can't tell you. But I'm sure the master would share the information if you asked him."

"You wouldn't believe me if I told you."

The words floated back to her from the dream, the man's voice sliding over her skin like a phantom caress. Maribel shivered.

"It's someone you trust. Only when that trust is broken will we be free."

"Do you know *why* the witch cursed him?" she asked, leaning closer.

The snake tilted its head. "Yesss. But ssso do you. He told you, didn't he?"

Maribel bit her lip. "And what he told me was the truth? The witch wanted to marry him and he rejected her?"

"You doubt hisss ssstory?"

"I only want the truth," Maribel moaned, rubbing a hand over her face. "Someone isn't being completely honest with me. Mother Briar told me that Daman was cursed by a witch that he scorned. The witch wanted to teach him a lesson about kindness and helping others. Mother Briar believed the fact that Daman fed and sheltered my father was some sign that Daman was changing, learning from his mistakes. She said to break the curse, Daman would have to prove he'd changed by falling in love and earning the love of someone else in return, that love was the most selfless act possible and only that would break the spell."

"Interesssting."

"But Daman contradicts that story." Maribel shoved herself off the bed and paced back and forth between the bed and the wardrobe. "He says it was the witch who was selfish, that the witch wanted his money and land and tried to seduce him to get it. He says she cursed him for rejecting her, and the only way to break the curse is for the witch to lift it herself."

"Two different ssstories."

"Exactly." Maribel paused, drumming the fingers of one hand against the opposite arm. Words continued to bubble up inside her, flowing from her mouth in an unstoppable stream. It seemed like ages since she'd had someone to talk to, someone that didn't...that wasn't...Daman.

"I don't like Mother Briar. She's arrogant and condescending. However, I can't deny that she's been a savior to my family. She fed us when we were starving, and she always takes time out of her day to help Corrine with her magic and me with studying all sorts of plants and herbs."

"Why don't you ssstudy magic?"

Maribel shook her head. "I don't have the gift for it like Corrine does. The only time I seem to be able to do anything extraordinary is if I'm working with plants and the land. Mother Briar says I speak to the earth and it listens to me." She shrugged. She'd long ago given up childish dreams of doing grand magic.

"Do you trussst thisss witch?"

"I have no reason not to. Besides, Corrine spoke about the rumors before Mother Briar did, so I don't think Mother Briar just made it all up."

"And your sssisssster?"

The snake's tone didn't change, but there was an inherent accusation in the words nonetheless. Maribel eyed the *cuelebre*. "Why would she make something like that up?"

"That'sss for you to tell me."

"She wouldn't." Maribel paused. "Well, I suppose she really didn't want me to leave," she admitted hesitantly. "I guess it's possible that she was trying to scare me away from coming. But that wouldn't explain why Mother Briar would agree with her. Even if she was only agreeing to help Corrine keep me home, she ruined all that when she encouraged me to go. She's the one who thought I could break Daman's curse."

"By falling in love with him?"

Maribel's traitorous mind flew back to the feeling of being in Daman's arms. In moments like those, he wasn't strange or monstrous. He was a man. A strong, handsome man who loved her cooking and enjoyed sitting outside with her in the garden. She cleared her throat. "I suppose that's what she meant."

"Ssso if you don't think your sssisssster isss lying, then do you think that Daman isss the liar?"

Was it her imagination, or did the *cuelebre* give the wardrobe a pointed look as it asked that last question? "I don't know." Maribel paused as she realized she was twisting the sheet in her hands, the nervous gesture betraying her inner conflict to the room. She marched behind the dressing screen, snagging a discarded gown on the way.

"I've enjoyed my time here with Daman," she admitted, finding it somewhat easier to voice her feelings now that she was behind the screen and protected from the snake's unnerving stare. "But I haven't known him long. How can I trust him more than my own sister?"

"Good quessstion."

"It's someone you trust. Only when that trust is broken will we be free."

Did she trust Daman? If the dream referred to Daman, then what did that mean?

"Do you trusssst your sssissster?"

The sibilant voice came from much closer than it had the last time. Startled, Maribel glared up at the snake. He'd left the bed and was hanging from the dressing screen, translucent wings she hadn't noticed before open to give him balance.

"Of course I trust her. But even if I didn't, she couldn't be the witch who cursed Daman, if that's what you're thinking. She would have had no reason to seek him out while we still had money, and she hasn't left the farm on her own since we've been there." Maribel paused. "I suppose…Mother Briar could be the one. But that doesn't make sense. I doubt she would come to Daman insisting he marry her so she could have all of his land and money. And if the other story is true and she cursed him for a lack of hospitality, then why wouldn't she have said that instead of saying she'd heard the same rumors?"

She looked up at the snake, but it'd vanished. She searched around her, even peering out from behind the screen to scan the room, but it was gone.

"That's getting beyond annoying," Maribel muttered. She swept out from behind the dressing screen, pausing awkwardly in front of the wardrobe.

"Well, I'm going to get going then," she told the furniture. She

waited, feeling as though it would be rude to leave without...
saying goodbye?

The wardrobe fluttered open a door in a wooden wave. "Have
a nice day, Maribel."

Maribel nodded, trying not to feel silly, then left the room.
Her head spun with unanswered questions as she strode through
the hallway and marched down the large staircase. Between the
dreams and the *cuelebre's* frustrating stream of half-information
and loaded questions, she was left with the distinct feeling that
she was being manipulated, but no idea as to why. She gritted her
teeth, grinding them until her jaw ached. *I hate being manipulated.*

She stormed out the kitchen doors, heading for the gardens
like a black cloud. Apparently, Daman was her only chance for
answers, and by the gods, she intended to get them.

A sudden cloud of dirt rising into the air caught her attention.
A flash of scales glittered in the sunlight, followed by a dull thud
and a litany of cursing that raised her eyebrows. Maribel crept
closer to the source of the sounds. Something thrashed around
on the ground and she had to clap a hand over her mouth to
avoid a squeak of surprise.

Daman was lying in the dirt, staring intently at a hole in the
ground. Something moved in the darkness and a creature she
couldn't identify leapt out and skittered across the garden.
Daman snarled and tried to snatch the creature off the ground.
His movements were too fast for Maribel to follow, but still the
creature escaped him and disappeared down another hole.

"Daman?"

"What?" Daman snapped. He looked up then twitched backward as if his brain had only just registered her presence. "I'm
sorry, I didn't mean to bark at you. You surprised me, that's all."

A few days ago the very idea of apologizing for being short
with her would have been ridiculous to Daman—knowledge she
based on having suggested he apologize on more than one occa-
sion. The fact that he'd offered it with no prompting on her part

sucked a considerable amount of wind from her blustering sails of a moment ago.

He rose out of the dirt and approached her, the long sleek muscles of his lower body sliding easily through the loose earth. "Good morning."

"Good morning." Maribel gave up on the shouting she'd been prepared to do—temporarily—and gestured at the holes. "What's going on here?"

Daman scowled. "Sprites. They're popping out of the ground everywhere."

Maribel's eyebrows rose. "Sprites."

"Yes. Annoying little pests." He glared at the ground. "I haven't seen one since I had to send my gardener away and tend the land myself. I thought I'd scared them off."

Tiny glittering eyes peered at Maribel from the darkness of one of the holes and she could have sworn she heard something giggle. "But they're not scared of you anymore?"

"Apparently not," Daman said darkly. His gaze flicked over the ground as if he could see the sprites moving even through the earth. "But I shall rectify that situation forthwith."

It took a bit of effort to keep the amusement from her face. The thought of Daman and all his gruffness throwing his weight around the garden chasing after the miniscule sprites did more than a little to leach some of the intimidation from Daman's presence. Of course, Maribel reflected, it really wasn't much different than a snake going after small rodents. A large predator waiting with deadly stillness, glossy black eyes unblinking as it waited for its prey. The small furry creatures venturing out into the light, never knowing that their death waited with the patience only a predator could manage...

Unease rolled through her stomach at the imagery her imagination was happily supplying her. Maribel blinked the pictures from her head. She cleared her throat and faced Daman with a weak smile. "Perhaps you're considering the situation in the wrong light," she offered. "Perhaps the return of the sprites is a good sign?"

"You have obviously never met a sprite. They are a plague, creatures who have nothing better to do than teach gofers how to steal food." He glared at the ground again. "How could they possibly be a good sign?"

The end of his tail slid slowly side to side and then his entire body froze, taking on that unnatural stillness that used to unnerve her so terribly. Maribel bit the inside of her cheek, sternly warning her thoughts to stay away from the darker side of nature's predators and concentrate on the man in front of her.

"Didn't you tell me once that your temper made you drive people away?"

Daman's silver eyes flicked to her, though the rest of his body didn't move. "Yes."

"Well, it sounds as though it was that same temper that frightened the sprites away. Perhaps the fact that they have returned is a sign that your temper is not as terrible as it once was."

Daman tapped the end of his tail against the soil. The motion drew the attention of another sprite, and the skinny creature snickered and flew at the scaled limb glittering like precious gems in the sunlight. At the last second, the tip of Daman's tail slashed through the air, smacking hard into the little fey and sending it sailing through the air like a falling star. A satisfied smirk twitched on Daman's lips. Maribel chuckled in amusement, but the sound quickly died when she found herself once again the sole target of Daman's intense gaze.

"You once told me I make you nervous. Tell me, do you find that—like the sprites—you are less...nervous, in my presence now?"

Maribel's mouth went dry, the rumbling bass of Daman's voice drawing her attention to his bare chest. It wasn't until that moment that she noticed he'd removed his shirt—the clothing that he'd started wearing for her benefit—apparently to keep it from getting destroyed as he shot around on the ground after the invading sprites.

Now there was nothing to block Maribel's searching gaze, nothing to hide the strange combination of unblemished human skin and glittering blue and green scales that traced the ridges decorating Daman's face and chest before disappearing in the cascade of scales that composed his draconic lower half.

She followed the lines of sinewy muscle over his pectorals, up around his biceps and the sharp lines of his throat. The scales should have given him a monstrous appearance, but at some point in the last week or so, they'd become less foreign. Now they were familiar, a defining feature that only served to decorate the already handsome veneer of the isolated lord. She'd seen them shining in the sunlight during the long days he sat with her in the garden, seen candlelight play over them as they ate dinner together and she happily answered all of the *naga's* questions about what ingredients she'd used, or what she was going to serve next.

The blue and green scales were warm, despite their icy appearance, slick under the pads of her fingers. She trailed a finger over one of the large ridges that traced Daman's collar bone, turning sharply at the line it met and following it up his neck.

I'm touching him.

Every muscle in Maribel's body seized at once, shocked and outraged at her own behavior. Tendons whiplashed, recoiling her hand with a speed surpassed only by creatures beyond the veil. She didn't remember moving, didn't remember reaching out to touch him. Dear gods, what had she been thinking?

His hand closed around her wrist, keeping her from retreating. She swallowed a squeak, her heart leaping into her throat.

"Maribel."

His voice was a low exhale that caressed every inch of her skin, even through her clothes. A thousand words rushed up only to halt without leaving her lips, choking her with too many things she couldn't say. She couldn't think with his hand on her skin like that, could hardly hear anything past the thundering of her heart. Sparks crackled in the air between them like pine logs baking in an open fire. *Dear gods, he's going to kiss me.*

Damn his eyes, his expression was unreadable, those silver orbs as good as mirrors, reflecting her own turmoil back at her without revealing anything about what he was thinking.

"Are you happy here?"

For a second, she would have sworn she'd heard some hesitancy in his voice, a slight stutter as if he'd been about to say something else and changed his mind in the last instant.

Would you let me go home if I wasn't? That was the question she should ask, the question that needed to be asked. After all, shouldn't that be her goal? Hadn't she told the *cuelebre* and the... wardrobe, that she was only here to save her father, that if it were up to her she'd go home? Wasn't that the truth?

The question refused to come out. Maribel's heart pounded and for a moment she felt she was being split in two. If she had the choice, she would have to go home, wouldn't she? It was the responsible thing to do, the right thing to do. Hiding here and basking in Daman's appreciation of her cooking, his attentiveness, his willingness to spend all day outside with her, digging his own hands into the dirt right alongside hers... It would be selfish to stay.

And the moodiness. His appreciation of her cooking and love of basking in the sun aside, more often than not he was short with her, curt, abrupt, *rude*. What sort of woman willingly stayed with a man like that?

Don't give me the choice.

"I've been having nightmares." She shoved the words out, her hesitation to share the dreams with him overridden by her desire to stop him from offering her the choice she didn't want to make.

The heat that had been burning steadily behind his eyes flickered, dimming like a lamp's flame behind a sooty shade. "Nightmares?"

Maribel nodded, the movement too fast, too jerky. She took a slow breath through her nose. "Yes. For a couple of nights now."

Daman studied her, his fingers still carefully wrapped around her wrist, claws held out so he didn't accidentally draw blood. The heat remained in his eyes, a faint glowing silver. "I'm sorry you are ill at ease. What is the nature of your nightmares?"

"I think… I think it's you."

The grip around her wrist tightened suddenly, a flash of pain shooting through her as a fraction of his strength squeezed her so hard she gasped. Daman released her immediately, the muscles of his lower body contracting and releasing as he backed away from her.

"Me."

It wasn't a question.

Unease rolled through Maribel's stomach and the hairs on the back of her neck rose in mimicry of her dream. She wanted to take her words back, stop this conversation from happening. It was only a dream, a nightmare. But as she stood there facing Daman now, she suspected he would not brush them off so easily.

"Perhaps nightmare was the wrong word," she said, hating how pathetic her voice sounded. "It's not a nightmare, not really, just a strange dream—a silly dream, there's really not even a reason to talk about it."

"Tell me."

His tone left no room for denial. She wouldn't get away from this conversation. She took a fortifying breath and told him about the dream, describing both the man and the dragon, including the chains and the man's cryptic words. Daman visibly withdrew farther and farther with every word out of her mouth, and she felt the distance like a physical pain, as though there were some bond between them being stretched, thinned to the point of snapping.

By the time she finished, Daman wasn't moving. More than that, his body had taken on that eerie reptilian stillness that no human could manage, a state so profoundly still that it was hard to believe he was still alive. Maribel's chest tightened and she realized she was wringing her hands in front of her. She forced herself to grab a handful of her skirt to stop the nervous motions.

"Daman, it's only a dream," she said finally, unable to bear the silence any longer. "I don't know what it means—"

Daman burst into a flurry of movement. A scream leapt from her lips, cutting off anything else she might have said. His tail lashed at the ground and he shot away from her like a bolt of lightning, his retreat so fast that by the time Maribel registered the movement, he was already gone. The air around her throbbed with lingering tension, her skin buzzing with emotion so strong her knees quivered and she nearly collapsed to the ground.

He was going to kiss me.

He was going to offer to let me leave.

Would I have let him kiss me? Do I want him to kiss me?

Would I have left? Do I want to leave?

Thought after thought swooped down on her, attacking her like screeching birds of prey, there and gone too fast for her to catch. She blinked at the spot where Daman had been, the spot he'd vanished from without a single word of explanation.

Anger cut through her confusion like a battleaxe, heating her blood with the desire to confront Daman, to challenge his retreat, demand answers. What did he think her dream meant? What had upset him so much that he'd fled, run away from…from whatever had been happening between them?

Maribel gritted her teeth. Her emotions were still chaotic, still a tangled web she couldn't quite see her way out of, but, by the gods, she would not cower away from them. She wasn't going to get any answers standing here alone. Daman was the one muddling her thoughts this way. It was his fault no one else would talk to her, give her any answers. She needed him to talk to her if she wanted to figure this mess out.

She glared in the direction he'd vanished.

You're not going to get away that easily.

CHAPTER 9

Daman dove into the lake, cutting through the water like a blade through the heart of an imaginary enemy. He could still feel Maribel's delicate wrist in his grip, the frantic beat of her pulse beneath the pads of his fingers. He pushed his hands, open-palmed—through the water, trying to rid them of the memory of Maribel's warmth. To think he'd been so close to...

"Are you happy here?"

His own words mocked him, ringing in his ears no matter how deep he dove into the lake, no matter how hard he tried to lose himself in the frigid water, the caress of the currents. What had he been thinking? What sort of question was that? What had he expected her to say?

So what if she was happy? What would that mean? Did he think it would be some sort of sign that he wasn't too scary to continue his duties, to start seeking out changelings in need again? Or was he truly so foolish, so deluded, so reckless...as to think it would mean more? What had he been thinking grabbing her, letting himself be overcome by the taste of her excitement in the air?

Where could it have gone?

He fought through the water, swimming deeper and deeper into the blackness at the bottom of the lake. The icy chill hardly touched him through his scales, but his upper body felt the bite. The sensation was a welcome distraction—a *needed* distraction.

I am a damn fool.

Spending the past few weeks with Maribel, playing in the dirt, basking in her laughter. He hadn't even tried to maintain the pretense with himself that he was trying to find her a new home, get her away from her witch of a sister. Every day it was easier to pretend she would stay here forever with him. That they would sit down together every night to eat a meal she'd prepared from herbs and vegetables she'd gathered right here on his land, with meat he brought her, he killed for her. It had been a pleasing and dangerous dream.

She dreamed of me as a human. Dreamed of the dragon as something separate, something terrifying—a nightmare.

What a fool he'd been to think she could be attracted to him in his current form. What woman would willingly come into the arms of a man more reptile than human?

Screams echoed in his memories, the screams of changelings he'd tried to help after the witch's curse—changelings he'd very nearly frightened to death. What had led him to believe Maribel would be any different?

Anger scalded his veins. Anger at himself for daring to dream of a life he had no business dreaming of. Anger at Maribel for putting that dream into his head. He'd been resigned to his fate until she'd come along.

His temper spiked again and not even the chill of the lake bottom could ease the burn. He cursed and shot up to the surface, breaking into the air in a surge of falling water. The sunlight seared his eyes and he blinked away the pain.

"Are you going to talk to me like a logical human being, or are you going to run away again like a sulking child?"

Daman spun in the water, sending a wave cascading

outward to the edge of the lake. Maribel stood there with her hands on her hips, glaring at him. Her blue eyes crackled with magic that he was more and more certain she had no idea she possessed and for a moment, he thought she might actually leap into the lake after him. A pleasant warmth curled up in his belly.

No!

"Go away." He sent another arc of icy water in her direction, spattering the edges of her skirt. "You shouldn't be here."

"I'm here because you're forcing me to be here," Maribel shot back, her chin jutting out in defiance. "*You're* the one who sent for me, *you're* the one who forced me to stay. And if you think I'm going to be ignored—"

"Go home, then. I release you."

He snapped his teeth shut, but it was too late. The words were out, the offer hanging between them, her freedom hers for the taking. A sharp pain in his chest caught him off guard, but he fiercely ignored it. He glared at the woman who'd given him false hope, part of him hoping she'd take his offer and leave, even as he realized how much he wanted her to stay.

Maribel looked as though he'd slapped her. Contrary to what he'd expected, there was no relief in her eyes, no joy. Her face fell as she dropped her arms to her sides.

"You're throwing me out?"

"Throwing you out? I'm setting you free." He crossed his arms, his tail swirling in furious circles to keep him afloat. "You're no longer my prisoner. Go home to your family."

"So you want me to leave."

Daman slammed a fist into the surface of the water, spattering more of his sensitive flesh with the frigid lake. "Why do you say it like that? As though I've hurt you in some way?" He shoved a hand through his hair, tugging on it in frustration. "You didn't want to come here, didn't want to stay here. Even in your sleep you know that this is not what you want."

Maribel straightened at his last sentence and Daman swore under his breath.

"What isn't what I want?" Her voice was barely loud enough to reach him.

"So like a female," Daman ground out, the sharp claws on his fingertips drawing warm beads of blood from his palms under the water. "Searching for praise, needing to be told how wonderful she is. Wanting to hear a man beg her to stay."

"You want me to stay?"

"I will not play these games with you. Leave!"

"I'm not leaving until you hear me out!"

Maribel set her shoulders, planting her feet more firmly on the ground. Daman clenched his hands into fists.

"What is there to hear? Your nightmares couldn't be any clearer. You dream of the man without the beast. Well, I'm sorry I cannot accommodate you. I am trapped this way. But even if I weren't, I would never be fully one or the other. The monster is as much a part of who I am as the man, and if that concept bothers you so, then leave."

"The only person here who has a problem with your form is you." Maribel suddenly dropped to the ground long enough to grab a pebble. She threw it at him, managing to bounce it off his shoulder before he could recover from his shock enough to move. "I don't care how much of you is snake and how much is man," she snarled.

The flicker of hope that flared to life at her words upset him more than anything else so far. Daman shot through the water, lashing against the bank until he stood only inches from Maribel. Her body tensed, but to her credit she refused to back down. The hope inside him flared brighter and he viciously threw it off. He grabbed her arm, digging his fingers into her flesh as he pulled her closer. She lost her balance and fell against his chest, her body falling flush with his.

He looked deep into her eyes as the scales of his lower body pressed against her, searching for the telltale fear or disgust he was sure he'd find. A muscle ticked in Maribel's jaw, but she didn't break eye contact. Water from his body soaked into her skirts.

"It would appear you have nerves of steel. But your mask won't do you any good against someone who can taste your fear."

Hating himself even as he did it, Daman opened his mouth enough to slide his tongue out, tasting the air. His forked tongue had scared her once, he was counting on the same reaction now. He was *praying* for that reaction now.

He didn't get it.

The air between them heated and a slight hint of musk coated his tongue. Daman closed his mouth abruptly. Pink tinged Maribel's cheeks, but her blue eyes were fierce, unwavering as they bored into his. Holding his gaze, she leaned more heavily against him.

Without giving him time to react, she wrapped her arms around his neck and pulled him down, standing on her tiptoes at the same time. Shock reverberated through Daman's system as she pressed her mouth to his.

It had been a long time since Daman had kissed someone. And he'd never kissed anyone while in this form. Bestial forms were for fighting, not...anything else. It was a disorienting feeling, like sitting in a bathtub fully dressed.

But not unpleasant.

Raspberries. She tasted of raspberries and...strawberries. Fruit that had ripened on the vine, warmed by the sun until they nearly burst. Sweet, and so very satisfying.

Maribel took advantage of his surprise and snaked her tongue into his mouth. Panic flared inside of him at the thought of her cutting her tongue on his fangs, chasing back the fuzzy cloud of desire that had eaten his good sense. He could imagine their mouths filling with blood, the horror that would cover her face, extinguishing whatever heat she was feeling now.

Scrambling to back away, Daman grunted as Maribel refused to loosen her hold. As he tried to retreat, she leaned closer, clinging to him like a stubborn coil of ivy. His balance wavered and they both fell backwards. Daman twisted his body, muscles straining as he fought to lower them gently to the ground. It was an acrobatic feat no human form could have managed, but was possible with the sinewy flexibility of his half-dragon form. Maribel didn't appear to mind the commotion in the least. Her legs slid to either side of his serpentine lower body and she pulled back to lick gently at his bottom lip.

Dear gods...

Without meaning to, Daman closed his hands around Maribel's hips, barely managing to keep his claws from pressing into her skin. He held his breath, giving in to the urge to kiss her back, if only a little. He chased that sweet flavor, rumbling deep in his chest at the wonder of it.

Maribel moaned in approval as he returned her kiss and he was careful to keep it shallow enough that his fangs didn't threaten her. He slid his lips against hers, their breaths mingling as they tasted each other. Slowly, Maribel teased the crease of his lips with her tongue, probing for entrance. He sucked in a shuddering breath, but pushed gently against her hips.

"My fangs," he warned, his voice hoarse.

"I'll be careful," Maribel promised softly.

There was a lazy weight to her voice that was nearly Daman's undoing. He groaned in surrender, parting his lips to let Maribel explore as she would. She traced her tongue lightly over his, carefully avoiding his teeth. He returned her passion with his own, chasing her tongue back into her mouth and exploring the silky depths. A new heat seeped through him, clouding his thoughts until he could think of nothing but the feel of her body in his arms, the press of her mouth against his.

The kiss lasted for an eternity that ended all too soon when

Maribel pulled back slightly, her labored breaths a match for his own.

"Now that we've established that you were wrong about your interpretation of my dream," she said, her voice breathy and uneven, "perhaps we could put our heads together and figure out what it really means?"

The mention of her dream popped the fantasy bubble that had been glittering around them, plunging Daman back into harsh reality. Fury singed his veins, a voice in his head mocking him with a phantasmal rolling laugh for so quickly falling under Maribel's charms. Whatever her kiss had tried to make him believe, the woman still dreamed of a human man. She held on to him only because she thought he would be human someday, that she could salvage a rich husband without having to live with a monster.

"I know you need someone to fall in love with you to break your curse."

He started to push Maribel away and lever himself up off the ground, only barely resisting the urge to throw her off of him with all the fury surging through his veins. *Is there no end to my gullibility?* The voice screamed in his head, so loud it hurt.

Maribel's legs slid around him as he rose, locking in place behind him. Startled, Daman gaped, too slow to stop her from locking her arms in a similar fashion around his neck.

"What are you doing?"

"You're not running away from me again." Maribel tightened her grip. "I'm telling you, I think the dreams mean something. And I want to know what it is."

Daman tried to extricate himself, holding his temper like a fiery shield around him, refusing to think about how her body felt against his, or the defiant tone ringing in her voice. Maribel responded by tightening her hold. There was no way to get her off of him without hurting her.

"I already told you what they mean." He looked down where

her body was wrapped around his, trying to ascertain the best way to pry her off of him. "There's no point in talking about it."

Maribel twisted against him as he rose and he bit back a groan as her body pressed harder against his. He was suddenly painfully aware of the fact that he was once again naked—not having planned on having a visitor during his swim. If Maribel didn't let go and let him get some space between their bodies, she was going to get a lot more than she'd bargained for. That thought inspired an interesting image and he half-choked as he shoved it away.

"They don't have to mean anything," he added, hating the tinge of desperation creeping into his voice.

"My sister is a witch, and I have some abilities too." Maribel tightened her grip stubbornly. "The dreams might mean something."

"Your kind are not known for prophecy." Daman groped behind himself, trying to get a grip on Maribel's legs so he could peel her off of him.

"Witches are human." Maribel pressed closer against him, fighting his attempts to lever her away. "If my sister is a witch, what makes you so sure I'm not?"

"You're not a witch," he huffed, "you're a—"

Daman cut himself off just in time. Maribel stared at him, the sharp look in her eyes telling him she'd caught what he'd said. He groped for some way to distract her, something that would cover his slip.

"What were you going to—"

"Didn't your parents ever teach you not to wrestle with a naked man?"

Maribel's muscles went slack, allowing Daman to wiggle free. He set her on the ground and hurriedly retreated to a safe distance, far enough away that she couldn't grab him again, but not so far that she accused him of running away. His words had apparently had the desired effect. Maribel stood there brushing at her skirt, her eyes firmly on the ground, on her dress, anywhere but on him.

"I didn't realize," she mumbled. "I wasn't thinking."

Daman cleared his throat, breaking the sudden, awkward silence. "Why don't we go inside and we'll see if I can't manage a meal for you? You've been cooking for me since you got here, allow me to return the favor?"

There may have been a hint of desperation in his tone, but neither of them seemed inclined to comment on it. Maribel busied herself with untying and retying the string of her apron, giving the task significantly more concentration than it merited. Apparent relief dragged her shoulders down when Daman moved ahead of her. She followed quietly behind him.

The silence was not as comforting as he'd expected it to be and Daman found himself wishing he could see her face.

"There really is nothing wrong with you, you know." She kept her voice light, conversational. "Man or beast, it doesn't matter. You shouldn't be so ashamed of your form."

"I am not ashamed of my form," Daman said stiffly, giving her a pointed look over his shoulder.

Maribel shrugged. "You're extremely sensitive about it. As a matter of fact, you seem determined to make it a point of contention between us." She focused fully on him, blue eyes severe. "But I'm not going to accommodate you. I will not pretend I give one whit about your tail."

Difficult woman. Though it is impressive she said tail without blushing. Daman ran a hand over his face. "My form is not the problem. It's…" He paused, trying to think of some way to explain his situation to make her understand. "Have you ever known a werewolf? Not a *loup garou*, but a true *lycanthrope*?"

Maribel's eyes widened. "No."

"Pity," Daman muttered. "Well, *lycanthropes* and *nagas* share a certain similarity in that we are dual creatures. Just as a *lycanthrope* is neither man nor beast, but something in between, so are *nagas* not wholly man but not wholly dragon. We have two forms, and they are separate, but even when we are one, we are no less the other."

"I...see."

Her tone made it perfectly clear that she did not see, did not understand. Frustration plucked at Daman's nerves like an archer's bow, threatening to launch his temper like a poison-tipped arrow straight into the heart of this budding conversation. He filled his lungs with the crisp spring air, furiously working to hold an image of his meditation candle in his mind. When he could see the candle flame without it exploding into a raging bonfire, he tried again.

"My dragon form is for hunting, for battle. When I am a wyvern, I am fighting to protect someone or something that I hold dear. When I am living my everyday life, eating, sleeping, conversing with friends and family, I am in my human form. This is not to say that when I am a wyvern, I am a mindless beast, nor to say that when I am human I have none of the wyvern's senses or instincts. However, staying in wyvern form when there is no threat of danger is like asking a warrior to stand in full battle regalia with his weapon in hand to go and purchase a loaf of bread. There is a certain...mindset that comes with this form, and it is not something so easily thrown off."

"You said you used to have people around you, friends and servants. You said you had to send them away."

A vice tightened around Daman's heart as he thought of those days. Men who'd fought beside him, who'd helped him rescue changelings and smuggle them to their new homes, had been forced to leave. "Many of them wanted to stay. Their faith in me was such that they couldn't imagine me bringing them harm."

Maribel swallowed hard. "Did you?"

Her voice was whisper soft, but the question hit Daman with the force of a much heavier blow. Bad enough to know that deep down she believed him capable of the same level of violence that he himself feared, but her question raised memories he'd been trying to forget.

"I sent them away for good reason."

He held the door to the kitchen open for her and she preceded him inside, seating herself at the table. For a moment, Daman allowed himself to think the subject had been dropped. Unfortunately, the tension in her shoulders told him the unpleasant part of the day was not yet over.

"Why do you want me here?"

Daman closed his hand, the tomato he'd been holding exploding in a mess of pulp and seeds. He flicked the mess away in sharp, angry motions, splattering juice over every nearby surface. "I told you that you're free to go."

A small sound escaped Maribel's throat, an interesting sound somewhere between a growl and a yelp of protest. Daman glanced over his shoulder to see her gripping the edge of the table, her lips pressed together in a firm line. She wouldn't meet his eyes, but there was a tightness in her jaw that spoke of frustration.

That same traitorous hope that had taunted him earlier burned as merrily as a holiday hearth fire. He clutched the rag he'd been using to sop up the tomato juice on his hands so hard that the fabric tore on his claws. "Do you want to stay?" he demanded gruffly.

"I have a sister at home who needs me." Maribel raised her eyes then, blue orbs glittering with silent fury. "A sister who's too sick to care for herself. I left her because I had to—I did it because she needs my father more than she needs me. I wouldn't have left her if I didn't have to."

An answering fury flickered inside Daman at the unspoken accusation. He slid closer, stopping at the edge of the table, gripping the wood to keep himself from coming any closer to her.

"Yes, I understand, I'm a monster for tearing you away from

your meek and innocent sister. I'm offering to let you go back to her—"

"Stop assuming you know what I want!"

Maribel shot up from her seat, her chair flying back to crash against the wall. She stormed around the table, charging him like an angry bull. For a moment, he thought she was going to slap him again, but she stopped short of arm's reach.

"*Maybe* I want to know why I was forced to make that choice to begin with!" She jabbed a finger at him, her hand shaking. "*Maybe* I want to know what's behind your sudden change of heart. Why you're suddenly only too eager to throw me away, to let me go now that you've flipped my world upside-down."

"Maybe you should stop asking questions you do not want the answers to." Daman slid forward, crowding her, raising himself higher as if he could scare her away and end this interrogation. Damn her, why was she so *stubborn*? Why did she have to push him now, now that he actually *cared* if he hurt her feelings?

"What's that supposed to mean?"

The words hovered on the tip of Daman's forked tongue. Oh, how he wanted to tell her. He wanted Maribel to know the truth about her sister, wanted her to know the truth about what Corrine was capable of. But no matter how strong his desire to make Maribel understand, he was no fool. Maribel's loyalty to her sister would not be shattered so easily, and he had no proof.

Daman lowered himself back down to his normal height, his shoulders sagging in defeat. "I'm going for a swim. Please don't follow me this time." He tried to go around her.

"I will follow you." Maribel side-stepped to stay in front of him. "I will follow you this time and every other time until you tell me why you wanted me here."

A dull pounding started in the base of his skull. He flexed his fingers at his sides, fighting to keep his arms down even as part of him wanted to grab her, rattle her, force her to see the truth. "Maribel, let it go."

"Not until you tell me."

This time when she raised a finger to point at him, she did poke him. She jabbed her finger into the center of his chest, her fingernail dragging along the scales on the center ridge, the one that led straight down. Before he was aware of what he was doing, Daman had snatched her wrist, had closed his fingers around it and hauled her closer. He put his face mere inches away from her own, searching her eyes for something he could reason with.

"What does it matter? I told you that you can go home, what does it matter why I brought you here?"

"Because coming here changed *everything!*" Maribel shouted.

The fervor in her voice made him lean back to see her face. Maribel glared at him and moved closer, not giving him an inch. The pulse at her neck fluttered, and Daman didn't have to taste the air to know she was near tears. He could see the telltale glimmer in her eyes and when she spoke, he could hear the thickness in her voice.

"I was at peace with the life I had, and now I don't know if I can go back. I was used to caring for my sister, putting aside my own dreams to make sure she was safe and happy. Then I came here. You freed me from responsibilities I was too guilty to even dream about abandoning, gave me a taste of a life I didn't think I could have, didn't think I *should* have." She tore her wrist from his grasp and he let her go, but she didn't back away. She stood her ground, jutting her chin out at him as if daring him to comment on her tears. "You changed everything for me, and I want to know why."

Daman's stomach dropped. She was right. He'd upended her life, torn her from her family. He'd realized his mistake right away, but instead of rectifying it immediately, instead of sending her home with her father, he'd forced her to stay. He'd told himself it was for her own protection, to keep her away from the witch, but he'd never really believed that. No, he'd wanted her to stay for himself. Because he didn't want to be alone.

Selfishness.

The pain lancing through him hurt too much. He needed to feel something else—anything else. And there was always one emotion waiting for him, ready to welcome him with open arms.

"It wass ssupposed to be your ssisster. Sshe'ss the one who wass ssuppossed to come here. Sshe would have removed her cursse from me, or elsse I would have *finally* had my revenge."

There. He'd said it. In a foreign, sibilant, inhuman hiss, he'd said it, the truth falling into the space between him and Maribel like boulders crashing down into a still lake, sending ripples of chaos out around them.

Maribel's mouth fell open, her brow furrowing over watery eyes. "You… You think Corrine's the witch that cursed you."

"I *know* sshe'ss the witch who curssed me." Daman sneered. "Sshe came to me covered in your blood. Sshe desscribed the ssame circumsstancess your father did—I vissited your farm. Your ssisster iss the witch who curssed me, and if it weren't for you, I would have her here now."

Maribel took one halting step back. "No. It's not true."

Daman slid closer, crowding her personal space until she took another step back. "Your ssisster iss ass incompetent a witch ass sshe iss a sseductressss. Like a child lacking even a sscrap of disscipline, sshe threw a tantrum when I refused her advancess, throwing her sspell like a handful of rockss. Not only did sshe trap me in thiss form, sshe dumped magic over my land." He watched the conflict dance in Maribel's vision. "Perhapss you've noticced a few sstrange thingss? Talking objectss? *A magic rosse?*"

He grabbed her arm, forcing her off balance. A ragged whimper fell from her lips as she put a hand on his chest to catch herself. Her hand touched him and she flinched.

There. You've frightened her. Are you satisfied now?

He ignored the voice in his head trying to shame him, bit back the apology that tingled on the tip of his forked tongue. He was tired of feeling vulnerable, tired of questioning every word, every gesture, every feeling. He'd been a fool to keep her here. She had to leave, and he had to do whatever it took to make her.

"You've given up your life and your dreamss to pamper your ssisster, and all the while sshe'ss been sseeking a way to leave you behind. And now you're jusst like her, wanting to usse me to esscape the pitiful circumstancess you've created for yoursself."

He leaned down until his face was only inches from hers, until his breath whispered across her skin and he could taste her tears in the air between them. "But I will not play thiss game. If you want to leave your ssisster behind, you will have to take that ressponssibility yoursself. I will not give you an excusse any longer." Some of his anger drained away even as he struggled to hold onto it. He shoved her away, steeling himself against the fresh stream of tears that fell as she stumbled. "Go home, Maribel."

CHAPTER 10

Corrine slid the lock on her bedroom door into the closed position. The iron clanked hard against its anchor, a loud, final sound. She strode across the room, not bothering to wait and see if her father came to ask if she was all right. She knew he wouldn't.

He knew better now.

She retrieved the pot of honey she'd tucked away in the small cupboard next to her bed, wrinkling her nose at the way her hand stuck to the jar. *Why is it no matter how many times you wipe off a honey container, there's always just enough residue left to make your fingers sticky?* She held her tacky hand out, searching for something to clean it off on so she wouldn't accidentally get it on her nightgown. The gown was new, her father's latest attempt to bribe Corrine into the same ignorant bliss that he'd so feverishly embraced. Her fingers tightened on the jar, nails carving grooves in the residue gluing it to her hand. She had no intention of taking the monster's hush money and leaving him to keep her sister.

Though she had kept the nightgown.

She stomped over to the window and shoved it open. The

creaking of the old frame and the grinding of the heavy wood against the sill grated on her nerves. Not so much for the noise, but because it was yet another reminder of how her status had remained the same, despite the rise in fortune. The workers who were steadily improving this farmhouse even as they built a new one had steadfastly avoided her room. Not a single shingle had been evened out, not a plank painted, not a hinge oiled. The entire house looked like a picturesque country cottage with her room sticking out like a deformed limb, rotting away from gangrene.

"If we had moved home, to our *proper* home," Corrine ground out, "the people would have better things to do than stew in superstition. No one there gave a flying fig about my illness, no one thought twice about it. They certainly didn't think I was being seized by demons, that I was...*evil*."

But here, oh, here was different. Country people wallowed in superstition. They left milk and honey out regularly, told horror stories about lights in the forest and dark shapes that moved under the surface of rivers and lakes. It had taken no more than one of Corrine's episodes to send the rumor spreading like wildfire in a drought—the farmer's daughter was a witch.

At first Corrine had cowered from their ire, but Mother Briar had quickly put a stop to that. Witches must command respect, and if it is not given then it must be *taken*. She'd coached Corrine, fed her confidence until she could meet the stares of the villagers with an answering stare of her own—and a stare was a great deal different when it came from a witch. As far as they were concerned, every glare from her was the Evil Eye, and they scattered like mice in the path of a hungry cat.

If she couldn't be loved, she would be feared. It would be enough. It had to be.

Corrine shook herself out of the reverie she'd fallen into, disgusted with herself for giving in to self pity. Reminding herself of her goals, she gazed out into the night sky. Searching.

"Where are you, little one?" she called out, keeping her voice as sweet as possible. "I have something for you."

There was a spark of light and something buzzed through the window to swirl around her head like a hyperactive firefly. The glow was faintly pink, and it spiraled around so quickly it could have drawn words in the air with its trail.

"Is that honey?" came a voice.

Corrine paused, slowly trying to parse out what the creature had said in her annoyingly high, squeaky tone. "Honey, yes. I have some honey for you. That is, if you have something for me...?"

The pixie halted as though it had somehow been crushed against the air, smashed into a smudge on invisible glass. Its eyes bulged as Corrine played her fingers over the lid of the small honey pot. "They're fighting."

Corrine's eyebrows shot into her hairline. "Fighting? About what?"

"The female wants to know why dragonman made her come there. Dragonman says it was supposed to be her sister. He says the sister is the one who cursed him."

Corrine's heart nearly stopped in her chest, her fingers going limp. Daman had told Maribel about what Corrine had done? No. No, Maribel couldn't know about that. Corrine couldn't bear it. The jar of honey started to tumble to the floor and she had to scramble to catch it as the pixie gasped and dove for it at the same time. Corrine caught it first and yanked it away from the fey. "And what did the woman say?" she demanded, her heart in her throat.

The pixie wrung her hands, eyes locked on the honey. "She's crying. Be careful you don't drop that!"

Crying? Corrine opened the jar and lifted the lid away. In the blink of an eye, the pixie dove into the honey and was instantly covered head to toe in the sticky mess. Corrine cringed and turned away, her thoughts racing.

"He's made his play." She paced the length of her room, nightgown tangling about her legs in a mad dance of silk. "The fight begins. I can't let him win her. If she believes him..."

The thought of Maribel finding out about Corrine's most desperate moment, her most humiliating memory, turned Corrine's stomach. There were few people in the world right now whose opinion mattered to Corrine, but Maribel was one of them. There had to be a way to get her back.

Corrine twirled a lock of her long dark hair around a finger, then stiffened as the strands stuck and tugged. She gritted her teeth, remembering the sticky residue she'd forgotten to clean off.

I. Hate. Honey.

After taking a moment to regain her composure, Corrine stormed over to her wash basin and dumped some water from the matching pitcher. She washed the lock of hair as best she could, along with both hands. Agitated ripples in the water drew her attention and she stopped. Were her hands trembling? She slowly raised them out of the water, ignoring the rivulets that ran down her arms to wet the silk of her nightgown. Yes. She was shaking.

Her gaze fell past her hands, down her body. The nightgown that had looked so sleek and decadent to her before now emphasized every sharp angle, every bone stabbing out against her skin. The soft, womanly curves sung about in songs and described with loving detail in poetry were nothing but a cruel dream, something a pathetic urchin like herself could only aspire to. She was starving, wasting away in a wilderness full of frightening monsters and mocking villagers. She was a skeleton draped in expensive cloth. The sick child that should have died in the cradle.

No, no, no...

She averted her eyes, not wanting to see herself anymore. Cruel fate dragged her gaze up and across the room to the large mirror hanging on her wall. A memory rose like a zombie from a grave to touch the silver surface of the polished glass. The episode she'd had earlier, her body twitching and unresponsive to her commands as she lay there, forced into a staring contest with her own reflection in the silver tray Maribel used to bring her meals on.

She'd seen her aura in that reflection. As her father had a hole in his heart, Corrine had a hole in her aura, a gaping mouth on the surface of the shimmering coat of color that fluctuated near-constantly. A bright tube of light led from that hole. It had once connected Corrine to Maribel, but now it was stretched so far, so thin, that Corrine couldn't feel anything on the other end of that link anymore. There was no energy flowing to her, no taste of Maribel's presence inside her. She was alone. *Vulnerable.*

"Maribel, you've ruined me."

Slowly, she clenched her hands into fists. "Why did you have to ask for that damned rose? Why did you have to draw *his* attention?" She bit the inside of her cheek, her throat suddenly closing, her heart twisting in her chest. "He'll keep you. He'll keep you or he'll take you away." She cleared her throat, warm tears threatening to spill down her cheeks. For a moment, thoughts of magic and illness fell away and an image of her sister hovered in her mind's eye. Her sister who had always been there for her, always loved her. Her favorite person in the world.

"Maribel, I miss you," she whispered.

Anger rose like an avenging angel, slaying her yearning for her sibling, her pain at being without her company, her laughter, her unwavering support. It hardened her soul, coating it in a protective, impenetrable shell. "She left me," she reminded herself. "Left without a second thought—*wanted* to leave. Why should I miss her?"

She wrapped her fingers into fists. A dull pain throbbed to life in her hands as her burned skin screamed in protest. The pain was a welcome distraction, exactly what she needed to focus on the future instead of wallowing in self-pity. Corrine lifted one of the small jars sitting on the end table. She twisted the lid off and the scent of lavender filled the air. The homemade cream was cool against her fingers as she dipped them in, ignoring the lumps of herbs and firmly rubbing the ointment into her skin. The wounds on her fingers burned, drawing her attention to the myriad of cuts.

She tried to imagine Maribel's face if her sister could see Corrine's hands, see what she'd been reduced to. Without Maribel close enough for the bond between them to let Corrine share her fey energy, Corrine had been forced to brew a different kind of potion to keep her strength up. The only potions strong enough to even come close to the fey power she was missing required powerful ingredients—including blood. Even with the addition of her blood, Corrine could feel the potions growing less and less effective. Mother Briar had told her it was a temporary fix.

She needed Maribel to come home.

"What is the dragonman's temper like these days?" she called out to the pixie, not taking her eyes off her own hands as she continued to rub the healing ointment into her skin.

"The sprites are back."

The pixie made the announcement as if it explained everything and went back to alternately playing in and eating the honey. Corrine pinched the bridge of her nose, the scent of the lavender ointment on her hands doing nothing to alleviate the growing headache pounding in her temples. "And do the sprites say he is in better spirits?" she ventured tiredly.

"The sprites wouldn't be there if it was too dangerous," the pixie scoffed. "They're cowards."

"So he is kind to the woman then? No bouts of temper?"

"Oh, yes, still bouts of temper. But it doesn't deter the woman." The pixie focused sparkling blue eyes on Corrine. "They were kissing."

"They were..." A tight, wrenching pain squeezed Corrine's chest and she closed her eyes. Of course. Of course he would want her. Maribel was a changeling, and Daman had always had a tender spot for changelings. Why shouldn't Maribel succeed where Corrine had failed? Why shouldn't Daman want her, kiss her, when he had cast Corrine aside like so much garbage?

"Are you sick?"

Corrine opened her eyes in time to see the pixie—still covered in thick, viscous honey—march over her coverlet to plop down on her lap. The miserable pest left a sticky trail all the way from the windowsill across the bed, and the sweet substance was now soaking into Corrine's silk nightgown. The fabric was ruined.

"Yes, little one, I am sick." Corrine snatched up the pixie, drawing a shriek of indignation from the creature. More disgusting honey oozed between her fingertips as she rose to her feet. "I'm *sick* of being pathetic. I'm *sick* of relying on others to keep me safe, to keep me *alive*." She tightened her grip. "I'm *sick* of needing *anyone*."

The creature in her grasp suddenly morphed into a scorpion, black insect body shining, and wickedly sharp stinger raised and ready to strike. A drop of amber venom beaded on the tip of its barbed tail.

"Save your glamour for someone who is unfamiliar with your kind," Corrine sneered.

The pixie snarled as she gave up the glamour, once again becoming the tiny person-shaped creature with translucent wings. "Let me *go*!"

Corrine stalked over to her wardrobe and tore it open, nearly ripping the door off its hinges. She retrieved a small birdcage, which she then opened so she could deposit the pixie inside. "Try to escape," she warned, "and the next place you go will be forged of iron."

The pixie scowled at her, sitting on the floor of the cage in a sticky honey puddle. "This was not part of our arrangement."

"I'm changing the arrangement." Corrine's mind danced over her options like a honeybee in a field of flowers. "I'm changing a lot of things."

There was much to do. After tucking the cage safely to the side, Corrine quickly washed her hand and gathered a few gowns from her wardrobe. She dragged a bag out from underneath the bed—the same bag she'd packed with her most precious clothes the day she'd had to leave her last home—her *real* home. She paused, staring down at the bag.

A memory flashed into her head. For a moment she was back in Daman's manor, standing beside him still covered in her sister's tacky, drying blood. He'd been so gentle with her then, so incredibly kind. He'd led her to that room and opened a wardrobe filled with beautiful gowns, each one more stunning than the last. All for her.

She slowly pulled the bag off her bed and went back to her wardrobe. Her potions rattled as she loaded them into the satchel, speaking to the pixie without looking up.

"What weakens a fey besides iron?"

The pixie crossed her tiny honey-thickened arms. "Why should I tell you?"

Corrine slid an iron file out of her grooming kit. She waved it at the pixie, letting the iron threat speak for itself. "If she's upset. Will that emotion make her stronger or weaker?"

The pixie scowled. "Weaker if she's sad, stronger if she's mad."

Corrine tightened her grip on the file, gritting her teeth as she fought the tremble threatening to rattle her fingers. "And if she's incredibly happy?"

That question gave the pixie pause. She tilted her head to the side. "What kind of fey is she?"

"I don't know. She's stronger if she's outside, and she's good with plants."

The pixie arched an eyebrow. "It would narrow the possibilities down more if she wasn't good with plants. Your sister's never told you what she is?"

"She doesn't know. She thinks she's human." Corrine hesitated, the file drooping in her grip. "I never... I never wanted her to feel like she didn't belong, so I never said anything. It didn't matter anyway, she's my sister no matter where she comes from."

The pixie blinked. "But...she's a grown-up now. You shouldn't have to tell her, there would be signs, her gifts would be obvious. Is she stupid?"

"No. There haven't been any signs."

"*You're* stupid," the pixie muttered. "If you think she doesn't know. No matter what she is, *there would be signs*. She has obviously been hiding them from you if you don't know about them."

Corrine gripped the cage, squeezing until the bars bent under the pressure. "You would do well not to insult my intelligence," she said, letting her anger warm her voice. "What if someone had been sharing her energy? Could that mute it enough to hide the signs?"

The pixie's gaze intensified with interest. It gave her a sharper appearance, carved more lines in her face, darkened her eyes into solid stones. It was an...unsettling look, and a trickle of unease dripped down Corrine's spine.

"You mean if a witch was draining her power?"

Corrine stiffened. "Not draining. Sharing. Symbiotically."

The pixie leaned against the bars of the cage, the motion somewhat predatory and completely at odds with the image of the honey-loving creature she'd been moments ago. "Symbiotically would suggest the fey got something in return. What does a human have to offer a fey?"

"Not merely a human," Corrine corrected through clenched teeth. "A witch."

The pixie shook her head slowly, that alien stare unnerving, unwavering. "Anyone who needs that sort of bond is too feeble to have anything to offer a fey."

Corrine snatched up the cage and swung it at her wardrobe. The metal banged against the solid wood, rattling the pixie until she cried out.

"My parents thought I would never live to see my first birthday. Did you know that? I wasn't supposed to live a *year*! I have not survived this long by being a coward—I have survived because I fight. I know what I want, I know what I *need*, and I am willing to do whatever I have to do to *get it*." The words flew from her, giving her strength as if claiming her courage, affirming her fortitude, somehow made it true. The fragility she'd been so sure of moments ago cowered from the passionate claims spilling from her lips now.

The pixie clutched at the bars of the cage, her head swaying back and forth as if dizzy. "So what are you going to do?" she demanded, slapping a hand to the side of her head as if to stop it spinning. "March up to the manor and demand the dragonman marry you? That did not work out so well for you last time."

"How..." Corrine gritted her teeth. She'd started dealing with the pixie a week ago because they were so very good at gathering information and she'd needed a spy. It shouldn't surprise her the pixie knew of her past. "I have no intention of trying to marry that beast."

"Again," the pixie added smugly.

Corrine slammed the cage down on the bed and its already honey-ruined coverlet. "I am going there to get my sister. I'm going to bring her home where she belongs."

"You should let her marry the dragonman," the pixie observed, sprawled like a starfish stuck to the bottom of the cage. "She would give you much money."

"I don't want her money." Corrine tore at the nightgown, fighting to loosen the ties so she could get it off. "I don't want to rely on *anyone*!"

"You already rely on her," the pixie pointed out, unperturbed by Corrine's show of temper. She winced as she pried her head from the floor of the cage, the suction of the honey making an audible sucking sound. "You need her energy, why not take her money too?"

"I don't *want* her energy, I just want—"

The silken tie on her nightgown broke under the pressure of Corrine's harried attempts to free herself of the gown. She stared at the string, loose threads curling into the air like the legs of a dead insect. Her eyelid twitched.

"Oh, boy," the pixie breathed. "Now, stay calm. It's going to be all right…"

Corrine's vision went red. Her entire body trembled, pulse pounding so hard in her neck it was difficult to swallow. She stepped closer to the cage and the pixie shrieked and tried to scramble away. The honey she'd so willingly coated herself with was slowly thickening to glue, and she was stuck to the floor of her prison. Corrine watched her squirm with a bone-deep satisfaction and stopped a few feet from the bed.

"I don't want to rely on anyone, but I need Maribel's energy. The blackouts are returning and it's only a matter of time before my flesh starts to rot away. There isn't enough food to keep me full, not enough blankets to keep me warm. I survived this long only because of the bond I managed to forge with Maribel— without her, I will die."

The trembling in her body grew worse and she had the sudden, awful realization that if she didn't calm down, she was going to plunge herself into another episode. Now was not the time to be helpless. Carefully, slowly, she removed the ruined nightgown. The patch of honey left by the pixie had soaked through to her undergarments, so she removed those too. Naked, she walked over to the wash basin with as much serenity as she could muster and began cleaning herself for what felt like the thousandth time that evening.

She could feel the pixie's eyes on her the whole time, though the fey wisely chose to remain silent. For once. Piece by piece,

Corrine dressed again, every clean garment, every slide of silk calming her, soothing her frazzled nerves. Finally dressed again, she faced herself in the mirror.

"Mother Briar has promised to help me," she said calmly, smoothing her hands down the rich green velvet of her skirt. "All I need is for Maribel to help me get the information she wants, and she'll teach me stronger magic. I won't need Maribel's energy anymore, I won't..." She closed her eyes and took several deep breaths, the tightness of the gown's bodice holding her in, holding her together even as she thought she would fly apart. "Maribel will help me."

"Daman will never betray the location of Mother Briar's daughter," the pixie muttered. "The old bat was too cruel to the goblin girl, Daman would never risk her life by telling anyone where she is—not even the woman who transfixes him so."

Corrine paused, a sudden thought occurring to her. She slanted a glance at the pixie. "Do... Do *you* know where the goblin girl is?"

"No. *Nagas* are much like their draconic ancestors in their ability to keep a secret. If the *naga* does not wish for the goblin girl to be found, it would take much to find her."

"But you *could* do it."

The pixie shook her head, frowning as her hair stuck to one of the bars of her cage. "No. Even if I wanted to help you—and at the moment I don't," she added, looking pointedly at the cage. "I would need help from my brethren. It would take me ages to find her by myself." She tried to pull her hair free of the bar, the effort drawing the skin from her face until her eyes were mere slits. "And there's no way I could convince enough of them to help— not when they would be risking the fury of the *naga* who wished the location to remain a secret." She grunted.

Corrine drummed the fingers of one hand against the opposite arm. *No help there, then.*

"Well, then I guess there's only one thing to do."

Ignoring the protests from the pixie, she packed the cage and some potions in her satchel and laced it up tight. After giving herself a moment to calm the last of her nerves, she marched to the door, thrust back the lock, and ripped the door open.

Her father jumped as she stormed into the main room of the cottage on her way to the front door. He was seated in the chair by the fireplace where an episode had struck her and left her lying helplessly with her hand on the hearth. The memory twisted her stomach and Corrine kept moving, determined to keep the memory from sinking its claws in deep enough to slow her down.

"Corrine," her father said, wariness in his voice. "Where are you going, child?"

"To get my sister back." Her hand tightened on the door handle, the aged metal creaking in her unforgiving grip.

Her father rose from his seat, wringing his hands in front of him. "Corrine, please. You have to accept your sister's choice—we both do. We cannot—"

"*We* are not going to do anything. *I* am going to get Maribel. Perhaps *you're* content to sit in that chair and do nothing, but I refuse to let that monster keep my little sister." She fixed her father with the glare that had been her most frequent expression for the last few days when dealing with her parental figure. "After all, *someone* has to do what's right for this family."

Her father flinched as though she'd physically struck him. Corrine wished she had something else to say, something else to throw at him to make him suffer as much as she was. Didn't he feel Maribel's absence? Didn't he think of her laugh, her smile, the way she hummed stupid little nonsense songs while she was cooking?

She was sick of seeing him go on with his life as if nothing had happened. After they'd lost all their money, their home, their friends, her father had picked up and moved on as though it were nothing. He'd bought this miserable farm, put his daughters to work, and acted like life was wonderful again. Then he'd lost Maribel, allowed her to go to that beast. And the bastard didn't even care about that!

"Corrine, you're always telling me that you're sick, that you're too weak to work outside. And yet now you're perfectly willing to go traipsing off through the forest—"

"Shut *up!*" Rage seized Corrine in a suffocating grip, raking claws over her voice until it was as rough as evergreen bark. "You don't get to believe in my illness when it suits you and forget it otherwise. You don't—"

She bit her words off, shifting her bag in her grip, trying to calm down. She couldn't leave in a rage, it was too dangerous to get that emotional when she was going to be alone. *Breathe...calm down...it's all right.* "I'm going to get Maribel back," she said, her voice only slightly breathless. She stared hard into her father's eyes, putting as much disdain as she could manage into her expression, wanting to be absolutely certain he wouldn't interfere. "Go sit in your chair."

As predicted, her father's face crumbled under her derision. He collapsed back into the chair like a marionette who'd had its strings hacked off, bones jarring with the impact as he hit the cushions.

Corrine gave him one last disgusted look and then left, heading into the dark forest to find her sister with her heart bleeding inside her.

CHAPTER 11

"Your ssisster iss the witch who curssed me, and if it weren't for you, I would have her here now."

Daman's words echoed in Maribel's head and she clenched her teeth. The dirt slicked rock slipped in her fingertips and she firmed her grip, heaving it into the lake. The rock landed with a satisfying smack on the water's surface. Water sprayed up into the air, disturbing the peace. She scanned the ground for another properly sized rock. As good as it felt to be throwing things into Daman's precious lake, she would have felt even better if she had enough rocks to fill the damn thing. *Let him try to swim in wet stones.*

She hefted another rock into the water. "That's for you, Daman." She gripped another, craggy rock. Heaving it with all her might into the lake, she grunted, "And that's for you, *Mother* Briar!"

That lying witch. Filling Maribel's head with ridiculous romantic notions of a beast who needed true love to save him from his curse. What a fool she'd been to fall for such nonsense. How simple-minded did she have to be to put one ounce of belief in such falderal? How desperate did she have to be to want to believe it?

"And you're even more foolish for not leaving immediately," she scolded herself. "He wants you to leave, so you should leave. How pathetic must he think you to see you staying where you're not wanted?"

"Not ssso foolisssh."

Maribel jumped and dropped the rock she was holding on the end of her toe. She shouted and cursed in a most unladylike manner, hopping on her uninjured foot as pain radiated with ridiculous intensity from her toe. When she was sure she could speak without spewing profanity, she faced the sound of the voice.

"You!" She pointed at the silver winged snake hanging from a tree branch like calcified ivy. "What do *you* want?"

"Jussst checking to sssee how thingsss are going." The snake looked pointedly at the rock beside her foot and then at the lake. "He ssswimsss when he isss feeling ssstresssssssed. Are you trying to keep him on edge?"

Maribel slanted a glare at the lake. "Why not? He'd driving me to the edge. Why should I be the only one to squirm?"

The snake blinked. "Sssquirm?"

"You probably knew all along though, didn't you?" Maribel muttered.

"Knew what?"

"Knew that he never wanted me here. You probably knew that the only reason he demanded my father send his daughter here to take his place was because he thought my father would bring my sister. He thinks she's the witch that cursed him and he wanted to bring her here so he could force her to lift the curse."

"Sshe would have removed her cursse from me, or elsse I would have finally had my revenge."

"Or worse," she added. Her stomach twisted at the last thought, dropping further at the memory of the hissing snarl

183

Daman's voice had become. Despite his temper, she truly hadn't wanted to believe Daman was capable of anything horrendous. The thought that he was serious about getting revenge, that he might have hurt Corrine...

"Ssso now you know about your sssissster?"

Maribel kicked a rock, crying out as her toe screamed in outrage, reminding her of its earlier injury. She collapsed to the ground, grabbing her aching foot. "I know that he *thinks* she's the one who cursed him," she ground out through clenched teeth. "What I don't understand is why."

"You think he isss missstaken?"

"All I know is that my sister has not left my side since we moved out here, the only time she's alone at all is when she's cleaning the house and I'm out in the fields." Maribel closed her eyes, wincing at the throb in her toe. "I don't see how it could have been her."

The *cuelebre* twined around the tree, corkscrewing down the trunk. "If it were within her power to get here on her own, without your knowledge, do you think ssshe would have attempted it?"

Maribel opened her mouth to say absolutely not, then hesitated. The rock in her hands was suddenly intensely interesting. The surface was damp, making the grey stone black, and it was coated in enough dirt to give it a gritty texture. "She's been hiding food again."

"Hiding...food?"

"Yes." Maribel shifted uneasily, feeling uncomfortable discussing Corrine's personal life this way. It was wrong to talk about her with a stranger, and yet... Dammit, she needed to talk to *someone*. Someone had to understand why Corrine couldn't possibly be the monster Daman believed her to be.

"When she was young, Father was always afraid she'd have an episode while she was eating and choke on her food. He used to limit how much he allowed her to eat." She bit her lip, focusing on the lake, on the ripples fading into glass-like smoothness. "His intentions were good, but I think it hurt more than it helped. Corrine panicked a lot, she worried about starving. She got better when she got older, and the episodes were further apart so Father relaxed the limitations on her food." She sighed and rubbed a hand over her face. "Then we came here."

"And the episssodesss worsssened?"

"Terribly so. I don't know if it was that one hard winter when food was scarce that scared her, or if there's something about being out here in and of itself, but she's nearly as bad now as she was before. Worse in some ways. Now she's afraid to go outside most times. She complains more, she's never happy, she..."

Daman was right. Maribel had used him as an excuse to leave, an excuse to leave Corrine behind because trying to keep her happy was becoming too...draining.

"Would being missstressssss of thisss manor have made her happy?"

"I don't know." The words were so quiet, so thin, they may as well have been echoes. There was no force behind them, no...certainty.

"Only when that trust is broken will we be free."

The voice from her dream echoed back to her and Maribel clenched her hand into a fist around the rock she still held. The sharp edges cut into her palm, the pain helping her to think clearly, to chase away the guilt long enough to consider, really consider, what the serpent was asking. "I—"

"Maribel!"

Maribel dropped the rock and spun around, heart pounding as though she'd been caught committing some sort of crime. "Corrine?"

She scrambled to her feet, sliding on the stones wet from the splashing water and took off into the forest. The figure coming through the woods was dressed in a stunning green dress, silk, satin, and fine beads embroidered into the bodice. There was only one person who would wear such garments on a trek through the woods. As she looked on, the figure swayed and collapsed.

"Corrine? Corrine!" Maribel shrieked and ran faster. She fell to her knees, taking her sister's limp hand in hers.

Her sister blinked, her head lolling from side to side where she lay on the ground. "Maribel. Maribel, I found you. I'm going to take you home…"

Her sister's eyes rolled up into her head, her eyelids falling closed. Maribel's heart leapt into her throat. She patted Corrine's cheeks, trying to force some color into the pale skin, to get her blood flowing. "Corrine, wake up. Corrine!"

Her chest tightened as her sister remained unresponsive, the pulse at her neck thready. Corrine's head lolled to the side as she laid her gently on the forest floor and stumbled to her feet. She raced back to the lake and half-fell onto the bank, shoving the end of her skirt into the water. When the material was thoroughly soaked, she lurched back to her feet and rushed to her sister. Water trickled down Corrine's face as Maribel pressed the soaked edge of her skirt to her sister's forehead. Her sister moaned and stirred. Maribel nearly fainted with relief as Corrine's brown eyes blinked open.

"Maribel. Maribel, I found you. I'll… I'll take you…home."

"Corrine, what on earth are you doing out here?" Maribel demanded, her voice faint with relief as Corrine's eyes remained open. She raised her head and scanned the forest, searching for some sign of an escort. "Are you alone?"

Corrine winced. "Yes. I had to…get away." She let out a deep breath and eased back against the ground, letting Maribel stroke her forehead. "Maribel, it's awful. There are so many strangers crawling all over the place now. Did you know that Father's building a new farmhouse? He never had any intention of moving back home."

Maribel didn't say anything to that. Part of her hoped that the reason her father was staying where he was had something to do with wanting to stay close to her. But even if that wasn't the case, she knew that she and her father shared something in common—they had both come to like living out here.

Her father had never said anything, but Maribel had seen a marked difference in him. The stress of the import business—pirates, unpredictable weather, cutthroat merchants—had melted away from him as he'd worked the fields, haggled good-naturedly with friendly villagers who enjoyed bartering as a favorite means of social interaction. He and Maribel had shared that secret, along with the guilt of knowing that they were getting happier and happier while Corrine became more and more miserable.

Corrine grabbed her hand suddenly and Maribel jumped.

"Maribel, I want you to know I never forgot about you," Corrine said seriously, locking her eyes on Maribel's face. "Every day I tried to think of some way to save you, some way to force that...monster, to let you go."

"He's not a monster."

Corrine jerked her hand back, a small tic twitching at her temple. "What do you mean he's not a monster?"

Maribel blinked. "I... I just mean, he's not all bad. He's got a temper, yes, and he..." She trailed off, the world fading a bit around the edges as her mind wandered back to Daman. *He's not a monster.*

"He what?" Corrine demanded.

"I think he's just been alone for a long time. He's going through a lot, and he doesn't have enough faith in himself—or others. But he's trying to change."

Corrine stared at her as though she'd lost her mind. Maribel understood how she felt. She herself was having a rather hard time understanding her feelings at the moment. She'd been so angry a few minutes ago, so ready to leave and say good riddance to Daman and his mood swings. But somehow, hearing Corrine call him a monster... *Oh, what is wrong with me?*

She gave Corrine a reassuring smile. "What I'm trying to say is, I'm fine. You don't have to worry about me here."

"Maribel, I don't know what's wrong with you, but I cannot leave you here." She grasped both of Maribel's hands in hers. "I've been talking to Mother Briar. The stories she's told me... He's done such horrible things."

"No, no, Corrine," Maribel hushed her. "He's not horrible, he's...very moody. But he's also kind and—"

"He kidnaps changelings!"

Maribel jerked back, startled as Corrine surged forward to grab Maribel's shoulder. She shook her so hard Maribel's teeth rattled, sending a dull pain through her jaw. "Corrine," she sputtered.

"I know it's true. He... Maribel, he..." For a moment Corrine's eyes glittered, her lower lip trembling. Then with a tiny sob, she burst into tears and collapsed against Maribel, burying her face in her shoulder. "Maribel, he kidnapped me."

Maribel's heart stopped, the entire world coming to a grinding, screeching halt. "What?"

"That day you had an accident in the field—you hit your head on the fence. Your blood was everywhere, even all over me. I helped Father get you cleaned up and into bed and I went back to my room. Before I could wash, he—" Another sob tore from her throat, punctuating her words. "He was suddenly there. He told me I had to come with him, that I didn't belong with you and Father. He told me I was a changeling, and he was going to take me back to my real parents."

Maribel shook her head, trying to process what her sister was saying. Her mouth had gone dry and she had a hard time swallowing. "But... But you're..."

"Oh, Maribel, I'm so sorry. I never wanted to tell you, I never wanted you to think... You're my sister, isn't that all that matters? I love you."

Maribel's skin felt cold, clammy. "You were covered in my

blood. He thought... He thought you were a changeling because...because I'm...?"

Corrine nodded, her face still buried in Maribel's shoulder. "I never loved you any less," she said fiercely.

"How did you get away?" Maribel's head spun, making it difficult to concentrate. She groped for the end of her skirt, raising the still damp section to her own forehead to wipe away the sudden sweat there.

"I used a spell Mother Briar taught me," Corrine sniffled, pulling away and wiping her eyes. "I was fighting him and he was trying to transform into a dragon. I tried to stop him, to hold him in human form."

"You... You are the one who cursed him into the form he's in now. You're the reason he can't go all the way back to one or the other." Maribel leaned back, hand scrabbling at the ground for support. No, it couldn't be true...

Corrine grabbed her hand, her grip so tight it was painful. "I didn't mean to! I was trying to get away."

An ache pulsed to life in Maribel's temples, throbbing with every laborious beat of her heart. "No. No, that can't be right. Even if he thought you were a changeling, he wouldn't have forced you to leave Father and me. He wouldn't have taken you from your home if you didn't want to go. He's not like that."

"Then why did he take you? Why did he make you come stay with him when you didn't want to be here?"

Maribel opened her mouth to respond then closed it. She couldn't argue that Daman had forced her to come here, that he would have forced their father to stay if she hadn't. But how could she explain his true intentions to her sister without frightening her? Maribel carefully avoided looking back at the manor, suddenly very nervous about the possibility that Daman may know Corrine was here.

"I... I think he's lonely," Maribel said weakly, kicking herself even as she lied. She pasted another smile on her face, hoping it didn't look as brittle as it felt. "Corrine, I'm fine here, really. Go back home, tell Father I'm all right."

"He wouldn't be lonely if he hadn't killed everyone else in the manor," Corrine snapped. "And I'm not going anywhere without you."

"He didn't kill everyone, Corrine, he sent them away." Maribel pulled her hand out of her sister's grasp. "Being trapped in the form he's in makes it hard for him to control his temper, and he was worried that he might hurt someone."

"But he doesn't care if he hurts you?" Corrine demanded incredulously.

Maribel pursed her lips. "He wouldn't hurt me. If he thought he was a danger to me, he'd send me away too. He's lonely, and he wants to try being around someone. He's told me about his meditation, about how hard he's been trying to deal with the temper being trapped in this form gives him."

"So you're saying it's all my fault." Corrine looked down at her skirt, swiped violently at the dirt clinging to the fabric.

"No, it's not your fault." Maribel grabbed a lock of her hair and twisted it around her finger, tugging as if she could distract herself from the mounting frustration inside her. "You were frightened, you did what you had to do to protect yourself. I'm only saying, it was all a misunderstanding."

Corrine narrowed her eyes and remained silent for an agonizingly long second. Then she nodded once, firmly. "All right then. Take me up to the manor. Let me see for myself how badly I've misjudged him, how wrong the stories are."

The blood drained from Maribel's face, leaving her cheeks cold.

"Sshe'ss the one who wass ssuppossed to come here. Sshe would have removed her cursse from me, or elsse I would have finally had my revenge."

"What's the matter?" Corrine held Maribel's gaze as she struggled to her feet, swaying a little before squaring her shoulders.

"Let's go talk with the lonely lord. Unless of course there's some reason you think that would be a bad idea?"

Maribel pursed her lips but didn't say anything.

"See?" Corrine jabbed a finger at Maribel. "You know he's a monster. Deep down, you know." She tugged on Maribel's arm. "Come home with me."

"No." Maribel faced Corrine, putting her determination in her face and stance. "No, I do have faith in him. He's not a bad man, and he wouldn't hurt you, not now that he knows how much you mean to me." Heat pulsed in her head, a warning that bringing Corrine to Daman was a mistake, that it would be pushing him too far. He was so angry already.

He is a good man. I know he is.

"Corrine?" she asked slowly.

"What?"

"Can you undo what you did? Lift the spell so he can shift form again?"

Corrine opened her mouth, then closed it. The skin around her eyes tightened and she wouldn't meet Maribel's eyes. "I don't know." She snapped a twig off an overhanging tree branch. "My powers aren't that strong..."

"Will you try?" Maribel asked, trying to keep her voice calm despite a flash of irritation. *What, does magic require too much effort as well as farm work?*

Corrine stared down at the twig as she turned it over in her hands. "Maribel...do you like him?"

"Do I..." Maribel dropped her gaze to the ground, trailing a finger through the dirt and fallen leaves. Her stomach flip-flopped in a strange and not altogether unpleasant manner. "What does that have to do with anything?"

"I think you do."

There was no accusation in Corrine's tone, no underlying heat. In fact, she sounded oddly detached. Maribel didn't look up, focused on the ground, the small sticks and stones scattered around her.

"Does he like you back?" Corrine pressed quietly.

Part of Maribel desperately wanted to confide in her sister. After all, wasn't this what sisters were for? Hadn't Corrine always been her confidant, the one she came to with everything? Well, until they'd moved to the farm. Until Maribel had emotions she had to hide from Corrine, emotions that would have only upset her.

She's not really your sister.

Maribel crushed that thought as soon as she had it. Corrine was her sister, in every way that mattered.

"Talk to me," Corrine prodded. She settled down on the ground next to Maribel and put a hand on her knee. "Please."

Maribel cleared her throat and started arranging some tiny pebbles in a circle. "I think he does. But…" She hesitated. "It just feels like there's too much between us. Too many misunderstandings."

"You mean about me."

"That's part of it," Maribel admitted. "I didn't believe you were capable of something like that. I didn't trust him when he told me it was you."

The twig snapped in Corrine's grasp and Maribel pulled her attention away from her pebble circle. "Are you okay?"

Corrine's smile was strained, but she looked away before Maribel could analyze her expression further. Corrine grabbed her bag where she'd dropped it and pushed herself to her feet.

"Well, misunderstandings are a problem. If you like him, and he likes you, then you need to clear the air." She took a deep breath and let it out. "I'll try to lift the spell." She dropped the pieces of the twig and started to brush her hand off on her skirt. She stopped with her fingers above the velvety material, then noticed that it was already filthy from her earlier fall. She pressed her lips into a thin line and brushed her hand off.

"But if I'm going to do this for him, then I want him to do something for you," she continued. "He has to be honest with you about who he is and what he's done. I don't know if the rumors I heard were true, but I remember clearly enough him kidnapping me. If there's a chance that he took others without their permission—perhaps others who were too afraid to tell him they didn't want to go—then he needs to make that right."

"I don't understand?" Maribel stood to face her sister, the excitement swirling inside of her at the prospect of ending Daman's curse tempered by sudden confusion. "What do you want him to do?"

"Ask him about the changelings he's relocated, make him take you to them so you can see for yourself if they're happy. Then there won't be any secrets between you and you can see where this might go."

"I…suppose that makes sense." Maribel wrung her hands in front of her, glancing from her sister to the manor. "Let me go ahead and tell him you're coming."

She'd expected Corrine to have a ready retort, something about how Daman wouldn't need a warning if he was really the good man Maribel claimed he was. To her surprise, Corrine simply nodded.

"Go ahead."

"Well, I'll help you get there first. You can wait in the gard—in the kitchen."

Corrine didn't comment on her slip. Maribel didn't meet her eyes, the memory of the Rose of the Mist too strong. Why Maribel had wanted it. What had happened because of it.

What Corrine might do with it if she had it.

Maribel tried to squash that last thought, grinding it as viciously as though it were a beetle going after her precious garden, but the memory of it remained. *You were wrong about her,* a voice whispered. *She did cast that curse. What else has she learned from dear Mother Briar?*

"You go on ahead, I can make it the rest of the way myself."

Maribel's eyebrows shot into her hairline. "Really?"

"I walked all the way here, didn't I?" Corrine said. Her smile didn't quite reach her eyes.

"Yes you did." Maribel took Corrine's hand in hers, holding it to her chest. "I'm so proud of you."

Corrine gently but firmly extricated her hand from Maribel's grasp. "Yes. Well, you'd be surprised how much I've managed in your absence."

Something in Corrine's tone urged Maribel to examine her more closely. Corrine had always sounded tired, weary, and more often than not, a touch afraid. Now there was...a certain steel in her voice. Maribel wondered exactly how hard life had been for Corrine since she'd been gone. And what effect it may have had on her older sister.

How well do you really know her now?

Maribel shoved those thoughts away, near desperation clutching her chest until she could hardly breathe. It was too much, she didn't have the energy to think about that now. First she would clear the air between her sister and Daman. Then she would figure out what her sister's revelation meant for her.

CHAPTER 12

The knock at his door echoed in Daman's ears. Every muscle in his body went taut, leaving him standing in the center of his room, body vibrating like a tuning fork. The rage he'd given into, the primal need to destroy, ebbed, but did not immediately recede. Like a lingering lover, it trailed hands across his mind, plucking at chords and whispering promises of its return.

The doorknob turned.

Pain made itself known as the haze of fury took its obliviousness with it, adrenaline dying to a trickle and leaving him to suffer the delayed consequences of his temper. He had barely enough time to register that his hands were bleeding from several jagged cuts and everything in his room that could have been shattered had been.

Then the door swung open.

"Daman?"

Say something, you idiot! The voice screamed inside his head, but Daman had no words. He had screams, shouts, bellows of rage and ragged howls of pain, but no words. And even if he'd had the words, he didn't dare speak them, not yet. Not when they would drip with sibilance. A reminder of why Maribel should not be here.

She stepped inside despite his lack of a response. Calmly, she surveyed the room, blue eyes dancing over the carnage with neutral consideration. No judgment. Something inside of him loosened, sobbing with relief. She hadn't gone, hadn't fled. She was here. With him.

Finally she met his eyes. "I don't want to leave."

He couldn't move. His gaze wouldn't leave her, wouldn't wander away for even a second for fear she was a figment of his fevered imagination. Blood trickled down his hands, warm and wet. He clenched his jaw, waiting for her to notice. Maybe if he pictured the disgust on her face now, it wouldn't be so painful when he saw it.

"You're right," she continued, casting her gaze around the room as she spoke. She stepped to a painting barely clinging to the wall, trailed a hand over the shredded canvas. "I was using you. Caring for my sister was hard, doing her work was hard. Harder still was feeling guilty any time I started to feel good. After all, it would be cruel to rub my pleasure in her face."

She lifted the scrap of canvas. Daman held his breath as she saw the picture revealed with the tatters in place. It had been a gift by one of the more artistically gifted changelings he'd helped —a painting of him in his human form. She'd said he was the perfect subject, given his ability to remain completely and utterly still, regardless of what form he was in. She'd joked that she could have crafted a sculpture with that kind of time. Maribel gazed at it and part of him searched her face for some sign of wistfulness, the look of a woman seeing something she wanted more than what she had.

Maribel dropped the shred of canvas as if the painting held no charm for her. Daman's breath came back in a rush.

"As long as you forced me to be here, I could do whatever I wanted. And there was no guilt because it wasn't as if I'd had a choice." The corner of her mouth quirked up. "The fact that you don't exactly live in a hovel helps too," she admitted.

A joke? She's joking?

Daman raised a hand to his head, probing for injuries. Maybe not a dream. A hallucination? Had he struck his head at some point in his rampage?

"I don't know how much of what you said, you said to try and scare me away, and how much was sincere." She plucked at her dress, brushing away a bit of dirt. "Actually, I guess I'm not sure how much I know about you is really you, and how much of it is a result of the curse that was laid on you, being trapped in that form. I know you said you're equal parts beast and man, but you also said being stuck in this form had consequences for your temper, so—" She stopped, shook her head. Finally she met his eyes. "I want to find out."

"Find out what?"

He managed to choke the words out past the sudden tightness in his throat, sending a brief thanks to whatever gods were listening that there had been no 's' sounds for his forked tongue to trip over.

"I want to get to know the real you."

Daman flexed his hands, remembered the blood, and slowly forced himself to move to the ruins of the bedsheets. He pulled a large swath of the material from the floor and cleaned his hands as best he could.

"You mentioned... The cursse..." He closed his eyes and counted to ten. "How do you intend to get to know the real me when you admit yourself that the curse makes that impossible?"

Maribel held her breath. "My sister has promised she'll try to lift the spell."

Stone. Cold stone, frozen stone. Ice. Lake, an icy lake. A cold stone at the bottom of an icy lake, frozen over. Dacian winters. Cold, cold, cold.

Daman struggled to hold on to the imagery, thought of

anything and everything to combat the heat that tried to blaze to glorious fury inside of him. The temper was back, tempting, familiar. Hot.

No! I will not give in, not again. Not when she came back.

"Your...ssiss—" He stopped, swallowed, and started again. *Cold. Dacian cold.* "Your...sister...is here?"

Slowly, so slowly, Maribel nodded. "She is."

His chest was heaving and Daman realized he was breathing too hard. He closed his eyes, counted to ten. Then twenty. Then thirty. At three hundred and two, he opened his eyes. "She says she will lift the cursse?"

"Yes." Maribel's throat worked as she swallowed. "She says she will try."

Try. Cold, cold, cold, cold.

"I will...be down to greet her...in a short while."

The words snagged on his tongue, on his fangs itching to come down. He could hardly see through the blackness eating at his vision, the fog that threatened to swallow him as every ounce of willpower rushed to battle the temper raging inside its cage. He thought about trying to smile reassuringly, but quickly abandoned the idea. He didn't want to know what a smile from him would look like right now.

Maribel's eyes examined every line of his face. He waited for her to tell him she would leave if he hurt her sister, to say something, some threat, some promise, if he slipped up. Some reassertion that her sister meant everything to her, and Daman would never compete with that.

She didn't say anything. Instead, she nodded once and left, closing the door gently behind her.

A tremble took over Daman's body. It started in his hands, traveled up his arms. In a minute his entire body was seizing, rattling his brain.

The witch is here. The witch is here. The witch is here.

A loud cry tore from his throat and he whirled around,

lashing out with his tail and shattering the remains of a heavy oak table. Splinters flew everywhere like miniature shrapnel. Daman struggled to draw in air, scrambling for his mantra, trying to hold the words in his head long enough to meditate on them. He reached for the winter imagery again.

"Thisss isss not promisssing," a voice said from above him.

The mantra and imagery kept slipping away from him, dancing out of reach like will o' wisps over a bog. "I'll tear you in two," Daman choked, glaring at the *cuelebre* hanging from the wall sconce.

The little serpent tapped the unlit candle with its tail. "Jussst an obssservation."

"You saw the witch?"

The *cuelebre* nodded.

Blood pooled in his mouth as Daman's tongue flicked against one of his fangs. The taste of copper crackled over his nerves, ignited the part of him that yearned for battle, for vengeance. His voice dropped an octave. "And it is the ssame one?"

Another nod.

"I've wanted to get that witch here for sso long." Daman twisted the scrap of material in his hands, claws kneading in slow, stabbing motions. If he closed his eyes, he could pretend it was the witch's neck he held. "All the hourss I've sspent planning..." His eyes flew open and his muscles bunched as he tore the piece of bedsheet into smaller shreds. "But now... How I am to have my revenge when—"

"When you've fallen in love with her sssisssster?"

For a moment, Daman wished he had the ability to breathe fire as he could in his full wyvern form. "I never ssaid I wass in love."

"I can sssee. I have eyesss." The *cuelebre* tilted its head. "Did you think you were being sssubtle?"

Daman lashed the floor with his tail, surging forward with all the speed at his command. The *cuelebre* had apparently expected the attack. This time it managed to dart out of the way in time, glittering slender body shooting through the air a hair's breadth ahead of Daman's claws.

"Temper, temper," the *cuelebre* chided him. "You'll have to do better than that if you want the witch to lift her cursssse."

"Sshe will never lift the cursse!" Daman flexed his claws, forked tongue slithering out as he gauged the distance between him and the *cuelebre*.

"Do not underessstimate Maribel'sss influenccce. Ssshe believesss that you are sssuffering. Ssshe will do whatever isss in her power to help you."

Maribel. The sound of her name flowed over him like a cool breeze against heated skin. Tension flowed from his muscles and Daman gazed back at the door as if he could still see her standing there. *She came back.*

The thought echoed in his head, soft with wonderment. He would never have expected it, never have believed it. It was too good to be true.

He stiffened. Too good to be true. It *was* too good to be true.

"If the witch ssent her here, sshe could be lying, ssetting me up to ssee me ssuffer."

"You are already sssuffering. What sssensssse doesss it make to go through all of thisss in an attempt to increasssse your misssery?"

"Or sshe could be trying to win my favor, to ssucceed where the witch failed." Daman eyed the pile of threads that had once been part of the bedsheet. His claws still ached with the need to destroy something.

"If that isss her intention, the witch will cccertainly not help her. You know better than anyone that the witch would not help anyone elsssse attain that which ssshe desssiresss."

That was true.

Maybe she does care for you.

He carded a hand through his hair, dancing his claws along

his scalp. The press of sharp points helped distract him, cleared his head. He turned his attention to his surroundings.

Everything was destroyed. Furniture had been reduced to splinters, fabric rent to shreds. The windows were no more than glittering dust and jagged fragments. Chunks of ceramic and jade spoke of statues and vases that were no more. The room looked as if it had been devastated by a storm the likes of which the world had never seen. Maribel had seen it all, had known that the storm had been his temper, the wanton destruction the result of his inability to deal with that anger any other way.

And she wants to stay.

"If her motives are not what she claims," he said slowly, gaze dancing over the carnage around him, "then she is either very brave, or incredibly foolish."

"It ssseemsss to me that the two often go hand in hand."

Daman inclined his head in acknowledgement. He took a deep breath through his nose and let it out his mouth. "If the witch does not, or can not, lift the curse... Do you think Maribel will stay anyway?"

The *cuelebre* flew off the wall sconce and draped himself over Daman's shoulder. The show of trust was not lost on Daman.

"I think Maribel isss going to be watching both of you very closssely. It will be very important that you do not lossse your temper."

Daman barked out a laugh. "With the witch in my home? That will be a challenge."

The *cuelebre* slithered around so its head was directly in front of Daman's. "Yesss. It will be."

No false reassurances there. Daman flexed his hands, open, closed, open, closed. The flames of anger inside him were simmering down into embers and leaving a tingling tension in their wake. Nervousness fought with temper.

"If she is lying...and I fall for it..." He shook his head. "I do not think my humanity would ever recover."

"And if ssshe isss not lying, and you let her leave. Will your humanity sssurvive that?"

Daman fell silent. Every nerve ending in his body tingled with awareness as if seeking some sign of the witch, some sign of her encroaching magic. Corrine was here, she was coming. This was the day he'd dreamed of, and yet now that it was here, he dreaded it with an all consuming, sickening anticipation.

Maribel's presence changed things. She loved Corrine, believed Corrine loved her back. More importantly than that, he was starting to let himself believe Maribel might lo—might care about him as well. If he exacted his revenge on Corrine, if he used force to make the witch lift her curse, Maribel would never forgive him. Perhaps the most shocking part of it all was that Daman found himself conflicted about what he wanted more. An end to his curse…or Maribel.

"Maribel wantsss to get to know you. It isss why ssshe wantsss ssso badly to break your curssse. You have made it clear to her that what you are now isss not the truth of you. If you are kind to her sssisssster, it will go a long way to ssshowing both of you who you are, curssse or no curssse." The *cuelebre* slithered around Daman's neck like a living, writhing boa. "If it isss in her sssisssster's power to undo your curssse, Maribel isss your bessst chanccce of getting her to do ssso," it added.

"And if she still refuses, I have other options." *Unless you want to keep Maribel.*

"It isss often bessst to talk firssst and ussse violenccce later," the *cuelebre* agreed. "Often the reversse order isss not practical."

Daman leaned away from the *cuelebre*, barely resisting the urge to grab it by its tail and fling it away from him. It had been a long time since he'd had company—having company quite so close was…stifling.

"I sent away people I cared for, people I respected because I couldn't be sure I wouldn't hurt them," Daman said, almost to himself. "And now I'm going to try and keep my temper with the person I hate most in this world."

"It will be interesssting."

Daman snorted. Several long moments ticked by.

"I suppose putting it off won't do me any good," he said aloud, whether for himself or the *cuelebre*, he wasn't sure.

"No good," the *cuelebre* agreed.

Daman didn't move. "If the witch cannot, or will not, lift the curse, I might still have Maribel. If I keep my temper."

"A dissstinct posssssssibility." The *cuelebre* flew into the air, hovering like a ribbon tossed to the sky. "*If* you can keep your temper."

"All right then." Daman cleared his throat and rolled his neck, the popping tendons audible evidence of how much tension he carried there. After eyeing the destroyed room one last time, he sighed and headed for the treasure room. The enchanted wardrobe would supply him with something appropriate.

Like bespelled armor.

Entering the treasure room was akin to stepping into the past. For a moment, Daman froze in the doorway, his mind flying back to the day Maribel had arrived. If he fixed his gaze on the middle of the room, he could see her standing with her father, both of them forgetting the chest of riches immediately as they begged one last time for their freedom. Daman's heart ached and he rubbed his chest absentmindedly as if he could soothe the pain there. If he'd known then what he knew now…if he'd known then how deeply Maribel would affect him…

Focus! This is a very poor time to let your concentration waver.

Stiffening his spine, he glided to the wardrobe and flung open the doors. As always, the wardrobe knew what was needed. A row of armor met his assessing look, a neat assortment of metal, leather, and hide. Daman considered each one, finally deciding on a chestplate forged from delicate chainmail. The metal links were formed of braided metal, copper, gold, silver, and iron. The working was so fine, it moved and bent as easily and cleanly as cloth and would allow Daman protection without inhibiting any of the acrobatic movements his serpentine body was capable of. The mix of metals would also afford him the largest range of protections against various types of magic the witch may have at her disposal.

As he settled the chainmail shirt over his torso, he glanced at the second half of the row of armor. There were pieces there that would fit part of his lower body, complete the ensemble so it more closely resembled an attempt at clothing himself as opposed to dressing for battle. After all, the chainmail was so fine, it could have been mistaken for cloth from a distance. And it was attractive enough that he could pass it off to Maribel as wanting to look his best, an outward reflection of his good intentions.

But he didn't want to put on armor over his lower half. Not only did he not need the protection there—his scales provided more than enough natural armor—he also wanted to show the witch that he was not ashamed of what he was. He wanted her to lift the curse, yes, but that was only because he wanted to be returned to what he was, what he was supposed to be. There was nothing wrong with this form, nothing he had to hide.

Besides, let the witch look on what she's done. Let her remember.

"Sssubtle."

Daman twitched, startled by the sudden presence of the *cuelebre* on top of the wardrobe. The serpent was shaking its arrow-shaped head.

"You are dresssssssing for battle."

"I am dressing for company," Daman said evenly.

The *cuelebre* snorted. "You may fool yourssself, but you will fool no one elssse."

"Shall I go naked, then?" Daman asked testily.

"That could be interesssting asss well."

"Well, then perhaps you'd like to suggest something." Daman

slammed the doors to the wardrobe closed, rattling the furniture so it rocked under the *cuelebre*. "Go ahead, open the doors. It will reveal whatever style of clothing you think is appropriate."

The *cuelebre*'s tongue flicked out. "You're ssstalling."

He wanted to argue. Oh, gods, he wanted to argue.

Seconds ticked by, then minutes. Daman stared at the *cuelebre*, unable to look away, unable to let this moment end for fear of what the next moment would bring.

"I will be here," the *cuelebre* said quietly. "I will not leave."

Daman opened his mouth to make a snide remark about the desirability of the *cuelebre*'s company, but then he closed it. He nodded once, slowly, in acknowledgement.

With a deeper breath than he'd taken in a long time, Daman left the room. His chest tightened with every step closer he came to the foyer, his nerves winding tighter with every inch. He tried to focus on Maribel, tried to focus on his breathing, tried to focus on anything but the witch waiting for him, the witch who had destroyed his life with a single moment of unbridled fury.

Apparently, he wasn't the only one who hadn't been in a hurry for this meeting. He arrived in the main foyer as Maribel was leading her sister inside.

Corrine.

The witch stood beside Maribel dressed in a gown that would have been suited more to the royal court than any other home within a hundred miles. The green satin was trimmed with velvet and silk, the corset hugging her torso and flaring at her hips to give her a perfect hourglass shape. The sleeves ended in deep points that fell to mid thigh on her—a ridiculous impracticality for anyone who actually had to work for a living. Which Corrine didn't. Her face was carefully blank, brown eyes revealing nothing of her thoughts.

Daman's mind superimposed the past over the present. The ghost of Corrine flew into his arms like a wild arrow, brown hair so dark it was nearly black flying behind her like a flag. She'd hit his chest with the force of a gale wind, the blood on her arms smearing over his shirt as she sobbed, begging him to take her in.

"My father lost his fortune... He is so angry all the time... He beats me... I am a slave in my own home."

Her voice echoed around him. He blinked, skin tingling under his armor with the memory of Corrine's body in his arms, the scent of tears and blood filling the air. He could still remember the way she'd pressed her soft body against his human form, the way she'd snuggled against him as if she were some kind of animal scent-marking him, claiming him as her own. He had never been a man to take advantage of a woman in distress, and he'd been a perfect gentleman, comforting Corrine and giving her privacy to bathe and change. It was only after she'd stood before him dressed in clean clothes and having scrubbed the dried blood from her body that he'd realized the blood hadn't been hers.

"Daman?"

Daman startled, realizing that Maribel was speaking to him. There was concern in her eyes, the blue orbs shining with unspoken questions. He had a moment of warmth that she should care about the turmoil raging inside of him. He started to reassure her that he was fine, but then Maribel stepped forward and to the side, putting herself between him and Corrine.

His burgeoning smile died on his lips. Her concern was not for him. It was for the witch who stood silently behind her.

"Maribel, perhaps this was not a wise idea." Corrine took a step back, shoulders hunching as if anticipating a strike. "He does not want me here."

"No," Maribel said slowly, firmly. "No, it's all right. Isn't it, Daman?"

Oh, I want her here. Daman pushed away the thought and the vicious inclinations that accompanied it. He bared his teeth in what he hoped would pass for a smile.

"Of course, you are welcome here."

Daman forced himself to bow, keeping his eyes on his new guest. "Welcome to my home." He nearly choked on the last words, but if Maribel noticed, she didn't say anything. Instead, she beamed at him and then Corrine. Her expression for her sister said, *"See? I told you it would be all right."*

So optimistic.

"It's so kind of you to have me here after how terribly our meeting went last time," Corrine said haltingly, prompted by something in Maribel's face. Her eyes dropped to the floor as if she were having a hard time meeting his eyes. "Maribel has told me how kind you've been to her. It's clear that you...care for her. She's helped me realize that perhaps the last time we met... Maybe I overreacted."

Daman bit back the response that leapt to his lips, managing at the last minute to twist them into a brief nod of acceptance. The tension in his shoulders threatened to tear the muscles from his bones and leave him gasping in agony on the floor, but he swallowed it back, fought to keep it from his face under the weight of Maribel's watchful eyes. He was still struggling to hold himself together when Corrine continued.

"I'm going to try to undo what I did." She brushed at some dirt on her dress, caressing the soft fabric. "My magic isn't as strong as I'd like, and I'm still learning, but..." She squared her shoulders and faced him like a soldier preparing for battle. "I will try my best."

Try? Try? Daman held his breath, desperate to keep any words or sounds from escaping his mouth. *I cannot do this, I cannot do this, what in the name of the gods led me to believe I could do this?*

"Daman, I've been telling Corrine about how good you've been to me." Maribel took Corrine's arm in hers, linking them together, but her gaze stayed focused on Daman's face. "I've explained to her that no matter what happens, I'll be staying here. With you."

Daman's mouth fell open. For a moment, he was a fish out of

water, lips parting and closing helplessly as his brain tried to process what was happening. Maribel hid her mouth behind her hand, her eyes shining with amusement.

Finally, he managed to get a hold of himself. He was smiling, responding to Maribel's merriment with his own, feeling lighter than he had in a hundred years. The feeling was so new, so unexpected. He grabbed onto it, held on for dear life. He faced Corrine and his smile grew wider.

The witch looked as though she'd swallowed a bug. She wasn't glaring at him, or scowling, nothing so obvious as that, but her face had a distinct green tint to it that suggested she wasn't feeling quite as good as she had prior to Maribel's announcement. There was a tightness around her eyes that hadn't been there, a brittleness to her posture.

It was wonderful.

"It is my sincerest hope that tonight we can lay all misunderstandings to rest," Daman said graciously. He bowed easily, the tension having flown from his shoulders to leave his body supple and energized once again. "I would be very grateful if you could...undo the spell you laid on me the last time we met." He looked at Maribel. "But if you cannot, I will bear you no ill will. Your curse has inadvertently given me more than I could have ever hoped for."

He might have been laying it on too thick, but he doubted anyone could blame him. It wasn't as if Corrine didn't deserve it. Maribel's cheeks grew a most becoming shade of pink. Maribel deserved it too.

"I'll try," Corrine said, her voice sharp.

Maribel glanced at her and for a moment Daman thought she might say something. He found himself childishly eager to hear Maribel chastise the witch in the way her body language had chastised Daman when she'd put herself between him and Corrine. Corrine's stomach grumbled, breaking the silence.

"Oh, you must be hungry," Maribel exclaimed. The frown that

had been tugging at her mouth a second ago vanished as she put an arm on her sister's shoulder. "I'll fix you some food. Do you want to come with me to the kitchen?"

Corrine kept her eyes on Daman, brown orbs darkening to the color of frozen earth. "I'll stay here and look through my spellbook. I think Daman has waited long enough."

Daman studied Corrine, wary of the strange light in her eyes. There was something in those eyes, something reflected in her voice, that had the hairs on the back of his neck standing up.

"Daman?"

Maribel's voice held a hint of concern and it was enough to snap Daman out of his daze. He smiled at Maribel, though this time it didn't quite reach his eyes.

"Of course, of course." He swept an arm in front of him and addressed Corrine. "If you would come with me into the sitting room, I'm sure you would be more comfortable."

Was it his imagination, or did Corrine give his armor a deliberate once over?

"Thank you." Corrine hugged her sister, holding Daman's gaze over Maribel's shoulder as she did so. "I'm so happy for you."

That set off warning bells. Daman's tail slid back and forth, tension returning to his muscles with the enthusiasm of an old friend. The witch was being far too kind. It would be one thing for her to try and help him, to leave her sister here if that's what Maribel wished. But there was no way she was happy about it.

Daman's stomach rolled. If Maribel's smile grew any wider, it would split her face. She did everything short of clapping her hands as Daman escorted Corrine into the other room. When she discovered Corrine's true nature, it would crush her.

If *she discovers it.*

Daman remained standing as Corrine settled herself into a broad-backed armchair beside the hearth. There was no fire, the days had grown warm enough that the house held a comfortable amount of heat without it. Corrine took great care tucking her skirt about her, behaving as though she were about to have her portrait painted instead of preparing for spellwork. Part of Daman expected her to drop the act immediately, to whirl on him and tell him how despicable he was and how she would worsen her curse if he didn't send her sister home immediately. He wouldn't have been surprised if she tried to blackmail him, tried again to get him to give over his estate to her or else she would poison Maribel against him.

"I got the spell from here," Corrine said briskly, drawing a book out of her bag.

The cover of the book was heavy, some sort of thick hide, and too worn for Daman to make out the title. He uncoiled his lower half, rising to see if he could peer into the depths of the bag the book had come from. Corrine quickly closed it, stopping Daman from gleaning any clues to the rest of the bag's contents.

Suspicion tightened his nerves and Daman moved behind a chair, gripping the back of it to keep his claws busy. Corrine opened the book and scanned its contents, one finger steadily trailing down the parchment. Her brow furrowed in thought as she perused the pages, deftly turning page after page. Suddenly, she gripped the book tighter. The pulse in her throat sped up. Daman found himself gripping the back of the chair he stood behind, leaning forward as excitement flickered inside him as well. His tongue tasted the air in front of him as if he could scent what she'd found.

"What?" he demanded, unable to help himself. He winced at the furrows he'd torn in the chair's material, the stuffing peeking out in silent accusation of his destruction.

Suddenly, Corrine's face fell. "A dead end." She leaned back in her chair, letting the book fall closed in her lap with a depressing and final *thump*. "There are pages missing."

Pages... The wood frame of the chair cracked as Daman's grip closed. His claws burrowed into the wood—the only thing keeping them from the witch's neck. "What game are you playing?" His voice was hot and rough, a sound dragged over burning coals.

Corrine kept her gaze on the book, refusing to meet his eyes. "This book belonged to a goblin. A girl not far from my own age who was studying with Mother Briar."

Daman went still, even his breath coming to a dead stop. *Jeanne.*

Jeanne was a goblin changeling who'd had the misfortune to be left at the tender mercy of Mother Briar. Unlike the *sidhe*, goblins didn't give one whit for what happened to their children after they left them and took home chubby pink human babes in their stead. The old witch had abused the poor goblin child with no fear of consequences, treating Jeanne worse than a slave, worse than an animal. The injuries he'd found on the goblin still haunted Daman's nightmares.

"And you need to speak with this girl," he guessed, horror dawning inside of him, wrapping flame-tipped fingers around his lungs. "In order to lift the curse."

"Yes. But I don't know where to find her."

Pressure built in Daman's chest, his temper stirring his insides like a cauldron about to boil over. He hadn't realized until that moment that part of him had believed Maribel, had believed that Corrine would really lift her curse. The wilting feeling inside of him, the sour, twisting sensation unique to dying hope, fell into the flames of his temper like an offering.

"Do you think I'm sstupid?"

Corrine finally met his eyes, brown orbs perfectly calm. If the sibilance creeping into his voice concerned her, she didn't show it. "I'm sorry?"

Daman held on to the ruined chair, using it to hold himself in place as every fiber of his being raged at him to leap at the woman who continued to torture him even in the wake of the curse that had stolen his life. The wooden frame groaned, broken boards shattering further as he squeezed.

"Mother Briar ssent you here, didn't sshe? Sshe ssent you here to find out where Jeanne iss sso sshe can track her down and drag her back to the pit sshe kept her in."

"The pit... What are you talking about?" Corrine raised a hand and touched the amulet around her neck. Her fingernails clicked against the surface of the crystal and a warm pulse spread through the room. "Mother Briar is a kind old woman. Don't tell me you've fallen for the horrible things people say about witches?" Her voice was full of reproach, condescending and pitying at once. "You don't believe we're all evil—"

"I have sseen no evidencce to the contrary." Before Daman was even aware of his intentions to move, he found himself in front of Corrine's chair, the thick scales of his lower body pressed against the cushion between her legs, one hand on each side of the chair's back. "What did the witch promisse you in return for Jeanne'ss location?"

"Nothing!" Corrine squeaked. She pressed back into the chair, trying to get as far away from Daman as possible. "She doesn't even known I'm here! I came to get Maribel back, that's all."

Daman bared his fangs. Corrine's face drained of all color as she scrabbled to firm her grip on the amulet. He should have backed away, sought some sort of shield, but he was too angry. He leaned closer, flicking his tongue out to taste the air. *Fear.* "You are jusst like Mother Briar," he sneered. "Too lazy to do your own work, you need ssomeone to be your sslave. What'ss the matter, Corrine? Did my gold not buy you enough workerss?" He paused. "Or are they mean to you?" he guessed. He tilted his head, studying Corrine's face. "Iss there not enough gold in that trunk to blind people to the monsster you really are?"

For the first time since Corrine had arrived, a spark of the woman Daman had known showed in her eyes. Her skin tightened over her features and she pressed her mouth into a thin line. She glared at Daman and for a split second, he expected flames to shoot from her eyes. Her hand tightened on the amulet and another waved of magic rolled off of her. Something tickled at the back of Daman's mind, some sort of warning. Corrine was angry. She was obviously wielding magic. Why wasn't she striking out at him?

"You think you know me so well," she ground out, her voice barely above a whisper. "You're so *superior*. You go around saving changelings, rescuing them from the people their own parents left them with, so determined to see that they get a better life—so *sensitive* to their suffering." A muscle in her jaw twitched. "You were kind to me when I came here too, but then you found out I was only human. You have no time for *humans*, do you? Don't care as much for their suffering." Her nose wrinkled. "Except of course for *Maribel*."

Daman seethed at hearing Maribel's name on the witch's lips. "You were not suffering. You were a spoiled child who wanted to be surrounded with money and servants so you wouldn't have to work yourself."

"How would you know what I wanted?" Corrine bit out. "You stopped listening to me as soon as you found out I was human. You couldn't have cared less what I had to say."

"I didn't have to hear what you had to say, I saw it with my own eyes. I went to your father's farm after you came here, saw for myself what your life was like. I saw your room, heard your father calling to you through the door since he thought you were still there. He begged you to come out and have your supper. His love and concern for you were obvious."

"And you still don't hear me, won't *listen* to me." Corrine's breath hitched, her brown eyes glittering. "You never asked me why I wanted so badly to marry you, to stay here."

"I didn't need to ask you," Daman spit back. "You couldn't have made it more clear."

"You think I was desperate to marry a man I didn't love, who didn't love me, because I wanted *luxury*?" Corrine seethed. "That is what you thought of me? *Think* of me?"

"You used your sister's blood to fool me, lied to me about your circumstances to manipulate me, and then tried to seduce me," Daman shot back. "That tells me all I need to know."

"Of course it does." Corrine slammed a hand down on the spellbook, glaring at Daman with hot tears in her eyes. "I'm tired of your judgment, your insults. You can stay in that form for all I care, let your anger eat away the rest of your humanity." She sneered at him. "It's not like you're using it anyway. And when your temper finally consumes the rest of you, Maribel's blood will be on *your* hands!"

Daman roared, the last shreds of control he had snapping as he reared up, fangs bared. He raised one heavy, clawed hand into the air. The tears spilled down Corrine's cheeks as he brought his arm down, slashing at the center of her chest.

Something struck his arm a foot away from her body, halting his strike with bone-jarring suddenness. Pain jolted down his limb, rattling the bone as magic prickled over his nerves in a sensation like buzzing insects. Daman's lips parted as he gaped at Corrine. Magic. She'd used magic to form some sort of protective shield around herself. She'd *wanted* him to attack her, had been goading him all along. Which meant...

"Daman, *no!*"

Maribel's voice shattered the sudden silence in the room, pierced the heated fog surrounding Daman. Dishes crashed to the floor as Maribel dove forward, shoving Daman away from Corrine.

Daman didn't fight her, couldn't collect his wits enough to do more than fall away. The fury that had been so hot a moment ago had frozen to hard, painful slivers of ice in his veins.

Daman couldn't move. The coil of his lower body had become heavy stone, his arm where Maribel had shoved him away ached in a way that had nothing to do with physical pain. Maribel was staring at him, not with anger or horror...but with hurt. Tears shone in her eyes, melting them to pools of blue so deep he could have drowned in them.

Those eyes would haunt him for the rest of his life.

Every scale on his body grew heavier, the fangs in his mouth growing larger until even closing his mouth didn't erase the thought of them from his mind, the image he knew must have greeted Maribel when she'd walked into the room. He would have appeared as a monster in her eyes, a beast intent on killing one of the people she loved most in this world. His attention flicked between Maribel and Corrine. The bond between them was as palpable as the distance between Maribel and himself.

There was nothing he could say to salvage the situation. No accusation he could rally against the witch that wouldn't cement the picture of him as the aggressor, not when he'd been caught mid-attack and she was cowering behind a shield, sobbing like a child.

A thousand words fought to escape his lips, but they all died on his tongue under the weight of Maribel's tears, the over-whelming sense of disappointment, of...loss. A howl built in his chest, gaining volume and power as it rose. He had to get out, get away before that sound broke free.

He fled the room.

CHAPTER 13

"Shhh, it's okay."

Maribel stroked Corrine's hair over and over, though whether she was doing it to calm her sister or herself, she couldn't be sure. Her mind was a jumble of thoughts and emotions too fractured to be rational. Daman holding her in his arms, kissing her. Daman standing in his room amidst destruction he'd wrought. Daman baring fangs longer than some kitchen knives, wicked, curved claws slashing at a crying Corrine.

Daman looking at her as though his entire world had fallen apart.

"What was I thinking? Great Goddess, what was I thinking? Bringing you here…"

"You love him," Corrine said, her voice thick with tears. "You wanted to believe the best of him, to have faith in him. I don't begrudge you that." Her voice broke. "I'm sorry I've ruined everything for you."

"Oh, Corrine, you haven't ruined anything." Maribel held her closer, partly to reassure herself, and partly to keep her sister from seeing her face. Maribel didn't know what emotion her sister might find there. She didn't know what she was feeling herself. Or maybe she didn't want to know.

"But I did! I know you, Maribel. I know you love me, and I know you love him, and I know that you'll never let yourself truly be with him while you feel it's a betrayal to me." She took a ragged breath and a fresh wave of tears soaked Maribel's shoulder.

A betrayal. Is that what it would be to love him now? Maribel closed her eyes. Was that why she'd brought Corrine here? Why she'd ignored her better sense, ignored the voice inside her head that had told her in no uncertain terms that she'd be insane to bring her sister into the home of the man she'd cursed? Had she needed Daman to prove that he could forgive Corrine, that the two could coexist, before she gave her heart to the half-monster who'd won her without even trying?

Ha. Who am I kidding? He won me trying not to.

"Corrine, what happened? For a while it seemed..." *It seemed like I could have everyone I love in my life.* "It seemed like you two could get along."

Corrine pulled back and wiped at her eyes. "Oh, Maribel, he's never going to forgive me. He thinks I'm evil and nothing I say will change that."

Maribel pressed her lips together. Every word out of her sister's mouth showed Daman in a worse and worse light, but there had to be *something* that had tipped the scales. Daman had allowed Corrine into his home, had claimed he was willing to give her a chance. For a moment back there—

What? For a moment you thought it wasn't going to matter? Like he was going to throw up his hands and say he didn't care about the curse anymore as long as he could be with you?

The voice in her head was mocking, derisive. Maribel shut it out, clenching her teeth as she fought to concentrate. Something must have happened to destroy that careful balance between

Daman and Corrine, and if she could understand what that thing had been, then maybe… "What. Happened?" she asked again.

Corrine's eyes flicked over Maribel's face for a moment—an assessment. "I told him it wasn't my spell. It was Jeanne's, a goblin girl who used to live with Mother Briar. I don't know how to break the spell, so I need Jeanne's help." Her lower lip trembled. "Daman doesn't believe me. He thinks Mother Briar told me to say that so I could get him to tell me where Jeanne is."

"Jeanne is a changeling?" The word tasted strange in Maribel's mouth. It was a word that could apparently be applied to her. *My father is not my father. Corrine is not my sister. My mother...* She shoved those thoughts away, locked them behind a solid door in her mind and chained it closed, throwing away the key. She wasn't ready to think about that. She didn't know if she'd ever be able to think about that.

"Yes. Daman stole her away from Mother Briar."

"Against her will?"

Corrine shrugged. "I don't know. Daman claims that Mother Briar was mistreating Jeanne, but…" She shoved a hand through her hair. "It doesn't matter. Without Jeanne's help, I can't lift the spell." The chain holding the amulet around her neck clinked as she fingered the crystal. "I told him that and he got angry. So angry…"

"He has trouble controlling his temper." Maribel rubbed her hand over her lap, trying to warm her hands that suddenly felt as though she'd bathed them in ice water. "It's part of the curse."

Corrine stiffened. For a moment, Maribel would have sworn she was angry, her chest filling with a sharp inhale as if preparing to shout. Then Corrine sagged against her.

"You're mad at me too. You still want him."

Maribel gently extricated herself from Corrine, but kept a hold of her hands. It was true, she did care for Daman. She wasn't ready to write him off yet, not without hearing his side of the story. But Corrine was her sister— in every way that mattered.

Even if she wasn't blood... Maribel pressed her fingers to her temples, trying to calm the burgeoning headache forming there.

"Your curse has inadvertently given me more than I could have ever hoped for."

The memory of those words mocked her now, taunting her with a happiness that seemed like a poor joke. Had he meant those words when he'd said them? If he had, what on earth could have pushed him to the edge so quickly?

Corrine laughed, but there was no humor in the sound. "I came back thinking I was going to rescue you, and here you don't want to leave."

"Corrine—"

"No." Corrine stood up, brushing off her skirts, obviously avoiding eye contact. "No, you're happier here." She snorted. "I can't blame you. It must be nice to live in such luxury, especially after the hard life you had on the farm."

"Actually, I do the same work here that I did at home." Maribel stiffened, her tone sharpening in self-defense. "I still cook, and I still work outside in the garden." She didn't mention anything about how much easier it was here, now that she could work without interruptions, or about how Daman was always very appreciative and interested in her cooking.

Corrine opened her mouth then closed it again. Her brown eyes twitched from side to side, scanning Maribel's face. She tilted her head, looked Maribel up and down. There was a question in that gaze that needed an answer. Maribel shifted uncomfortably, feeling like livestock up for auction under that level of scrutiny. Finally Corrine rubbed the bridge of her nose.

"I want to help him, Maribel. But if I'm going to break that spell, you need to convince him to tell me where Jeanne is. I'll go to her myself and ask for the counterspell. Maybe he'll trust you enough to tell you."

Maribel's spirit rose and she leaned closer to Corrine. "You would still help him?"

"Of course I would." Corrine offered her a half smile. "I'm really not all bad."

"Oh, Corrine." Maribel drew her into a hug, holding her tight for a moment as gentle waves of guilt lapped against her. "I know you're not bad."

"How?"

Corrine's voice was small, muffled against Maribel's shoulder. The vulnerability in that voice stabbed at Maribel and she tightened her hold.

"Because you're my sister. Because you're terrified of going anywhere by yourself, or exerting yourself, but you did both because you were worried about me. Because you can see feelings in me that I've only barely acknowledged, and you're trying to help me to be happy even if…"

Even if the man I care for hates you, tried to hurt you. Even if being with him means I'll be leaving you behind.

At some point the hug changed, became more about Corrine comforting her than the reverse.

"I love you, Maribel."

"I love you too."

They stayed like that for a long minute, locked together, each one offering comfort and receiving it in return. It was a reflection of how things used to be when they were young, if they were frightened, or even just sad. It was comforting in a way Maribel hadn't expected, but had needed nonetheless.

Finally, Maribel pulled back. Corrine dropped her gaze, not meeting Maribel's eyes.

"I can't help him if he won't tell me where Jeanne is," she said, her voice thick with some emotion Maribel couldn't quite identify. "Get him to tell you where she is, and I'll do everything in my power to undo the damage I did." Her voice grew hoarse and she cleared her throat. "I'm sure he'll trust you enough to tell you."

"Corrine, are you all right?" Maribel touched Corrine's arm, flinching when her sister jerked away.

"I'm fine." Corrine half-shrugged. "Only I'm...so tired. Would it be all right... Is there a room where I could rest before going home?"

"Oh, Corrine, I'm so sorry. I've been going on and on about me, about my problems, and here you're probably ready to collapse."

Nice. Ask her to help the man who tried to cut her to ribbons and completely ignore the fact that she travelled all the way here by herself.

"Of course I can show you to a room where you can rest. Follow me."

They stood and Corrine paused, gaze fixed on the mess where Maribel had dropped the dinner tray. Chunks of chicken and thick slices of mushroom lay in a nest of broken crockery, all of it spattered with thick white sauce. The scent of tender shallots and warm Marsala wine perfumed the air, still enough to tempt Maribel's senses despite the dinner's ruined state.

"Chicken Marsala." Corrine inhaled deeply and her stomach growled. "Now that is a sad sight."

"I have more," Maribel offered. "The sauce is keeping warm over the fire, and it doesn't take long to cut up a bit more chicken."

Corrine shuffled over to the mess and started to kneel. Maribel's lips parted in shock as she plucked pieces of broken plate from the ground.

"Let me help you clean up this mess," Corrine said, still eyeing the food as though she wanted to cry.

"I..." Maribel cut herself off from the automatic response that wanted to assure Corrine that she didn't need to do that, that Maribel could clean it up. She squared her shoulders. If Corrine wanted to help, that was good—admirable. "Thank you," Maribel told her seriously, kneeling beside her to help.

Corrine nodded, but didn't speak. They worked together for a while, gathering what they could and piling it onto the silver tray. There was only so much good the napkins could do them, so they had to leave somewhat of a mess behind, but Maribel assured Corrine that it would be taken care of. They were both silent for several minutes as Maribel led Corrine to a room, careful to choose one as far from Daman's quarters as she could.

Finally the silence started to feel uncomfortable. Maribel glanced at Corrine and noticed the amulet around her neck. She recalled the scene she'd interrupted between Corrine and Daman, remembered seeing her sister holding the amulet in her fist.

"That amulet is new, isn't it?" she asked.

Corrine automatically raised a hand to touch the item in question. She looked down at the gold-encased crystal. "Yes. Mother Briar helped me make it. She took some of my blood and infused it with her own magic, then used it to make this crystal." She tapped a fingernail on the slick surface of the glittering red stone. "It gives me power to fuel my spells."

"It sounds like you've been making a lot of progress." Her voice came out higher than usual, exited. Maribel winced as she realized how she must sound. "I meant, it sounds like you're becoming the powerful witch you always wanted to be," she amended quickly. "I wasn't trying to—"

"It's all right," Corrine interrupted. A strained smile tugged at her lips. "I know what you meant." She dropped the amulet and ran her hands down the silky surface of her skirt. "I don't want to get your hopes up though. This amulet is Mother Briar's magic, not mine. It'll need recharged soon."

"Still, the spell I saw you using seemed impressive." Maribel tried to keep her voice encouraging even as Corrine's words pricked at her high expectations for her sister's ability to end Daman's curse.

"A basic shield spell." Corrine snorted. "Child's play for any witch with even a speck of talent."

She obviously didn't want to speak of her magic, so Maribel gave up. They journeyed the rest of the way to the room in silence. Finally Maribel stopped at a door.

"You can use this room. I'll come in and help get you settled—"

"This isn't my first time here, Maribel, remember?"

Maribel's teeth clacked as she shut her mouth abruptly. "Oh, right."

Tension crept between them, a sudden awkwardness that hadn't been there a moment ago. Corrine cleared her throat.

"I'm tired, so I'm going to go lie down."

"Okay," Maribel said, perhaps too quickly. "I'll bring you up some food."

Corrine opened the door and stepped into the room. She turned to close the door, but then paused. "Maribel?"

"Yes?"

"I'm glad you're happy. Just… Try to get him to tell you where Jeanne is. I can't help him if he won't trust you enough to tell you."

There was something about the way she said that last part that sounded out of place, a hesitation to her voice like there was more she wasn't saying. Was Corrine trying to tell her something?

Mother Briar's words came back to her, the story of how trust was the key to breaking Daman's curse. Was this part of that? Was this the proof of his trust? Maribel searched Corrine's face for some sign, some clue. "All right. I'll try my best."

Corrine nodded, but there was that same hesitation in her body language, the tension in her shoulders and arms screaming at Maribel that there was more she wanted to say. Before she could push, Corrine closed the door gently, but firmly.

Maribel hovered in the hallway, her mind tearing her in a thousand different directions at once. Should she stay and press Corrine for more information? Was she making a mistake keeping her here? Would Daman trust her with Jeanne's location? Would he let Corrine leave unmolested if she couldn't lift his curse?

At some point, she must have started walking, because suddenly Maribel found herself standing in front of the door to Daman's room. She stopped and listened, holding her breath as she strained to hear any evidence that Daman was lost to his temper again. It wasn't until several long moments dragged by in complete silence that Maribel realized she'd expected to hear rending cloth, shattering glass and ceramic, splintering wood.

Perhaps he's destroyed it all already, she wondered, remembering the state of his room earlier.

"Daman?" she ventured carefully. She knocked on the door, then pressed her ear to the heavy, polished wood. "Daman, are you in there?"

There was no answer, but she heard something. The heavy slide of scales against stone and something else, something softer. It was familiar, but she couldn't quite place it. She had her answer, though. Daman was in there and he was moving. She tried to picture him and what he might be doing inside and an image popped into her head of the carnage she'd witnessed the last time she'd been in that room.

Suddenly she questioned the wisdom of standing there with her head pressed to the door. She didn't believe Daman would ever willingly hurt her—even seeing what he'd tried to do to Corrine didn't change that. Still, if he lashed out in a fit of temper, not knowing how close she was to the door... She backed away a few steps.

"Daman, may I come in?"

There was a burst of movement, something scraping the stone, something different than the now familiar slide of scales, but still a sound she knew but couldn't place.

"Oh, this is ridiculous," Maribel muttered. She grabbed the door handle. "I'm coming in." Without waiting for an answer, she turned the handle and shoved the solid door open, well-oiled hinges not making a sound.

The room was spotless.

Well, not spotless. There was still some dust on the floor, some jagged glass fragments sticking out of the window frames. And the mattress still bore deep gouges bulging with stuffing. But the broken vases and statues, the shattered wooden furniture, and the scraps of ruined blankets were all gone.

Daman stood in the corner. His hair stuck up at odd angles as though he'd been tugging on it, some of the pale strands coated in the dust dancing merrily through the air. Maribel's lips parted as she noticed he was holding a dustpan and a brush. The sound she'd heard, the one she'd known but couldn't place. It had been the sound of a broom and dustpan.

She closed her mouth, wrinkling her nose at the sensation of dust coating the tip of her tongue. Waving her hand in front of her face to disperse the dust provided a distraction for her mind as her eyes continued an unabashed examination of the *naga*.

He was no longer wearing the glittering mail shirt that he'd worn to greet Corrine—or anything else for that matter. Rather he stood before her bare—in more ways than one. There was a raw look in his silver eyes, a slight hunch to his shoulders. He stood there like a man expecting bad news. The pain she saw in his eyes stole her breath.

She must have stared at him longer than she thought because he finally gave in and spoke first.

"You came back." His voice was low, hoarse with dust, emotion, or both. Slowly, he leaned down to place the brush and dustpan on the floor, his serpentine body more graceful than any biped could ever hope to be. "You came back...again."

"You cleaned up." *Brilliant, Maribel, lovely opening.*

Daman's eyes didn't waver from her face, as if he were afraid if he looked away she would vanish. "I had to believe you would come back. I wanted to show you..." He started to gesture at the room, stopped. "I wanted… I don't know what I wanted." Frustration pinched his mouth and he shoved a hand through his hair. "I didn't want you to see me like you did last time." He gestured around the room, the movement jerky, almost angry. "Sitting in ruins like some sort of barbarian."

It was strange to be standing there talking about the room's state of cleanliness when they were both thinking about Corrine, and what had happened in the sitting room. It wasn't lost on Maribel that whether Daman realized it or not, what he was doing by cleaning his room was trying to show Maribel that he was in control. She knew a little something about organizing the world around her when the world inside of her was…a bit conflicted.

"Do you want to talk about what happened back there?" She kept her voice calm, nonjudgmental. Open.

Daman's face tightened, but to his credit, he didn't look away. "Are you offering me a choice?"

"I am. We don't have to talk about it. I know you well enough to know you met with my sister with the best of intentions." She lifted one shoulder in a shrug. "And it's not as if you haven't told me from the beginning that you…struggle…to control your temper."

Something in Daman's eyes sharpened suddenly and he leaned toward her ever so slightly. There was a scrutiny in his expression that had every nerve in Maribel's body alive and buzzing with awareness.

"You know your sister goaded me," he said slowly, his voice low with something akin to awe. "You… You are not convinced she was the victim she played so convincingly."

Maribel snapped her mouth closed. Heat rushed to her head and her hands fluttered around her, helpless to do anything with the nervous energy suddenly sizzling along her skin. *Deny it!* a voice screamed inside her. *She is your sister!*

"Perhaps we don't have to talk about it," she managed meekly.

The intensity remained in Daman's eyes as he slid toward her, his posture improving as if a weight had been lifted from him. The black slit that bisected his silver irises grew wider, and Maribel could suddenly see her face reflected in his gaze. She looked…mesmerized.

"You still want to stay with me."

Maribel's throat went dry. He was so close. The heat from his body kissed her skin and she could already imagine the weight of his scales pressing against her legs, could practically feel his arms sliding around her waist. She leaned closer to him.

"Yes."

There was something she was supposed to tell him, ask him. Or something she should be doing. Whatever it was, it was lost when his mouth closed over hers.

He tasted exactly as she remembered, hot with a trace of the flavors she'd used in her last meal. Sweet Marsala wine. She moaned and deepened the kiss, parting her lips in invitation. Daman's arms tightened around her, dragged her against his chest.

She inhaled sharply at the first touch of his forked tongue against her own, the sensation strange and new. Tension sprang to life in Daman's arms and he started to pull back, arms stiffening as if to push her away. A small sound of protest escaped Maribel's throat and she threw her arms around his neck and hung on.

Daman stilled, hesitating, then a deep chuckle reverberated in his chest. Maribel swallowed the sound, pleased when he continued the kiss. Tentatively, she drew her tongue over his, playing with the different points. Daman's breath quickened, became more ragged.

He pulled away with a gasp. His mouth moved, but no words came out. The black slits of his eyes had thinned, nearly vanished. The sight tightened things low in Maribel's body and for a long minute she could do nothing more than stare into those eyes.

"You…" Daman started. His voice was hoarse and he had to swallow before continuing. "You understand now that my curse has nothing to do with love or trust. Your…feelings for me will change nothing. Your sister will not—or cannot—lift the curse. I am now as I will always be."

"I don't care," Maribel said fiercely. She stroked one hand through his hair, laughing at the dust that rose into the air. "I'm not going anywhere. You're stuck with me."

Daman leaned closer, laid a gentle kiss on her lips. "A most pleasing situation."

Warmth blossomed in Maribel's chest as his lips slid from her mouth across her jaw in a trail of gentle kisses. Suddenly she remembered what it was she'd come to ask him.

"I don't care what form you have," she managed, closing her eyes as he laid a particularly hot kiss against the pulse at her throat. "But you should know you may still have a choice."

Daman went still in her arms, that strange, alien stillness that no human could attain. "What?"

"My…my sister says she may still be able to lift the curse." Maribel pulled back so she could think. "She just needs a little help."

The air changed, cooling between them even as he still held her in his arms, only inches away from his chest. Something snagged at her dress and some distant point of Maribel's mind registered the fact that his claws were dancing at the small of her back, sharp tips catching the material of her bodice.

"Does she now?" Daman took a deep, slow breath. "And would this help need to come in the form of a goblin girl?"

His scales shone in the light streaming through the shattered windows, illuminating his heaving shoulders and the tip of his twitching tail. His eyes gleamed more than human eyes ever could, the black slit down the middle emphasized by the brilliance of the silver. His tongue flicked out from between his lips.

Was he doing that on purpose as he had before, intending to intimidate her, drive her away?

A wave of unease washed through Maribel's stomach, but she pushed it back. "She doesn't have to come back here, I just need to speak with her. Won't you trust me to let me do that?"

"Oh, so now it is a matter of whether or not I trust you?" Daman pulled away, his face closing down until he wore the same indifferent mask he'd worn so often when they'd first met. "Let me guess, your dear sister has told you that if I trust you, I will give you Jeanne's location."

Maribel bristled at his tone. "I told you once that I didn't care what form you're in. I still don't."

Daman's jaw twitched, but he nodded. "I believe you."

"But it's also clear to me that whether or not I care…you care. I have to wonder if you'll ever be really okay with yourself if this curse isn't broken. If you'll ever be able to…let me close to you." A blush tickled her cheeks, tried to distract her from what she was trying to say, but Maribel stubbornly ignored it.

Daman averted his eyes, peering out the broken windows. Shadows danced through his eyes, over his face. The sun was setting and for a moment that dying light was the only warmth on Daman's features.

"I do trust you," he said finally. There was a tiredness around his eyes when he faced her again, an exhaustion in the way his shoulders sagged. "But even if Corrine is being truthful, and she wants to find Jeanne for no other reason than to ask for her help, I could never betray Jeanne by revealing her location. I swore to her the day I pulled her out of Mother Briar's grasping clutches that she would be safe, that no one would ever find her. Not even to save my own sanity could I betray her trust." His gaze grew unfocused, as if he wasn't seeing anything now before him. "That trust was not easily given. It is far too precious to break."

Maribel studied him carefully, her heart softening. "It sounds like she meant a great deal to you."

"They all do," Daman said simply. "So many changelings are left by their parents. There are all kinds of reasons. The *sidhe* do it to keep their bloodlines strong, to bring in fresh blood. The goblins and trolls often do it because they find human babes more appealing than their own kin. And then there are others who do it out of boredom, or to chase some random prophecy or another. Whatever the reason, it is seldom that they do their research before leaving their child. They assume that humans will care for the creature they think is their own, and they leave it at that."

His eyes sharpened and he once again focused on Maribel, grim determination etched in the lines of his face. "But that is not always the case. Mother Briar knew in a moment that the child screaming in the cradle was not hers. She kept her anyway—probably because there is more work to be gotten from a goblin girl than a human child. But the way she treated Jeanne..." He shook his head, as if the end to that sentence was too horrible to vocalize.

It wasn't until that moment that Maribel realized what was truly driving Daman mad. "Daman, what have you done since you stopped rescuing changelings?"

"What have I done?" His tail slashed across the floor, flinging up a fresh cloud of dust. "I have done nothing. I am far from my homeland and there are very few creatures who are familiar with my kind around here. To the changelings of this land, I am a monster, something to terrify, not comfort. They are already abused, taught that the world is a hateful, violent place. They do not trust easily, and this form makes it difficult to even approach them, let alone gain their trust enough to convince them to come with me, to let me help them."

"Oh, Daman, you can't just turn off that kind of passion, that kind of dedication." Maribel took his face in her hands, cupping his jaw in her palms. He vibrated in her grip, silver eyes shining with some sort of inner light. She smiled ruefully at him. "No wonder you feel like you're going insane."

"*Nagas* do not change their purpose once they have found it," Daman whispered, his voice a bitter mix of longing and despair. "I cannot simply take up a new mission."

"Do all *nagas* work alone?"

Daman frowned, his handsome face twisting with the expression as he focused on her eyes. "What do you mean?"

"Your problem is that you cannot approach the changelings because you are physically frightening. You need them to know you mean them no harm, you need them to know you before they see you." She raised her eyebrows. "You need an introduction."

She could see the moment he realized what she was suggesting.

"You... You want to help me." His brow furrowed, eyes going hazy as his mind turned the idea over. "So...I would find the changelings, but you would approach them first. You would get to know them—"

"And after I've earned their trust, I would tell them I know someone who could help them," Maribel finished. "I would introduce you in a controlled way, after preparing them."

Daman dropped his head, no longer meeting her eyes. His entire body trembled, a violent shaking that had Maribel's heart leaping into her throat.

"Oh, Goddess, did I say something wrong?" She tightened her grip on his face, tried to make him look at her. He resisted her efforts, shaking his head, and her heart pounded ferociously in her chest. "Daman, please, tell—"

A strangled cry tore from somewhere deep in Daman's chest. The next thing Maribel knew, she was being crushed against his chest, his mouth covering hers in a possessive, searing kiss.

CHAPTER 14

Daman's head spun under the wave of heat that flowed from where his mouth was pressed to Maribel's, melting down his body to pool below his waist. She tasted as sweet as he remembered, her lips the same velvety texture that haunted his dreams. Her words echoed in his ears, dragging hope kicking and screaming from the depths of his body.

She wanted to stay, no matter what his physical form, she wanted to stay—she wanted him. To be offered a chance to get his life back, the purpose he lived for, he needed to keep him sane, on top of that was...

A surge of passion washed over him and he wrapped his arms tighter around her waist, careful not to drag his claws over her body as he held her like a lifeline. She'd done herself in now—he'd never let her go.

Maribel moaned into his mouth, her sharp intake of breath stoking the flames inside of him. It took more effort than it should have to keep from deepening the kiss. His fangs retracted against the roof of his mouth, but there was still a good chance Maribel could cut herself if the kiss went too far. Adrenaline was adrenaline, and he had very little practice with passionate kissing in this form.

This was a dream. It had to be a dream. Somewhere in reality, Maribel was running as fast as she could away from him, her arm around her two-faced sister. She'd come in at such a horrible moment, caught him at his worst, towering over her sister with what must have been a demonic expression on his face, fangs bared. She wouldn't have stayed. She wouldn't have come to him when her sister was working so hard to poison her against him.

Maribel pressed her lower body against his, her hips sliding against his scales. A growl trickled unbidden from his throat, his body rolling in an undulating motion against her. He swallowed the sharp gasp that fell from her lips, the taste of her desire sending a fresh wave of liquid heat through his veins. His head swam as a ferocious urge to drag her to the ground tightened his muscles, demanded that he take what she offered so willingly.

Daman broke the kiss with a sharp inhalation of breath, the last scrap of sanity he'd managed to retain warning him that he was letting things go too far.

Stop now. Don't throw it all away.

Maribel's head fell back, exposing the long, pale line of her throat. Daman's honorable intentions to put some distance between them melted away, the light scent of vanilla wafting up from her delicate flesh beckoning him closer, drawing him in to taste that silken flesh.

Memories overwhelmed him, reminding him of days spent in the garden, nights spent hovering in the kitchen, watching Maribel coax untold delights from the simplest of ingredients. Even now he could see the pleasure on her face, the slight quirk at the corner of her mouth as she swatted him away from tasting the meal before it was finished. Those were the nights he couldn't sleep, kept awake by thoughts of what he couldn't have, of the day she would leave and never return. The day he would scare her away for good.

"I'm not going anywhere."

He groaned in surrender as he dropped his mouth to her silky flesh, dragging hot kisses against her skin, tasting the scent of the garden that always clung to her.

Maribel's hands slid over his shoulders, trailing along the thick ridges there. Despite the half-crazed desire pounding a throbbing beat against his skull, Daman froze. Maribel's fingers danced over his scales, stroked the heavy silver flesh that was more like armor than skin. The urge to pull away seized him and it took every ounce of his self-control to remain where he was.

"The only one who has a problem with your form is you."

He would never convince changelings not to be afraid of him if he couldn't be comfortable with himself. Maribel cared for him, had no fear of this form. He would not get a more welcoming reception, so perhaps it was best to start here.

He concentrated on breathing through his nerves, holding still as Maribel's fingers slid into his hair and combed through the short strands. His heart slammed against his ribcage with every beat, his nerves taut as he let her explore as she would, waited for her reaction. She'd already kissed him, had been sprawled over his body, but she'd never touched his scales this way. It would make it harder to ignore what he was, harder to imagine he was human.

She lifted her head and gazed at him, her eyes cloudy with desire and a lazy smile on her lips. One hand slid from his hair and she ran a fingertip lightly over the heavily scaled ridge over his eye, following the curve around to his cheekbone. Bit by bit, tension eased from his body as she touched him, caressing the parts of him that should have scared her away.

A heavy, languid feeling wove through his muscles, making his body pliable. He didn't even realize his tail was moving until the thick coil had risen behind Maribel, pressing against her and holding her to him.

She pulled his head closer for another kiss and Daman surrendered, releasing the last of his worries, his insecurities. His mind was fracturing, breaking apart and rebuilding into something better, stronger. He didn't have the concentration to worry anymore, not when there was so much else that required his...attention.

Maribel traced her tongue over his lips and he parted them willingly, letting her dart inside his mouth to explore as she would. He held as still as the desire coursing through him would allow, willing her to be careful, but not warning her away. Her tongue found his fangs, and Maribel slowed the kiss, carefully avoiding the sharp points as she continued to explore with small licks and playful nips.

By the time she pulled away, Daman's head was spinning, a heated mess of pleasure and desire. He stared down at the willing woman in his arms, hungry for more of her, tormented by thoughts of her pale, naked body spread out before him. Never in his life had he wanted a woman so badly.

Her fingers trailed down his chest, not stopping at his waist. A half-choke escaped his mouth and he grabbed her wrists, closing his eyes as if not seeing her would give him back some semblance of control.

"Maribel," he rasped.

Maribel went still and he opened his eyes to see a deep blush staining her cheeks. She met his eyes, but the strain in her neck betrayed how hard she had to try to keep from looking away.

"Don't you want—"

Daman nearly swallowed his tongue, the huskiness in her voice very nearly too much for his increasingly fragile self-control. "Yes," he said hoarsely, not strong enough to let her finish that sentence. He swallowed hard. "But you deserve more than... I can't ask you to..." Words abandoned him as quickly as his sanity and all he could do was look down at his draconic half.

Understanding dawned in Maribel's sapphire blue eyes. "It's okay," she said softly.

"No. It's not. I can't..."

The color in Maribel's face deepened to a near-purple hue. "Can't?"

An answering heat started at Daman's neck and consumed the flesh between it and his hairline like wildfire. "Not like that," he mumbled. "I can, but I..." He cleared his throat, consciously pulling his tail away from the small of her back, forcing himself to withdraw his arms from her waist. "I couldn't ask you to—"

Maribel frowned at his retreat, but didn't move to hold onto him. Her hands slid away from his body as he pulled back and she wrapped her arms around herself as if she were suddenly cold.

"Corrine says that without Jeanne's help, she can't lift the curse."

Daman tensed, blinking through the haze that clouded his mind in the wake of Maribel's kiss. "So you said," he said carefully. Unease trailed sharp claws down his back. Hadn't they already discussed this?

Maribel kept her eyes on the floor for several long moments. "You won't tell her where Jeanne is. And you won't go see Jeanne, ask her for the rest of the spell yourself?"

Every nerve in Daman's body tightened, one by one, slowing the maddening flow of desire through his veins. "It would be too risky. I never see the changelings again after I've found them new homes. There is too great a risk that the ones who abused them might follow me and I would never lead such danger into their lives."

"Then you'll be in this form forever," Maribel said, almost too quietly for him to hear.

The tightening of his nerves increased, causing a sickening sensation in Daman's stomach. He forced himself to keep looking at Maribel, scanning her face for some sign of where her thoughts were, what her purpose was for this line of conversation. A voice in his head was screaming at him to give her whatever she wanted, do or say anything to get her back into his arms. A voice from lower in his body bellowed at him for ever letting her out of his arms to begin with.

"Yes." He steeled himself against the shriveling hope being strangled inside of him. He could not betray Jeanne's trust. Not for any reason.

Maribel raised her eyes to his and stepped closer until a deep breath would have had them touching. "Then that bares the question, will you keep yourself from me forever?"

"I—What?"

Maribel held his gaze as she touched his chest, slowly trailed her hand down. Daman's skin sizzled with an anticipatory buzz and his throat went dry.

"Your scales don't bother me," Maribel said firmly, sliding her hand farther down until it brushed his ribs. "Your tail doesn't bother me." Her fingers danced over his stomach, trailing the line of scales that led farther, farther down. "Your teeth and claws don't bother me." She stopped, holding his gaze, her hands closer than she knew to the point of no return. "If this is to be who you are, then this is who I want to be with."

Molten heat flowed up Daman's body, melting his veins until the fire from his blood spilled through the rest of him. He couldn't think, could barely see.

"Maribel," he choked.

She stopped then, tilted her head. Words failed him as she slowly raised her hand to lift her hair off of her neck, pivoted slowly until her back was to him.

"Help me?"

Daman stared dumbly at the fastenings of her dress. Laces and buttons mocked him, suddenly requiring great feats of intellectual and physical skill that were far beyond his mortal brain. His hands moved of their own accord, his body not sharing any of his brain's doubts. Horrified, he saw himself drag a claw down the laces, slicing them one by one. His shame was mitigated by the intense appreciation of every inch of skin bared by his heavy-handed tactics.

"I owe you a new gown," he managed, his voice rough, barely intelligible.

"You gave me this one," Maribel answered in a voice almost musical with amusement.

He didn't bother trying to come up with a response, his breath quickly leaving him as the material finally released, parting to reveal smooth, creamy skin. The breath left his body as the gown fell away like flower petals opening to reveal a gorgeous bloom. The soft swells of flesh beckoned to him, called to him to drag his mouth and hands over every hill and valley, to worship the perfection that was Maribel's feminine form.

Maribel turned around, her pink cheeks the only crack in her confident façade. Her gaze faltered and fell as if her bravado had suddenly abandoned her.

Daman surged forward, outraged that she could be anything but gloriously arrogant of the body she'd bared so willingly for him. One arm locked around her waist, dragging her naked body against him, the other rose to cup the back of her head, holding her still so he could ravage her mouth. He didn't know if he imagined it or not, but Maribel tasted different now, warmer, more exotic. He followed that flavor into her mouth, stroking his tongue along hers, fighting to get closer, deeper, wanting to meld their bodies together until it was impossible to tell where one ended and the other began.

He shifted the hand holding the back of her head, carding it through the silky brown waves as he slid it down her body. Her skin caressed his palms, so supple, so different from the harder planes of his own body, mottled as it was with scales. Warm curves melted into his hand as if yearning for his touch, every sound falling from her lips encouraging him to explore further, touch more.

Maribel caught her breath in a sharp gasp as he cupped the swell of her breast, claws pressing ever so lightly against her skin. The sound drove a sharp ache of want deep inside him and he muffled a groan against her mouth as he put just enough space between them to let him lift her breast in his palm. Maribel gasped, breaking the kiss as her head fell back. A whimper escaped on a sharp inhale as he flicked his thumb over the hardening bud of her nipple. Her hands groped against his shoulders then slid up and clutched at his hair, anchoring herself to him.

The movement lifted her breasts and Daman licked the line of her jaw approvingly as he slid his other hand around to cup her other breast. He pushed his tail farther out behind him, lowering his torso in a swift, limber motion no bipedal creature could manage. Maribel gazed down at him with heavy-lidded eyes, her breath coming in heavy pants, doing wonderful, sinful things to her breasts. Daman kept his eyes on hers as he closed his mouth around one succulent nipple.

Maribel cried out, a delicious, passion-rich sound that urged Daman to lave at her nipple, nipping gently at the puckered flesh then soothing it with his tongue. There was a split second of hesitation as his forked tongue caught his attention, the moment the two points were on either side of her nipple, framing it and mocking him at the same time.

He glanced up at Maribel, searching her face for some sign of repulsion. Maribel held his gaze as she pressed her breast more firmly against him, fire sparking her blue eyes to flame. Hot satisfaction rose inside Daman and he renewed his efforts, cupping her breasts and holding them to receive his equal attention.

Her skin tasted like the air on the first day of spring, fresh and sharp, holding a small bite of winter. An odd thought skittered across his brain, the impression that she had to be some type of nature spirit, perhaps a *sidhe*. Any further speculation drowned on a wave of hunger as he slid his mouth down the taut line of her stomach, his hands drifting along her sides to clutch her hips. He tightened his grip and lifted her until her feet left the ground.

Maribel gasped, clutching his head to keep her balance as he swung his body in a rapid arc, positioning himself so that she straddled him. He kept his grip on her hips, holding her firmly as he brought his mouth between her legs.

"Daman!"

Maribel's voice rose to a fevered pitch and her entire body tensed at the first touch of his tongue against her wet, heated flesh. Daman groaned, sending vibrations into her body as he dipped his tongue between her velvety folds, licking at the nectar that clung to her. Maribel writhed in his arms, her fingers tightening spastically in his hair, and his muscles bunched as he held her through her contortions. He focused his attention on the bundle of nerves throbbing before him, begging for his attention.

Maribel's hips bucked rhythmically in his hold, her body striving for the release his mouth promised her. His ego swelled, filling him with the masculine satisfaction only a passion-drenched woman could give. He watched her up the line of her body, watched her eyes close, her lips part. She was beautiful in her abandonment, free and wild as she was always meant to be.

He licked and sucked at the bundle of nerves, his own hunger building as her movements became erratic. Her hair tumbled around her in waves that bounced with every movement, the curling tips caressing her nipples, still hard and straining from his earlier attention. Suddenly her entire body tensed, her fingers digging into his scalp as her head fell back. Her mouth parted, but no sound came out, only strangled breath as her hips thrust in tight little jerks against his mouth. Her passion lasted for wave after wave, and then the tension melted from her body, and she was boneless in his arms.

Reluctant to abandon the sweet taste of her, Daman continued his ministrations for a few moments more, committing the flavor of her to memory. Slowly, he slid up her body, letting her weight press against him as he lowered her to her feet. She whimpered and writhed as his scales dragged against her over sensitized flesh, each bump of the vertical ridge down his chest kissing the swollen bundle of nerves still throbbing between her legs.

Maribel groped at his shoulders, her movements sluggish as if she were having a hard time making her body do what she wanted it to. He grinned wickedly, careful to support her as he pulled his lower body between her legs and then started to push against the floor to straighten himself into a standing position.

As his coil left her body, lowering to the floor, Maribel abruptly closed her legs, trapping him there. Daman faltered, scrabbling to redistribute his weight farther down his tail to keep his back from hitting the floor.

Shock shot through his system as Maribel grabbed a handful of his hair. She flexed her legs and shimmied down until his coil was once again pressed against the wet heat at the apex of her thighs.

"No," she ground out, still breathing heavily. "You're not going anywhere."

Daman inhaled sharply, desire spiking so strong inside him it was a wonder it didn't draw blood.

"Maribel," he rasped. "Are you sure?"

Maribel surged forward, the suddenness of the motion catching Daman off guard. He grunted as he fell back, his tail flexing to keep them both from hitting the floor. Maribel slid her legs more firmly around his body. With one hand clutching his hair and the other holding his shoulder, she dove toward him, pressing her mouth against his neck. There was a sharp pain on his skin, the sense of her teeth digging into his flesh in a lover's bite.

It was the last straw.

Daman hissed as the hot heated length of his cock swelled,

pressing up through the slit in the scales of his lower body. A groan wrenched itself from the depths of his being as he thrust against Maribel, sliding between her legs. Maribel cried out against his neck, her hips thrusting instinctively, trying to impale herself on his shaft. Heat filled Daman's head in a rush, melting coherent thought, leaving only instinct, raw want. He growled and grasped her hips, claws grazing her skin as he held her still.

He didn't have the sense to doubt anymore, too lost to the desire eating him alive from the inside out. He thrust into her with savage intensity, the vice-like grip of her body an achingly sweet agony. Maribel screamed, riding him as he eased them back onto the floor.

Pleasure rose like a wild desert storm, lashing through Daman and twisting his body in wild ripples. He surged beneath Maribel, thrusting deeper and deeper, driven mad with the need to get closer. Every stroke stole more of his breath, every clench of Maribel's muscles robbed him of more control. He thrashed underneath her, surging up higher and higher, trying to bury himself as deep inside her as any man could. Her breasts swayed above him as she held on to his chest, her eyes closed as she chased her own pleasure. He wanted to touch her breasts, wanted to raise himself up to take them in his mouth, but it was all he could do to hold on to her hips while the desire whipped him into a frenzy.

His climax hit him with all the force of a gale wind, twisting his body into a tight mass of knotted muscle. He roared as he came, his grip tightening to bruising force on her hips. Maribel screamed a moment later, her delicate body fluttering against him. A shine came from somewhere inside her, light dancing over her skin like sunbeams playing with new spring leaves. Daman blinked, but the effect was gone before his addled brain could make sense of it.

As the last ripple faded, Maribel collapsed against his chest. Her tangled hair fell over him and the floor, a beautiful puddle of warm chocolate. He stroked her naked shoulder with the backs of his claws, floating peacefully on the warm waves of pleasure still washing over him in gentle laps. In that moment, he was truly present, here and nowhere else. The past didn't matter, the future didn't matter. He was here, Maribel was here.

It was enough.

CHAPTER 15

Corrine stared into the mirror as the images she'd conjured faded away. As the last vestiges of her spell wore off, she slowly became aware of her own reflection again. Her brown eyes were glassy, blank. For a moment, she swore she could still see Daman's silver eyes flashing, glowing with passion as he…

Her stomach rumbled, twisting itself into a painful knot. It seemed that she would have to go searching for food on her own. Maribel was…occupied.

Energy fluttered inside her like wild butterflies, her skin buzzing with the sensation of marching ants. The bond between her and Maribel had been renewed now that they were so close, and the amount of energy pouring through that link was more potent than any potion Mother Briar could manage. Corrine stumbled as she rose from the vanity, having to lean heavily on the furniture while she waited for her head to stop spinning. She was energized in a way she could scarcely remember ever feeling. She should be happy.

"If you help me get my daughter back, I will teach you magic stronger than any you have ever dreamed of… You will have the land, the money, and the power to support yourself—forever."

"You love him."

"Oh, Corrine. I know you're not bad."

"I love you, Maribel."

"I love you too."

"Get him to tell you where she is, and I'll do everything in my power to undo the damage I did."

Corrine crossed her arms, hugging herself as the voices danced around in her head, each one tearing up her emotions, throwing them around like so much confetti. Everything had been so clear yesterday, the plan had sounded so easy.

"She's in love."

She said the words out loud, tasting them, testing them. Bittersweet.

Using her bond with Maribel to cast the spell that allowed her to see things through her sister's eyes had been one of the most painful experiences she'd ever been through in her life—and the most educating. It had hurt more than she wanted to admit to see Maribel...giving herself to a man who'd no more than an hour ago threatened to kill Corrine. See her coupling with him, lost in the moment, when she'd supposedly been so concerned about Corrine, so willing to fetch food from the kitchen for her to keep up her strength.

"It took so little time for her to forget about me."

The anger that should have rushed to warm her at the sound of those words wouldn't come. The resentment that she had a right to, the indignation...none of it would comfort her now as it had in the past. Not when the happiness in her sister's voice was so blinding, even in memory. Maribel was in love. True love.

"Oh, I was so close," Corrine continued, talking to herself despite the way her dull, lifeless tone fell like stones into the room. "I had him. I had him exactly where I wanted him, where I needed him. She was going to ask him—no, not ask him, *make him* tell her where Jeanne was." She pressed her hands flat to her skirt, increasing the pressure, pushing them harder and harder against her thighs as she fought the tremble beginning in her shoulders and threatening to flow down to her fingertips. "He probably would have forgiven her. They could have still lived happily ever after. And then I would have my mentor, have the help I needed to be strong on my own."

She stared down at the small clay bowl on the dresser in front of the mirror. The herbs she'd used in the spell still smoked gently, filling the room with the scent of burning rosemary and sage. She picked up the pestle and half-heartedly ground the herbs to dust until the smoke faded and the ashes cooled. A trail of fading smoke followed her as she strode over to the window and dumped the remainders over the windowsill. They floated away on the breeze, carrying her dreams with them, leaving her alone and bereft...again.

A muffled squeaking erupted from inside her bag. Her mind still muddled with conflicting thoughts, Corrine stumbled over to her bag in a daze. The squeaking grew louder as she opened the laces and fished out the small cage.

"About time!" grumbled the pixie. She glared at Corrine, but the expression was somewhat ruined by the fact that the honey she'd so willingly covered herself in had dried into a glue-like consistency. Her wings were stuck together and her hair was twisted into hard clumps. The eyelashes of one eye were stuck to her eyelid, and her dress was bunched into a hard knot of amber-hued glue plastered to her body.

Corrine stared at the fairy, but her mind was still in that other room. With her sister. Watching her forget about Corrine as she built a new future with Daman. *Get angry, Corrine. Use the fury. You can still salvage this, still get the information you need. New love is such a delicate thing...* Her anger was a phantom scent on the wind, there, but gone before she could follow it. She blinked at the fairy without seeing her.

"I need a bath," the fairy said slowly, careful to enunciate each syllable.

Corrine strode over to the small table holding the tea tray that had been waiting in her room on her arrival. She poured the hot water that had been meant for tea into the empty teacup and then cooled it with some water from her washing pitcher. Mechanically, she opened the cage door and set the teacup inside. The pixie struggled to stand, hissing as she pried her sticky arms from her legs and she limped over to her bath.

"I don't know what to do now." The words went out into the air like orphans, meek and pathetic, searching for help in mewling tones.

The pixie sighed happily as she sank up to her chin in the warm water. Blue eyes blinked lazily as she gazed up at Corrine through the faint cloud of steam. "Eh?"

"I can't do it. I mean, I didn't want to do it. I did it anyway, at least I tried. It didn't work though. He wouldn't tell her, and she wouldn't press him. They just..." Corrine trailed off. "They're in love," she said simply. "What right do I have to take that from her?"

The pixie splashed gently in the water, shifting around as though trying to let the water get at as much of the sticky honey as possible. "Her? Maribel? Is that the sister you've been draining?"

A hot retort lit on Corrine's lips, but snuffed itself out with her next breath. She rubbed her temples in small, soothing circles. "I'm so tired."

"You shouldn't be. This close to Maribel you should feel like a barrel of honey."

The familiar burning sensation of tears made Corrine close her eyes all the way. She sank down on the side of the bed.

"I never wanted to hurt Maribel. Never. I don't care if she's my blood or not, she's my sister and I love her, no matter what anyone else thinks. I just..." She opened her eyes, holding her breath until she was sure she could speak without losing her words to a sob. "I'm scared."

The fairy dunked her face into the water again, vigorously scrubbing before popping back out. Water sloshed over the side of the cup, landing in wet splats against the floor of the cage. She tried to blink, scrunching up her face as she pried her eyelashes from her eyelid, face contorting as she did so. One eye rolled in Corrine's direction. "Why do you think you're so sick anyway?"

Corrine traced the velvet pattern worked into the silk stretched across her lap. The material caressed the pad of her finger, calming her nerves. "You're fey. What would you know about feeling weak?"

"Nothing," the fairy agreed. "I'm very strong."

"Well, I'm not." Corrine shifted, pulled the gold braided cord knotted about her waist out from under her where she'd sat on it. The braid was slick and supple in her hands as she twined it around her fingers. "Sometimes I think I was meant to die as a child. Father said I came close. Not many children who are taken by the Evil Fire survive."

Memories flooded back to her, the early days when the episodes had been new. The pain. The convulsions. The horrible images that would frighten her until she screamed, and not even her mother could comfort her. They were terrifying enough now that she was older. As a child, they had nearly destroyed her.

"The Evil Fire," the fairy mused. "I've heard of that. Had convulsions did you?"

Corrine shuddered. "I nearly bit my tongue off during one of them. I still get them now and again."

"Saw frightening things if you closed your eyes?"

"I didn't even have to close my eyes," she breathed. An eerie shiver slithered down her spine and she instinctively fixed her gaze more solidly on her lap, avoiding the windows and shadows. *If you don't look, you can't see them.*

Silence dragged on. Encouraged by the stroll down memory lane, the nightmares from the past paraded across her mind's eye, as horrible and terrifying as they had ever been. Shadows moving when they shouldn't, long spindly fingers reaching out for her. Faces peering at her from outside her window that was far too high for any human to peer through.

Gradually she became aware of a rasping sound. Her heart leapt into her throat, her skin tightening to the point of pain. It took several seconds to register that she was scratching her skirts, the rasping sound just her fingernail rapidly clawing at the velvet. She stilled her hand and tried to slow her breathing.

Corrine caught the fairy staring out of her peripheral vision and angled herself to face the pixie more fully. Something about the expression on the fey's face gave Corrine chills. That serious, soul-penetrating gaze didn't belong on that insolent little countenance, surrounded by hair still sticking up in stiffened clumps on top of her head.

"You've been studying magic with Mother Briar, yes?"

"Yes." The answer slipped out before Corrine could think and she pressed her lips into a tight line. *You know better than that, Corrine. This is exactly the mistake others so often make, the reason the tiny folk always know everything. So tiny, so nonthreatening. No one ever gives a second thought to answering their questions, speaking in front of them. To speak in front of a pixie is to risk your words traveling abroad without your knowledge, being shared with who knew what or who. You are smarter than that!*

"And how exactly did this apprenticeship come about?" the pixie prodded.

"I'm not her apprentice," Corrine corrected automatically. "I'm not really a witch, at least not a powerful one. I'm just a human with a little skill for spells."

The fairy arched an eyebrow. It stuck to a glob of honey under her hairline and stayed there in an expression of perpetual amusement. "Mother Briar told you that?"

Corrine nodded. Then she kicked herself for answering so easily even after remembering the risk.

"Did she also tell you that you wouldn't be able to work magic without her help?"

Corrine bit the inside of her cheek, holding her answer in. She fought not to raise her hand to touch the amulet resting between her breasts.

"I am perfectly capable of casting spells without help," Corrine corrected the pixie stiffly. "I told you, I have *some* natural talent for it."

The fairy disappeared under the water. A long second dragged by. Curiosity ate at her and Corrine peered down into the teacup. The fairy blinked up at her through the honey-clouded water, blue eyes piercing even through the ripples. She blew a stream of bubbles that rustled the surface of the water and completely blocked her from Corrine's view. Corrine rolled her eyes.

"Corrine?"

Corrine tripped over her skirt as she lunged off the bed. She managed to keep her feet, but just barely as she stumbled into the table the tea set was resting on. The china clinked together and rattled against the tabletop. The pixie's makeshift bath tilted wildly to the side. The fey popped her head out of the water with a yelp and Corrine hissed and plucked her out of the cup with a muttered "Shush."

The pixie glared at her, but didn't say anything as Corrine dropped her into the cage and fastened it closed before shutting it away in her bag once again.

"Corrine, are you awake? It's me. I want to talk."

Corrine quickly dumped the honeyed water out the window and half-flew to the washing basin, rinsing out the cup and drying it quickly before rushing to replace it on the tray. She searched for any signs she may have missed, evidence of her spellwork, or her fey guest. No need for Maribel to know what she'd been up to. It didn't matter now anyway.

She stood there for a moment, smoothing down her hair and

dress, trying to regain control of her breathing. Finally, she straightened her spine and walked with slow, measured steps to answer the door.

Maribel stood there, her cheeks flushed with the evidence of what she'd been doing, making the wild tumble of her hair and the wrinkles in her gown all the more damning. Her eyes were still bright, her lips fuller, slightly swollen. Every detail pierced Corrine like the blade of a dagger, stabbing at her, torturing her with the double-edged sword of her sister's happiness. It didn't help that every physical sign was paired with the memory of it happening, the curse of the spell she'd used.

You cold-hearted heathen, be happy for her! When was the last time you saw her smile like that?

"How are you feeling?" Maribel asked.

Corrine twisted her mouth into her best attempt at a smile. "I'm feeling better. I was about to have some tea. I don't suppose you have time to join me?"

Maribel's face crumpled and her hand flew to her mouth. "Oh, Corrine. Your dinner. I forgot."

"It's all right, really." Corrine focused her full attention on the teapot. She had no idea what expression was on her face right now, but whatever it was, she wanted it to remain private. Maribel deserved this happiness, and she would not ruin it for her. It was time to get out of her sister's way.

"No, it's—"

"I'm not going to stay the night."

Maribel snapped her mouth closed and half-fell onto the bed. "Oh, Corrine, please."

"I think it's for the best," Corrine said firmly, her voice thick with the cursed tears trying to come back. She poured a cup of tea for Maribel and slid the saucer closer to her side of the small table. Then she poured a cup for herself.

"Why?" Maribel asked quietly.

Corrine made no move to pick up her cup of tea, barely

caressing the saucer with her fingertips. "You're happy here, Maribel. There's nothing I can do to make it better." She let out a long breath. "And so much I can do to make it worse. It's better if I go. Really it is."

The silence that fell between them was thick, charged with emotions the way the air before a storm is charged with the promise of lightning and the distant rumble of thunder.

"I miss you."

Maribel's words crept toward Corrine, hesitant, as if afraid of the reception they'd receive. A sob lodged itself in Corrine's throat.

"I've missed you too." Her vision blurred. "Maribel, there's something I have to tell you."

"No." Maribel seized Corrine's hands, her blue-eyed gaze boring into Corrine as though she could stop her from speaking through sheer force of will. "It doesn't matter. Whatever it is, it doesn't matter. We're starting with a clean slate—all of us. I'm going to make sure you and Father have all the help you need—and you're going to come visit—all the time." Maribel's eyes turned glassy, the threat of tears turning them into twin blue ponds. "Or you could stay here. I'm sure—"

"No, no, I can't stay here." Corrine pulled a hand free, rubbing the arcane mark as the tattoo started to itch. "It's better if I go. But I'll…I'll visit, yes."

Maribel smiled, sniffling and blinking away her tears. "If you're sure."

No! I'm not sure.

Panic reared its ugly head, wild eyes and screaming mouth painting a horrifying image on the inside of Corrine's mind. Her sister's words echoed in her head, and suddenly it hit her—*really* hit her.

Maribel was staying. Corrine was going home alone. Alone. Alone to face those horrible people, alone to watch her father sink further and further into depression. She wouldn't have Maribel's energy anymore. The nightmares, the monsters...

Her heart leapt into her throat. Mother Briar. She would be furious with Corrine for not getting Jeanne's location. She would shun her, stop helping her, stop teaching her. She would be alone then, truly and utterly alone. Vulnerable.

Dying.

The bond between Corrine and her sister pulsed, throbbing like a second heartbeat. It glowed like a bright gold thread inside her and Corrine tugged on it, desperate, needing more energy to keep her sane. She needed more, more to get her through, more to keep her safe. Oh, Goddess, she was going to make the journey home alone. Again.

The string gave easily under Corrine's panic-fueled tugs, pouring a churning, roiling rush of energy down the connection. Corrine startled at the power of the flood, the weight of it. That shouldn't be. Maribel was too strong, Corrine shouldn't be able to pull so deeply from her. Until now, calling on that bond had only fed her minimal amounts of energy, like water dripping from a silent pump. It was as Mother Briar had said, she couldn't take much from Maribel because her sister was so much stronger than Corrine.

Unless...

The amulet around Corrine's neck had begun to glow. Red flame lit the crystal, pouring warm power out over Corrine's body. It invigorated her, making her feel stronger, more confident. Secure.

Corrine jumped as Maribel suddenly collapsed on the bed, blue eyes glazing over, shifting from a bright sapphire to a muted winter sky. Her head lolled from side to side and she let out a soft sigh as if she were falling asleep.

I just need a little more. Just enough to get me home, to last me for awhile until I find some other way.

Corrine held her breath and pulled harder on the thread,

tugging at the energy that was so abundant in Maribel. The power came like a flood from a shattered dam. Corrine pulled again, trying to make the flow faster, to get what she needed quickly so she could get out of here, away from Daman and his smug face, away from Maribel and the temptation to use the arcane mark, to keep leeching energy from her. This was it, the last time, and then Corrine would break the link for good.

Energy like nothing she'd ever experienced before washed over her. Her muscles swelled, flexing as if dreaming of great feats of strength. Her heart pounded, a firm, steady beat that invigorated her entire body. Her mind sharpened and it was as if she were thinking clearly for the first time in her life, as if a curtain had parted and she could finally see.

CHAPTER 16

Maribel's head throbbed, sending a pulsing wave of pain over her scalp to the back of her head. It flowed back like an angry tide, rose, and flowed forward again, bringing its agony with it like foam laced with broken shells. She closed her eyes and pressed her forehead into the down coverlet on Corrine's bed, seeking relief.

"Corrine...something's wrong." Her voice came out heavy and slurred. Her tongue felt too big for her mouth and she could barely hold her wits together long enough to swallow.

"Maribel? Are you all right?"

Corrine laid a hand on Maribel's shoulder and Maribel rolled her head to the side to rest it on her hand, grateful for the comfort. Her sister's skin was cool against her feverish cheek, a welcome balm to the miserable heat holding her in its suffocating grip. Corrine cupped her jaw, whispering soothing, nonsense words.

A second later, Maribel's stomach lurched. Something twisted inside her body, like a string was being pulled from somewhere deep inside her, a string connected to her heart and stomach both. The sensation wasn't exactly painful, but strange and nauseating. Maribel leaned away from Corrine and the pulling sensation intensified and she groaned.

"Corrine, I don't feel well."

Corrine's grip followed her, her fingers digging more firmly into Maribel's shoulder. "It's all right. Everything's going to be all right."

Corrine's voice had changed. There was an excitement in her tone, a fluttering nervousness that left her words breathy. Maribel forced her eyes open.

The paleness that had always given Corrine a haunted, ghostly pallor had been replaced by a rosy-cheeked glow. Her brown eyes shone bright and lively, more brown than the black they usually appeared as. She was curled to hover over Maribel, but her posture was different, more confident, nurturing instead of slumped under some invisible weight.

Maribel tried to raise a hand to pet Corrine's cheek, but her fingers were too heavy. "You look wonderful."

In an instant, the peaceful expression on Corrine's face cracked, revealing wide, panicked eyes that darted from side to side, scrutinizing Maribel from head to toe. Her fingers curled into claws, digging into Maribel with painful stabbing motions.

"Maribel? Maribel!"

Maribel kept smiling, the fuzzy feeling in her head flowing down her body like warm honey, leaving her muscles limp. "It's so nice to see you looking so healthy." She blinked slowly, lethargically. "You'll be fine. I'll stay with Daman and you can go home… I'll send you…so much money. You'll be…"

Pain exploded in her cheek as Corrine landed a ringing slap across her face. She grabbed Maribel's head in her hands and shook her, Maribel's body barely rocking where she lay on the bed.

"Maribel!" Corrine screamed.

"Get away from her!"

Daman's voice broke over the room like a tremendous clap of

thunder. There was a flash of glittering scales and a jagged shriek tore from Corrine as a clawed hand wrapped mercilessly around her biceps and flung her halfway across the room.

Maribel's heart pounded, an acidic wave of adrenaline washing over her, pushing back the pain and nausea enough for her to struggle into a sitting position. She swayed, feeling like a small boat being tossed to and fro on a raging river, and braced both hands on the bed to hold herself up so she could see what was happening.

Daman was on the floor, his tail wrapped around Corrine's waist. The large bluish green scales of his lower body covered Corrine from her ribs to her hips in a punishing vice. His silver eyes blazed like liquid starlight, his lips pulled back to reveal two sets of wickedly curved fangs. He lunged, reaching out for Corrine's throat with a hand tipped with vicious, sharp white claws.

Maribel tried to scream, tried to yell for Daman to let Corrine go, to stop. Then her gaze landed on her sister and the words faded away under a flood of awe.

Corrine's eyes were no longer the dark brown of pure bitter chocolate. They were green, a vibrant, glowing emerald like paintings Maribel had seen of the lights in the Dacian winter sky. Corrine was gripping Daman's hand by the wrist, muscles trembling as she fought to keep his claws away from her throat. At the same time, she groped for his face with her other hand, straining for his eyes as if she would blind him. Only Daman's grip on her wrist kept her from gouging out those silver, glowing eyes.

"Stop!" Maribel tried to shout, but her voice came out a breathy plea. She closed her eyes but opened them immediately when the room started to spin. The tugging on the string inside her grew worse, the nausea threatening to empty her stomach. She swallowed hard and focused on the couple fighting on the ground.

"Daman," she tried again. "Stop. Please."

"Sshe wass hurting you." Daman lurched forward another inch, claws flexing as he strained to rake the tender flesh of Corrine's throat.

"I was not!" Corrine's voice rose an octave, her eyes wild. She risked a glance at Maribel. "Maribel, are you all right?"

"Do not pretend you care for her!" Daman bellowed, rage tearing his voice to shreds on his fangs. "What were you doing to her, witch?" His tail flexed, squeezing Corrine until she gasped. "Tell her!"

"Daman, stop, please," Maribel shouted hoarsely. "Don't hurt her."

Daman faced her, reptilian eyes widening even as the black slits narrowed to the width of a hair, almost completely lost to the silver. "Sshe hurt you."

Maribel cursed as the haze refused to lift and every movement sickened her further. "I'm fine. Maybe a little tired."

"Perhaps you wore her out," Corrine snarled, the strain in her voice betraying how hard she was struggling. "Being taken on the floor like an animal can be hard on a woman."

Maribel sputtered, her cheeks suddenly scalding. "You..."

Daman focused glittering eyes on Corrine. "You have been sspying." His voice dropped to a deadly hiss and his coils flexed as they covered more of Corrine's body. "Why are you really here, witch?"

"I'm here to get my sister back." Corrine choked, her voice growing raspy as her chest was constricted by the scaled body clutching her tighter with every breath she released.

"No. No, that iss not why you're really here." Daman flicked his forked tongue into the air between them, so close to Corrine he could have licked her. Corrine shrieked and angled her face away. "You tasste of magic. What sspell have you been working on your ssisster?"

A garbled sound came from Corrine's throat, but no words. She thrashed feebly and the hand holding Daman's away from her throat trembled. His claws inched forward, closing the distance, tips brushing pale skin.

Maribel shoved herself up, ignoring the fresh wave of nausea that swept over her and nearly threw her out of the bed. She thrust out a hand as Daman's claws dimpled Corrine's skin, sharp points pressing in.

"Daman, *stop!*"

Corrine tried to suck in a breath, but it came out a skin-crawling wheeze. Her face darkened to purple, green-glowing eyes dulling.

Maribel lurched, shoving herself off the bed. Her feet hit the floor and her legs threatened to give way, half-spilling her to the rug. She grabbed the edge of the bed, holding on, waiting for the room to stop spinning. Panic sent adrenaline through her system like an acid wash, and she gritted her teeth.

"Daman, get away from her."

Daman's gaze was locked on Corrine's neck, followed a drop of blood that had welled out around one of his claws. "You are too closse, you cannot ssee the truth right in front of you. Sshe caress nothing for you, Maribel! You are a changeling, a child left at her housse in the middle of the night. Whatever sshe'ss ssaid to you, sshe caress only about your power."

His face twisted with fury. "Sshe'ss done ssomething to you. I know sshe hass. Sshe wass holding you and you were getting weaker while sshe sseemed only to grow sstronger." The muscle in his jaw tightened and he flexed his muscles, leaning forward. Corrine's arms trembled, but she held him back. "Don't you ssee how much sstronger sshe iss? I know there iss a connection."

Every word out of his mouth was another needle in Maribel's heart, another strip of skin peeled away to leave her raw and vulnerable. It was only minutes ago she'd been so happy, every-thing had been settled, all was right with the world. What was this nightmare, where had it come from? She stared at Daman, willing him to listen. "You're the one who can't see what's right in front of you. Corrine has been studying magic in the hopes of coping with her illness. It makes sense that she's getting stronger. That's why she studies magic, why would she continue to study if it wasn't working?"

"Do you hear how sshe defendss you?" Daman pulled Corrine closer, constricting, tightening his coils around her. "Do you hear the love in her voicce? Sshe musst feel what you've done to her, ssomewhere insside her, sshe musst know. And sshe defendss you anyway—lovess you anyway. How heartlessss musst you be to usse her?"

Corrine's eyes flashed, then the green light died, leaving them a brown so dark it was nearly black. Her gaze flicked to Maribel, her face a sickening shade of bluish purple. Maribel tried to meet her eyes, tried to offer her encouragement, support, some sign that she had more faith in Corrine than Daman did. Corrine's eyes glistened with tears and she looked away.

Maribel stifled the roll of unease at the way Corrine wouldn't meet her eyes. "Daman, please. I care so much for you, and I do want to stay here. But Corrine is my sister. If you hurt her... I don't know how I would ever move past that."

Daman's face twisted in pain. "Maribel..."

Suddenly his entire body spasmed. A muffled choke garbled from his mouth, his coils going limp around Corrine as his body arched back, face going taut. The blade of a dagger protruded from his chest, just to the side of his heart. Ruby red blood welled up in the wound, spilling down his body and outlining his silver scales with rivulets of crimson. A trickle of blood escaped his mouth as he blinked down at the weapon, the black slits of his eyes flickering, silver irises shifting from silver to dull iron. Maribel screamed and stumbled forward.

Corrine gasped, choked, the ragged sounds speaking to the condition of her ravaged lungs. She lay on the floor like a ragdoll, half of her body still lying on Daman's coils where she'd fallen. Brown eyes too wide, she lay on the floor, staring up at Daman like a sinner on his deathbed, gazing into the face of an avenging angel.

The hand that had been trying to claw at Daman was free, extended toward the *naga* as though she'd thrown the knife. Her bag was open on the floor beside the bed, a silken scarf trailing out of it as though something had been pulled in a hurry from the depths of the satchel. By magic.

Maribel hovered in front of Daman, afraid to touch him, afraid that she would only bring him pain. Tears blurred her vision and she spoke to her sister without facing her. "Corrine?"

Corrine heaved herself away from Daman, scurrying away from his coils as if they might grab her again. "He was going to kill me." Her voice was a broken rasp, each word sounding like a struggle. "I had to do something."

A sob broke from Maribel's throat, tears welling up to blind her. Daman was still frozen, whether from shock or pain she didn't know. He wasn't looking at her. Rather, his leaden gaze was zeroed in on Corrine.

"Daman…"

The *naga* dove for her sister with more speed than a human, but less than he'd been capable of before. His silvery-scaled body flashed, his arm rising above his head, slick white claws spread. Corrine opened her mouth to scream, but the noise never made it past her lips. Daman brought his hand down, slashing her throat and upper chest. Maribel screamed again as Corrine fell back against the wall, sliding down into a crumpled heap.

"I won't…let you hurt her," Daman rasped.

Time slowed, becoming thick and palpable. Maribel had all the time in the world to see the light die in Daman's eyes, the tension melt from his face as a ripple moved from one end of his body to the other. His torso hit the ground with a dull thud and a rustle of scales. He didn't get back up.

Maribel's heart constricted in her chest, so tight she could scarcely breathe around the solid weight of it. Panic, fear, desperation all braided together, forging strength that rushed through her body with nerve-sizzling intensity. She half-fell toward Daman, hands out, choked cry lodged in her throat. A wet wheezing sound came from behind her.

Corrine.

The sound drew Maribel, some instinct telling her that she might be too late to save Daman, but her sister was still alive. Corrine held her neck with one hand, blood seeping through her fingers. Her face was deathly pale, her lips nearly white. Blood soaked her gown, some of it hers gushing from the wounds in her neck and chest, flowing down her body in a broad ribbon, and some of it Daman's splattered over her like some macabre rain. She didn't speak, just stared at Maribel.

"No!" Maribel sobbed and fell to her knees beside Corrine. "No…"

Corrine's lips moved but no sound came out. Maribel searched the floor around her, searching for something, anything to staunch the flow of blood. She spotted Corrine's bag on the floor, but Corrine's hand scrabbled at her arm.

"Maribel…"

Her voice was so faint, Maribel nearly missed it. She clutched Corrine's hand in hers, fingers slipping in the slick coating of blood. She leaned closer so her ear was right next to Corrine's mouth.

"S…sorry…"

Maribel shook her head, warm tears streaming down her face. "No. No, don't be sorry, don't be sorry, Corrine." She hesitated before brushing Corrine's hair behind her ear, stroking her cheek. "I'm sorry. I'm sorry I left you, I'm sorry I brought you here, I'm just," she choked, "sorry."

Corrine's eyes drifted closed. A long exhalation rolled out from her body, flowing from her nose and mouth on a sigh that came from somewhere deep in her body. Something inside Maribel loosened, the phantom string she'd felt so keenly earlier. The nausea and pain she'd had a moment ago vanished, so quickly it made her head spin anew. She blinked, startled at how much more vibrant the world seemed suddenly, how much clearer her mind was. Strength flowed through her and she pulled in a deep, soul-cleansing breath.

Corrine slid to the floor, her head lolling to the side. A small smile played over her lips.

"Sshe wass holding you and you were getting weaker while sshe sseemed only to grow sstronger. Don't you ssee how much sstronger sshe iss? I know there iss a connection."

"Sshe musst feel what you've done to her, ssomewhere insside her, sshe musst know."

Maribel's hand stilled on Corrine's cheek. Slowly, tilted her head down so she could look into Corrine's cloudy brown eyes. "You were taking energy from me."

Corrine blinked once, slowly.

Dread curled in Maribel's stomach, sent icy shards bobbing into her bloodstream. "Corrine?"

"Y…yes."

The confession was so breathy that Maribel had to strain to hear it, and even then she thought she might have imagined it. Her heart pounded, hope shooting up inside of her like a geyser, explosive with its force. She grabbed Corrine by the shoulders. "Do it again," she commanded. "Take more, take everything you need."

Corrine's teeth clacked together from the force of Maribel's jostling. She could tell the moment the words registered because Corrine's eyes flew open, the haze over the brown orbs retreating. "No," she rasped. "Will kill…you."

Maribel shook her head, unable to keep from looking at Daman's body lying a few feet away. He hadn't moved, hadn't shifted. There was no rise and fall to his body, no twitch in any flesh from the top of his head to the tip of his heavy tail. He was gone. She bit her lip to hold back a sob. "I won't watch you die too."

Corrine tried to push herself up, hands scrabbling at the ground, pushing her back against the wall in a vain attempt to shove herself upright. Her dress tore, the sound of wet fabric tearing jolting Corrine out of her futile attempts. She stilled, studying Maribel from the corner of her eye. A spark of green lit somewhere deep within the brown irises.

Maribel recognized the pull when it started. It was the same string, the same nauseating tug that had laid her out earlier. Even prepared for it as she was, she couldn't help but curl her arms around her stomach as if that could ease the discomfort. The invigoration of a moment ago seemed like a dream as the adrenaline fizzled out, left her drained, listing to the side.

She blinked trying to stay conscious, needing to reassure herself that Corrine was getting better. Images blurred into watery blobs of color and gray ate away at the edges of her vision. Her heart lurched as she fell back...

And into a pair of strong arms.

Maribel blinked, breath chilling to ice in her lungs. "Daman?"

Daman's eyes looked into hers from where he hovered over her. Well, sort of Daman's eyes. They were the same beautiful silver, but the pupils were round like a human's instead of slitted like a reptile's. Her brow furrowed, brain fighting to process the other changes. His skin. It wasn't pale silvery-blue anymore. It was the pale flesh tone of a human. The scales were gone, the ridges that had traced his brow, curled down his shoulders...gone.

"Maribel?" Daman held her face in his hands, gently, as if afraid of hurting her.

"Daman!" Maribel thrashed in his lap, desperate to sit up, to see for herself that she wasn't dreaming. Arms akimbo, body stubbornly refusing to do as she instructed it, she let out a cry of frustration.

"Easy, easy," Daman hushed her.

The strong arms around her flexed, became steadying. Maribel's hands landed on his shoulder, dancing over his skin, his jaw, his face. He held still, let her touch him, reassure herself he was all right.

"Oh, Daman, what happened?" she breathed. "I thought you were dead, and Corrine—"

Daman's face tightened, pain in his eyes. His grip on Maribel tightened and he tried to pull her to him, tried to keep her from turning around to where Corrine would be.

"Daman…" Maribel struggled against him, straining to look behind her. Daman put his hands on her face. Slowly, he shook his head. Panic rose like a wild thing in Maribel's chest and she renewed her efforts, thrashing, needing to see for herself.

Daman had to let her go or risk hurting her. As soon as he relaxed his grip, Maribel spun, heart in her throat.

Corrine was lying on the floor, her eyes open, but drooping. Her chest rose and fell slightly. Or did it?

"Corrine!" Maribel tried to go to her sister, but her body wouldn't support her. She collapsed, sobbing, stretching for her sister, but only grasping the edge of her skirts. Daman's hands closed around her, lifted her and carried her to Corrine's body.

"I don't understand," Maribel sobbed. "What happened?"

A muffled shouting from somewhere close by drew Maribel's frazzled attention to Corrine's bag. She pointed, too disoriented to verbalize what she needed. Daman followed her hand and nodded. After carefully settling her against the wall—moving so slowly Maribel wanted to scream—he fetched the bag and brought it to Maribel. She fished around in the bag and removed a small cage.

A tiny creature was inside, roughly the size of a raven, but thin and humanoid. She had pale pink skin and her clothing was sewn from some sort of gauzy material that was darker in some places and clung to her body as if it had dried funny. It swiped it's long ponytail out of its eyes and glared at Maribel, translucent wings fluttering angrily.

"Let me out!" the fairy demanded. She stared at Corrine's body slumped on the floor, face creasing in consternation. "Let me out or she'll die!"

Maribel flicked the latch on the cage and opened the door, barely resisting the urge to shake the cage to get the loud creature out faster. The fairy zipped out in a flash of glittering lights and landed on Corrine's shoulder.

"Who are you? What happened to Corrine? How did Daman—"

"Agh!" the fairy shouted, covering her ears. "Too many questions! I can't concentrate! Shut up!"

Maribel snapped her mouth closed, as the fairy laid her hand on Corrine's cheek and spoke in a voice too quiet for Maribel to make out what she was saying.

"Is she going to be all right?" Maribel leaned to the side, grateful when Daman put an arm around her and held her tight. She laid her head on his shoulder, too tired to hold it up anymore.

The fairy didn't answer. Her eyes lit up and a second later she was gone.

A second later she was back, holding a flower in her hands. Broad white petals glittered with gold dust, a warm pulse flowing out from its shining center. The energy washed through the air, flowing over Maribel, infusing her muscles with heat and vitality. She sat up, still in Daman's embrace but no longer leaning on him.

"The Rose of the Mist," she breathed.

The pixie nodded. "Use it. Save your sister."

Maribel caught the rose as the pixie half-flung it through the air. As soon as her hand closed around it, the invigorating sensation she'd felt before increased, pounding through her like a sledgehammer of adrenaline. She sucked in a breath, blinking through the buzz of power.

"Don't go getting drunk on me yet," the pixie barked. "Heal your sister first!"

"I… I don't know how to use it, I don't have the…book."

The fairy crossed her skinny arms. "You're *sidhe*. I'm not sure how this is confusing you."

"She?"

"Not 'she,'" the fairy corrected her. "*Sidhe*."

Maribel blinked. The fairy rolled her eyes.

"You're a changeling. A *sidhe* changeling. The plants listen to you. Just…" She waved her arms in frustration. "Listen to the flower! Talk to the flower. Tell it what you want it to do."

Tears burned in Maribel's eyes. "I don't know how." Corrine's chest hitched, her body going stiff. Her eyes drifted the rest of the way closed.

"No!"

"Maribel, look at me."

Daman's voice sounded far away. Pressure on either side of Maribel's head made her turn, held her still no matter how hard she tried to focus on Corrine and that dreadful stillness creeping over her body. Finally she became aware of Daman's eyes, the fact that she was looking at his face from inches away.

"Listen to me, and take deep breaths," Daman said calmly.

Maribel pulled at his grip, but he held her firm.

"Corrine is going to be fine," he said firmly. "You are going to listen to me and you are going to heal her. She will be fine."

"You don't know that." Maribel sobbed, her voice hitching as a fresh wave of hot tears spilled down her cheeks.

"Yes, I do. Now close your eyes, and take a deep breath. Hold the flower."

Maribel pressed her lips together to hold back another sob, but did as he told her. She clutched the rose so tightly the stem snapped, smearing her hands with liquid that smelled of spring and newly churned soil. She whimpered and opened her eyes, crying out when she saw what she'd done.

"It's okay, you haven't hurt it," Daman soothed. "Close your eyes."

More tears spilled as she obeyed, her closed lids sending them washing over her cheeks in sheets.

"Concentrate on the flower. Do you feel the warmth? The pulse?"

Maribel nodded, holding the thought of that warm throbbing beat in her mind.

"Picture the glow, feel the warmth." Daman cupped his hands around hers, cradling her grip around the rose. Slowly, he lowered her hands to Corrine's wounded flesh.

Blood slicked her fingers as she pressed the flower to Corrine's skin. The jagged edges of the slash marks had started to curl, some blood clots making the flesh tacky. Maribel swallowed a scream, concentrating on the rose, on what she wanted desperately for it to do.

Please work. Please work. Please work. Oh, Corrine, come back to me.

"Ssso the witch isss going to live."

Daman didn't take his eyes off the mirror, gaze still locked on his legs.

Legs.

"Yes, she is." He angled his body to the side, stepping carefully. He'd dreamed of having this form back for so long, but it had never occurred to him how hard it would be to get used to walking again. He'd fallen over the first time he'd tried to stand up.

Which is to say, he would be very embarrassed, if he weren't so overjoyed.

"You're not very upssset about it. Consssidering you ssseemed to put sssome effort into killing her, I find that ssstrange."

Daman had been staring into the mirror long enough now that he figured he was bordering on vanity, so he tore his attention away from his reflection and focused on the *cuelebre*. His houseguest was hanging from one of the wall sconces again, wings tucked neatly against its slender body. It had fixed him with the usual beady-eyed stare, tapping its chin with the tip of its tail.

"Sssomthing'sss different about you."

"Can't fool you," Daman said dryly, crossing his arms. "What do you want?"

"Jussst checking in." The *cuelebre* wound its head around one hundred and eighty degrees, peering at Daman from its upside-down vantage point. "You're ssshorter."

Daman opened his mouth then closed it. He slanted a glance at the mirror and realized the *cuelebre* was right. He furrowed his brow and looked down at his body, then back at the mirror. Now that he thought about it, it felt strange to have his height so… consistent. In his *naga* form, his height changed depending on the flex of his muscles, how much of his tail he raised off of the ground. His human legs remained the same. He didn't bob up and down as he stood either, there was no flexing of muscles subtly raising and lowering him.

His hair remained the same, so that provided some transition. His eyes were similar, metallic grey, only with a circular pupil instead of almond-shaped. He ran his hands over his stomach and arms, tracing the skin where once there had been scales and ridges.

"I'm sssurprisssed your lover isssn't with you."

Daman tensed, hands stilling on his stomach. His temper flickered inside him, familiar and alien at the same time now that he was in this form. *Your lover.* His heartbeat echoed in his ears as he slowly faced the *cuelebre*. "How do you know she's my lover?"

The *cuelebre* twitched, tongue flicking out and back in. "Oh, isss ssshe? I meant the word in itsss purest form, lady love and sssuch, you undersssstand. But can I take your ressssponssse to mean thingsss are now physssical—"

The change came to him with the enthusiasm of an old friend returning from a long voyage. Daman's body swelled and twisted. Scales clattered down his body in a rain of thick, plated glitter and his muscles and bones stretched, broke, reformed. He opened his mouth in a wide yawn, a snout extending from his face, full of razor sharp teeth and four curved fangs the size of short swords. His claws scrabbled at the floor as he whirled to face the *cuelebre*, his thick tail swishing behind him. He snorted at the flying pest that seemed all the tinier next to his full wyvern form.

"No need to be ssso touchy," the *cuelebre* grumbled. He perked his head up, beady gaze suddenly fixed on the door behind Daman. "Your...*lover* isss coming."

Daman swirled around in a chaotic swirl of scales, muscle, and claws, commanding the same grace as he had in his half-and half form, the tail more familiar to his brain than two legs. Footsteps echoed in the hallway beyond the door and he cursed and called the change again.

Dizzy from changing twice in such rapid succession, he stumbled a bit as he grabbed the clothes he'd pulled out earlier and dressed as quickly as he could. The *cuelebre* snickered behind him, a pleased hissing sound that would have earned it a knock upside its tiny head if Daman had had the time. As it was, he had barely fastened his trousers when there was a knock at his door.

"Daman?"

There was a tone in the voice that came through the door, a note of uncertainty, colored with fatigue. That voice made something in Daman's stomach clench, a tight sensation of dread tugging at his guts as if it would spill them out onto the floor.

He abandoned his shirt and rushed to the door, snarling as his legs threatened to dump him on the ground. A moment of concentration and he got them under control enough to reach the door. He flung it open and came to a dead halt.

Maribel stood there in a simple mint green dress, the cotton hugging her curves like beloved treasures. She'd bathed, and her skin was scrubbed clean of blood, along with what he guessed was a layer of skin. Her clothes were rumpled as though she'd been sleeping in them, and her face was still flushed as though she'd only just woken up. Though any thought that she may have been sleeping was disillusioned by the slight redness in her eyes and the droop in her shoulders.

"You've been crying. Are you all right?" Daman asked gently.

Maribel nodded tiredly. Her gaze roved over Daman, skittering over his new form as if she still couldn't quite believe it. She hadn't really had time to see him properly earlier, not with her hands covered in her sister's blood, Corrine's life force leaking away from wounds Daman had inflicted. Maribel hadn't taken her eyes or her hands from her sister until golden light had spilled from the bloody gashes in her neck and chest, melting the wounds closed like hot wax being smoothed into perfect skin.

Daman had helped her get her sister into bed and left them together. As much as he'd wanted to stay, there had been a tightness in Maribel's posture that…frightened him.

"How is Corrine?" he asked, unable to stand the silence any longer. He tried to keep the question light, but emotion battered his words, showed his uncertainty in all its inglorious light. He desperately wanted to ask Maribel if she'd forgive him, if she'd ever be able to forget that it had been his claws that had nearly cost Maribel her sister. But he was afraid of what the answer might be.

"Sleeping still. The rose seems to have worked."

There was an awe in her voice that reminded Daman of how sheltered Maribel had been from her heritage, how human she had been raised. It would be interesting to see how she adapted to the knowledge that she was anything but human.

He hoped he would be around to see it.

"Would you like to come in?" Daman stepped back and to the side. His steps were still shaky in this form and he moved as though he had splints on. It was irritating, but in that moment he was grateful for the distraction it provided.

"Not yet."

Daman's heart hardened to rock in his chest, a painful weight that ached with every breath. He shuffled back to stand in front of Maribel again, studying her carefully.

"Corrine and I talked a lot before she fell asleep," Maribel started slowly. She wrung her hands in front of her. "She told me about the bonding spell." She took a deep breath, stilled her hands. "I guess she knew what I was right away—I mean, that I wasn't…"

She cleared her throat. "The fairy says that Corrine's illness wasn't really an illness, that really it was some entity that had decided to grant Corrine power. She called it a 'patron.' She says that's why Corrine had hallucinations and seizures, it was the power she had inside her. I guess without a familiar or anyone to properly train her, a witch isn't able to fully process her abilities, and it can cause a lot of problems. For Corrine, she used too much energy just fighting to stay sane. The magic was manifesting itself in nightmares and things that scared her, so she was constantly trying to suppress it entirely. It weakened her body and that's why she always felt so ill."

Daman nodded slowly. "I have heard of that. There are many such patrons out there who bestow power on individuals at their own discretion, without telling them why. No one knows what motivates them, if it is some cosmic game or if it is done deliberately as part of a greater scheme." His arms ached to reach out for Maribel, but he didn't dare. Not yet. "It is unfortunate that this patron caused your sister so many problems."

"That's why she bonded with me," Maribel said. "Corrine thought she was actually sick, that she was dying, and she thought that bonding with me, sharing my energy, would help her keep up her strength. As a *sidhe*, she thought I'd have plenty of energy to spare. The fairy said that she was using my energy to sort of heal herself, help her body handle the strain of constantly battling back so much magic." She looked down at her hands. "I still don't really understand it."

"Magic is complicated and far beyond my meager experience." Daman took a cautious step closer, searching Maribel for any sign his nearness was unwanted. The pulse at his neck fluttered like a living thing trapped beneath his skin. "The fairy will help her."

Maribel nodded, eyes unfocused. "Yes. She'll be fine."

There was another long, awkward silence. Plenty of time for Daman's imagination to torment him with images of Maribel leaving him, declaring him violent, a monster no matter his form. Putting her arm around her sister and leaving him. The images were so real, Daman imagined he could see the sunlight on her hair as she left, feel the chill in the kitchen where he would eat every meal alone. No one to talk to. No one to laugh with.

Finally, Daman couldn't stand it anymore. "I'm sorry I hurt your sister," he blurted out.

Maribel flinched. Her throat worked as she swallowed, nostrils flaring with a long inhalation. She was coming to a decision, and from the deep line between her eyebrows and the stiffness in her shoulders, it would not be altogether pleasant to hear. Daman pressed his hands to his thighs, wishing he had something to hold on to, something to keep his hands busy.

"Maribel, I thought I was dying and I thought once I was gone, she was going to kill you." Desperation tightened Daman's voice, pushed him to slide closer to her, caution be damned. "When I came into the room and saw you lying there, saw her putting her hands on you, getting stronger while you faded right in front of me…" He closed his eyes, the memory playing in sickening detail behind his eyelids. "I couldn't bear the thought of leaving you alone with her."

She tortured him with another long silence. Daman shifted from foot to foot, but not even that familiar, but alien motion was enough to distract him. She held his future in her hands.

"You tried to tell me about her and I didn't listen."

Her voice was so low, Daman almost didn't hear her. He ran a hand through his hair, tugging at the short strands as if that could take his mind from the pulse-pounding trepidation eating him from the inside out. "She's your sister and you love her. That's a bond not so easily broken by the accusations of a stranger."

Maribel's blue eyes glittered at him, with tears or emotion he wasn't sure.

"But you weren't a stranger. I know you, I—" She looked away for a moment as if regaining her composure. Her hands toyed with the material of her skirt, bunching it up, letting it go. Finally she met his eyes again. "I cared about both of you, and I was so worried about hurting one of you that I buried my head in the sand. I could have tried to find out the truth, but I was willing to let both of you believe what you wanted to while I tried to find some way of making you both happy." Her voice hitched, tripping over her breath. "And because of that, I could have lost both of you."

A tear rolled down her cheek and Daman couldn't help it. He pulled her into his arms, tucking her head against his shoulder and resting his chin on the top of her head. "Shhh. It's all right. Everyone is all right."

"I thought you died," Maribel sobbed. She folded against him, hands pressed to his bare skin, roaming in small circles as if reassuring herself he was really there, really all right. "All that blood…"

"Shhh, it's okay. Maybe you were right in the end. Corrine may have lied, but you believed that deep down she did care about you, and you were right. You offered her your energy, told her to take whatever she needed. She could have drained enough to heal herself, traded your life for hers. But instead, she took just enough for one more spell. She lifted my curse so I could heal, and I know she did that because she knew I would take care of you. In the end, she chose you over herself. I can't think of more convincing evidence of someone's love."

He was somewhat taken aback at the words coming out of his mouth, more so that he could feel the truth of them on his tongue. Corrine had chosen Maribel in the end, had been willing to make the ultimate sacrifice. Even Daman couldn't have asked more of her than that.

"Maybe if I'd given her more attention, I would have seen there was something wrong." Maribel pressed her cheek against his chest. "Part of me always resented that she didn't do more work, that I always had to take care of her. But maybe if I'd really listened—"

"You know nothing of the world beyond humans." Daman rubbed small soothing circles on her back, fingers pressing into the knots her muscles had worked themselves into. "There's no way you could have known what was happening."

Maribel stiffened. The knots beneath Daman's fingers grew to the size of large hailstones.

"But Mother Briar did."

"In all likelihood, yes." A warm, burning anger stirred in his belly, soothing in its familiarity. "She probably knew right away what both of you were, that you were *sidhe* and Corrine was touched by a patron. That witch hasn't lived as long as she has without learning how to manipulate people." His fingers stilled as his mind raced, followed the line of thought leading into darkness. "In fact," he said slowly, "it wouldn't surprise me if she set this whole thing in motion just to find Jeanne."

The scent of spring wafted past his senses as Maribel stirred against him, raising her eyes to his. "That sounds terribly complicated," she said doubtfully. "To manipulate Corrine into coming here, your curse, the Rose of the Mist, me."

"But what if Corrine was her plan A?" Daman kept his arms around Maribel, the feel of her warm body comforting in the midst of the discomforting thoughts churning in his mind. "She knew Corrine's weaknesses well enough after spending so much time 'training' her. She could have easily planted the idea in Corrine's head that marrying me would end her misery, give her a safer life. Then after that failed, she might have seen you as a viable plan B. You would do anything for your sister, after all."

Maribel clenched her hands into fists where they rested against his chest. "Corrine got worse after we came out here, got worse with every season that passed. You're saying it was that witch, that Mother Briar was twisting her mind, feeding her fears so she would be desperate enough to manipulate into coming here?"

A supple lock of her hair tickled his finger and Daman absent-mindedly toyed with it. "Possibly, but Corrine may have gotten worse from being in a rural area instead of the main village."

"What does that have to do with anything?"

"When you're this close to nature, working with the land, vulnerable to any change in the weather, superstitions have a much stronger hold. Belief in creatures beyond the veil is stronger, and people are more vigilant of them, more fearful. That kind of emotion has a tangible effect on magic. Corrine may have gotten worse, because her power grew stronger out here, fed by the fervent faith of her neighbors."

"And Mother Briar would have known about that too," Maribel guessed.

"Most definitely."

Maribel clenched her teeth. "She can't get away with what she's done."

Daman rubbed a hand up and down her back, offering what comfort he could. As much as he wanted to dispose of Mother Briar for Maribel—taking his wyvern form and eating her seemed a viable idea—part of him was loathe to take on a witch so soon after breaking his curse. He had underestimated a witch once, it would be foolish to do so again.

"We will need to speak with Corrine," he said finally. "She should have some say in this."

Maribel pulled away, peering behind her down the hallway in the direction of Corrine's room. "She's sleeping now, I don't want to wake her."

The sadness and stress that had weighed so heavily on her when she'd first arrived pinched Maribel's features, pushing her shoulders down until she stood hunched over, defeated. Daman pulled her back into his arms, tilting her face up to his with one hand under her chin. "We will make Mother Briar pay," he promised. "There is more than one way to burn a witch."

Maribel tensed and leaned back. "That's a hideous thought."

Daman flushed. "I didn't mean—"

"No, it's all right," Maribel interrupted. She folded herself back into his arms. "For Mother Briar, it's appropriate."

Daman bit back the urge to apologize again. Witches had been evil in his mind for so long, it was going to take some time to adjust his thinking now that saying anything against witches would be saying things against the sister of the woman he…

His thoughts trailed off. He only meant to glance at Maribel, but once his gaze landed on her, he couldn't look away. It wasn't until she shifted, her cheeks taking on a pleasing pink hue, that he realized how long he'd been staring.

"About what happened before you went to see your sister…"

Maribel bit the inside of her cheek, but she didn't take her eyes from his. "Yes?"

"I'd still like you to stay. If you still want to be part of my life."

"I'd like that," Maribel said, putting her hands on his shoulders.

"I love you." The words hurt coming out, hanging back, too afraid of rejection to stray farther than his tongue. But he'd almost lost her, almost died without telling her how he felt. Never again.

"I love you too," she half-sobbed.

Daman tightened his arms around her, dragging her against his chest. Happiness more profound than any emotion he'd experienced in some time nearly overwhelmed him, left him feeling as if he could fly, human form or no. He bent his head to press his lips to Maribel's, sealing the promise of their new life with a kiss.

CHAPTER 18

"Your sister has gone, you can stop pretending to be asleep now."

Corrine slowly opened one eye, just enough to test the veracity of the pixie's claim. True to the fey's word, the bed beside her was empty, the rumpled sheets all that remained of her sister. Slowly, Corrine sat up, wincing as the skin in her neck tightened and pulled. Her wounds were closed, already pink with new skin, but the pain lingered.

As did the memory.

"I'm sure your lack of a formal expression of gratitude is merely a result of your exhaustion and emotional turmoil," the pixie assured her. "Don't feel too terribly about it."

Corrine eased herself into a sitting position, resting her aching back against the firm cushion of the headboard and pressing a hand to the sensitive skin on her neck where a fatal wound had once been. The puckered skin felt strange under her fingertips, the slick texture at odds with the harsh memory of what had caused it. She stared at the door, imagining where Maribel must be. In Daman's arms, most likely.

A small flicker of warmth eased some of the tightness in Corrine's chest. She'd expected to feel jealousy, or resentment, at the thought of her sister finding happiness in a life she could have no part of. But there was none.

"You're happier."

The corners of Corrine's mouth rose, the expression foreign to her in ways a smile should never be. She laughed and ran a hand over her face.

"I am happy," she admitted. "Happy-*er*."

"I don't doubt it. Wounds like yours take an incredible amount of energy to survive, even with a *sidhe* using a magic flower to heal you. All that magic you've been fighting to suppress has probably been nigh exhausted." The pixie fluttered down from her perch on the bedside table where she'd been lounging in a teacup filled with faintly steaming water. Droplets of water plopped onto Corrine's skin as the fey marched up her arm to sit on her shoulder, running in warm rivulets to leave wet spots on the sheets.

"What?" Corrine started to roll over, but stopped, wincing at the sensation of the wet spots left by the pixie soaking into her nightgown. She craned her neck to see the pixie's face. "What magic? I haven't been suppressing anything. I've been trying to get all the magic I can." She groped around her neck, stiffening as she discovered the amulet was missing.

Panic prickled over her nerves like a dozen sharp needles and she thrashed to the side, searching for the crystal. The pixie shrieked as she fell off her shoulder, her body twitching in the air as her wings burst into a flurry of movement to keep herself from falling.

"Careful! Warn a pixie before you go jumping about, you could have squished me."

"Where is it?" Corrine ran her hands over the sheets and under the pillows, bunching up the comforter, feeling for any sign of the missing magical item.

"Where is what?"

"My amulet! The one Mother Briar gave me."

"You mean that rock on a chain? I gave it to the wardrobe."

Corrine gaped at the pixie. "You…what?"

"I gave it to the wardrobe," the pixie repeated slowly. She crossed her arms, drumming her fingers along her rose-tinted skin. "Maybe you should go back to sleep. You still seem a bit—"

The rest of the fey's sentence was cut off by a squeak as Corrine shoved herself out of the bed and dashed over to the wardrobe. She flung open the doors, searching for some sign of the crystal. "Where is it?" she muttered, a lump forming in her throat. She pulled open the drawers one by one, growing more frantic by the second. "I need that amulet. It's all I have left." The last drawer failed to yield results and Corrine slammed it and whirled to the pixie, pointing a shaking finger at the flying creature. "Why would you put it in the wardrobe? Don't you know they're enchanted? Who knows where it is now, I may never get it back."

"I gave it to the wardrobe, because it *asked* for it." The pixie sniffed, examining her nails as though she were bored. "I don't like it when you shout at me."

The floor rushed up to meet Corrine as she sank to her knees, tears burning behind her eyes. "That's it then." Her voice grew thicker and she put her back against the wardrobe and drew her knees up to her chest. "What do I do now?"

A small weight pressed down on her head and the pixie's voice floated down. "Why are you upset? It was only a crystal. The wardrobe promised to give you some particularly exquisite clothes for it." A little hand stroked her head, toying with her hair. "You like pretty clothes."

"You don't understand. That was the only magic I had left from Mother Briar. She'll never help me now, not after I failed so terribly to get her what she wanted. And Maribel is staying here…"

"Why would you want Mother Briar's magic?"

Corrine didn't respond. There was no point. She was tired of trying to explain how she felt to people, tired of having to justify why she needed magic, why she needed help.

"When you came here, I thought you were going to try and break up your sister and Daman."

The pixie's voice had turned thoughtful, with an undertone of something more serious, more…calculating?

Corrine leaned heavily against the wardrobe, letting it hold her full weight. For a moment she thought her mind was playing tricks on her, making her think the furniture was shifting, trying to make her more comfortable.

"I wanted to," she admitted, her voice as numb as the rest of her. "Part of me thought I could kill two birds with one stone. If I could convince Maribel to make Daman tell her where Jeanne was, I could give Mother Briar the information she needed, and possibly make Daman angry enough with Maribel to send her home in the process."

"But you didn't."

An image of Maribel floated through Corrine's mind, her sister's face while she talked about Daman. The spark in his eyes when he looked at Maribel.

"Everyone thinks I'm selfish, that I use Maribel and don't really care about her." Corrine raised a hand, offering a perch to the pixie. The tiny fey accepted and settled into her palm so Corrine could bring her down to face her. "They're wrong. I'm not proud of everything I've done, but I never wanted to hurt Maribel. I was scared, and I'll admit there wasn't a lot I wasn't willing to do to feel safe, but…"

She swallowed, blinking back the tears threatening to fall. "I never hurt her. Never. I was never evil, I… Today when I… When she…" She clenched her teeth, breathing through the sudden burn of impending tears. "I didn't mean to. I stopped as soon as I realized…" Words failed her, sounding pathetically inadequate even to her own ears. She covered her face with her free hand as though she could hold the tears in. "I couldn't take that happiness away from her."

A hurried tapping on her fingers made her lower her hands. The pixie's face hovered in front of her, lit with a brilliant smile. "You have a good heart," she declared. "That's what we needed to hear."

"We?"

"Yes." The pixie jumped into the air, wings beating furiously. "Come with me."

"Wait, where? Who's we?" Corrine stood, but made no move to follow the pixie. Her brain was having trouble processing the abrupt change in conversation and what she really wanted to do was go back to bed. The silky sheets and thick blankets looked awfully inviting.

"She was right, you know. You have a lot of raw power. I don't know who your patron is, but they really poured it all into you." She pursed her lips. "Not very kind if you think about it. They didn't give you a familiar or a mentor. Just let you go. No wonder you always felt like you were dying." She perked up. "No matter, though. It'll all work out now."

The faint stirrings of a memory came back to Corrine, hazy voices she'd thought she'd dreamt up, people talking over her, about her, while she lay unconscious. Patron. Power. Evil Fire. "You're saying I have power."

The pixie arched an eyebrow. "You're just now picking up on that?"

"But Mother Briar said my magic wasn't very strong."

"Which makes her a dirty liar."

"But the amulet, the potions... She needed to make them for me."

"She created them for you because you didn't know how, but she used *your* blood. That's where the power came from. That amulet was a trick of the mind, a way to pass your magic off as hers so you would think you needed her." The pixie snorted.

"That old bat doesn't have the juice to do half of what you did today. Do you know how rare it is for a witch to work a spell through sheer willpower?" She paused. "Of course, being near death tends to give one quite a bit of extra oomph. I doubt you'd have been able to do that on an average day. Obviously I wouldn't recommend it as a *first* course of action…"

Corrine's head fell back, banging against the wardrobe. She hissed and jerked forward, rubbing the back of her head.

"You pulled energy from a *sidhe* too," the pixie continued. "Pulled enough from her to hurt her. Even panicking as much as you were, that was impressive. Not sure you could have done that if you hadn't already been taking from her for so long, but still."

Maribel. Corrine had a flash of seeing Maribel collapse, remembered the euphoric feeling she'd been lost in, how long it had taken her to register what she was doing, what effect she was having on her sister.

"I could have killed her." Saying the words out loud made her blood run cold.

The pixie tilted her head, eyeing Corrine from her new position on a tented portion of bedsheets. "Surprisingly, yes. Well, maybe not killed her. *Sidhe* are creatures of the earth, and the land around us is vital. She may have survived even if you did attempt to drain her."

Corrine covered her face with her hands, trying to shove the memory away. "I never wanted to hurt her."

"Witches left untrained with no familiar and no mentor often hurt people without intending to. Your patron must have had a terrible sense of humor. Not atypical, mind you, but terrible nonetheless."

A surge of anger flared bright and hot, chasing back the pain. Corrine dropped her hands to glare at the pixie. "You've been dropping information like breadcrumbs, tempting my appetite, but providing nothing of substance. Is it your intention to continue to torment me, or do you plan to explain exactly what you know about me?"

The pixie put a hand on her chest. "You would accuse me of being vague?"

Corrine narrowed her eyes.

"Humph," the pixie muttered. "That's gratitude for you. Oh, all right. I suppose I could answer a few questions before we go."

"Go where?"

"To Mother Hazel."

That got Corrine's attention. "You can't be serious. You want to take me to another witch? After everything Mother Briar did to me?"

The pixie crossed her arms. "Fine. Figure it all out for yourself. How hard could that be?"

Corrine bristled at the sarcasm dripping from the pixie's tone, but she bit back the scathing response that readied on her tongue. The fey had agreed to answer some questions. Best not to look that gift horse in the mouth.

"What's a patron?"

The pixie took her time settling down, getting comfortable. By the time she finally answered, Corrine was ready to leap off the floor and strangle her.

"A patron is someone or something very powerful. It can be a god, a spirit, or a very, very, very, very, very, very, very, very—"

"Is that really necessary?"

"*Very* powerful person," the pixie finished with a glare. She sniffed. "The patron might reveal herself to the witch or she might not. She might have a reason for giving the person power or she might not. She might be giving the power to the person for a good reason or—"

"She might not," Corrine finished. Impatience licked at her and she had to clasp her hands in her lap to keep from reaching for the fey.

"Or she might not," the pixie finished pointedly.

"Is there any way to find out who my patron is?" Corrine's heart throbbed in her throat, her nerves singing as she felt herself getting close to the answers she needed.

"Not if she doesn't want you to know. At least, I've never heard of anyone tracking down a patron. You'd have to be some sort of crazy investigator."

Corrine slumped back against the wardrobe, but her mind continued to whirl. The pixie eyed her for a minute then continued.

"Normally, the patron arranges for a mentor, either by formal introduction or as some sort of apparent coincidence. The witch can either find a mentor, or a mentor can find a witch. It's the mentor's job to help you balance the power that's making you 'ill' and to help you learn new spells."

The way the fey said "ill" made Corrine study her more closely. "Why do you say 'ill' like I'm not really ill?"

The pixie gripped her head in both hands. "You haven't figured it out yet?" she half-shrieked. "After all I've been saying?"

"What? Just tell me!"

"You were never sick," the pixie shouted. "Your patron just decided to let you think that. All that nausea, dizziness, hallucinations, weakness—it was all raw power! You didn't know what you were, you had no one to help you. Your power was making you mad."

A fine trembling shook Corrine's body. Never ill? All those years...all that time...all that *fear*. The pixie shifted as though suddenly uncomfortable. Then she cleared her throat and slid down the incline the bed sheets had made. She jumped off the bed and flew over to land on Corrine's folded hands. Slowly, she leaned down and put her tiny hand on one of Corrine's fingers.

"All this time... All the things I've done." Heat swamped Corrine's head, making it hard to think. She could only sit there, helpless as images danced across her mind. All those days she'd spent in bed, terrified of falling and hurting herself, of losing herself in one of those horrible waking dreams. The stares she'd always gotten from others, the whispers. The times an episode had left her in physical danger, cut, burned, or bleeding. The bonding spell she'd used on Maribel.

"It's not your fault," the pixie said softly. "I know you're feeling guilty about what you did to Maribel, but there was nothing else you could have done. You were drawn to magic, it was inevitable with that much power inside you, but you didn't understand what you were. You bonded to your sister because she was the only one 'other' that you knew. You were driven to do something to prevent true madness." The pixie scowled. "Whoever your patron is, she's a sick one."

"You keep saying 'she.'" Corrine tried to focus on the pixie. "How do you know it's a she?"

The pixie shrugged and leaned back. "I don't. But I resort to female when dealing with any kind of creative magic. Women are the creators, after all, not men."

Corrine mulled that over for a while. Her hands grew clammy as an unpleasant thought unfurled in her mind. "Could Mother Briar be my patron?"

The pixie snorted. "No. Mother Briar isn't powerful enough. That's why she's so desperate to get Jeanne back. She wants the girl to be her slave, to do all the work she's too lazy to do and doesn't have the power to do magically. If the old bat put half as much effort into her own work as she did trying to find Jeanne, it would all balance out and she wouldn't even need the poor goblin girl. I mean, look at how much work she put into manipulating you."

Corrine stared into space for a moment. "Maribel knows about Mother Briar's part in…everything."

The pixie shrugged. "Seems so."

"Maribel will want her punished." Inner turmoil tightened Corrine's voice, threatening to choke her with emotion she didn't want to deal with right now. "Maribel has always been very protective of me."

The pixie pressed her lips into a thin line. "It would be foolish of Maribel to go after Mother Briar. She's not all that powerful as far as witches go, but that's still a lot farther than a *sidhe* who's believed she was a human her entire life. Even Daman would do well to keep his distance unless he wanted to end up cursed into a shape significantly worse than the halfway form he's been living in this past year. Even a poor excuse for a witch like Mother Briar could manage to change him into a wild boar or something." The pixie paused. "Well, perhaps not a boar. *Nagas* are too powerful for something so mortal. But a river, that could likely be managed."

"Is Mother Briar more powerful than me?" Corrine asked carefully, her mind parsing through different scenarios in which she might make Mother Briar pay for all she'd done.

"In terms of raw power, not likely," the pixie mused. "Mother Briar comes from a line of witches capable of little more than parlor tricks, there isn't much power in her bloodline. And she's never been foolish enough to barter with a bigger force for more power. You, on the other hand, have been touched by a very generous, if cruel, patron." The pixie eyed Corrine. "Still, all the power in the world won't do you any good if you don't know how to use it. You're nowhere near ready to take on Mother Briar."

"I can't let Maribel go after her and get hurt. I have to do something."

"Well, there are all kinds of ways to keep your sister from challenging the old crone," the pixie assured her. "Why, I could teach you a spell to lay a fog around the old crone's house that would disorient and turn away anyone who tried to go in. Or we could try wiping the memory of Mother Briar from your sister's mind. Or—"

"No," Corrine interrupted. "Fog would only lead unwary travelers astray. And I will never interfere with my sister's mind again." She tapped a finger against her thigh. "I'll be honest with Maribel. It's the least I can do to make up for the deception of the past."

She slid out of the bed and searched the room until she found parchment and a pen. She quickly scribbled a letter to her sister. Her eyes watered as she penned a pathetic apology along with an insistence that Maribel leave Mother Briar to her, since it was she who had been manipulated. She swallowed hard as tears streamed down her cheeks, then forced herself to finish the letter with a plea that Maribel not try to find her.

"Pixie?"

"Yes?"

"Can you help me get out of here without being seen?"

"Oh, yes. Glamour is easy."

Corrine hesitated before asking the next part, but there was no point putting it off. "And can you help me find somewhere to stay until I can support myself?"

"Mother Hazel will help you." The pixie tilted her head. "Why don't you stay here? Your sister obviously wants you to stay, the *naga* lord has no reason to attack you now." The pixie glanced around. "Isn't this exactly what you wanted? To live like a queen?"

"Not on someone's else's coin!" The words came out louder and harsher than Corrine had meant to say them and she pressed her lips into a thin line as she took deep breaths. After some measure of her control had returned, she addressed the pixie again. "All I want is to be self-sufficient. I don't want to rely on anyone."

"That wasn't your attitude before," the pixie pointed out. "You were quite firm on the point that you wanted to be rich and wealthy with lots of servants—"

"That was when I thought I had need of such things." Corrine pressed her hands to the table, concentrating on the solid support of the wood. "That was when I thought I was ill, that I couldn't do things on my own. If what you've told me is true, I don't need to rely on anyone. I don't need to surround myself with wealth and servants, to protect myself from the world. I can handle the world." She cleared her throat and looked away, suddenly uncomfortable with the pixie's piercing gaze. "I just need a little help to get there."

"And you would take that help from Mother Hazel, but not your sister?"

Corrine cleared her throat, mentally threatening to dig her eyes out of her head if they dared to drop another tear. "I have taken enough from my sister." An ache in her chest prompted her to massage a spot just under her collarbone. Where once there had been an arcane mark, the symbol of the bond linking her with Maribel, there was now only a scar. The last remnant of her link to her *sidhe* sibling, severed by a sheer force of will in what she'd thought would be her last act on this plane of existence. She gave the pixie a defiant glare. "Besides, isn't it my mentor's job to help me? Isn't that what this Mother Hazel is offering?"

The pixie ignored her tone, not blinking an eye. She stared at Corrine for so long that the gaze gained a weight to it, bored straight through Corrine and dragged over the tender fabric of her very soul. She clenched her hands into fists, determined not to squirm. Finally, the pixie nodded.

"I will take you to Mother Hazel. But I will tell you now, Corrine. The life you're choosing for yourself will not be an easy one. Magic is a fierce beast that can hurt you or help you, depending on how you try to use it and how seriously you take your studies. To learn that life surrounded by loved ones and comforts is one thing. To study alone…"

"Perhaps it's time I was alone." Corrine stood straighter, squared her shoulders. "But mark my words, pixie. Someday I will repay my sister for her kindness. I will make up for all I have done." She stared out the window at the land. "I swear it."

EPILOGUE

Kirill, vampire prince of Dacia and member of the ruling council for the New Kingdom, led Daman into the study. The castle had only recently been completed and everything was shiny and new, every golden wall sconce gleaming with perfection, every inch of the marble floor polished to a glossy shine. The art hanging on the walls had come from his own personal stock, and the vibrant colors made the images come alive. The entire castle screamed of money and power—exactly as Kirill intended. It was precisely the scene he wanted as he invited his first prospect to meet with the rest of the council.

"I'm still not sure I understand why I'm here?"

Kirill smiled at Daman, not bothering to hide his fangs. Daman was a *naga*, with a half dragon and full dragon form—a set of fangs was not going to startle him. "All will be explained very soon." He tilted his head. "I trust your honeymoon was pleasant?"

The corner of Daman's mouth quirked up in an expression that said more than words how much he'd enjoyed his vacation with his new wife, Maribel. "Indeed. Your suggestion was most welcome."

"Glad to hear it. So few people are aware of that island. It makes it the perfect spot for a private getaway."

"Did you honeymoon there as well?"

Kirill paused, keeping his face neutral as he studied Daman. From the way the *naga* had behaved when Kirill had first appeared at his home, he'd assumed the *naga* was unfamiliar with the royal family of Dacia. How had he known Kirill was married?

Then it dawned on Kirill and he glanced down at his left hand and the ring that matched the silver band he'd given his wife Irina. "No," he answered finally. "My wife and I didn't travel for our honeymoon, though I did suggest it."

"Your wife does not like to travel?"

Kirill fought not to roll his eyes. "No. She doesn't like to leave the kingdom. My wife is very interested in"—*social reform, interfering in my political machinations*—"charity work. She is quite dedicated."

"She sounds like a lovely woman," Daman said politely.

This time Kirill's smile was a full flashing of fangs as he thought of his beautiful bride. Heat stirred in his body and he composed himself before his mind could travel too far ahead in the evening to the time he would once again have his wife in his arms. "She is that."

Finally they arrived at the study. Kirill opened the door and gestured for Daman to precede him. Daman warily glanced into the room, body held loose, prepared to leap at any sign of danger. After a moment, he stepped over the threshold. Kirill followed him.

There were four men in the room, the rest of the ruling council of the New Kingdom. Kirill stepped slightly ahead of Daman to begin introductions.

"Daman, may I introduce you to my compatriots." He gestured toward the window. "Prince Etienne of Sanguenay."

The moonlight spilling through the window illuminated Etienne, casting his shaggy brown hair in shadow and making his dark blue waistcoat appear black. His brown eyes glinted with a momentary flash of gold, a hint of the wolf within him peeking out at the visitor. He bowed slightly. "Pleased to meet you."

"And this is Adonis, Prince of Nysa." Kirill paused and put a hand to his head and rubbed his temple. "Adonis, didn't we discuss this?"

The demon standing at the fireplace crossed his arms, the smoldering cigarette tucked between two fingers filling the room with the smoky scent of cloves. "You said he was a *naga*. Don't tell me horns and wings are going to frighten him?"

"That's not the point," Kirill argued tiredly. "Is Etienne in wolfman form? Is Saamal appearing as a jaguar or a gust of wind?"

"Patricio's wings are out," Adonis objected.

"Patricio is an angel, he has no choice."

"Well, I'm an incubus. This is what I look like, to look otherwise would be deceptive. Hardly the sort of first impression you want to make when you're inviting someone to move into your kingdom and take up a position of power in the court."

"Move? Position of power in the court?" Daman leaned back from the other occupants of the room. "What court? What kingdom?"

Kirill clenched his teeth, struggling not to bare his fangs. "Thank you for that subtle revelation, Adonis. And here I was worried about how best to broach the subject." He straightened his clothes, counting his weapons as he kept a careful eye on Daman out of his peripheral vision.

"If I may continue with the introductions, all else will soon be revealed."

Daman studied Kirill for a moment. Finally he inclined his head once. "Very well."

Kirill noticed that he remained with his back to a corner, keeping all five members of the council in view while remaining close to the door. Silently, Kirill congratulated him on his choice.

"Now where was I? Ah, yes. The gentleman standing next to the table is Prince Patricio of Meropis and the gentleman seated in front of the fireplace is Prince Saamal of Mu."

Daman nodded to the towering angel, surprisingly unintimidated. Not many men could look at the over seven foot angel with his massive wingspan without taking a step back out of sheer instinct. The massive sword hanging at his side didn't help him appear any more approachable. Saamal, despite being the most powerful being in the room, was also the least intimidating physically. It wasn't until the god chose to use his powers that he could be seen for the terrifying being he was.

"A pleasure to meet you."

Saamal's voice was gentle and calm as always, and not for the first time, Kirill found himself wondering how much of the god's placid exterior was genuine and how much was an attempt to put others at ease.

"The pleasure is mine," Daman answered amicably. He glanced back to Kirill with an expectant expression on his face.

He has Adonis' patience. Kirill muffled a sigh. "All right, let us get down to business then. Daman, you will no doubt have noticed that the land you now find yourself in is as yet untouched by civilization, other than the palace around you."

"I have."

"Well, due to circumstances that are unimportant at this time, my fellow council members and I find ourselves in the rather unique position of populating this new land by invitation."

Daman's eyebrows rose. "You're looking for settlers?"

"In a manner of speaking. It is important when taking on an endeavor such as this one that—"

"We're willing to let you relocate abused changelings here in exchange for your willingness to relocate as well and help us govern as part of our new court," Patricio interrupted.

Kirill pulled one hand inside his cloak, closing long fingers around the hilt of his favorite dagger. The texture of the blade's grip soothed him, helped him keep hold of his temper in the face of the angel's blatant disrespect.

Patricio crossed his arms and faced Kirill down without a sliver of apology in his blue gaze. "Some of us would like to get home at a reasonable hour. Not all of us are nocturnal."

"What do you know about the changelingss?" Daman's pupils narrowed to draconic slits and his fingers twitched, tips sharpening into claws the color and shape of a crescent moon.

"Thank you for putting our guest at ease, Patricio," Kirill said tightly. "Done with your usual flair for comfort. Marcella would be so proud."

"Leave my wife out of this." Patricio's wings rose in the wind of his agitation.

"Who wouldn't want to join this family?" Adonis joked. He blew a smoke ring at the ceiling, blue-white tendrils curling outward as it rose. He winked at Daman. "Our winter solstice parties are unrivaled."

"Winter solstice..." Daman blinked.

Not for the first time, Kirill was impressed with Adonis' ability to put others at ease. His political guile was deplorable, but his genuine likeability was lethal.

"Daman," Kirill said, facing the *naga*. "The angel, in all his ham-fistedness, is correct. We are building a society here from the ground up. I have heard much about you, many stories from grateful changelings who have found happiness with the families you find for them. I have seen for myself how dedicated you are. You are precisely the type of man that could help us build a court to be proud of, respected. In exchange for your guidance, your participation in our endeavors, we would be pleased to let you bring changelings here. Surely there is no place they would be safer than a land accessible only by invitation?"

He didn't look around the room at the other princes, silently willing them not to contradict him. After all, for the most part, it was true that this new kingdom could be accessed only by invitation. Though it was possible for the unwary to accidentally stumble through the portal if they passed close enough to the world tree.

Daman glanced from one man to the other, but Kirill could see his mind working behind his silver eyes. The *naga*'s first responsibility was to his charges, his changelings. This land was safe for them, open to them.

"What do you want from me?" Daman asked finally.

Kirill smiled. "Etienne? Won't you escort our guest to the map room so he can pick a location for his new home?"

"I'm not your lapdog," Etienne snapped.

The handle of his dagger was soothing, as it always was. For what felt like the hundredth time that night alone, Kirill toyed with the idea of burying the blade somewhere in Etienne's thigh. Not to kill him, or even lame him—lycanthrope physiology would protect him from any lasting damage—but just to let the beast know that his dismal attitude would have consequences. With a sigh, he pulled his hand from the weapon.

"Saamal?"

The god's lip quirked as he pushed away a smile. "It would be my pleasure."

Daman, who had watched the exchange between Kirill and Etienne with a sharp silver-eyed stare that was far too discerning for Kirill's taste, amiably followed Saamal out. Kirill waited until the door closed behind them and their footsteps faded away down the hall.

"Etienne, for the love of all gods and demons everywhere, must you *always* be so disagreeable?"

The lycanthrope folded his arms, muscles bunching with the movement. "Must you always be so manipulative?"

"Manipulative? I thought we'd all agreed to invite Daman into our realm? What, pray tell, have I done to deserve such ire from you on this matter?"

Golden eyes darkened to hard amber. "Do you think I don't

know about the pirate? Tyr, I believe he's called? Aging pirate with one hand?"

Kirill paused, careful to keep the tension from his face and shoulders. "What about him?"

"Do you intend to tell Daman that it was you who arranged for pirates to steal Maribel's family fortune? That it was your scheming that sent her family from their home at court to the farm where her poor sister suffered so?"

Damn his eyes. "You've been talking with shady characters, my friend. Who would tell such stories?"

"Wow, that's a long game even for you," Adonis piped up.

Clove-scented smoke wafted past Kirill as the demon spoke, and he waved it away with a sharp flick of his hand. "I'm sure I don't know what you're talking about."

"How many seers do you have working for you?" Patricio demanded, feathers rustling as he straightened to his full height. "Who is giving you such information that you can arrange events so far ahead of time?"

Three. Kirill gave Patricio a blank stare. "What seers?"

"He won't tell you," Adonis informed them. "Kirill plays his cards close to his dagger-laden vest."

"This is never going to work," Etienne muttered. "Some high council we are. How could Eurydice ever have thought we could rule a kingdom together?"

"Oh, don't be so sour, my wolfish friend," Adonis insisted, sauntering over to clap a clawed hand on Etienne's back. "We're all getting along swimmingly. Just a few growing pains, that's all." He took another puff from his cigarette and patted Etienne on the back. "You just need to accept our vampire companion for who he is. Fangs, weapons, seers, and all."

"This kingdom is doomed," Patricio muttered.

"Oh, take heart, angelic prince," Kirill soothed. "Wait until you see my next candidate..."

Sneak Peek:

BLUE VOODOO

Book two in the Blood Realm series

CHAPTER 1

"I can't believe you put your faith in this swamp witch."

The butler's censure fell over Dominique like an upended drawer of cooking knives, sharp tones cutting and brash. It wasn't the first comment he'd made during her short visit, nor did she think it would be his last. Unacceptable, considering he had never been invited to witness this meeting in the first place. *Breathe.* Dominique didn't look at the butler, didn't give him the satisfaction of reacting at all. Instead, she picked up the small pouch of soot set out amongst her other ingredients on the stone floor beside her. Singing under her breath to the *loa*, Agwe, she added the soot to a hollowed pumpkin gourd, letting it drift down to join the powdered lizard, red precipitate, and the soil she'd gathered this morning from a local crossroad.

The warm caress of her power hummed through her finger-tips, infusing the concoction with the energy of the *loa*, the mystical messengers that bridged the void between humans and the great god Bondye. The sensation was as familiar and soothing to her as her own heartbeat. Energy built, spreading outward in ever growing circles, filling the room with the kiss of magic.

Her client, a cook named Widelene, sat on a stool near where

Dominique worked. Even as her body remained slumped in her seat, she tracked every movement with sharp curiosity. The lines around her eyes were deeper than they should be, painting the woman's exhaustion over her face for the world to see. It was no wonder she'd come to Dominique for help. The poor woman hadn't had a decent night's sleep in over a week.

But that was about to change.

Dominique rubbed oil into the wick she'd pulled from her bag, then suspended it over the ingredients in the gourd with two slivers of ivory bone. "Those dreams won't bother you anymore, Widelene. Take this and hang it from a tree in front of your house. Light it at sundown and douse it after you wake. The ingredients must be replaced every week for seven weeks and then you must throw the whole thing into the sea and say a prayer of thanks to Agwe. I will come to check on you next week and will bring fresh ingredients then."

Widelene's cloudy brown eyes bounced from Dominique to the butler behind her. "Th-thank you so much, Madame Laveau."

Dominique inclined her head, the tail of her sunset-hued cotton head wrap sliding over her shoulder to brush the neckline of her white blouse.

"Don't thank her." The butler took an agitated step forward. "She hasn't done anything but make a fool out of you."

More color drained from Widelene's face until her normal ebony complexion was nearly as light as Dominique's own sienna hue. Her gaze flicked from Dominique to the butler and back. The sour man was above her in the house hierarchy and could make her working life miserable if he chose. But Dominique was a voodoo priestess, someone with power and influence amongst the *loa*, messengers to Bondye. The lines on her face deepened even more, her breathing becoming ragged.

Dominique rested a hand on Widelene's knee, offering silent support. She rose to her feet from the position she'd been kneeling in for the last half hour.

Slowly. Slowly.

Keeping an iron grip on her balance, Dominique gained her feet in one smooth, unhurried motion, careful not to betray any of the sharp stabs of pain that pricked her knees and ankles from their time spent holding still in an uncomfortable position. She turned to confront the butler like an actress in a play, the movement graceful and dramatic, giving the man plenty of time to reflect on what she might say—what she might do. Her eyes locked on his.

"Gerard Xavier Roche."

She enunciated every syllable, rolling them on her tongue. The skin at Gerard's temples tightened, but his lip retained its derisive curl. His impeccably groomed hair was liberally sprinkled with grey, providing a contrast to skin the color of water on a moonless night. "So you know my name. You think that frightens me?" He snorted. "If that's all you have, *voodoo queen*, then be on your way." He glared at Widelene, his voice rising the deeper she huddled into her shawl. "You've gotten all the fool's adulation you're going to get here."

Dominique slashed her hand through the air, halting with her fingers inches from his head. The butler tensed, but held his ground, hands balled tightly at his side like he was bracing for impact.

"Gerard. Xavier. Roche."

With a flick of her wrist, Dominique plucked a hair from Gerard's head, holding the strand inches in front of the butler's nose. He pressed his lips together, firmly biting back whatever words he wanted to let fly. Power pulsed inside her, waiting to be used, but she ignored it. She didn't need power for the likes of him. She leaned forward and put her lips a hair's breath away from the shell of his ear.

"The gambling tables can be so cruel. Can't they, Gerard Xavier Roche?"

The flinch that rattled the butler's body was quick and

violent. He swayed a little as though he would step back, but foolish pride was enough to help him stubbornly hold his ground.

"Time to count the family silver." Dominique's breath ghosted over his skin, leaving a trail of gooseflesh in its wake.

Gerard staggered back like he'd been struck, the full weight of his body pulling his shoulders down and his jaw sagging open. Widelene—the source of that particular bit of knowledge—let out a strangled whimper before she quickly remembered herself and covered her mouth. Dominique made a show of putting the hair into the pocket of her skirt, patting it as she looked down her nose at its origin.

"Respect is very important, Gerard Xavier Roche. Those who do not know whom to give it to will often find the lesson that follows to be very...unpleasant."

With that parting shot, she swept out of the kitchen. Pointedly ignoring the servants' exit, she strode up the stairs to the main house. Her burgundy skirts swirled around her legs, the heavy material rubbing against her like a friendly cat. She hauled it over her boots to keep her petticoats from tangling around her in an undignified fashion as she flowed through the foyer to the front doors.

"Madame Laveau, I didn't realize you were here."

The deep voice vibrated Dominique's insides with the strength of the baritone. She recognized it immediately and spun around with open arms. "Leonaldo, what a pleasure."

The lord of the manor strode across the foyer with the ambling gait of a man comfortable with himself and his environment. His skin was as dark as his voice was deep, his teeth a brilliant crescent moon in a night sky. He held his arms out and Dominique allowed him to fold her into his embrace, chuckling as he squeezed her and rocked her from side to side.

"You do not come around enough," Lord Mercier told her,

pulling back to see her properly. "You grow more beautiful every time I see you."

"Shameless flattery is always welcome." Dominique responded to her host's joy with a full smile of her own. "And you are looking handsome as well."

Lord Mercier rolled his eyes. "Are you sure about that? Have I not gone completely grey, then?"

She eyed the lord's head of dark, well-groomed hair. There was a fair dusting of silver strands making themselves known, but he was far from being completely grey. "Something is driving the color from your hair, then?"

"Pah!"

Intrigued by that succinct response, Dominique followed the direction of the lord's stare to the back of the house and caught a glimpse of a young servant biting his lip in deep concentration as he struggled to balance a tray full of dishes. His blue eyes were locked on the porcelain as if he could will them to stay put, his pale cheeks holding a pink tint that spoke of more exertion than such a task warranted. The tray teetered precariously and she had to avert her eyes or be overcome with a case of sympathetic nerves. "A new recruit, I see. He does not appear to be from Ville au Camp?"

"He is not." Lord Mercier winced and looked away as if he too couldn't bear the suspense of waiting for the tea set's death. "A good friend's daughter grew sweet on the boy during a visit to Nysa, and when they moved here to Sanguennay, she begged me to employ the lad so he could come as well."

There was a gasp from the kitchen and Dominique tensed, her nerves screaming as they predicted the inevitable crash. "I'm sure he'll fit in after he's had a bit more time."

"You have been away for a long time," Lord Mercier pointed out tersely. "He's already been here for *seven months*."

She winced. "Oh dear."

"He sticks out like a sheep in a horse herd," Lord Mercier

grumbled. "Practically glows in the dark. My wife got up in the middle of the night and nearly fainted dead away when she glanced out the window and saw him chasing down the dog he'd let out. Swore there was a ghost trying to eat her *petit chien*."

Choking back a laugh, Dominique covered her mouth with her hand. The only reason the boy stood out so painfully was because Lord Mercier made it a point to only hire people from his homeland of Ville au Camp. Rumor was the lord had been run out of his homeland after he'd been falsely accused of fixing the games of chance in his gambling establishment to ensure no one would win without his consent—a deadly serious crime amongst a people who so dearly prized their games. He couldn't go back home, and so he strove to make his manor here in Sanguennay into a replica of his beloved Ville au Camp, from the fanciful colors of the curtains to the dark skin of his household members.

"I had to take him off gardening duty," Lord Mercier confided. "Boiled like a lobster before he'd been out an hour." He rubbed a hand over his face. "Perhaps you're right. I shouldn't be so hard on him."

Crashing porcelain shattered the stillness of the air, followed by the unmistakable clamor of a serving tray. Lord Mercier's right eye twitched.

"I should go." Dominique bolted out the door with as much dignity as she could muster, not wanting to compromise her reputation by running, but not wanting to compromise it by laughing herself silly on the floor, either.

She emerged from the manor's heavy doors, and warm, balmy air enveloped her like the embrace of a family member who always overstayed their welcome. Lord Mercier's manor was located right at the edge of town, close enough that the sounds and scents of the village danced in the air. They called to Dominique, leading her down the path from the manor to the main road that wove like a writhing serpent through the center of town and all the shops that fought for space on this most precious real estate.

Lifting her face to relish a passing breeze, she inhaled deeply, savoring the scent of freshly baked bread, the musk of livestock, the perfume of liquors and wines, and the myriad odors of herbs and plants. The Midsummer Celebration was approaching.

Of all the celebrations that lit up the calendar, Midsummer was her favorite. It was a time to worship and praise not one, but all the spirits. A time when the most important thing was joy. Joy for everything they'd been given, joy for everything they loved. There would be food, dancing, games, and costumes. It was a time for pleasure and fun. Class and status didn't matter, and behind the safety of masks and the dark of night, the wealthy would mingle with the poor, strangers would become friends, and the entire village would be...free.

Her smile grew brittle as a memory threatened to sour her good mood. A Midsummer Celebration that had been both the best and worst of her life. The night that—

Stop it. Stop it or you'll make a fool of yourself.

Dominique slid her hands into the pockets of her apron, doing a spontaneous inventory of the various objects she carried with her. Satchels of powdered herbs, bits of string, a few coins, slivers of wood and bone, two small empty bottles, and a hodgepodge of stones and pebbles. Each one gathered at the subtle guidance of the *loa* to be used when the time was right.

As she made her way through the village to her home on the edge of the bayou, she took the time to acknowledge every individual she passed. If she knew a person's name, she used it—first if they were a friend, first, middle, and last if they were not—and she stopped to chat and introduce herself if she didn't know them at all. The former was more common than the latter, a fact that filled her with a deep sense of satisfaction. She wasn't royalty by blood or combat, no, but here? In this part of Sanguennay, among these people? She was a queen. The voodoo queen of Sanguennay.

"Madame Laveau!"

Monsieur Hugon swept out of his tavern with a broad wave, large hand obscuring his face as it passed. The wedding ring on his finger caught the sunlight, a pleasant golden glow that took the edge off his gruff demeanor and mitigated his above-average stature. Dominique deviated from the cobblestoned road, keeping her strides slow and measured, not rushing nor dawdling. She would come at his summons, but she would arrive in her own good time.

"My throat is a bit dry," she said as she approached. Her practical flat-soled shoes were silent on the wood porch leading up to the tavern.

"Allow me to offer you a drink then." Monsieur Hugon stepped back and gestured for her to enter ahead of him. "You are, of course, always welcome here."

The scent of the tavern was a personality all its own. The robust character of liquor, the teasing perfume of wine, and the frothy aroma of beer tickled her nose and mingled with the scent of wood polish and clean silver. She seated herself on a stool at the long bar that stretched from the wall near the door across to the other wall where a door led into the small kitchen. As Dominique settled her skirts around her, Monsieur Hugon bustled around on the other side of the counter, drawing out a plain, but clean glass from its fellows lining a shelf beneath the bar. He filled it with two fingers of bourbon.

The rich, amber colored liquid glittered behind the glass like a precious stone. Dominique waved it under her nose, inhaling the bouquet with an appreciative sigh. "Soft, mild with very light oak, subtle sweetness and herbal grass notes. Such a heavenly scent."

"Only the best for you, Madame Laveau."

She took a sip, holding her tongue to the roof of her mouth to fully appreciate the flavor. It *was* the best bourbon—but then she'd known that already. She was the one who'd supplied it.

"I hope you'll enjoy a glass yourself, Monsieur Hugon."

The large man leaned on the bar, the wood creaking in muted protest. "Would that I could, Madame Laveau. But I'm afraid our stores are rather low, and I would not want to take such fine liquor from the mouths of my customers."

Ah. "Have a glass, Monsieur Hugon. The *loa* always provide for the faithful."

"From your mouth to their ears." The tavern owner cleared his throat, the sound louder than it needed to be.

Madame Hugon appeared a moment later, so quickly one might have thought she was fey and had simply been hiding behind a veil, waiting for her husband's signal. Her red hair had long ago faded to a tarnished blonde, but there were still rich streaks of auburn combing through the waves pinned close to her head in a casual plait. Her dress was plain brown cotton, but it was clean. Her cream-colored apron bore stains like badges of honor, marking the proud woman as someone who worked for a living. She beamed at Dominique as she set something colorful on the bar in front of her.

"Please accept this gift, Madame Laveau." She caressed the material with the back of her fingers, holding Dominique's gaze as she did so. "I wove it myself. A token of our appreciation for all you do for our community." She patted the material again. "I hope it pleases you."

Dominique amicably stroked a hand across the wool. Something hard and curved met her fingertips—gold coins wrapped in the scarf, tucked carefully into the pocket created by Madame Hugon's clever folding. The amount felt right for two cases of bourbon.

"It is beautiful, Georgina." She lifted the garment, careful not to jar the coins from their nest as she gently tucked it into a large pocket in her thick skirts. "I will wear it tonight for the festival."

She swirled her glass, watching the play of liquor against the sides. "You'll be going to the festival as well, won't you? I'm told there will be a stunning display of fireworks by the harbor tonight. I have friends who will be there at eight o' clock. They're coming all the way from Dacia and their ship is called the Adze. Do say hello to them for me if you see them."

Monsieur Hugon bobbed his head, eyebrows knitted as he focused on trying to memorize the ship and the time. She would have told him to write it down if she weren't so certain his wife would remember.

"Excited about tonight, I hope, Madame Laveau?"

"Of course." Dominique took another sip of her bourbon. "The *loa* have been very good to us, I look forward to showing my gratitude and celebrating with my people. We must always be careful to remember from where our good fortune comes."

Madame Hugon nodded, but it was an absent-minded gesture. "Of course, of course, but I was referring to Monsieur Marcon."

The whiskey scalded Dominique's windpipe as she gasped mid-swallow. Her eyes and nose burned, and she blinked slowly, clearing the sheen of sudden tears from her eyes as she fought off a deep cough.

Madame Hugon appeared blessedly unaware of her struggle and bunched her hands in her skirts and leaned forward, waiting with bated breath for Dominique's response.

Marcon. Julien Marcon. He's back? When? Why? It can't be him.

She hushed the voice in her head brimming with questions and painted serenity over her face in as thick a layer as she could manage. "As you know, I have a great many duties to perform tonight for the Midsummer Celebration." Despite her intentions, emotion made her voice hoarse, threatening to betray her calm facade. She took another slow sip of whiskey. "I cannot promise my time to any one person."

"Oh, but Madame Laveau, you being one of their most dedicated priestesses, surely the spirits would be only too pleased to witness your engagement during this special time."

"It's unseemly for a gentleman to announce his engagement without his bride being present." Monsieur Hugon scrubbed at a glass that was already clean. "And that beard of his—"

His wife slapped his stomach, the lines in her face suddenly deeper, her other hand tightening on the edge of the bar in a white-knuckled grip. Monsieur Hugon's eyes bulged. "I-I of course meant no disrespect," he rushed to add. "I'm sure he would not have announced such a thing without your blessing, Madame Laveau. And his beard—"

The glass of whiskey in Dominique's hand shattered. Warm blood seeped through her fingers, mingling with the stinging bourbon as it pooled on the surface of the well-worn bar.

Bluebeard had returned then. And he'd claimed to be her... fiancé.

I'm going to kill him.

ABOUT THE AUTHOR

Jennifer Blackstream is a USA Today bestselling author of fantasy/paranormal romance. Urban Fantasy will soon be joining her repertoire, and if she doesn't get hold of the insidious roving gang of plot bunnies, there's going to be steampunk sprinkled in there too...

For news, new releases, and a free copy of What Big Teeth You Have, sign up for Jennifer's mailing list here on her website at jenniferblackstream.com

Jennifer has unfailing affection for the authors who have influenced her, including Laurell K. Hamilton, Jim Butcher, and the sorely missed Sir Terry Pratchett. Her books include humor, romance, and action, with enough darkness to keep things very interesting.

When Jennifer isn't writing, she can be found binge watching iZombie, Castle, or Once Upon a Time with her sibling (or Bones, Lucifer, and Miss Fisher's Murder Mysteries if she's alone). She also spends an inordinate amount of time arguing with herself over whether it's too late for another cup of coffee. To find out more about Jennifer, visit her website at jenniferblackstream.com

DID YOU FIND A TYPO?

Typos are the jack-in-the-boxes of the reading world. There you are, reading an amazing story, when suddenly—BAM! A typo rips you right out of the groove. At Skeleton Key Publishing, our editors do their best to correct the typos that slink by our authors, but sometimes they escape and go on their ruinous rampage.

So here's the deal. If you found any typos, go to our website at www.skeletonkeypublishing.net and report it. Every month we will put the names of everyone who reported a typo into a hat and pick one out. That person will then be offered a $25 gift certificate.

That's right...you can win a gift certificate just for reporting a typo. If you find more than three typos, send us a copy of your receipt and we'll send you an updated version of the book.

Thank you for helping us improve the reading experience for later readers.

- The Skeleton Crew